PRAISE FOR ELIZABETH DYER

"An excellent blend of suspense and romance—I was sucked into the story from page one!"

—Susan Stoker, *New York Times*, *Wall Street Journal*, and *USA Today* bestselling author

"Funny, clever, and suspenseful—I couldn't put this book down! The world needs more nerdy-hot heroes and fierce-hot heroines."

—Penny Reid, *USA Today* bestselling author

"Sexy, suspenseful, and downright hilarious in places. *Defenseless* had me gripped with the perfect balance of romance and intrigue. A tightly crafted plot combined with a beautifully told story as well as characters I was rooting for meant I couldn't put it down."

—Louise Bay, *USA Today* bestselling author

"*Defenseless* from Elizabeth Dyer is my favorite romantic suspense debut of 2017. Fast-paced action, heart-pounding passion, and a cat that rides a Roomba! I love it when the tension in a book is tempered with humor, and this author delivers in spades. Georgia Bennett and Parker Livingston are meant for each other. She's the type of woman you'd want to be friends with. And he's '. . . lazy Sunday mornings after sex-against-the-wall Saturday nights.' Love it!"

—Dana Marton, *New York Times* bestselling author

RELENTLESS

ALSO BY ELIZABETH DYER

Somerton Security

Defenseless

RELENTLESS

SOMERTON SECURITY, BOOK 2

ELIZABETH DYER

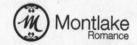

Montlake Romance

Text copyright © 2018 by Elizabeth Dyer
All rights reserved.

Published by Montlake Romance, Seattle

www.apub.com

Amazon, the Amazon logo, and Montlake Romance are trademarks of Amazon.com, Inc., or its affiliates.

ISBN-13: 9781503901759
ISBN-10: 1503901750

Cover design by Eileen Carey

Printed in the United States of America

For everyone—reader, author, blogger or friend—
who made Defenseless *so incredibly special.*
Relentless *exists because of you.*

PROLOGUE

One Year Ago

Protect your sister.

As Natalia Vega sat in the darkened quiet of a home that wasn't hers, waiting for a man she hardly knew, she let her father's words—the last he'd ever said to her—flow through her. Let the promise she'd made harden her, keep her.

It was bend or be broken, she reminded herself, and Vegas didn't break.

Not under threat of a knife.

Not under pain of betrayal.

And not beneath the weight of desperate choices and no-win situations.

As always, Natalia would do what she had to in order to protect Ana Maria.

A key slid into the lock, the door opened on quiet hinges, and Garrison Coates let himself into his apartment. Natalia had chosen her moment well. Returning from the gym, Garrison had his headphones on and blasting loud enough that Natalia could hear the thread of a heavy-metal guitar from across the room. He was tired, slicked with the sweat of a punishing workout, and most important, unarmed—his Glock securely stowed in the safe by the door.

Foolish. But then Garrison had marched into the cartel on an ironclad recommendation and backed his competence with a sense of ruthless disinterest and swaggering confidence. The ultimate yes-man, he'd risen through the ranks quickly, earned her uncle's regard, caught Ana Maria's eye, and snared Natalia's suspicion.

He slipped his keys on the hook, hit the lights, then turned and froze. For a long moment, he stared at her, his face open and surprised, the honesty of his expression smoothing away jaded lines and adding youth to his thirty-two years. When it came to looks, her sister had good taste. Six feet tall, Garrison had wavy brown hair, moss-green eyes, and the tapered physique of someone who swam as much as he lifted.

"Natalia," he said slowly, his surprise ebbing away beneath a tide of careful calculation. She could see the questions, the running assessment. Why was she here? How had she found him? What did she want?

None of it mattered.

"Expecting my sister?" she asked, letting a foot drop from the rung of the bar stool where she sat.

"She's never been here." He left his bag by the door and slipped out of the shoes he hadn't bothered to lace. "But then, you already knew that, didn't you?"

"I did."

"Here to warn me off?" he asked, glancing toward the side table with the safe on top before wandering toward the kitchen. That was the problem with responsible gun ownership—access. One of the many reasons Natalia preferred her knife.

"You never should have gone near her."

Garrison shrugged and pulled open the fridge. "She's a sweet, sheltered kid."

"And an easy mark," Natalia agreed. "My fault. I was so busy protecting her from the men within the cartel, I failed to warn her against those who'd come with easy smiles and studied interest."

"She loves me."

"I know." Natalia sighed. It was why she'd come herself rather than send one of her uncle's men. It shouldn't have surprised her that Ana

Maria had fallen in love. She was young and beautiful and so very lonely. For Natalia, it made everything that much worse, that much more dangerous. For Garrison, it would make everything so much easier—even if he couldn't possibly appreciate it.

"I love her, too, you know." He pulled a knife from the butcher block and cut into an orange he'd pulled from the fridge along with a bottle of water.

"I'm sure she believes you when you say it."

"But you don't?"

"You targeted her, used her, manipulated her, and for what? Access to an organization I'd sell my soul to free her from?" Natalia shook her head. "No. Whatever you might have come to feel—respect, responsibility, affection—it's not love."

"So . . . what? You're here to tell me to leave her alone? To walk away?" He took a long drink of his water, his throat working even as his gaze met hers over the rim.

"It's far too late for that." She rose from her stool. Watched as his body stilled and readied. He set his water down on the counter, then emerged from the galley kitchen and around the peninsula, knife held loosely at his side.

It wasn't his weapon. It was there in the way he held it: too tight, too forced. Like the grip of a gun instead of the hand of a friend. It was a complication, a distraction, but not a danger.

"Who else knows about you two?" she asked, squaring off to face him.

"No one knew." His grin slipped loose, a thin rueful thing. "But here you are."

When she didn't say anything, simply stared him down to parse the truth from the lie, he added, "I would never put her in danger, Natalia. I meant it when I said I'd get her out of this life. That I'd give her a future free of your uncle, of the violence and constant danger. It's not a promise I made lightly—and it's one I intend to keep."

3

She stood there, absorbed the shock of the blow, and pushed back the tide of regret. She believed him. Maybe it was because she understood the conviction, the desire. Knew what it looked like, how it felt, the suffocating weight and the comforting warmth of a goal that justified the means. An intimate feeling she knew well, had carried for years, and was able to spot in others.

It should have made this so much worse, so much more difficult.

But it didn't. Garrison Coates couldn't save them. He couldn't even save himself.

"Hernan has you on video removing product. He had you followed to a meet—you've been exposed."

Fear, milky white and cold, spilled across his face, stealing the flush of exertion and dulling the smug tilt of his chin. Good. At least he'd understood the risks. Had gone into this with his eyes open.

"Shit." Garrison tugged a hand through his hair. "Your sister send you to warn me?"

"Does she know what you are?" Natalia asked, shifting toward the door, closing off the angles, and asking the only questions that mattered anymore. How much did Ana Maria know? How deeply had Garrison compromised her?

What would their uncle do if he found out?

"Of course not," Garrison scoffed. His fist tightened around the knife, and his eyes went to the gun, safely out of reach.

A lie. Easy to spot in the dismissive tone and lack of eye contact. Somewhere along the line, in a stolen moment or between the sheets, Garrison Coates had told Ana Maria one secret too many.

And she'd said nothing. Not to Natalia, who might have found a way to avoid this, or to their uncle, who would certainly kill her for the betrayal.

If he found out.

Natalia couldn't let that happen.

"I need to disappear."

4

"There's no running from this, Garrison. Nowhere you can go—"

"You don't know—I have resources. People. Thirty minutes. One phone call. I'm *gone*."

"I didn't come alone." It would have been better. Safer. For her, anyway. "There are men on all the doors. I said I'd talk you down, get you into a car."

"And then?" he asked.

She shrugged. He knew the answer. Interrogation. Torture. A life lost and an example made. It wouldn't be easy or quick, and in the end, he'd beg. They all did. She could spare him that, at least.

"You aren't here to warn me, are you?"

"It's too late for that."

"Then, why?" he asked, widening his stance, preparing for the fight. "I've been close to Vega long enough to know this isn't your scene; you leave the torture and interrogation to those better suited to it. The people who enjoy it. That's not you."

"You risked my sister. Plied a betrayal from her. When you break—"

"I won't—"

"You will. We all do," she whispered. "I won't gamble with her life."

"I can help you, Natalia," he promised, his voice taking on a desperate, pleading edge. "One call, that's all it would take."

"Signal's blocked. Has been since before you walked in the door."

"I can hold out long enough for you—"

She shook her head.

"You'd really do this? Kill a man in cold blood?" he asked, pivoting, bringing his weight forward and ready.

She didn't say anything. Didn't have to. Let him read the answer in her expression, in the way she turned her body to meet him, in the cold metallic *snick* of a switchblade. He rushed her on a shout, butcher knife raised—all desperation, strength, and fury. With a gun, he'd have the advantage. In hand-to-hand, they'd be well matched. But with a knife?

No contest.

She let him come, stepped into and beneath the arcing slice he aimed at her face, and dropped to a knee, plunging her knife through the skin along the inside of his thigh, twisting, then withdrawing in a move that took seconds to execute and years to learn.

She stood as his leg crumpled beneath him. Sheathed her blade as he tried to stand but collapsed.

She plucked the butcher knife from his hand, watched as blood pooled against the gray fabric of his sweats. In a stroke, she'd severed his femoral artery. Death would be quick, at least. And the only comfort she could offer him.

She knelt next to him. Picked up his hand and laced their fingers together as shocked disbelief bled to agonizing horror and reality dawned on his face.

"I'm sorry," she said, her tone flat and distant. Resigned. The guilt would come, as it always did. But later. When she was alone. Then the memory of how easy it had been, how she hadn't hesitated or flinched or allowed herself a shred of doubt, would creep in like a predator in the night. "I'm sorry," she repeated, squeezing his fingers as he fought to keep his eyes open. "But you never should have involved my sister."

CHAPTER ONE

There was something stoic about Washington, DC, in the heavy, darkened gray of early morning. The sharp, nearly metallic scent of the waters of the Potomac. The eerie, quiet resilience of the monuments, still lit against the darkness. Whether running along the Mall or rowing past the shoreline, Ethan found a way, as often as possible, to begin his day here. In the strange silence that only a major city could offer in the hour before most people woke.

Ethan breathed through another catch and extract, enjoying the way rowing felt when he hit that perfect, balanced stroke. It had been far too long since he'd made the time. As the Lincoln Memorial came into view, he realized how much he'd needed the exercise. Needed to clear his mind, challenge his body, find his center.

Now, more than ever, he needed that sense of balance, of purpose. He'd been off-kilter and out of commission for too long.

Recovery, it turned out, was almost worse than the three bullets to the chest that had demanded it.

As Ethan pulled through another clean catch and extract, his single-man scull sliding through the water, the music in his earbuds cut out, and a voice announced, "Good morning, Captain Coxless."

"Can't you call me like a normal person?" Ethan grimaced, fighting to recover the easy rhythm he'd set up over the last half hour. "You know I hate it when you hack my phone."

"Want me to hang up?" Parker asked, far too alert for five thirty in the morning. "Call back? I can say, 'Ahoy, Captain Coxless' this time."

Ethan started to suppress a smile, then, since he figured Parker wasn't there to witness it, set it free. "Glad to see all those early-morning rowing lessons weren't entirely lost on you." A whole summer of dragging Parker out of bed or away from the computer at 5:00 a.m., and the only thing the man could be bothered to recall was the one vaguely dirty term.

"I don't know what you expected, forcing me out of the house at an ungodly hour of the morning and down to some pretentious yacht club—"

"Rowing club," Ethan corrected, dipping his oars in the water, rotating his hips forward, then straightening his legs, his scull silent and smooth as it cut a path along the shore. "The lack of sails should make for an easy distinction."

"Like I said, pretentious. You wouldn't even let me have coffee first," Parker whined. "So really, what did you expect?"

"That exercise coupled with the quiet atmosphere might have a calming effect on your otherwise erratic personality?" he huffed, wondering why he'd ever believed something so nuanced would appeal to Parker.

Parker snorted. "Idiot."

"Obviously." For someone who could mentally process multiple issues at the rate of a supercomputer, Parker was laughably bad at simple brain-body coordination, to say nothing of his complete lack of anything resembling patience. Ethan counted it a win that he'd never dumped the pair of them into the Potomac.

"Now, if you're quite finished with the cock jokes, bring me up to speed."

"I'm never finished with the cock jokes," Parker replied, though all enthusiasm and humor had fled his voice. "And I'd rather try, *again*, to talk you out of this."

"We've had this discussion, Parker." Ethan grunted, forcing himself not to muscle the oars through the water, to keep his strokes and his mind calm, his thoughts and his body centered. It was a mentality he was going to need in the coming days, and one he'd have to constantly cultivate.

One wrong step, one moment of weakness, of indecision—one tiny error, just one, and Ethan would be dead. And worse, he'd condemn every single person counting on him.

"That's bullshit and you know it." Parker heaved a breath over the line, as if surprised he'd had the temerity to openly challenge Ethan. A few months ago—hell, a few *weeks* ago—he wouldn't have. It was just one more example of how much could change when Ethan took his eye off the ball, when he delegated instead of led, when he forgot to account for all angles, all options, all eventualities.

His failures as team leader were piling up fast and stacking high.

"I distinctly recall you, present and accounted for, when we had this conversation more than a week ago."

"There was no conversation," Parker said, the clatter of a dropped pencil accompanying his frustrated sigh. "You came in, decision made. No contingencies, no plan B. You asked me to compile a report on the Vega cartel, to find a way in, but stupid me, I assumed you'd take the time to weigh all our options—not go rushing headlong into one of the most violent organizations on the planet!"

"Parker—"

"Don't, Ethan, just don't. If you think you're going to treat me like some desk-jockey tech analyst full of information but lacking opinions, then you've seriously misjudged the situation."

"What I misjudged," Ethan replied through gritted teeth, "was Charles Brandt." A senior official with the Department of Defense, Charles Brandt had operated with a frightening degree of autonomy—a necessary evil when it came to off-book military units. The man had taken Parker's predictive analysis technology and used it to line his pockets, completely betraying both the men under his command and the country he'd sworn to serve.

And Ethan had *missed* it.

"You couldn't have known, Ethan."

Except, as usual, hindsight was fucking twenty-twenty. Ethan should have seen what was happening, stepped in sooner. The Cyber Warfare Unit was his team—and his responsibility. It didn't matter that they'd reported in to Brandt and, through him, in to the DoD. At the end of the day, Ethan was the one responsible for everything that went on in the field. He'd been the one to recruit the team members, to train them, to prepare them, to *risk* them.

And he'd been okay with that. Risk—of injury, of death, of capture— those were all known quantities in the realm of Special Forces. As a SEAL, he'd trained for those eventualities, survived some of them, lost friends to others. And always, *always*, he'd weathered it, moving forward with the surety that at the end of the day, the scales still tipped toward the greater good.

How wrong he'd been.

"What I should or shouldn't have known is irrelevant," Ethan replied, his heart rate ramping up to match the pace of his strokes. "It's done. Now I have to fix it."

His rhythm slipped, and for a moment, Ethan fought the current, muscled his oars. His left pectoral stretched and burned, and his lungs ached against the cold air and heavy exertion, reminding him of the consequences of his negligence. If only three bullets—two to the vest, one to the meat of his shoulder—had been the worst of it.

Bruised ribs, a collapsed lung, loss of muscle mass and dexterity in his arm—those were all costs he was willing to pay. They were *his* costs, after all, paid for with *his* mistakes.

No, it was the collateral damage that kept Ethan up at night.

The thought of Parker, who had no field experience, no tactical training, standing over the body of a man he'd killed in self-defense because Ethan hadn't *listened*.

Of Georgia, who Ethan had assigned to Parker's security detail, blowing past every reasonable expectation of her job to keep Parker whole and healthy, as a selfish prick with all the assets at the disposal of the US government tried to kill not only them but the entire team Ethan had painstakingly built from the ground up.

And of Will, Georgia's brother and Ethan's best friend, who even now languished in some South American hellhole, held by the very cartel that Charles Brandt had sent him to destroy. Not for liberty or justice or basic human decency. Just pure, uncomplicated greed.

"*We* have to fix it," Parker said, the sound of a ceramic coffee mug landing in the sink clattering through the line.

"What?"

"You said, 'I have to fix it.' I'm correcting you," Parker explained with a grunt as a drawer squealed open, then slammed closed. "You're not the only one who feels responsible for this, Ethan. And you aren't the only one who wants—needs—to bring Will home safe." A cabinet door opened, then snapped shut again. "Fuck," Parker mumbled. "She expects me to use a fresh mug *every time*, but I can never freaking find them anymore."

"Check the dishwasher." Ethan rolled his eyes as Parker mumbled something barely intelligible about missing artificial sweetener and the dangers of a reduced sugar intake. The way Parker had folded Georgia into his life and his space, as if he'd always had a place for her there, lessened *some* of Ethan's guilt.

But it wasn't enough. Not by half.

"My point," Parker continued, switching tracks as hot water gurgled in the background, "is that the team you built is a family, and that means—"

"Quote *Fast and the Furious* and I'm hanging up."

Parker snorted. "I was going to say no one stands alone—something I learned from you, by the way."

"I hate it when you use my words against me," Ethan scoffed, jerking the oars and bunching his shoulders, rocking the scull precariously as his anger destroyed his form.

Which really shouldn't have surprised him. For all that brotherhood appealed to him—always had, always would—it was a role he seemed doomed to fail in. Connor, a brother by blood he couldn't save. Parker, who Ethan should have believed in the first place. And now Will, who Ethan had left behind to rot.

Ethan made for a shitty family member.

"Will's out there, Parker. I can't accept that. I won't."

He'd met Will—a Delta operator with an easy grin, a wicked sense of humor, and a soft spot for his tough-as-nails little sister—in Afghanistan. Assigned to the same joint task force, they'd forged a friendship based on fast cars, *Call of Duty*, and Coke—never Pepsi—that was as simple as it was enduring. They'd taken leave together, spent holidays together, and shared too many laughs—and a few too many fights—over a pitcher of beer and a Patriots game. Even when duty and family and desire had taken them to far-flung corners of the globe, the friendship had remained.

As enduring as it was uncomplicated, their friendship was one Ethan had come to rely on. On Will's agile mind, his sharp bark of laughter, and his constant admonishments that Ethan, despite all evidence to the contrary, wasn't all-knowing or all-powerful. A true peer in a world where Ethan often felt isolated by his experience and leadership.

Bringing Will into the Cyber Warfare Unit had just made sense. The fledgling team had needed experienced Special Forces personnel who could be pulled from their assignments and dropped in with the permanent team members for temporary missions on an as-needed basis.

Will, with his easygoing nature and lethal, tactical skill set, had been a perfect choice.

A choice that, up until a few weeks ago, Ethan believed had cost him his life.

"You didn't know, Ethan. None of us did. No one blames you for this. Not even Georgia," Parker said, his tone going soft and warm and comfortable.

Parker meant well, but he was wrong. Even if Georgia didn't blame him—and she had every right to—Ethan blamed himself. When news had come that Will had died during a raid against a cartel compound in the South American jungle, Ethan had handled it the only way he knew how—by bearing Will's flag-draped casket, saying his goodbyes, and pressing forward. Cold, maybe. But also necessary. Will, like Ethan, had known the risks, known what he was signing up for.

Except it was all *bullshit*.

Because Will *hadn't* understood the risks. Brandt's greed had seen to that. And worse, so much worse, was that Will hadn't known what he was signing up for, what he'd been risking his *life* for. Patriotism? Please. Charles Brandt hadn't given two fucks about love of country. He'd been all about the money, about getting rich off Parker's program and the hard work of people like Will, who, in the end, had been nothing more than cheap, expendable labor.

That alone would have been enough to keep Ethan up at night.

But to find out that Will hadn't died? That his actions, his sacrifices, had ultimately led to more than six months of captivity? To interrogation and torture and suffering that Ethan couldn't begin to contemplate, and worse, that Charles-fucking-Brandt had *known*?

There wasn't a level of hell deep enough to bury Charles Brandt—or Ethan's own sense of culpability.

At any time, Ethan could have listened to Parker, listened to his own goddamn gut telling him something wasn't right. Maybe it had been Ethan's trust and belief in the chain of command. Maybe it had been the manifestation of his grief over losing Will—it hardly mattered. Bottom line: if he'd been paying attention, if he'd been doing his job, then Will wouldn't be out there, alone, suffering, wondering if the entire world had forgotten him.

And Ethan wouldn't feel so fucking *helpless*.

So yeah, he didn't give a shit about the risks or the costs. Right now, the only thing that mattered was bringing Will home. There wasn't a price Ethan wasn't willing to pay to see that done.

"There are other ways, Ethan," Parker said softly. "Less dangerous options we can explore—"

"With what time?" Ethan grunted, struggling against the tide of the Potomac and the swirling current of his own worries that it might already be too late, that Will's body may have already given out, his spirit given up. It took everything in Ethan to maintain his calm, find his stroke, his rhythm, and force back the bubbling rage that would solve nothing and help no one.

"Every day that passes is another day Will is at the mercy of the cartel, another day closer to the moment that giving up becomes easier than holding out. I don't care about the risks. I can't leave him there, not now that we know he's alive."

"You sound like Georgia."

"Can you blame her? She's already mourned her brother once—do you really want to ask her to do it again?"

"Low blow." Quiet descended between them, stretching out as Ethan pulled his scull across the water's surface and under the Theodore Roosevelt Bridge. Birdsong and the hum of early-morning traffic carried across the water as pink tinged the horizon. Only the sound of Parker sipping his coffee assured Ethan he hadn't been hung up on.

Finally, after Parker rinsed his mug and dumped it into the sink, he said, "I love her. More than I ever thought I'd love anyone. There's not much I wouldn't do to bring Will home to her—"

"Then stop fighting me on this—"

"I said there wasn't 'much' I wouldn't do," Parker said, his voice hissing into Ethan's ear. "But if saving Will's life means sacrificing yours, then I'm sorry, but no. That's not acceptable to me. And you know what? Will would agree with me."

Ethan bit back a curse. "And you accused me of low blows."

"Someone had to say it. The Vega cartel's reputation precedes them—they're violent and ruthless, and all evidence points to the fact that they have no respect for law enforcement and little regard for human life."

"Exactly!" Ethan said, slapping the water with the broadside of the paddle, his scull sliding sideways in the water. "There's no decency in a cartel, Parker. No humanity. I don't know why they kept Will alive or what they hope to gain by holding him, but the second he's no longer useful, he's dead. We're not going to get a second chance at this, and we are running out of time." Every minute, every second, they debated this was another moment of agony and desperation for Will—assuming he was still hanging on, still hoping. "So please, just do what I asked you to in the first place and find me a way inside the cartel."

"I already have," Parker said with a sigh.

"Tell me."

Parker grunted, and the sound of his chair sliding heavily across wood flooring filtered through Ethan's earbuds. "Best point of entry is going to be Stephen Milner, Vega cartel accountant and all-around stain on humanity's record."

No wonder Parker had made one last-ditch effort at pointing Ethan toward caution. If Stephen Milner was compromised, if they could use him as a way in, then Ethan didn't have to waste precious time arguing all the reasons why he should be the one to take the risk—the argument made itself. Ethan was the only one on the team with a forensic accounting specialty. He had a head for numbers, always had, and now, finally, that boring degree and near-perfect GPA were going to be useful.

And shut down any of Parker's objections.

"Give me the rundown," Ethan said, sighting the dock in the distance and slowly settling back into a rhythm made easier by finding both purpose and direction.

"I leveraged the program, accessed every public database readily available, knocked on the back door of a few others—"

"Parker . . . ," Ethan warned, "we talked about that."

"Yeah, yeah. Hacking bad. Bite me, Mr. I Want It Right the Hell Now. This was a lot easier when my program had instant access to every government database known to man."

Ethan winced. It had taken all of Somerton Security's in-house attorney's sway to cut a deal that liberated both Parker and his predictive analysis software from DoD control. One of the downsides had been agreeing to disconnect from all government-controlled databases and to request information or access via the ordinary channels. A process that was as frustrating as it was slow.

"Just be careful, okay? The last thing I need is for our office to get raided by some jumped-up fed looking to make a name for himself—"

"Or herself," Parker interjected, no doubt grinning as he did. "No need to be sexist while painting the feds with a broad brush."

More of Georgia's influence in action. Miracle or menace, the jury was still out on the woman and the effect she'd had on Parker. Really, anyone who could wrangle Parker 24-7, let alone volunteered for the job, was inherently suspect in Ethan's book.

"You know what I mean."

"Yeah, yeah. Careful hacking. Got it. Anyway, there wasn't much for the program to work with. Cartels, unlike terrorist cells, still believe in the power of anonymity. They aren't using Twitter, Facebook, or any of the other standard social media outlets. I couldn't pull up much beyond public record of past crimes and known family members. So I cast a wider net."

"And?"

"And jackpot. Because while cartels might need to keep their business off book, they still need people to cook said books. It didn't take the program long to come up with a likely list of firms willing to get their hands dirty and, from there, a list of accountants with ties to the Vega family."

"Stephen Milner."

"Right. Ivy League educated. Midfifties. Worked his way up through two of the big accounting firms before finally landing at Whitney, Smith and Brindle. Made VP there—"

Ethan let loose a long, low whistle. Landing a job with a top firm was tough. Keeping the job even tougher. Most people burned out within the first five years. So the man wasn't stupid, just greedy.

"I can't believe that Whitney, Smith and Brindle would risk their reputation by doing business with the cartel. Most firms are too afraid of the criminal penalties if they're caught laundering funds for cartels or terrorist organizations."

"They're not—not on paper, at least. According to his tax records—"

"Parker!"

"Yeah, yeah, hacking, blah, whatever. Like I was saying, Milner's been an independent consultant for the last ten years—or from the moment he resigned from his position at Whitney, Smith and Brindle."

"Okay, but you said 'on paper.' If he's an independent contractor, then what does an international accounting firm have to do with this?"

"Well, that's where things get interesting. Because as it turns out, they have a relatively high attrition rate across executive and VP positions."

"Retirement?"

"That's what I thought, or loss to competition. And some of the time, that was the case. But in about ten percent of instances, employees left and transitioned to independent contracting." Parker paused, the *tap tap tap* of his pencil against the desk marking his thoughts. "Here's the thing, when I turned the program on that ten percent? None of them had extensive client lists, their websites are bland and basic—just enough to pass the sniff test on a Google search."

"Most likely outcome?" Ethan asked, the pink on the horizon bleeding into orange as morning crept up on the Capitol.

"Program says!" Parker chirped, doing his best *Family Feud* impression. "When a high-risk client comes to Whitney, Smith and Brindle, instead of sending them away, they headhunt for the right candidate internally. They're staffing cartels, terrorist organizations, and God knows who else with their own employees, then getting them set up as independent contractors and cashing in a nice referral fee and, if I had to guess, an ongoing commission. They share resources but maintain plausible deniability should one of their former employees come under investigation."

"Can we prove it?" Ethan asked, lifting his oars as his scull slid the last fifteen feet to the dock.

"For the purposes of criminal prosecution?" Parker asked, his desk chair squeaking as if he'd leaned back too far. "Not without a lot of time, money, and resources spent investigating."

"But . . ." And Ethan knew there was a but. There had to be. He'd spent eighteen months tearing down Parker's incessant need to know and share every single mundane detail until they'd finally reached an understanding. Ethan didn't give a shit about interesting details, only relevant facts. What qualified as relevant, they didn't always agree on, but Ethan was generally game to give Parker a bit of room for the windup. The man was never so happy as when he got to make a reveal.

"But we've got enough to scare them stupid. Play this right and Whitney, Smith and Brindle will fall all over themselves to place you inside the cartel."

"Great," Ethan huffed, pulling himself up onto the dock and ignoring the way his shoulder trembled in exhausted protest. "Their backing will go a long way to getting the job done. But how do we get Milner out?"

"Oh, he's done our job for us on that score. His finances and personal lifestyle read like an idiot's guide to skimming money from your employer. Couple that with the evidence of an ongoing drug problem and a taste for young girls—trust me when I say we've got plenty to send him running."

If Milner had been dumb enough to take from the cartel, there might not be a corner of the world far enough to run to. They'd want his head, no question. If Milner had any sense at all, he already had an exit strategy in place. And if he didn't? Well, that wasn't really Ethan's primary concern. No one had forced Milner into bed with the cartel. No one had demanded he accept their money—or steal it, for that matter. And anyone laundering money for a cartel knew just where that money came from. Drugs. Guns. Human trafficking.

Stephen Milner had made his choices, and now Ethan would make his.

"Time frame?" he asked, hefting the scull from the water and making his way toward his storage berth.

"Six, maybe seven days." Parker's chair creaked and complained in a steady back and forth of perpetual motion, Parker's default setting. "I'll have Isaac make the approach. Leading with 'I'm an attorney with the Justice Department' ought to have the accountants ready to piss themselves—and that's before he slaps down all the data I'm compiling."

"You've got seventy-two hours to get it done."

Parker groaned as Ethan disengaged the alarm on his Land Rover. "I know I make it look easy, but that sort of stuff takes time."

"The longer this takes, the longer Will suffers. Make it happen."

"You know," Parker said, the clatter of keys already filling the line, "for someone who claims to be a morning person, you sure are bitchy before sunrise."

Ethan shrugged, turned on the ignition, and put the car in gear. He'd been called worse. "Anything else?"

"Yeah, I got a preliminary prediction back on the mole within the Vega cartel."

"And?" Ethan asked, unease bunching muscles that had just begun to unwind under the relentless blast of the heater. There were always unknowns when it came to planning an operation, quantities and contingencies that couldn't be accounted for. That went double for an undercover operation. Ethan had dealt with those realities before, but this was different. This was someone acting against the cartel and, presumably, against their own interests. It made them both unknown *and* unpredictable.

Which made Ethan's stomach churn.

"Program indicates Ana Maria Vega is the informant who's been tipping off the FBI over the last five years and the person most likely to have sent in that video of Will."

"Have you had any luck tracing that back to the source, by the way?"

"No," Parker bit out, sounding both frustrated and defeated. "The file was scrubbed clean of any identifying data, and the e-mail isn't traceable. Whoever sent it in knew what they were doing. It's a dead end."

"You mean someone out there got the better of Parker Livingston, noted tech genius and persistent pain in my ass?"

"No one got the *better* of me, you jerk," Parker said, his disdain lacing every syllable. "You're going to pay for that."

Of that, Ethan had no doubt. Parker was nothing if not creative when it came to revenge, and Ethan knew exactly which buttons to push to set Parker off. But if it redirected Parker, kept him focused and engaged, if it prevented him from worrying he wasn't doing enough, then Ethan would consider it worth it.

"What do we know about the girl?" Ethan asked, searching his memory for any details that had been covered in the briefings. They'd pulled every resource they could—he still had requests pending with Isaac's contacts at the FBI, DEA, and Homeland Security—but there'd been precious little information on cartel family members.

"Not a lot," Parker admitted. "She's Hernan Vega's niece. Early twenties. College kid. Other than that? Basically one giant question mark."

"Hernan's head of US operations for the cartel, so she'd have access, I suppose." It was one piece of the puzzle but not the one Ethan most wanted. It didn't tell him why. Didn't explain what her goal was or why she'd risk turning informant. "Send me the file, we'll go from there when I get to the office."

"Done."

Ethan hung up.

Until he knew what drove Ana Maria Vega, he couldn't predict her. Certainly couldn't trust her. Which made everything more difficult.

But then, Ethan had never really cared for safe or easy.

He was all about the challenge, the risk. Always had been, always would be.

Even now, the first drop of adrenaline slid through his veins, awakening that part of him that lived for the mission, for the action. Too long, he'd been on the defensive.

It was time to change all that.

He might be walking into a nest of vipers, and there was a lot Ethan still didn't know and couldn't account for, but one thing was certain: Ana Maria Vega would never see him coming.

CHAPTER TWO

The scent hit her first, and on its heels, a memory. Warm and whole and welcoming, as seasoned and satisfying as the empanadas on the stove. For a second, Natalia allowed herself to linger on the back steps of her parents' DC home, hand on the doorknob, feet firmly planted in the present but her heart lodged painfully in the past. She took a deep breath of oil and meat and spices. Heard her mother's laugh. Saw her sister's grin. Felt her father's hand, warm and large and gentle on her shoulder.

And let the loss, the pain, the rage, envelop her. Harden her. Remind her that there wasn't anything she wouldn't do to keep what little she had left.

In Ana Maria, her sweet, shy little sister, Natalia found purpose and drive, if not forgiveness. And she could live with that. Ignore every line she crossed and every sin she committed by focusing only on the promise she'd made.

Protect your little sister.

And she would, even if that meant tucking away the mounting stress and anxiety and sense that things were unraveling, faster and faster with each passing day. That they were nearing a breaking point—an end or a beginning, she wasn't sure, but change was coming, violent and permanent all the same. It was an unnamed threat Ana Maria didn't need to know about, so Natalia took a breath. Forced herself to calm down and wait on the back steps until she could transition from problem solver to big sister.

Pulling a smile to her face, Natalia pushed open the door to her childhood home in Washington, DC, and stepped into the kitchen. "You're trying to make me fat, aren't you?" She hung her purse on the fancy scrolling hook by the door her mother had installed to keep track of her father's perpetually missing keys.

"It's my fondest wish." Ana Maria stood at the lemon-yellow Lacanche French range their father had bought their mother one long-ago Christmas, turning an empanada with a practiced flick of her wrist.

"We agreed years ago—you're the brains, I'm the beauty. It seems unfair you should have both," Ana Maria said, carefully spooning three more pastry shells into the popping grease.

"Remind me. Which one of us made the dean's list last semester?" Trying to force away the thoughts of just what Ana Maria's education had cost, the concessions Natalia had carefully extracted from their uncle, the things he'd demanded in payment. She turned her thoughts to the only thing that mattered—a ten-year-old promise that had become the strength that convinced her to fight. For her mother. Her sister. Both soft, delicate, and so easily broken. Natalia had thought of them as her uncle's associate—a nameless man whose face she would never forget—had plunged inside her, his hands wrapped around her neck, his eyes wild and dark and excited.

It was the one and only time Natalia had allowed herself to consider escape. She'd been so close. So tempted. But as her attacker's face had grown fuzzy, as her cries had turned rough and inaudible, painful scrapes of sandpaper against her vocal cords with nowhere to go and no one to hear, she'd thought of the sister she'd leave behind. The sweet, naive girl who hadn't spoken a single word in the three months since their uncle had murdered their father at the dinner table. Of the way Ana Maria had lost weight, lost light, lost hope.

And she'd thought of the promise she'd made.

It had been enough to send her fingers scrabbling until they met the heavy crystal of the highball on the nightstand next to her, still half-full of the cheap whiskey she'd never forget the scent of. Had given her the strength to slam it against her attacker's temple and, finally, to thrust a broken shard into the soft skin at his throat, severing the carotid artery by luck as much as desire.

When she'd walked from the room, dress torn, chest and face covered in blood, she'd expected her uncle to kill her.

Instead, he'd found a new use for a niece he'd considered expendable. And Natalia had found her only source of leverage.

But she'd survived. Grown. Changed. Until she became lethal, feared, relentless. Until everything she'd ever been or hoped to be had been stripped from her, leaving behind only the promise she'd made and the determination to see it through.

No matter what it cost her in the end, Natalia would see Ana Maria out of this life, away from their uncle, and out of the cartel. Free to pursue the dreams Natalia had once held for herself.

A yell echoed down the stairs followed by the shatter of glass against the wall. Wonderful.

"His temper's been foul all day," Ana Maria whispered, her eyes still trained on the ceiling. "Started drinking early, too."

That explained the empanadas. Ana Maria only ever cooked when she was stressed or upset about something, and they both knew from experience the best way to manage their uncle's drunken temper was to smother it with food and keep well clear until it passed. Hopefully, the empanadas would do their job, because there'd be no avoiding Hernan Vega tonight. Not for Natalia, at least. He'd want an update, good news she didn't have.

"Where've you been, anyway?" Ana Maria asked, turning back to the range and flipping over the three pastry shells to reveal a perfect golden hue. "You're usually here when I get home from class."

"I had a meeting with Mitchell Grimes."

"The private investigator?" Ana Maria asked. "Why?"

"*Tio* needed some work done." Natalia pulled a glass from the cabinet and filled it with water from the fridge, mostly to keep herself busy. Nothing good could come of Ana Maria's involvement—a lesson they'd learned the hard way.

"What's wrong?" Ana Maria turned to where Natalia had taken a seat at the butcher-block island. "And don't say nothing—I know you too well to believe it."

"Company business." Natalia shrugged and took another bite to buy herself a little time.

For the most part, Ana Maria escaped their uncle's attention—and avoided the worst of his temper. So much like their mother, Ana Maria was soft-spoken, gentle, and acquiescent when confronted—she was neither threat nor asset where the cartel was concerned, which was half the reason their uncle permitted her a degree of freedom. The other half was that with every passing day, Ana Maria grew into a more beautiful, refined version of their mother—a woman their uncle often claimed to have loved beyond all reason.

But how much of the violence, of the danger, did Ana Maria need to know about to stay safe? And how much could Natalia share before the knowledge began to stain her sister in small but irreparable ways?

There was no place in the cartel for a woman with a soft heart and a gentle disposition.

"It's nothing for you to worry about, just a problem with our accountant."

Ana Maria turned back to her cooking, her grip tight on the spatula, but otherwise didn't move as the empanadas sizzled in the pan. "Stephen's always so polite—he hardly seems like the type to cause trouble."

Natalia repressed a frustrated sigh. She spent so much time working to keep Ana Maria untouched by the world around them. Sheltered. Innocent. Even a little naive. But every now and then, Natalia's success had unintended consequences. It seemed almost inexplicable that

Ana Maria could be so trusting of the people around her, that she could still see inherent good in just about everyone, that she'd mistaken Stephen Milner's wandering eye and taste for beautiful things as anything remotely genuine. But then, history had shown her otherwise. Somehow, Ana Maria still wanted to believe the best of people.

Natalia knew better.

"Have you seen him lately?" Natalia asked, studying her sister's profile. Surely she would have said if Stephen had been coming around.

"No." Ana Maria placed the last of the empanadas on the cooling rack and flicked off the burner. "Is he all right?" she asked, joining Natalia at the kitchen island.

"He's missing," Natalia explained, leaving out the part where Milner had made off with millions. "If you see him, I want you to call me, okay? Don't talk to him, not even to say hello."

"That would be rude," Ana Maria said, sprinkling flour across the work surface, then rolling out a new sheet of dough.

Natalia caught Ana Maria's wrist, firmly lacing her fingers around the delicate bones. "I mean it. Promise me that if you see him, you'll walk away and call me." The last thing she needed was Ana Maria caught in the cross fire or for Milner to try to use her as leverage. When it came down to it, their uncle would choose money and vengeance over his niece, no question and no hesitation.

Ana Maria huffed, then rolled her eyes. "Fine."

"Thank you." Natalia withdrew her hand and watched as Ana Maria cut the dough into long diagonal strips, then again going in the opposite direction until she had rows of neat triangles.

If Milner had any sense at all, he'd eat a bullet before he'd let Hernan's thugs take him alive when they found him.

And they *would* find him. Of that, Natalia had no doubt. Her uncle wasn't the smartest man, and generally too prone to fits of temper and decisions made in the moment. But when it came to a grudge, to an insult, perceived or real, he was nothing short of possessed. There was nowhere in the world Milner could hide that Hernan would not find him. If it took one month or ten years, her uncle would neither forget nor forgive.

Everyone who worked in Hernan's orbit understood that defiance and betrayal were bought and paid for in blood and death. He'd only ever made a single exception, spared one life.

Some days, Natalia wished he hadn't.

"Is that why he's so angry?" Ana Maria asked, casting her gaze to the ceiling, though the upstairs office had fallen quiet.

"Yes. Try to stay out of his way, okay?"

Ana Maria nodded, then pulled the muslin cover off a bowl full of spiced fruit. With movements born of plenty of practice, she scooped spoonful after spoonful onto the pastry she'd cut, then sealed together the two triangles of dough with the tines of her fork. It was something Natalia could watch her do all day, the rhythm familiar and easy and almost enough to make her believe that their circumstances were different, that their lives were normal.

Someday, she reminded herself. Though lately, "someday" was beginning to feel more and more like a promise she'd never be able to keep.

Cartel business was mercurial at best, but throw in a botched assassination attempt and millions of dollars that, sooner or later, the company would come to collect . . . The pressure would turn far stronger men insane with paranoia.

But the precarious situation made it almost impossible for Natalia to interfere. The constant movement of drugs, she could live with. Even her own father had never managed to turn all their family's holdings legitimate. No, it was the human trafficking that kept her up at night. The knowledge that where her father had held some level of compassion, some sense of boundaries and decency, her uncle did not. For him, every life held only the value he assigned it. No more, no less.

The thought of where those women and children ended up haunted her. She knew all too well the life that awaited them. It was short and brutal and devoid of any warmth or comfort. And even under the best of circumstances, there was so little Natalia could do to help. Not without risking her own life, and therefore Ana Maria's safety.

It had been months since Natalia had dared make any sort of tip. No matter how much it ate at her, she couldn't weigh the life of a stranger against the life of her sister. If Hernan caught her, there'd be no pity, no second chance. Under the best of circumstances, he'd kill her.

She didn't have to wonder. Didn't live in fear of the unknown. She knew *exactly* what he'd do. Years ago, he'd sat her down and laid out every detail. It was the only time she'd seen him stone-cold calm.

Natalia shivered.

"What the fuck is all this?" Hernan asked, stumbling down the last few steps and into the kitchen. Natalia straightened in her chair, even as Ana Maria pulled a strained smile to her face.

"Dinner, *Tio*. I thought you might be hungry." She turned and used a pot holder to pull a heavy white plate piled with empanadas from the warming drawer. "Here, I'll set your place at the dinner table and bring you something to drink." She moved to brush past him, but he caught her forearm and jerked her to a stop.

"I'll eat here," he said, pulling her around to the island. "You," he said, jerking his chin at Natalia, "make me a drink. Then get back in here."

Quietly, Natalia rose and cast her sister a careful look as she went into the dining room and the dry bar they kept fully stocked. When she returned, Ana Maria was back in front of her work area, neatly arranging fruit into pastry triangles. Natalia did her best to ignore the way the skin at her sister's forearm was still red and angry-looking.

"I have to replace the fucking accountant," Hernan said as Natalia set a glass at her uncle's elbow. "Where's the goddamn ice?" he asked, staring into his drink. Given his mood, Natalia had no doubt that if she'd served it that way to begin with, he'd have slapped it off the edge of the counter and demanded it neat. She went to the freezer and withdrew the tray of square ice cubes, reminding herself she couldn't afford to react to the whims of his mood.

"I'm sure you'll find someone suitable, *Tio*," Ana Maria offered, turning back to the stove and lighting the flame beneath a new cast-iron pan of oil.

"Has Whitney, Smith and Brindle recommended someone?" Natalia asked, popping an ice cube into his drink.

"Fucking bastards are falling all over themselves to replace the thief they sent me." He grunted and crammed half an empanada into his mouth. "Should tell them to go fuck themselves for the trouble they've caused. Instead, they throw a party."

A party? That sounded like Whitney, Smith and Brindle. It would no doubt be both opulent and public—the perfect venue to mitigate her uncle's unpredictable nature. He was just too stupid to see it for the attempt at control that it was.

Hernan tossed back the last of his whiskey. "They're sending some asshole with an expensive degree looking for an illegal thrill and a cartel payday. *Pendejo* probably spends his nights jerking off to *Narcos*." He snorted. "I want you," he said, jabbing his finger at Ana Maria, "to introduce yourself to the accountant."

"But why?" Natalia snapped out before she could think better of it. "Ana Maria's got no experience in the business, no head for numbers—"

Hernan cut her off with a harsh look. "Your sister has everything she needs—a woman's body and her mother's looks; it's time she put them to use."

Panic dropped, thick and heavy. "No, I—" Lightning fast, her uncle struck out, the back of his hand catching Natalia across her cheek and snapping her head to the side, the power of the blow driving her to her knees. Before she could recover, Hernan was on her, his fist in her hair and his other hand wrenching her arm up behind her back. In moments, he had her bent over the stove, her face hovering inches above the hot, popping grease.

"You think to question me? To tell me *no*?" he hissed. "You forget your place."

With her free hand, Natalia scrabbled for purchase, her fingers gripping the edge of the stove. She flinched, the grease turning hot enough to pop, little flecks landing against the smooth skin of her cheek. Her own stupidity had led her here; she couldn't afford to make it worse. She forced herself to go still and calm, to relax against her uncle's unrelenting hold.

Now is not the time, she reminded herself. If she struck out or fought back, the situation would turn fatal for one of them.

And she couldn't guarantee she'd win. Or that Ana Maria wouldn't be hurt.

Out of the corner of her eye, Natalia watched, absorbing the little pops of grease without so much as a flinch, as Ana Maria rushed forward. "No!"

But it was too late; the second Ana Maria touched Hernan, he used the hand he'd planted in the middle of Natalia's back to strike out, catching Ana Maria across the cheek.

Silence descended on the kitchen, the *sizzle, pop, spit* of the grease the only thing Natalia could hear above the buzz of rage filling her head.

"*Tío*, please," Ana Maria implored, her voice soft and scared. Trembling fingers touched the skin of her cheek, her large cornflower-blue eyes blinking away tears that were probably as much a product of shock as they were pain. "She didn't mean it," she whispered.

Natalia held herself perfectly still, willing herself to wait, to let the situation play out. The moment Hernan had removed the hand from her back, he'd given her the opening she'd need to twist away. But now, as he stood stock-still, as if he couldn't quite believe he'd hit Ana Maria—something he'd *never* done before—Natalia forced herself to remain still and compliant, to rein in the urge to take him apart, bit by bit, and damn the consequences.

"She's only protective of me," Ana Maria whispered as she lifted a trembling hand and slid her palm along Hernan's arm, down toward his wrist and out of Natalia's sight. "As are you. *Please.*"

On a curse, he jerked Natalia away from the stove, away from the heat and the grease and the very real fear that this time he'd go too far, that this time he'd hurt her too badly, and pushed her toward her sister.

"You," he said, advancing on Natalia even as she pulled Ana Maria behind her, "will not contradict me again. And you," he said, jerking his chin to Ana Maria, who at least had the good sense to stay still and quiet behind her, "will do as you are told. A man never opens his mouth so much as when a woman opens her legs. I trusted our last accountant—a costly mistake I won't make twice."

Natalia stood, still and quiet, barely daring to breathe as he stared them down.

"I'll take care of him, *Tio,*" Natalia whispered, her body tight under the weight of the risk she was taking. She knew better than to openly oppose him, knew that managing him required subtle and careful manipulation. But she'd sooner find a way to put a knife in her uncle's back than send her sister to some ambitious asshole's bed. "It's like you said, he's looking for the cartel experience—an illicit thrill—Ana Maria can't give him that." True, and they both knew it. Ana Maria, although beautiful, was far too gentle to entice someone who wanted to take a walk down a darker path. Most men who looked at Natalia's sister saw something lovely and fragile, something they wanted to possess and cosset. A trophy to place on their mantel. And those who didn't? The men who saw something they could break or defile or ruin? They feared Hernan's wrath enough that they kept their thoughts to themselves. So no, Ana Maria couldn't offer this accountant anything he hadn't already experienced at his fine schools and fancy parties.

But Natalia could. "He wants the cartel life—let me give it to him."

Hernan stared at her a long time, his dark eyes dilated with booze and rage. "And if he proves a problem?" he asked slowly.

31

"Then I'll give him that experience, too," Natalia offered quietly, bile building in the back of her throat.

"Fine, but I'll hear no complaints. You'll take what he gives, and you'll do it without protest." He stepped forward, pulling himself up to his full height and glowering down at her. "Fuck him. Break him. I don't care so long as you find out if this *pendejo* is who he says he is. Because if you don't, if he cheats me, I'll kill you right after I dispose of him. Are we clear?"

Natalia swallowed and nodded.

"Good. Then get this shit cleaned up." He grabbed his drink off the counter and stomped his way back up the stairs. When the door to his office slammed shut, Natalia took her first full breath since he'd held her over the stove. To her horror, tears stung her eyes even as pinpricks of fire stung her cheek.

Ana Maria stepped around her and quietly flicked off the burner. The sight of her trembling fingers against the heavy steel knob had Natalia pulling herself together.

"You're so stupid sometimes," Ana Maria mumbled.

"I know," Natalia agreed on a relieved sigh. "But I'll take care of *Tio*, and I promise, no matter what, you don't have to deal with that accountant."

"Right. Because you *will*," Ana Maria ground out, her voice a strangled, garbled thing. She pulled away, her eyes dry and her mouth a firm, tight line. "You can't protect me from everything, you know."

"Sure I can," Natalia said, a fond smile pulling at her lips. When her sister frowned, when her lip curled in distaste and her eyes creased with frustration, she looked as indignant as a wet cat . . . and so damn young it hurt.

"We can't keep doing this," Ana Maria whispered.

It was a statement Natalia had thought a thousand times before but never given voice to. That Ana Maria had let it slip from her lips as a toneless, leaden fact settled heavily on Natalia's shoulders. Because no, they couldn't keep doing this. Not anymore. Hernan had crossed a line Natalia could not ignore—he'd struck Ana Maria. And though Natalia had seen the shock on his face, felt the hesitation in his grip, the door was open. She couldn't afford to pretend it wouldn't happen again.

Or that the next time wouldn't be worse.

For so long, Natalia had allowed herself to linger in the fragile peace she'd brokered with Hernan—defiance had always been too dangerous, too risky, the odds of success too narrow and the consequences of failure too great.

But now, all that had changed. She couldn't wait anymore. Couldn't hope things would get better.

She just didn't know what to do about it. Somehow, everything— and nothing—had changed.

"You don't have to look out for me, you know," Ana Maria said, turning away and slipping a roll of plastic wrap from the drawer.

"Of course I do," Natalia scoffed as Ana Maria used shaking hands to cover the fruit-filled empanadas she hadn't cooked. "You're my baby sister. If I don't watch over you, who will?"

"But who's looking out for you?" Ana Maria asked on a whisper.

Natalia swallowed hard around the truth she'd known for a very long time and forced a smile to her lips. "You, of course."

Natalia had never, not once, doubted how much Ana Maria loved her. And in so many ways, so many little, normal, sisterly ways, Ana Maria did take care of her. Made sure there was always a fresh home-made meal. Kept up with the house, called when she was late. Kept yellow—a color they both agreed Natalia could never pull off—out of her closet.

But when it came down to it, when it was life or death, Natalia was on her own.

Always had been. Always would be. And nothing and no one was ever going to change that.

CHAPTER THREE

The time for rest and recovery had passed, and thank fuck for that. Because no amount of planning, strategizing, or consulting was going to get Ethan back on his feet like diving headfirst into fieldwork. He needed to put his boots on the ground and get his hands dirty.

Ethan wasn't built to idle or let other people handle things in his stead. He delegated when he had to, and he had the utmost faith in the team he'd built. But at the end of the day, his team was his responsibility. He gap-filled for them, not the other way around. It had taken just three shots to the chest to blow that all to shit. To render him little more than deadweight.

Obsolete.

Ethan rolled his shoulders within the confines of his tailored suit. After all the prep and planning—blackmailing the accounting firm, helping Parker create a vast digital trail to support Ethan's alias—he hadn't expected incursion into the Vega cartel to come by way of a fucking cocktail party. Heavy artillery and close-quarter combat he could handle. Subterfuge and covert maneuvers he was trained for. But sipping cocktails, listening to insipid corporate gossip, and otherwise schmoozing his way through an evening? Well, his parents had trained him for it, but it was still the worst sort of boredom.

But the executive team at Whitney, Smith and Brindle had *insisted*. They'd been adamant—no backroom introductions, no low-key deals. In their rush to provide Ethan an in and to avoid a federal investigation, they had explained that high-risk, high-profile staffing was always handled via a "networking opportunity" for plausible deniability. Host a large enough event, let enough people mingle, and the firm could wash its hands of any discussions or career decisions that took place.

Which was why Ethan stood near a floor-to-ceiling window overlooking the Washington Monument, making dull small talk with two middle-aged lobbyists while he waited for someone from within the cartel to make contact. Once again, he'd been put on the defensive, forced to wait for somebody else to make the first move.

Patience, he reminded himself. Unlike tactical incursions, undercover assignments required a different type of endurance and finesse. Much as he wanted to, he couldn't afford to rush things along.

Bringing Will home was the priority, and always at the forefront of Ethan's mind, consuming his thoughts and driving his every decision. But now it was time to tuck that away and focus less on the big picture and more on the individual pieces. One step at a time, until Will was taking his first steps home.

"Mr. Sullivan," a voice announced, drawing Ethan's attention from the window and back to the conversation at hand. As he turned, both the lobbyists he'd been largely tuning out went still. "Hernan Vega." The hair on the back of Ethan's neck rose at the deep, slightly accented voice. Ethan pivoted, coming face-to-face with the man of the hour.

"Ethan." He shook hands with Hernan, nodding as one of the men he'd been standing with mumbled something about refreshing his drink and left, the other following in his wake.

"Have a seat," Hernan said, pointing to one of the ridiculously high-backed leather chairs flanking the window. When Ethan didn't move, Hernan canted the glass he held in the palm of his hand, the amber liquid dipping toward the rim, and repeated his command. "Sit."

Subtle. And everything Ethan had expected of the man he'd researched and studied.

Convenient. But a little disappointing, too. Just once Ethan wanted to test himself against an adversary who surprised him. Who was more than the sum of their deeds. Who wasn't motivated by basic, boring instincts like greed or power or lust. Someone a dossier or rap sheet couldn't capture.

Someone dynamic. Someone interesting.

But not here. Not today. And certainly not Hernan Vega.

The man didn't say anything, simply stood there, sipping at his drink and running an assessing gaze over Ethan. For his part, Ethan crossed an ankle over a knee and reclined against the gold leather of his chair and waited. He and Parker had spent endless hours preparing for this moment, had leveraged all the power of Parker's predictive analysis program to create a persona for Ethan that Hernan Vega would buy into.

He'd been burned once already by an arrogant white-collar employee who'd had next to nothing in common with a man born and bred in a culture of violence. Ethan Sullivan had been crafted from a meticulous blend of competence, arrogance, and deferential respect. Someone who came from nothing but didn't intend to accept that as his due.

Someone willing to get his hands dirty to achieve his own ends.

Someone Hernan could recognize as a peer. Someone he could predict, if not control.

It was a delicate fucking balance, and in that, at least, Ethan found the challenge he was looking for.

"Are you enjoying yourself, Mr. Sullivan?" Hernan finally asked, staring down at Ethan from a face that had seen too much sun and too many fists.

"Not particularly," Ethan answered, clinking the ice of his empty drink against his glass.

"Oh?" Hernan shifted, glancing out the window. "Is it the view you find lacking?" he asked, indicating the Washington Monument, glowing white against the inky black of the night sky. "Or perhaps the free booze is not to your taste?"

Ethan cut a tight-lipped smile. "I don't care for the company. Men who inherit an empire don't know what it means to build one, to bleed for one."

The corner of Hernan's mouth, the one bisected by a deep, curving scar, tilted up. *"Pendejos."*

"All of them," Ethan agreed, sucking a piece of ice between his lips and crunching.

"All?" Hernan asked, his dark-brown eyes boring into Ethan, the flicker of a challenge in their depths.

"Most," Ethan conceded with a careless shrug.

"But not you?" Hernan asked, his rigid frame and tense posture settling into something ready but relaxed.

"My father left me his looks . . . and nothing else. Everything I have, I earned."

"Bled for."

"Or drew blood for."

Hernan *tsk*ed and took a slow sip of his drink. "A dangerous game, taking what does not belong to you."

"That depends on who you're taking it from."

"Something your predecessor failed to realize."

"Then he was a fool, and you are well rid of him."

"I certainly will be," Hernan said, his face going hard and grim and cruel, giving Ethan his first glimpse of the monster beneath the suit. The Hernan Vega he'd read about was as mean as he was brutal. Ruthless. The sort of cartel player who not only embraced the violence but delighted in it.

Not for the first time, Ethan hoped that for his sake, Stephen Milner was a better ghost than he was a thief. There would be no easy death if Vega caught him.

"And you, Mr. Sullivan?" Hernan asked, his voice frigid and sharp.

"Me?" Ethan asked, rising to his feet as Ana Maria Vega, the person he had most hoped to meet that evening, appeared at her uncle's elbow.

"*Tio?*" she asked, her voice high and soft and sweet as a freshwater spring. "I freshened your drink," she said, gently slipping her uncle's near-empty glass from his fingers and replacing it with a new one. With a soft smile and curious blue eyes, she turned to Ethan. "I hope I'm not interrupting."

"I was just asking Mr. Sullivan if he was a fool," Hernan barked, his gaze never leaving Ethan's.

"What man isn't when it comes to cards, cars, or beautiful women?" he said, shooting a pretentious wink at Ana Maria. The corner of her mouth twitched in amusement, and to Ethan's shock, an innocent blush rose across her chest and up the fair column of her neck. This . . . was not the woman he'd expected. Before he could get lost in that train of thought, he forced himself to turn back to Hernan. "But not so foolish as to pass up drinking another man's liquor"—he shook his glass, rattling the ice against the sides—"or to forget that nothing tastes sweeter—or goes down smoother—than what a man secures for himself."

"I suppose we'll see," Hernan grunted.

"I look forward to working with you," Ethan said.

"You assume too much. I've offered you no job."

"Forgive me," Ethan said, shifting his stare back to Hernan. "I thought that was why we are all here tonight."

"We're here," Hernan said with a sneer, "because the last accountant was a liar and a cheat—very soon he'll be nothing at all—and now I've discovered he was incompetent, too. What guarantees do I have you're not exactly the same?"

"None," Ethan said. "But then, you aren't a man who deals in guarantees. Just in facts and the control they bring."

"And what are the facts, Mr. Sullivan?" he asked.

"That while Milner and I share an education and a work history, we share little else. That I'm not interested in a quick payday or boring career." Ethan met Hernan's gaze head-on. "And that when I say I can or will do something, I back it up."

"Easy words."

"Easy to test," Ethan countered.

"What did you have in mind?" Hernan asked, his expression growing calm and curious.

This, too, Ethan had discussed with Parker. Given Hernan's own history and the general culture within a cartel, Ethan would likely need to prove himself. His willingness to do so without being asked or challenged could only work to his benefit.

"Grant me access and I'll tear through Milner's files until you know down to the last cent what money he stole and how he spent it. Give me a week and access to your systems and I'll provide you a full accounting." Ethan loosened his stance and slipped his hands into his pockets. On a shrug, he said, "I'm good. Certainly better than Milner, but talk is cheap." He watched Hernan consider his proposition, his face a blank slate Ethan couldn't quite read. "Judge a man by his actions and you'll never have to wonder if he's lying to you."

"Very well," Hernan acquiesced. "I'll have Milner's computer delivered to your home—you'll have full access to his files but not mine. Not yet."

Ethan suppressed a wince. Full access had been a long shot, but ultimately tomorrow's problem. With any luck, Milner's files would provide the answers he was looking for.

"I'll have a full accounting for you by the end of next week—"

"You'll have it Wednesday afternoon," Hernan corrected.

"Done," Ethan said. He'd asked for more time than he'd need—he and Parker had already compiled half the picture where Milner was concerned, but still, he'd hoped for more time to look for anything that might lead them to Will. But it didn't matter. Ethan would deliver on his promise, and Hernan would pull him into the fold and one step closer to bringing his friend home.

"I have business to attend to," Hernan said, dismissing Ethan and their conversation. "My niece," he said, pulling her forward by her elbow, "will see to it that the rest of your evening is more to your liking."

"It's looking up already," Ethan said, extending his hand to Ana Maria as Hernan turned and walked away. "Ethan Sullivan."

"Ana Maria Vega." She slid her long, delicate fingers against the roughened skin of Ethan's palm, suppressing a shy smile as he brought her knuckles to his mouth for a kiss. "It's lovely to meet you."

"The pleasure is mine," he said, allowing her to slip her hand from his. The photos he'd studied of the woman before him hadn't done her beauty justice. At first glance, Ana Maria reminded Ethan of an exhibition he'd seen years ago at a museum in Paris. It had featured one-of-a-kind drawings that the artist had created by setting pen to paper only once, creating beauty in one seamless, fluid stroke.

In Ana Maria, Ethan saw the same long, fluid lines, delicate curves, and fragile planes. Had she been petite, as her build suggested she should be, she would have been no less beautiful and yet significantly less striking. As it was, she rose nearly eye to eye with Ethan's own six foot two. A feat, even in heels, for a woman who looked as if she should barely reach his shoulder.

"Are you enjoying yourself, Mr. Sullivan?" Ana Maria asked, blinking up at him with wide blue eyes Ethan could only assume she'd inherited from her mother's European lineage. Certainly, judging by the few Vega family photos Parker had dug out of some Internet database, she looked nothing like her father and even less like her uncle.

"Ethan," he corrected. "And the evening has certainly taken a pleasant turn." True, insomuch that Ethan hadn't had to track down Ana Maria or force an introduction on his own. But strange in that the woman before him was nothing like he'd expected. His own fault. He knew better than to make assumptions based on half-formed impressions or details found only on paper.

Still, Ana Maria wasn't the sort of surprise he'd had in mind. Nothing about her felt like a challenge or an enigma. Even on first impression she felt too open, too inclined to please the people around her. She was exactly the sort of woman Ethan dated—beautiful, accommodating, uncomplicated—for a month, six weeks if he was traveling. Until hot sex turned to questions about the future and vapid conversations about celebrity scandals and reality TV.

This was the woman who'd been tipping off the authorities for *years*? Appearances could be deceiving, but good God, if that were the case, then this was one hell of a disguise.

Ana Maria's chin dipped, her gaze going briefly to the nearly empty martini glass she held. "I'm glad to hear it."

They settled into an awkward silence, the din of 150 or so of Whitney, Smith and Brindle's most valued clients filtering into the space stretching between them. Ethan shifted, searching for a safe topic of discussion. He'd thought conversing with Hernan would be the difficult part of his evening, but with every passing moment, it was becoming clear Ana Maria really didn't want to be here, and yet, she stayed. Because her uncle had instructed her to? Because she had nowhere else to be?

Or because she was waiting him out?

Leveraging a long pause and an uncomfortable interaction to see what he'd fill it with? As manipulation went, it was a good one. A tactic taught in interrogation training. Most people tried to fill an awkward or uncomfortable silence, and inane chitchat often revealed more than the speaker intended. But as Ana Maria stood there, chewing on the corner of her lip as she twisted the diamond bracelet at her wrist, Ethan had to admit that if this stretch of silence was intentional, if Ana Maria was playing him, then she was the best operator he'd ever come across.

Because *nothing* about this woman felt shrewd or calculating or manipulative. And with each passing moment, Ethan's faith in the program's conclusion that Ana Maria Vega was the informant within the cartel, the one risking her *life* to tip off a handful of federal agencies, grew less and less certain.

Ethan's gut against Parker's program. There was a showdown he didn't want to have, and definitely not without something more concrete than a "feeling" to back it up. And if Ana Maria was determined to wait him out, to let him step into the silence, well, then, who was he to disappoint her?

"Any moment, I'm going to remark on the weather," Ethan said, letting a small smile curl the corners of his mouth. "Tell me about yourself and save me the embarrassment?"

Ana Maria laughed and sipped from her martini glass. "What would you like to know?" she asked, turning away from the window and giving Ethan her full attention.

"Anything you'd like to tell me."

She arched one fine blonde brow. "What, like where I go to school? My favorite color?"

Ethan shrugged. "Sure. For a start."

"George Washington and red, though I'm afraid it suits my sister better." She tipped her head to the side, and Ethan followed her gaze, spotting Natalia Vega cutting her way toward them through the room. He had neither the breath nor desire to disagree. Red was most certainly Natalia's color. In a sea of black suits and starched white shirts, she approached like the sunrise, a bold slash of color brazen enough to challenge the night, determined and steadfast enough to win. Bright and beautiful and hot enough to burn.

And the *worst* sort of temptation. The kind of woman who pushed a man to possession, to distraction, to lust.

Natalia Vega, in that bloodred cocktail dress and stormy expression, had the dangerous allure of a woman who could slide to her knees, only to drive a man to his.

"There you are," Natalia said, stepping close, her hand going briefly to the small of her sister's back.

Had she been a man, Ethan might have found the gesture a hollow attempt at posturing, but when Natalia glanced to Ana Maria, there was no mistaking the warmth, the love, the devotion. And when her gaze slid from the gentle cut of her sister's profile to meet Ethan's stare, there was no mistaking the warning in that look or the ice in her tone. "And you are?"

"Ethan Sullivan," he said, extending his palm. Natalia slipped her hand in his, the slide of her skin smooth and firm and confident. Ethan didn't bother to bring her knuckles up for a kiss—he knew without question such a gesture would not only amuse her at his expense but that even the barest taste of her would prove a distraction he could not afford.

"Natalia," she said, dismissing him with a glance that did nothing for his ego but helped bring him back to the present reality where any attraction, to say nothing of the montage of dirty thoughts he'd just had about a *Vega*, would be incredibly inconvenient.

"Have you had something to eat?" Natalia asked, glancing at the mostly empty martini glass her sister held.

"Yes, Mom." Ana Maria rolled her eyes and turned to Ethan. "You'll have to forgive my sister, she tends to be a little overprotective."

"Who can blame her?" Ethan asked, lifting the glass from Ana Maria's fingers and setting it on a passing server's tray. "I'm sure you look out for each other." Ethan didn't need to spend days, hours, or even minutes with the two women to see how close they were. It was written in the way Ana Maria had relaxed the moment Natalia had joined them. The way her shy smile and stilted efforts at conversation had immediately changed to full, familiar grins and easy exasperation.

"It looks like you could both use a fresh drink. Why don't I see what I can do about that?" Ethan stepped aside, gesturing toward the bar flanking one long wall and overlooking the view of DC.

"The bartender is set up at the end of the room," Natalia said, nodding toward the line of suits milling about a smaller bar at the far side of the space.

"I had something else in mind," Ethan said, slipping beneath the break in the bar top and pulling a fresh martini glass and a stainless-steel tumbler from the stack behind him.

"Oh," Ana Maria gasped, her eyes flitting across the room. "I don't think you're supposed to be back there."

"I won't tell if you won't." Ethan smiled and shrugged out of his jacket. "Now let me see . . . Ana Maria, if memory serves, you had a martini, yes?"

"I did," she agreed. "Gin. Extra olives."

"A classic, and coming right up," Ethan said, shrugging out of his jacket and rolling up his shirtsleeves. "Though you weren't supposed to tell me. How am I supposed to impress you with my bartending prowess if I can't even guess your drink?"

"And what would you have guessed?" she asked, her smile full and playful. "Wait, don't tell me. A *Cosmo*."

"Nothing wrong with a little cranberry juice," he said, pouring a measure of gin into the tumbler. "But not your style."

"No?" she asked, leaning forward and bracing her elbows against the countertop. Natalia settled in next to her on a huff and a roll of her eyes. "Why not?"

"Too predictable. Too *pink*. A Cosmo has become a ready favorite of bachelorette parties and sorority girls. It's fun, a little frivolous, and the message it sends is, 'I'm just here to have a good time.' It's the cotton candy of mixed drinks."

"And that's not me?" Ana Maria asked.

"Nope." Ethan shook the tumbler, eyeing Ana Maria's open interest and amused expression. She was a sweet kid. Smart, he'd bet, in a bookish, sheltered sort of way. The type of student who studied hard, rarely partied, but was always willing to play the designated driver. Intel had told him as much, though now Ethan wondered who was keeping her sheltered and protected—Hernan or her sister, who hadn't stopped glowering at him as if she could flay him with the edge of his own flirting. "*This*," he said, pouring her freshly mixed martini into the glass he'd set on the bar, "is the right drink for you. Classy. Uncomplicated in its elegance. With a dash of interest"—he plopped a skewer of three olives into the drink—"and just a hint of surprise."

Delighted, she laughed, picked up the glass, and took a sip. "Very nice. But what's the surprise?"

"The gin." Ethan shrugged, braced both hands on the bar, and leaned in close. "I'd have pegged you for vodka."

"It seems you don't know me as well as you think," she said, her smile wide and pleased. For the first time all night, Ethan wondered what else might lay behind her expression. A sense of humor, maybe. A quick tongue to go with a sharp mind. But nothing else. Certainly nothing dangerous or calculating.

"Something I hope to remedy as we work together."

"Ana Maria doesn't work for the family business," Natalia interjected. "So I'm afraid there will be little reason or opportunity for you to *get to know each other*." She might as well have gone ahead and used air quotes, the way she'd emphasized the last few words of her statement. It hardly mattered. Beautiful she may be, but Ana Maria didn't hold Ethan's interest. And not just because it was taking all his self-control to keep his focus on Ana Maria when Natalia stood beside her. It was like basking in the pale glow of the moon when the sun was just there, waiting to bathe him in warmth.

"I'm going to go check on *Tio*. Maybe replace his drink with a plate," Ana Maria said, sliding her fingers along the back of Natalia's hand. "I'll be back?" The way she said it, more question than comment, had Ethan watching the interplay between the sisters.

Natalia smiled and dipped her chin in a little nod. "Take your time."

"I'm afraid you'll have more of a challenge with my sister, Ethan. No one's pegged her yet." Ana Maria grinned, mouthed *Good luck*, and turned and made her way toward the far side of the room. She had a polite smile and a kind word for everyone who reached out, said hello, or stepped into her path.

He was almost, *almost* looking forward to telling Parker that his program was wrong. Since that basically amounted to telling *Parker* he was wrong, it was something Ethan didn't get to do often. No question, there'd be a fight. A bunch of four-syllable words and geek-speak Ethan didn't understand and wouldn't care to decipher. And, when he finally wore him down, he'd get to hear his favorite phrase.

You were right; I was wrong.

Though to be fair, the program's conclusion *had* made sense.

Ana Maria had a full life and presence outside the cartel. She was an honor student at George Washington University. Had volunteered at a local women's shelter. Her digital footprint, while not as open or extensive as most of her peers, had revealed her as an intelligent, educated woman, with a soft spot for animals and at-risk women and children. And yet, by all accounts, she still lived beneath her uncle's roof, paid for her education with cartel money. She was as close to the major players as anyone yet had been exposed to a life beyond the power and privilege organized crime provided.

So yeah, Ethan got it. Ana Maria *should* be their person of interest.

Though the tips came anonymously and sporadically, they'd almost always had one thing in common—human trafficking. Women. Children. Sometimes in shipments the authorities intercepted coming into the country, sometimes in small busts of local row houses or seedy motels. Only on the rare occasion did a tip lead to the recovery of drugs or money or weapons. As tips went, these did little to disband or destroy the cartel's business. Something that had bothered Ethan to no end.

What did the informant stand to gain? This wasn't a rival cartel trying to destabilize the Vega empire. And it wasn't someone within the organization looking to make a grab for power. No. This was someone's guilty conscience. Someone on the inside who didn't like what they saw but who could do little about it. Someone willing to take the risk, patient enough to wait for the right opportunities, and smart enough to know how to get away with it.

No question, Ana Maria had the brains—a 3.8 at George Washington University didn't happen by accident—and from what Ethan could tell, she had the sort of soft heart that would bleed for the victims of her uncle's business.

But the only thing she lacked was the only thing that really mattered—the nerve to go through with it. Careful or not, she had to know that if she were caught, if her uncle realized what she'd done, there'd be hell to pay. Rumor had it Hernan Vega had killed his own brother—Ana Maria's father—to secure his ascent to power. A man like that didn't quibble about killing women or children. His own niece would be no different.

So the question remained, was Ana Maria the sort of woman who'd risk her life to save someone else's?

Parker's program said yes. Ethan's gut said no.

CHAPTER FOUR

"I do like a challenge," Ethan said, allowing himself to turn his full attention to Natalia Vega. Something about the woman invited his interest, tempted him to live dangerously. With Ana Maria, he'd wanted to set her at ease, keep things light and comfortable. Everything about her had been soft and sweet and open. But with Natalia, Ethan wanted to slip past that stern expression and rev things up until she had to let her foot off the brake and let go of all that pent-up control. This wasn't a woman who'd be felled with pretty words or casual compliments. Everything from the set of her jaw to the full pout of her lips said she recognized bullshit when she heard it and a player when she saw him.

Good. He'd been looking for someone shrewd. Someone who could divest him of the lies he wore.

He just hadn't expected to want to divest her of everything from clothes to inhibitions in return.

"Excuse me?" Natalia's eyes flashed and her lips thinned. Someone didn't like to be teased or taunted.

Only made Ethan want to do it more.

"Your sister. She said you'd be a challenge." He set his palms against the edge of the counter and beat back the ruthless, primal pleasure that coursed through him when Natalia's gaze lingered on the flexing muscles of his forearm.

"I'm not interested in your cheap party tricks that wouldn't work on the dumbest sorority girl—"

"On behalf of the girls at Penn, I'm insulted."

Natalia continued as if he hadn't spoken. "And I don't care if you like a challenge—so long as you understand my sister *isn't* one."

"No?" Ethan asked, stepping back and wiping his hands on a fresh towel.

"No."

"But does she agree with you?" he asked, pushing, if only to see how she'd react. No question, the sisters were close. But was that a source of strength or weakness where Natalia was concerned? Both, he'd wager. "Ana Maria is a grown woman. Perhaps she's looking for a challenge of her own."

"You have a high opinion of yourself, Mr. Sullivan."

"Ethan," he corrected, rinsing out the stainless-steel tumbler he'd used to make the martini. "Are you implying that I'm easy?"

Natalia raked him with a scathing glance that said she'd sized him up the moment they'd met—and was uniformly unimpressed. "In my experience, most men are. Particularly when there's a beautiful woman involved."

"Ouch."

"You deny it?" she asked, her lips quirking up into a biting smile, even as her tone dared him to challenge her.

"That your sister is a beautiful, charming woman who could likely have her choice of men?" He wiped his hands on a fresh dish towel, then set it aside. "No. Not at all."

"And what do you intend to do about that?"

"Nothing."

Natalia scoffed.

"You don't believe me?" he asked, oddly annoyed with the reality that she *shouldn't*. He was, after all, lying to her about his name. And would continue to lie to her about that and just about anything else that served his best interests. It shouldn't have bothered him—he'd known what he was signing up for—but it did.

"I don't know you."

"Let's rectify that."

"I'm afraid your charming lines and attractive smiles are wasted on me, Mr. Sullivan."

"Ethan." He didn't like the way Sullivan slipped like snake oil from her full, tempting lips. "And that's all right—I'm more than happy to be the recipient of yours. Tell me," he said, leaning close over the wooden top that separated them, "what else of mine do you find attractive?"

Natalia rolled her eyes on a huff and pushed away from the bar. "Stay away from my sister and we won't have any problems." She turned to go, but Ethan caught her wrist before she could escape.

For a long moment, nothing happened. As if time and the universe were all on his side, Ethan held Natalia in the moment of first contact but experienced it in pieces that allowed him to commit each detail to memory.

Still, contained, neither fight nor flight kicked in, and Natalia allowed herself to linger in his grasp. The skin beneath Ethan's fingers was warm and smooth and so tantalizingly soft. Were the circumstances different, were they alone, had a bar not separated them, were Natalia not a goddamn person of interest in a high-stakes investigation, Ethan might have pulled her close, crowded her in against his body, and waited. For her to breathe, to move, to fight or succumb.

Her choice. It would always be her choice. But fuck, he wanted her to make it. There was a fire there, banked but burning, just waiting for the right moment to combust.

As it was, he allowed himself to luxuriate in the way her muscles— firm and strong—bunched beneath his hand even as her pulse beat against his palm. When Natalia turned, stared first at where he'd had the audacity to restrain her, then lifted her gaze to his, Ethan was struck by the contradictions laced through her body and written across her face.

Anger and desire.

Scorn and interest.

Predator and prey.

A confusing, if potent, cocktail of contradictions that set Ethan's heart racing and his body tightening.

One of the most basic battles waged across her face as she studied him. Stay or go. And as her expression smoothed over and her body relaxed, Ethan realized he'd been played. She'd baited him. Challenged and dismissed him. Then turned to walk away . . . except now it was clear she'd expected him to stop her. But he didn't think she'd expected to want him to, or to react to his touch. Knowing desire had snared her as surely as it had him soothed his ego.

A little, at least.

"I promised you a drink," he offered, when the moment stretched beyond what either of them could afford. "If nothing else, I'm a man of my word," he said, the statement measured and poured in exacting increments. A declaration of truth he hadn't intended to serve up quite so soon. And yet, it bothered him, the idea that Natalia might dismiss him. Might write him off as the ego he'd projected for most of the evening.

He dropped her wrist.

"Let me guess . . . Cosmo?" He quirked his lips as she rolled her eyes but fought a smile.

"I strike you as someone who indulges in froufrou cotton-candy drinks?"

Not even a little bit. "As you said, we don't know each other." He had her curiosity, if nothing else. Who was this woman? What drove her? There'd been little in the way of public record, though Parker had dug through an extensive array of databases. But it was almost as if, at seventeen, Natalia Vega had simply ceased to exist. It was one of the reasons the program had favored Ana Maria as the likely informant. There simply wasn't much of anything to find where Natalia was concerned. All the information, impressive though it had been, concerned a teenager who'd disappeared from public record and public life for nearly a decade.

But Ethan knew better than anyone that little to find did not mean little to know. There were hidden depths to this woman, interesting layers he doubted many people bothered to see or explore. But then, Ethan had never been one to settle for the easy or obvious answer.

"I'm beginning to see why you left bartending for accounting," she said, sliding onto a high-backed red leather stool and tucking her legs up under the bar. "Tell me, Mr. Sullivan, did you assume that a single drink and a charming smile would keep your tip jar full and your bed warm? Or are you just like every other accountant I've met—good with numbers but terrible with people?"

"So I'm either lazy or predictable? You're doing wonders for my ego," he said, reaching for two short bottom-heavy glasses even as he ran through a catalog of drinks. She could make fun all she wanted, but people were reflected in the choices they made. Even in simple ones, like the cocktails they favored. "And I've asked you repeatedly to call me Ethan."

"Yes, you have." Her eyes flashed amusement, and too late, Ethan realized he'd tipped his hand. He *wanted* her to use his name. To hear it fall from her lips. To taste it on her tongue. And now she knew it, too. Out of spite, or amusement, or simply because she enjoyed the power of having something he wanted, Natalia denied him.

And unless or until he could surprise or impress her, she was going to hold her ground.

Finally, a challenge.

"As I make it a point to avoid becoming both lazy *and* predictable, I'll have to step up my game." Ethan studied her, wondering how often Natalia indulged in anything fun or frivolous. "No Cosmos, which probably rules out lemon drops and appletinis." No, nothing fun or flirty or with sugar lacing the rim. Nothing she'd have picked up in a college bar or on the arm of some trust-fund brat who thought money could buy taste.

He didn't yet know what or who Natalia *was*, but everything she *wasn't* became clearer by the second.

"Your deductive powers are truly astonishing."

"Thank you." He nodded and continued as if she wasn't tossing insults as freely as he assigned physical training. Still baiting him, he concluded, mildly annoyed she'd so effectively caught his interest. Yes, he wanted to talk to her. And yes, he was interested in ways he hadn't anticipated. But she didn't have to be so damn aware of it. "I'd say a glass of wine, but we aren't at dinner, and you don't strike me as the sort to lounge in bubble baths with a buttery chardonnay and the latest book-club pick."

"Too many large words?" she asked sweetly.

Of all the self-deprecating conclusions she could have jumped to, she'd gone straight to stupid. Insecurity or confidence? The latter, if he had to make a guess. Early school records had revealed Natalia Vega as both determined and intelligent. The sort of grades that reflected a dedicated student and a curious mind, rather than a God-given brilliance.

Ethan knew as well as anyone that talent was wasted without hard work, and if he had to choose one over the other, a strong work ethic won every single time.

"Only an exceptionally stupid man would presume beauty and brains to be mutually exclusive." He laid the glasses on the bar and draped a napkin over the top of each.

"I thought we agreed my sister wasn't a topic of interest where you're concerned, Mr. Sullivan." Her eyes went sharp and her tone flat, her hostility returning in a rush that stole something open and honest from her expression.

"I'm not talking about Ana Maria."

The edge of surprise, there and gone in a second, snagged Natalia's otherwise-composed expression. Ethan still saw it in the way her throat worked as she swallowed, in the way her shoulders came back and her chin tipped up. Almost immediately, she reined herself in, adjusted her appearance to something bland and unimpressed, and said, "Flattery. How predictable."

"Can't have that," Ethan agreed. This wasn't the time or place to discuss the merits of Natalia's beauty, though part of him wanted to. From the moment they'd met, she'd used the long stretch of her caramel-colored skin and endless, sloping curves to command his attention and challenge his focus. That it hadn't been a calculated attempt at misdirection baffled him almost as much as it aroused him.

Whatever else she was, Natalia was not a woman who'd deny herself an advantage.

Again, the need to know her, to peel away the layers until she was utterly bare before him, struck hard and fast. Time to see how much of the picture he'd managed to put together.

"Club soda with a twist," he announced, watching as Natalia sat a little straighter. "That's your drink of choice."

Her lips parted, and she sat back.

"Neither classy nor surprising. How boring of me," she said, watching him for a reaction. He'd made a point of turning Ana Maria's drink into a compliment; no doubt Natalia expected him to attempt the same with her. Tempting, but no. Surprising her was much more fun and far more revealing. She didn't often let an expression slip that she hadn't tried on a thousand times before, perfecting the lie until she wore it like a truth, but every time he got close, every time he acknowledged something she hid well or others dismissed, he caught the edge of something real and open and beautiful.

"Some would agree with you," he said, rooting around behind the bar for the sugar cubes. When he found the tray, he plucked two Demerara squares the color of Natalia's eyes and set them on top of the napkins.

"Tasteless," Natalia agreed, drawing her index finger along the wood grain of the bar, then tracing a knot in a simple, arcing swipe that had Ethan swallowing hard. "Controlled. Invisible. Immune to a good time."

"For someone who takes things at face value, yes." He was still pulling the pieces together, still figuring out who and what the enigma before him was, but he was damn sure that even if she believed she was all those things, she was wrong. That she was hiding behind who she had to be, which made Ethan wonder who she *wanted* to be.

What had happened to her at seventeen? After her father's death and her virtual disappearance? Who was she before, and who had she become?

"But not you?" Smug expectation looked good on her, but like everything else she wore, he was determined to strip it away.

"Not me," he agreed, twisting the lid off the bitters and shaking out six or seven drops to soak each cube. "If I saw you, in that dress, in this place, surrounded by men in thousand-dollar suits with hundred-dollar haircuts, sipping on a club soda and lime, I'd be captivated."

"By club soda?" She arched one thick, curving eyebrow.

"By the mystery of the woman drinking it. Because yes, it looks like a club soda with lime, but it could be a vodka tonic. Or a gin and tonic. A glance won't tell you. You've got to get close . . ." He snatched away the napkins so the soaked sugar landed in the bottom of each glass. Leaning in, he said, "You've got to take your time, then steal a taste. A woman drinking a club soda and lime? She's not easy. Not looking for a casual hookup or an anonymous encounter. She's too purposeful, too driven for that. She's work, and that scares men off."

"But not you," Natalia repeated, though this time her words were thick and slow and heavy. An unwitting seduction in place of her calculated flirtation. It drew him in just the same.

"I like a challenge, Natalia. A little mystery." He pulled back, retrieved a muddler, and set to work pulverizing the sugar in quick, efficient motions. "You're an overprotective sister, suspicious of others and cautious—so very cautious—but any man who thinks that's the extent of who you are? He's not paying attention." Satisfied, Ethan poured two measures of whiskey, deftly dropping them into each glass. "There's more to you than meets the eye, Natalia Vega, and to a man like me, that might as well be foreplay." He handed her a lemon and paring knife as he took an orange for himself. "Give me a hand here?"

She accepted both and settled in to remove the rind. "Yet you're not making a club soda and lime," she said, nodding to the glasses of whiskey on the bar.

"No, I'm not. But I'm hoping to tempt you, anyway." He twisted the orange rinds, running the bright side along the rim of each glass, then garnished the edge with the twist he'd made.

"Your preferred drink?" she asked, her knife turning graceful arcs around the lemon she held.

"When I'm drinking, yes." He pulled a tray of perfectly cubed ice from the fridge to his right and set three in each glass.

"You know, Mr. Sullivan, the thing about bartenders is that they're full of lines and fancy drinks, and, the good ones, at least, are full of shit, too."

Ethan pushed away from the bar but bit off a laugh. Feisty, this one. And direct when she wanted to be. "Am I?"

She lifted the glass he pushed toward her and took a sip, her eyes closing on a sigh he was almost certain had been manufactured to stroke his ego. She swallowed, set the glass down, then met his gaze head-on.

"This isn't your drink any more than it's mine," she said, drawing her finger along the rim of the glass. "Oh, I'm sure you order it often enough. When you're surrounded by men in thousand-dollar suits with hundred-dollar haircuts." Her smile unfurled, wide and sharp and predatory. "A cultured, refined classic for a man pretending he's both."

"Turning the tables, Miss Vega?"

"It's only fair," she said, lifting one exposed shoulder in a casual shrug.

"Then, by all means, proceed. I'm dying to know just what you've made of me."

She slid from her stool, standing straight and tall, though she let her fingers curl around the glass he'd given her. "You'll order an old-fashioned when the situation calls for it—in the company of people privileged enough to judge their peers by something so frivolous as the clothes they wear or the drink they order."

Ethan kept his wince back, but only barely. She couldn't know just how close that blow had landed, how many embassy parties he'd attended where those judgments had been passed around like party favors.

"You find a usefulness in the steps of creating the cocktail. It isn't hard, but it *looks* impressive, and you've learned that with most people, looks are all that matters. But you don't actually care for the routine. It's there in the way you muddle the sugar with jerking, impatient motions. In the way that your citrus curl was just a short, thin scrape of orange peel. Perfunctory. Sufficient."

She held up the perfect, endless spiral of lemon she'd cut at his behest, which he'd completely forgotten about. "Artistry isn't important to you, which means you don't hold any real affection for the drink itself."

Ethan grinned, caught in the lie but not sorry for it. Every word from Natalia's mouth was a damnation, but a revelation as well. He'd have to watch himself around her, because this one? This one was cut sharper than his combat knife.

"So if not this?" he asked, wondering what she'd decided.

"Something simple. No muss, no fuss. The only prep required is a handful of ice, and even that's negotiable." She smiled at him, a little patronizing, a lot wicked, and 100 percent aware of how she held his attention. "I certainly hope you're not so . . . cursory in all aspects of your life." She tapped her lips with her index finger when he scowled. He'd never had any complaints. "I suppose time will tell."

"Are you hitting on me, Miss Vega?"

She smiled at him, the tilt of her mouth secretive and smug and a little bit condescending.

"I'm told accounting is a detail-oriented profession, Mr. Sullivan. One that requires intense focus and complete devotion to each and every detail. I certainly hope you're up to the task."

"I don't do anything by halves," he said, helpless to do much more than watch the way her mouth moved as she mocked him. "Rest assured, when I turn my attention to something, I take note of each and every detail. Study it. Catalog it. Commit it to memory." She didn't blush or sigh or even go tense and uncomfortable. But her bottom lip dropped ever so slightly, and her eyes went warm and molten and dark. It was Ethan's turn to grin. "When I spread the ledgers, nothing—no matter how small or hidden or secret—goes overlooked. But please, feel free to provide a detailed review of my work."

"That won't be necessary," she said, pulling away from him.

They'd played this round to a draw, it would seem. Disappointed, he watched as she withdrew into herself, dismissing her own attraction as easily as if it had meant nothing at all to her. It made him wonder what she was after. If it was satisfaction. Or pleasure. Or even just the sweet taste of victory over a man who'd challenged her. Ethan was confident enough in his assessment and in his gut reactions to believe that her interest and attraction had been real rather than manufactured. But he was also sure that it had caught her by surprise. She'd said all the right things, played him as if she'd known him for far longer than a cocktail party, and yet she hadn't followed through.

Practiced and confident yet caught off guard and flustered. It was an odd combination with few easy answers or ready explanations.

"If you're sure," he said, wanting to leave the door open but unwilling to push when he couldn't be sure what he was pushing her toward.

"As to your drink?" she said, the ghost of a smile returning to her lips as she picked up the thread of their previous conversation. "Imported scotch, I think, when you're feeling indulgent or hosting close, personal friends. But when you're on your own, when there's no one to charm or influence or impress? Whiskey. American and neat."

Ethan pulled a rough breath in through his nose and forced himself to remember where he was and who he was with. What had started as a game had suddenly turned on him. "Like I said. Only a foolish man believes beauty and brains are mutually exclusive."

"Unlike you, I don't care for a mystery, Mr. Sullivan. You're an over-confident flirt and a man who thinks he's smarter than his peers. But anyone who looks at you and believes the lie you present the world, well, then, she's a fool with a reckless heart and thoughtless disposition." She laced the edge of her lemon curl over the rim of his glass, letting it dangle there to mock him. "You're not who you claim to be, Mr. Sullivan, and to a woman like me," she said, catching his gaze, "that might as well be provocation."

Shock seized him before he could rein it in, but she just smiled and stepped back from the bar.

"It would seem you could flay a man with more than your tongue, Miss Vega," Ethan said, tracing the edge of the lemon and wondering just how much he'd enjoy being at the mercy of her mouth.

Natalia cast a long look over her shoulder. "And you'd do well to remember it, Mr. Sullivan."

CHAPTER FIVE

"Whoa." Parker stumbled back as the elevator doors slid open and Ethan finally stepped into Somerton Security's main office. "Sasquatch sighting."

Ethan pushed his sunglasses up the bridge of his nose and into his hair on a heavy sigh, and tried not to scratch self-consciously at the stubble covering his jaw.

As promised, Milner's computer had been delivered to Ethan's condo—a space Parker had sourced, rented, and forged a history for, and one Ethan hadn't attempted to conceal. Still, he hadn't expected Vega to find it quite so quickly. It meant Hernan likely had a PI on payroll, and that Ethan would have to be hypervigilant. He'd expected as much, but still, it made everything that much more difficult.

From the moment Ethan had received Milner's computer, he'd fallen into the work, pushing himself to sleep less and discover more, breaking only for coffee and a protein bar. It had been closer to 4:00 a.m. than midnight when he'd stumbled his way into the bathroom and beneath the spray of the hottest shower he could stand, then collapsed, naked and damp, into bed, only to rise three hours later, shove himself into a suit, get into the car, and spend the next two hours driving aimlessly through DC's city center to ensure he hadn't been tailed to the office.

So yeah, he hadn't shaved. A rarity for a guy who made his bed every morning, got his hair cut every month, and shined his shoes every Sunday.

But the last twelve hours had been a whirlwind of revelations, complications, and one incredibly difficult-to-read distraction.

And then there was Milner, who in addition to being a thief, turned out to be lazy and incompetent as well. Untangling the mess he'd left behind would take the average accountant several months, even with a full staff and a huge retainer. Ethan had just two days, which meant he had a better shot of teaching Parker how to combat rappel out of a Blackhawk helicopter at 150 feet.

But Ethan specialized in lost causes and hopeless situations. This one was just going to make him work for it.

But first, caffeine and a lot of it.

"Please tell me that's for me," he said, nodding to the huge black travel mug Parker was carrying but not drinking, which really should have been answer enough.

"Yep. Pulled it fresh from the lounge when security logged your car coming into the garage." He handed it over, his lips twitching as if he was fighting a smile.

"There better not be sugar in here." Why people felt the need to dress up coffee, Ethan would never know. It, like everything else in Ethan's employ, had a job to do. If it couldn't do it without bells and whistles, he had little use for it.

"Nope." Parker grinned. A clear indication Ethan just wasn't asking the right question.

"Syrup, nutmeg, milk of any kind?"

"Nope, nope, and nope. Plain and boring, just the way you like it."

Ethan grunted. "Doesn't need to be fancy to get the job done. Functional works just fine for me."

"If only you had such an enlightened view about the dress code."

"Don't start." Ethan sneered at Parker's shoes, the laces mismatched—one green and one blue—the heel of one rubber sole making an odd flopping sound that probably meant the Gorilla Glue he'd used to fuse the rubber back to the canvas had failed. Again.

Parker *claimed* the damn things were lucky—something about MIT, pranks, and expulsion—and that he wore them only during "difficult" assignments.

Ethan was pretty sure Parker just liked watching the vein in Ethan's head throb when they squeaked in time with Parker's perpetually bouncing leg.

Mug in one hand, Ethan flipped on the lights and slung his keys on the desk. "Last chance. Because I swear, after the amount of sleep I've had, if I find so much as a single grain of sugar or one drop of whatever not-milk milk you imported-coffee-drinking hipsters are raving about now, I will ship you off to Ranger school in the Pacific Northwest, where the only stimulant you'll receive is some pissed-off master sergeant's boot up your ass, where dinner is what you can forage, and toilet paper doesn't exist." For good measure, and because he was feeling a little bit mean, he said, "And if that doesn't work, I'll tell Georgia where you keep the secret stash of artificial sweetener and Pop-Tarts that I know you have."

"Sadist." Parker scowled.

"'Fess up or pay up," Ethan ground out.

"I solemnly swear that though I'm always up to no good, the only thing you'll find in that mug is hot black coffee."

"I better," Ethan said, raising the tumbler to his mouth as he pulled his laptop out of his bag. Tamper-free dark roast hit his tongue at the same time the mug erupted in Darth Vader's mechanical inhale-exhale. "I swear to God, one of these days I'm going to donate you to a lab."

Parker shrugged unapologetically. "Been there, done that, got the MIT diploma to prove it."

"Then to a Girl Scout troop looking to earn their science badge by making slime."

Parker just slid onto the edge of his desk and grinned. "Someone's cranky this morning."

"I'm functioning on three hours of sleep, two hours of DC traffic, and coffee from a cup better suited to a six-year-old's hot chocolate. Don't push your luck with me." Ethan yanked open his bottom desk drawer; pulled out a mug that had zero writing, no logos, and did *not* sound like a pissed-off, asthmatic robot; and dumped his coffee into it.

"Good, you're here," Isaac said, stepping into the office before Ethan could strangle Parker. "You tell him yet?" he asked Parker, who kept his distance. The pair had figured out how to work together, which seemed to mostly consist of pretending the other didn't exist.

"Tell me what?"

"Nah, wanted to let the coffee kick in first."

"Tell me *what*?" Ethan ground out, unable to believe he was being ignored in his own damn office. It was *his* name on the checks, for fuck's sake. A little respect wouldn't kill anyone, would it?

"I heard from my contact at the DEA," Isaac informed him with a grim tone. "We need to talk."

"Conference room?" Ethan asked, though he was already heading for the door.

"Everyone's there and waiting," Parker offered with a shrug, then followed him out of the office and down the hall.

Ethan swung open the conference-room door, found the rest of the team waiting as promised—a bad omen if ever there was one—and took his seat.

"All right. Let's hear it."

"Our initial requests for information were met largely with silence, and when I pushed, everyone gave me the same name—Curtis Strauss. He's a senior agent with the DEA," Isaac began, taking a chair and lacing his fingers over a knee. "Took a while to track him down—he's in the field—but turns out that eighteen months ago he was the agent in charge of an operation aimed at taking down the Vega cartel."

"Foreign or domestic?" Ortiz asked.

Isaac met Ethan's stare across the table. "Domestic."

Well, shit.

"I'm assuming the investigation is no longer active," Ethan said. If it were, the DEA would have been on his doorstep the minute they'd caught wind of Ethan asking questions. And since the cartel was still active and operating in the United States, Ethan was willing to bet a lifetime of drinking out of one of Parker's mugs that he wouldn't like the reason the DEA had pulled out.

"It's not, no." Isaac sighed and rubbed the bridge of his nose. "They got close—really close."

"They had someone on the inside," Ethan realized aloud.

Isaac dipped his chin. "Curtis wouldn't give me the details, but they managed to place a man within Vega's inner circle, and slowly the information started flowing." Isaac sat up, trailed his fingers along the faux wood grain of the desk. "They were careful, Ethan. Deliberate. Had all kinds of intel but decided to play the slow game. To position Vega for a narco-terrorism charge."

"Did the intel support the idea?" It wasn't unheard of, cartels doing business with terrorists, trading drugs for guns or money or both. But it was a risky play for authorities that involved walking the line of entrapment.

"Curtis wouldn't confirm that, and in any case, it's irrelevant. The operation was scrapped." Isaac sent Ethan a heavy look. "The costs were deemed too high."

"Their agent was exposed."

"Then murdered and dumped for someone to find. Cartel wanted the DEA to know, Ethan. Message sent and received—only saving grace was that the end was quick." Isaac sighed, as if the thought of an operation he'd had no part in weighed on him anyway. "The DEA wasn't willing to put another man at risk—"

"And without someone on the inside pulling Vega's strings, their play was dead."

"Ethan," Parker said, shooting a worried glance toward Georgia, "if the *DEA* deemed the situation too volatile . . . I think you have to at least reconsider what we're doing here."

Ethan shook his head.

"Fuck. Just, fuck." Ortiz swore and dropped his head into his hands. "Ethan, man, this was supposed to be quick. Undercover recon, I think you called it?"

"None of that's changed," Ethan assured his team, who, to a man, looked utterly strung out. Except for Georgia, who just looked ready to air-drop into Colombia with a machete and an attitude problem. Ethan couldn't blame her, but he also didn't have the luxury of managing her with kid gloves. Or any gloves, for that matter. "I'm the one taking the risk, I get to decide if it's acceptable or not—"

"Ethan—"

"I'm not having this discussion again!" Ethan silenced Parker with a look but didn't miss the mulish expression or the narrow-eyed glare that said the tone was both received and resented.

The room went silent, everyone exchanging cautious looks and heavy sighs. No one wanted to quit—Ethan knew that—but they didn't really understand. Georgia did, in some ways, at least. She knew what it felt like to be left behind, to be forgotten. Loyalty, as much as love, drove her. But it wasn't the same. Death, Ethan could accept. Knew how to process. It was the dying that he found so goddamned hard. Every day that went by was another step toward the end. Somewhere, right now, if he wasn't already buried in a shallow, unmarked grave, Will was fighting a losing battle against his captors, against the elements, against disease, and, most of all, against himself.

Because Ethan knew the day would come, if it hadn't already, when Will decided it was easier to let go. To give up. To leave behind the pain and the suffering and the exhaustion and embrace what came next.

From there, the end would come quickly. Ethan had seen it before.

Antiseptic and illness and the humid tang of his own breath inside a surgical mask rose from the depths of his memory. Ethan swallowed hard and pushed away scents that weren't real, weren't present, and weren't wanted.

"We need to focus on what we can do and handle complications as they arise," Ethan said. "Right now, I have to prioritize proving myself to Hernan Vega. So far, Milner's financials are providing plenty of proof of what an incompetent asshole he was, but it's not bringing me any closer to Will."

"Maybe while you continue to put together that picture," Isaac said slowly, "we assemble another one. We know that someone bought an outcome—the hit on the South American compound. Ortiz and I can start working backward from there, see what we turn over, maybe even see where the money leads."

Ethan nodded; it was as good a plan as any, and definitely better than inaction.

"What do you need to get the job done?" Parker asked, his voice firm if resigned.

"More hours in the day, for one," Ethan said, running through a list of everything he needed to do. "I'd hoped to spend the majority of my time digging through digital records, looking for transactions that would lead us to property holdings, payoffs, Colombian associates—anything that could trace back to Will. But for now, I have to focus my resources on providing Vega answers—and even then, there's no guarantee he gives me full access. He's paranoid but not stupid."

"If access is the problem, then I might be able to help with that," Parker said, a slow, satisfied grin curling his mouth. "A little program I've been working on in my spare time—highly experimental, and should anyone at the NSA, Homeland Security, or Interpol ask, entirely theoretical. Harmless."

"Some kind of worm or virus?" Ethan asked.

"Please," Parker scoffed. "That's like calling Longclaw a paper opener."

Ethan rubbed his forehead. "Translate for the culturally uninformed, please."

"It's a sword on Game of—oh." Parker laughed. "You meant the important part. Right." At Ethan's glare, Parker continued. "The problem with worms is that unless they're targeted to something really specific—searching for a single type of file, for example—they're slow and unreliable. Basically the inelegant solution of the lazy amateur."

There wasn't enough coffee in the world to make sense of tech speak. "Conclusions, Parker. I don't give a shit how it works, just tell me what the hell it does and how it helps us."

Parker deflated and mumbled, "Get me access to a networked computer and I can deploy a two-step program that will clone their network on one of ours, which I can guarantee makes their tech look like a T-15." When Ethan cast him a blank stare, Parker explained, "Obsolete."

"Star Wars humor," Ortiz offered when Ethan cast a baleful look down the table. "Right. Not the time. What's step two?"

"Huh?" Parker asked.

"You said two-step program. I'm counting, and so far I've got step one as 'clone.' So what's step two?"

"Oh, right. I can then set it up so that our network is designated as primary—every transaction sent to the Vega network goes through ours instead." Parker tossed Ethan a smug grin. "All those times you bitched about the 'asinine cost' of Somerton Security's IT? Get ready to thank me."

"And you can do this completely undetected?" Isaac asked.

"Yep. The 'worm,'" he said, with air quotes and a roll of his eyes, "only has to run once, and I can disguise it as a deployed security update."

Ethan sighed, the tension in his neck and shoulders easing off the tiniest bit. "What's the catch?"

Parker grimaced but said, "I can deploy via a Trojan, but the fastest way is with a direct-access upload, which means you have to get your hands on a cartel computer that's paired with their network."

"Any chance Milner's computer will work?" Georgia asked.

Parker shook his head. "No, I've already explored that option. All the security protocols have changed, and if Vega is as paranoid as you say, he's probably set an alert to tell him if you try accessing anything you shouldn't from Milner's laptop, which would raise questions we don't want to answer." Parker shrugged. "It's a complication, but if you can get to a paired device—a cell phone, even—the rest is easy peasy."

Sure, because a man as paranoid as Vega left computers lying around. But Ethan didn't complain. Parker handled the tech details; Ethan handled the fieldwork. He'd hold up his end. "I'll get you access."

"That simple, huh?" Ortiz asked with a smirk. "And this from the man who's torched three satellite phones, two field laptops, and countless cell phones. Right."

Yeah, yeah. Ethan and technology were in a long-standing war. Which side had fired the first shot was a detail lost to time, but more than once, Parker had threatened to saddle Ethan with a flip phone circa 2004.

"Access is the easy part," Parker said. "The hard part will be building a recursive algorithm to interpret all the data, filter out the terabytes of irrelevant shit—I *seriously* hope this guy isn't cruising porn every night." He kissed the back of Georgia's hand. "I'm gonna need the pink packets of awesome, babe. My brain only functions at fifty percent on organic sugar and half caf. This calls for the double-barreled, artificial guns, 'kay?"

"Fine." She rolled her eyes, then turned back to Ethan. "You got a plan for handling access?"

An idea, but it was *monumentally* stupid . . . and yet his gut said it was the right approach. There was someone within the cartel who had the access they needed. Someone who, if she couldn't be incentivized to act in her own self-interest, could be convinced to do so for her sister.

"Let's work on some options," Ethan said, flipping open a new page in his tech-free yet totally functional legal pad. "Before any of us leaves today, we need to have a plan in place, and I need to know exactly, down to the smallest step, how to deploy the worm. And, Parker?"

"Yeah?"

"I'm going to need you to run a few more outcomes through your program." For the first time since Darth Vader had ruined Ethan's first sip of coffee, Ethan smiled. "Seems you—it, sorry—got a few things wrong."

Parker spluttered and sat up in his chair, an irritated scowl marring his face. "What?"

Ethan waved him off. "I'll explain later." Because while the program *had* been wrong about Ana Maria, it had still led Ethan to the person who'd been tipping off the authorities for years. He still wasn't sure why Natalia cared—guilt, probably; a battered heart, maybe. But now he needed to know if a woman who appeared to be hanging on by the thinnest thread, spun from the love she had for her sister, had finally reached her breaking point.

If she could be persuaded that there was a better life waiting for her, and for her sister . . . if she would only be brave enough to reach for it.

CHAPTER SIX

Cold, brittle air seared her lungs as indecision chased Natalia up the sidewalk. Usually, running exhausted her body and cleared her head. Decisions and risks and consequences that felt insurmountable in mile one began to simplify at mile five, make sense at mile eight, and become manageable at mile ten. But as her parents' home came into view and twelve miles echoed through her legs, Natalia admitted defeat.

She had a choice to make, one that even a few weeks ago would have been simple, if not regrettable.

Ethan Sullivan had *lied*.

Experience and the weight of her uncle's expectations marked him for death.

She'd certainly considered it when she'd discovered his real name earlier that afternoon. Contemplated the best way to do it—quick, unexpected, merciful. A fast knife and fatal plunge. He'd have been dead before he'd closed the door behind him.

It was what her uncle had demanded of her, and she knew the cost of defiance.

But as she'd stared down at the picture she'd found, as she'd tasted his name on her tongue, as she'd wondered about the man she'd read about—the ace student, the champion crew member, the double major in finance and accounting, the man who'd pledged a fraternity, then given it up for charity work—she'd hesitated.

Nothing about Ethan felt vile. Dangerous, yes. But not evil. Determined but not ruthless. The truth was, for reasons Natalia still didn't fully understand, she didn't want to hurt Ethan Somerton.

And she didn't believe he wanted to hurt her, either.

Life would have been so much simpler if he'd turned out to be everything he portrayed. Vain. Greedy. Willing to get his hands dirty for a payday. She wouldn't give a shit about what happened to that man.

But this one . . .

Desperation and hope—an insidious weed she should have rooted out the moment it sprouted—stayed her hand.

For now.

She had time—a little, at least. She'd been careful. Discreet. It had taken less than twenty-four hours and a quick trip to Philadelphia to discover what Ethan had lied about but not why. Not yet. And though the reasons had never mattered to her before, today they did.

Because maybe, just maybe, he could help her.

Maybe there was a way out.

Maybe this could all finally end.

She turned up the drive, slowing to a walk and struggling to catch her breath, and scowled against the memory of the way Ethan had teased her. Pushed back against the way his smile had struck her. Ignored the way his gaze, watchful and alert and assessing, had felt on her skin.

She *liked* him, she realized as she rounded the back of the house. Or could, given the time.

But did that make him more or less dangerous? Her gut had been right about so much, but this . . . this was something else entirely.

Wishful thinking, maybe.

Dangerous, definitely.

And for now, a problem with no immediate solution.

She climbed the back porch steps, her fingers fishing for the key she'd tucked into an interior pocket. Why hadn't the floodlight sensed her? The hair on the back of her neck stood straight up in warning, even as she took a step back, then drew up short when gravity threatened to topple her off the concrete stairs she'd just ascended.

"*Damasiado lento.*" The voice struck, viper fast, with large, bruising hands in place of fangs.

Shit. She'd lost focus, let herself be trapped in thoughts of problems she couldn't solve, forgotten where she was, and blinded herself to the danger around her.

Too slow, indeed.

But the killing blow didn't come. A knife didn't sever her carotid, her brachial, her femoral—all arteries this man could slice with little effort and no care.

No, Natalia thought as rough hands jerked her down the steps and spun her toward the wall, this wasn't about death. This was a test. A tease. A reminder that the student had not surpassed the teacher.

She prayed she never did.

"Carlos," she said as he pushed her back against the wall, the force of the blow stealing her breath in a rush. There'd be a knot on the back of her skull—she hadn't been able to brace for the whiplash—but she'd live. Today, anyway.

"*Tú recuerdas?*" he said, his scarred vocal cords—the product of a hit gone wrong—a tangled rasp of hissed syllables.

Of course she remembered. There were few who heard Carlos's voice and lived to speak of it. For years after the bullet that had nearly taken his life—and permanently marred his voice—Carlos had held to silence. Refusing to speak or give voice to the only failure he carried. But with time, what had begun as shame had morphed into legend. Even now, people whispered stories of the man with no voice. The demon who came in the dark to slit their throats. The devil who, according to some, whispered goodbye in the second before he struck.

Lies, of course, though Natalia suspected Carlos encouraged them. After all, *sicarios* were nameless, faceless vermin. One died and another rose to take his place.

Replaceable. Forgettable. Generic.

Carlos had taught her as much. Beat it into her until it became a hardened truth that protected her. Everyone was replaceable.

But there were exceptions. Men, and even the rare woman, who lasted decades where others rose and fell in the span of months. *Sicarios* dealt in death and, in the end, accepted it as their due.

But sometimes, the man didn't die—and the legend was born.

And legends lived forever.

"Did you miss me?" he asked, digging his fingers into her throat, threatening to cut off her air.

"No."

He laughed, a hissing rasp of air that sounded like the warning rattle on her mother's old pressure cooker. His grip tightened and black spots danced before her eyes even as he drew the fingers of his free hand along the curve of her cheek.

Control and condescension—tools he'd used often and to his advantage. But tools he'd used to teach her fearless resolve and deadly skill.

With time and the heavy weight of failure, he'd made her relentless.

And she had not forgotten.

She let her eyelids flutter, drew a grasping breath of air that felt like sucking oxygen from a straw, then scrabbled uselessly at the hand he held to her throat . . . and waited for the laugh. He'd never learned to hide his amusement at her failures, at her repetitive attempts, at her ability to pull herself to her feet.

And he didn't disappoint her now.

The moment he chuckled, his hand twitched—and she struck. Hard.

Gripping his wrist, she drove her closed fist straight for his throat— he'd gone for her weakness, exploited a terrible memory; she could do the same.

Carlos stumbled back, his hand at his throat but a smile on his face. He nodded. *"Bueno."* Then held up his hand, palm out, when she took two determined steps forward. *"Esta bien. Esta bien."*

"What are you doing here?" Natalia snarled but let her feet take root and keep her from carrying forward into a fight that was ill-advised at best and potentially deadly at worst. Mentor or not, Carlos would weather only so many blows to his ego.

"You've become careless?" he asked, his head tilted to the side as he considered her.

She bristled, and when he smiled, she realized she'd failed another test. Reacted against another testing prick.

"Three days I've been here. Watching. Waiting. Three days you run. Same path. Same time." He shook his head and clucked his tongue. "Careless." The smile fell from his face, and his plain brown eyes went flat. "I taught you better."

Yes, he had.

"Did you become stupid in your years away, as well?" he asked.

"No."

"Then tell me, *gatita*, why am I here?"

Another test. Another riddle designed to see if she was paying attention. But ultimately one she'd been working at even as she stood on the steps. Change. An ending. A beginning. It didn't matter. Carlos was the harbinger—the cartel wouldn't send him unless things had reached a breaking point.

"My uncle?" she asked.

"Is a careless man."

A careless man who'd let his accountant steal an untold amount of money . . . and get away with it. There would be payment, of one kind or another.

And Carlos had been sent to collect—a message, a warning, and a promise in one.

"How much does he owe?" Natalia asked, wondering how thoroughly her uncle had damned them. If it was already too late to mitigate the damage. If every sacrifice she'd ever made would all be wiped away by the careless actions of her uncle, the man who'd put her in this position to begin with.

"No se." Carlos shrugged, rocking back and forth on his feet. Always poised. Always ready. Never caught resting or unaware or off guard. "I'm here first for Milner. An accountant who steals—an example must be made." He stilled, and his white teeth flashed and bit through the dark like the warning of a predator circling in close. "Then we see."

Who lives. Who dies. He didn't have to say it. Natalia had been in this life long enough to understand the message.

In so many ways, life had been easier when she'd believed things were black and white, right and wrong, good and bad. But Carlos . . . he defied all categorization. He wasn't the sort of man to lose sleep over the lives he took, but neither did he relish the kill. It was a contradiction that had taken Natalia time—and her own first, fumbling kills—to understand.

Carlos had grown up poor in the slums of Medellín, survived the rise—and more impressively, the fall—of Pablo Escobar. He'd navigated the tumultuous year that came after, survived the infighting, the government sweeps, the CIA hits. Sober, he'd claim that luck and careful planning had ensured his survival. But once, long ago, beneath the fog of tequila and an opium-laced cigar, he'd told Natalia the truth. He didn't pick sides. He wasn't emotional or vain or ruled by his reputation.

He pulled a trigger or sliced a vein. With neither care nor regret, he killed.

Ruthless but typically dispassionate.

But this, Natalia knew, he'd enjoy.

After all, Hernan had been responsible for the bullet that had stolen Carlos's voice. But politics and power plays and good old plausible deniability—to say nothing of the protection afforded by the Vega name—had stayed Carlos's hand. Until now. If her uncle couldn't find Milner, couldn't retrieve the money stolen on his watch, Carlos would kill him.

But where would it stop? What would satisfy Colombia?

"Collateral damage?" she asked, glancing toward the door.

"Your pretty sister, you mean?"

Natalia took a breath, reminded herself that Carlos was always pushing, always prodding, always looking for the chink, the weak spot, the wound he could press until emotion or reason or information bled free.

"The family has never cared for us, one way or the other."

"But you hope I might," he reasoned, the side of his mouth drawing tight—the equivalent of a lopsided grin lost long ago to the cut of a blade that had severed a nerve along his jaw.

"A warning, at least."

"And would you run, *gatita*? Or use your claws?"

Little cat. He'd called her such for years, always teasing her for her tiny, trembling rage; her pitiful hiss; and her sheathed, but always present, blades. He'd given her the moniker the first time he'd beaten her for failing one of his many impossible tests. But what had once been a slur was now an endearment, odd as it was.

"I can't kill everyone."

"Perhaps you will not have to. Colombia wants their money more than they want Hernan dead. I've come to ensure they get it back."

"Ana Maria is innocent—"

He shrugged. *"No me importa."*

"Then why are you here?" she asked on an angry step forward she wouldn't, couldn't, take back. "To toy with me? To scare me? You lost that power long ago."

His expression changed, the quirk of his mouth going flat and limp, disinterest painted in thin but obvious strokes.

"Still emotional. Still weak." He sneered at her. "You should have cut such ties long ago."

Even now, all these years later, Natalia's heart seized at the very idea. It was, after all, one of the first things Carlos had told her.

Your sister will be your death.

She'd asked him once what he'd have her do.

Kill her. Sell her. Shed the weakness like old skin and live again.

Harsh, cold words, whispered across a table and over a meal. As if they'd been discussing a bad habit or an old shirt. But words Carlos lived by.

He'd never understood Natalia, never reconciled that she'd become so lethal yet remained so loyal. It was, she suspected, one of the things he liked about her. The puzzle. The mystery. He wanted to see her fail, to crack and crumble and become the detached *sicario* he'd trained her to be . . . But there was a part of him, too, that wanted to see how long she'd last. How far she'd go. He'd never admit it, but Natalia knew on some level he hoped she'd stay the course. Continue to be unmoved by promises of freedom or money or power.

He studied her a long moment, waiting for her to ask for help, for an exception. To pretend that no matter what perverse affection had rooted deep then slept and crept and leapt like a tangled, thorny vine over the years, that he wouldn't still kill her the moment the order dropped.

He would, without question or hesitation, the only kindness in the smooth stroke of a knife he'd never let her see coming.

An assassin's courtesy.

She'd never, not once, begged him for anything. Understood, even at seventeen, such pleas would fall on deaf ears. She wouldn't start now.

"Stephen Milner will be found and the money returned." She turned her back on him, the heaviest insult she could lob at his head, and reached for the door. When her hand met the cold metal of the knob, she looked over her shoulder and delivered a warning of her own. "And you'll stay away from Ana Maria."

"You reveal too much, *gatita*."

"Nothing you didn't know already."

He laughed, a hissing rustle of noise, like dead leaves blown along a frozen sidewalk.

"Walk carefully, little cat. Cornered men lash out."

"And cornered women?"

"Suppose we see." He shook his head, his smile fond but his eyes sharp.

Carlos walked away, his hands stuffed into his pockets as he ignored the drive and disappeared into the heavily shadowed yard. As quiet descended and the sounds of suburbia filtered in—the hum of electricity, the pass of a car, the gentle, mellow tone of the neighbor's music—the porch light flickered back to life and cast Natalia in a dim yellow glow that did nothing to chase away the gloom.

Carlos had come to see her, to scare her, and, in his way, to warn her.

Time was nearly up.

She could run—and never stop looking over her shoulder.

She could fight—and lose against the power of the cartel.

Or she could trust in hope . . . and do something far more dangerous.

Twelve exhausting hours after the meeting with his team, Ethan tossed his keys on the counter and shrugged out of his jacket, draping it over the back of a stool. He left his gun safely tucked in his shoulder holster. Slowly, he turned to face the living room and the floor-to-ceiling windows that showcased the vibrant city lights of the DC skyline.

"American, just as I suspected," Natalia said, her voice low and steady and just a little bit smug. He watched as she ran her finger along the rim of a cut-crystal glass. She'd left the bottle of Jack Daniel's Single Barrel on the counter where he'd tossed his keys. Intentionally, no doubt, though the warning took nothing away from the picture she made. Ensconced in one of his leather club chairs, the DC skyline a silent sentinel at her back, Natalia quietly watched him as if she couldn't quite decide what to do with him.

He, on the other hand, had *plenty* of ideas about what to do with her. Dozens of thoughts of just what her leave-little-to-the-imagination activewear concealed. On what it would feel like to put his hands on her hips, to pull the black runner's fleece over her head, to press her, naked and willing, between the heat of his body and the cold plane of the window.

There wasn't a man alive who wouldn't consider all those things and more.

But only a stupid one would try it when there was a gun within easy reach on the table beside her.

"Full of surprises, aren't you, Miss Vega?" he asked, fighting back the surge of desperate arousal that could very well get him killed.

"You've no idea."

Regardless of what Natalia Vega was, Ethan couldn't let go of what he wanted her to be.

Friend. Ally. Lover.

So damn *stupid*. He'd met beautiful women before. Taken more than a few of them to his bed. But not a single one of them had ever been a threat to him. Most saw either the polished prestige of an old family name or a dangerous Special Forces operator—a man they could take to bed once and tell stories about for years.

But Natalia . . . Natalia saw Ethan for what, if not who, he was. Controlled. Skilled. Deadly.

Her enemy, maybe. Her equal, definitely.

Turned out, lust didn't give a shit about convenience, stupidity, or danger. Because as Ethan stared at Natalia, comfortable and relaxed in his home, drinking his liquor, questions lingering in her eyes and poised on her lips, all he could really think about was all the things they could do in bed.

And what it would take to earn her surrender.

No doubt she'd make him work for it.

He prayed he got the chance. The fact that she was here, that he wasn't dead, told him he just might.

She tipped back her drink, draining the last of the alcohol she'd poured for herself. "We need to talk, Mr. *Somerton*."

CHAPTER SEVEN

The last time Natalia had broken into a man's house, she'd murdered him. She couldn't guarantee tonight wouldn't end the same way.

But she couldn't pull the trigger. Not yet. Not until she knew why.

Not until she knew if Ethan, friend or foe or something else entirely, posed a threat to Ana Maria. Then, and only then, could she forge a path forward.

The idea of killing him, of holding his hand as he died, chilled her. But if push came to shove, she would.

She prayed Ethan would give her a reason to look the other way. Stupid and dangerous and so unacceptably naive of her, but Natalia believed the man she'd spent the day uncovering, researching, and piecing together was a *good* man.

Smart. Kind. Compassionate.

The yearbooks—five of them in total, because *of course* he'd been a fifth-year MBA—had painted a picture of someone driven but also down-to-earth. Someone who tutored high school students and ran 10Ks for cancer research. Someone who'd likely had six-figure job offers but, according to a profile in the University of Pennsylvania paper, had chosen the military instead. None of it made sense, and until it did, until he explained himself, Ethan Somerton lived.

"Doorman let you in?" Ethan asked. He'd crossed half the distance between them but stopped there. Wary. Careful. "Can't decide if I should file a complaint or slip him a tip."

"I took the stairs." She rose from the chair but lingered near the gun. She had her knife—she always had her knife—but against a man like Ethan, she'd need surprise to get close enough to use it. "Then picked the lock."

"Handy," he said, the corner of his mouth twitching up in a grin. "And made yourself at home. Pity you didn't make one for me." He tipped his head toward the empty glass by her side. "Mind if I do?"

"It's your house." Though it didn't suit him. It was too . . . pulled together. Too "designed." As if he'd rented it fully furnished or turned over the decorating to some top-end designer who equated taste with expensive things.

"And my whiskey," he agreed, turning his back on her and heading to the kitchen. Bold. Confidence . . . or stupidity?

Natalia took the gun, held it loosely by her side, and followed him when he rounded the L-shaped bar, but she kept the wide expanse of grainy gray granite between them.

"I figure," he said, pulling a glass from the cabinet where she'd found them, then unscrewing the lid on the Jack Daniel's, "you aren't going to shoot me in the back if you went to all the trouble of breaking in, tipping me off to your presence, and waiting where you could be certain I'd see you."

He lifted the glass to his mouth, took a sip, and swallowed. When he set it down, he placed it atop the University of Pennsylvania yearbook she'd lifted from the library. She'd left it open for him, turned to the page with the photo of him, ten years younger but just as potent, just as compelling, just as intriguing. Determined but not dangerous. Not yet. The Ethan who'd attended one of the nation's best schools lacked the edge, the experience, that, once gained, was worn forever.

"Can't account for hard copies," he said, running a finger across the page. He looked up at her, took another sip of his drink. "So you know who I am."

"I know who you were," Natalia corrected, the taste of his real name still fresh on her tongue. "You're going to tell me who you are."

"Am I?" he asked, his mouth unfurling in a wide, pleasured grin. Like a cat that had woken from a sun-warmed nap, only to spot an overly ambitious mouse. "And if I don't?"

He didn't think she'd pull the trigger, she realized. It shouldn't have surprised her, but it did. He wasn't *afraid* of her. Wary, yes. Uncertain, absolutely. Curious, definitely.

But not afraid.

What a fucking *idiot*. She only wished it made him less attractive.

The suit he'd chosen for today, neatly tailored and pressed, was a deep blue and skimmed his body as if it had been cut for him specifically. It may well have been. She knew by the way he moved, the way he turned, the way his muscles and tendons flexed beneath the skin she could see, that he was built. Not in a gym. Oh no. He was too compact for that. Too well proportioned. Nothing excessive or obvious. Just stone-cold competence wrapped up in winter-blue eyes; thick, dark hair; and smooth, fair skin. The man certainly left an impression.

"If I leave here with questions, I'll be voicing them with my uncle over breakfast." Natalia drew back and raised her gun as Ethan pulled his from his shoulder holster, checked the chamber, and ejected the magazine. He set the bullets on the counter and slid the gun into a kitchen drawer.

"I can well imagine how your uncle asks questions." Ethan drained his glass, set it in the sink, then came around the bar, his hands up and palms out. "I think I'll pass, thanks."

He stalked toward her, his gaze alive and vibrant, dancing over her with the spark and fluidity of a blue-toned flame along a power line. Mesmerizing, but guaranteed trouble all the same. She matched each forward step of his with a backward step of her own.

"That's far enough," she warned, her voice steady but her palms slick with sweat. Why was he challenging her? He had to know that if he forced the issue, she'd shoot him. She'd aim for muscle, something fleshy and painful—his ego presented a large enough target. She stopped, planted her feet, and told him again. "Stop. Now."

Finally, he did as she ordered, drawing up just feet away. Too close. Far too close. But she couldn't continue to retreat; he'd only follow her. It was time to stand her ground and see what happened. It was why she'd let herself into his home and into his life.

She so desperately wanted to be *right* about him.

"That's not your weapon," he said.

"Yes"—she thumbed off the safety—"it is."

"Your gun," Ethan agreed, "but not your weapon. It feels wrong in your hand. Too heavy, off-balance. Blunt and unnecessary." He watched her, his stance loose, his hands still open and up where she could see them. "Put it down, Natalia. I'll answer your questions if you answer mine. But not with a gun in my face."

Make me. She didn't say it, though she knew the second Ethan moved, he'd heard it loud and clear anyway. In the span of a breath, he was on her. Striking out with his open palm, he grabbed her wrist at the same time his other hand grasped the barrel. Natalia stumbled forward as Ethan plucked the gun from her nerveless fingers, then used her own momentum against her to jerk her closer, sidestepping at the last second so he could insert himself behind her and pull her in tight, her back to his front.

Hot breath slid across the shell of her ear. "Like I said," he whispered, the release and clatter of the magazine against the floor mocking her, "not your weapon." He held her close, the weight of his arm, corded with heavy muscle, tight across her chest. His fingers still gripped her wrist, her own arm trapped and useless over her breasts. "Empty." He chuckled after he'd checked the chamber. "Thought so." He nudged her forward, his hips grinding into her ass, his steps carrying them both a few feet toward the kitchen. He set the pistol on the bar. "The gun doesn't suit you, sweetheart," he taunted, tilting his head against hers and breathing deep: a lover's hello. "My guess?" he said, his breath drawing goose bumps from the skin along her neck. "You're a decent shot—necessity would demand it in the cartel—but your strengths lie in close-quarter combat. Give you a knife and a man dumb enough to underestimate you . . . and I'd give you the edge every single time."

"Keep your edge. I don't need it." If he thought he'd surprised her for more than a split second, that she hadn't let him grasp her wrist and pull her close, then he was as egotistical as he was beautiful. Because no, the gun didn't suit her. It wasn't natural, though she practiced with it as often as she could.

But up close and personal? *That* she could do.

She took a breath, let her body go limp, and stepped to the side, ducking her head beneath the elbow he'd used to block her in. He'd kept his grip loose, could have gone for a rear choke but hadn't. Arrogant and stupid. He'd thought to toy with her.

She intended to make him pay for it.

The moment her head slipped free of the crook of his arm, she could have stepped aside, pushed away, and gone for distance. Instead, she moved in closer, slid her leg behind his, locked her arms around the back of his knee, and lifted him straight up off the floor. He was heavy, but she leveraged his shock and used her firmly planted foot to tip him over her leg; the moment his feet left the ground, he went down.

Hard.

His breath left him in a rush, and he blinked up at her from hand-scraped wood floors. Stunned but still smiling.

"Stick to accounting, *sweetheart*. Though the position suits you."

He quirked an eyebrow at her. "Like me on my back, do you?"

She stared down at him, unwilling to admit that, yeah, she did. That she liked the way he looked up at her from hooded, almost sleepy, eyes. Liked the way he watched her, a pleasured touch to his mouth. Not a smile or a grin, something lazier, something indulgent and satisfied. Liked the way his gaze slid up and over her legs, around her hips, along the curve of her breasts, mapping each and every turn as if charting a course—the long way around, judging by his hungry expression. Under his hands, his mouth, his control, it would be all scenic detours and exhausting rest stops.

She hated that she wanted to take that journey with him. That even now, standing over him, she could all too easily imagine his hands on her, in her, pulling her hair and parting her thighs.

Attraction, as natural as it was foreign, thrummed between them.

He sat up, curled in a leg, and planted a foot on the floor. Instead of pushing to his feet, he stared up at her and extended a hand. "A little help?"

Natalia rolled her eyes and stepped to the side. "You can't be serious." The second she had her hand in his, she'd be on the floor, and they both knew it.

"Didn't think so," he agreed, then struck, his leg darting out to catch the back of her calves. Natalia went down hard, braced for the hit, prepared to twist away, but Ethan was there, absorbing the impact by pulling her over him and then rolling until she was laid out on her back, his smug face smiling down as he straddled her hips.

She planted both feet, rocked from side to side, brought her hands up, only for him to catch her wrists against the floor. Pinned and breathing hard, she stared up at him. "You're toying with me." He'd gentled her fall, and they both knew it.

"You're testing me," he replied with a shrug. "Truce?"

And let him go out on top? Not in this lifetime. She slid one arm over her head, moving the hand pinning her to the floor within grasping distance of her other one. The moment she had her fingers around his wrist, she planted a foot and *pushed*. She used the hold she had on his arm and the torque of her hips to flip their positions.

He wheezed out a laugh. "If you wanted to ride me, all you had to do was ask." He went loose and relaxed beneath her. Well, most of him did. Still panting, he pulled his wrists free and slid his hands up the back of her legs, his fingers spreading wide to cup her thighs and pull her in, settling her more firmly against him. "Loved the cocktail dress," he said, trailing a finger up the inside seam of her pants. "But activewear suits you."

He drew one large, heavy palm up her leg and over her ass, fingers tracing the seam up the middle, thumb brushing over the curve of her hip, then traveling along her spine and finally coming to rest at the back of her head, spearing into the hair she'd pulled back in a ponytail.

Her heart pounded in her ears, and goose bumps rose along her nape as his grip tightened. He pulled her head down and close to his face. Their noses brushed, the first slide of skin against skin little more than a tease whispered in the dark. "Natalia." Warm breath, spiced with the bold aroma of whiskey, spilled across her face, tickled the wisps of hair by her ears. Ethan pushed up, chasing her mouth as she pulled away, maintaining only the razor's edge of indecision between them. One moment, the smallest weakness, the briefest indulgence—that was all it would take.

Utter surrender. She'd never been so tempted.

Natalia drew back as Ethan sat up, pulling her hips in until she straddled him, her knees against the floor, her legs curled beneath her and flush against his thighs. There was no mistaking the hard length of his cock for anything other than what it was.

Attraction. Lust. Desire.

For *her*.

Would his reaction have been the same if she'd let him win? If she'd allowed him to back her into the wall, into a corner?

She didn't think so.

The interest had been there. Of that she was certain. The chemistry between them surging and sparking from the moment she'd met him at the bar. Even then, she'd seen beyond the flirt, the ego, the persona he'd crafted for one reason or another. She'd claimed she didn't like a challenge, that she wouldn't play his games.

She'd lied.

"You're still teasing me," he whispered against her mouth. "Dangerous thing to do to a man."

"You've no idea what I can do to a man," she said, then grabbed the back of his neck and brought her mouth to his, stealing his moment and taking what they both wanted.

He didn't waste time with shock or surprise. Didn't bother with slow and easy. This wasn't an introduction or a cautious, gentle hello. This was shots fired—the opening salvo and the final battle all wrapped up into one bruising, biting kiss.

With a pull of her hair, he tipped her neck back, scraped his teeth and tongue up the long column of her throat. With his hand still tangled in her ponytail, he brought her mouth to his, pried her lips open with his tongue, and conquered.

She may have stolen his moment, but it was the only victory he seemed inclined to allow her. He kissed the way he moved. Deliberate. Precise. As if he'd considered every possible option, cataloged every potential outcome, and simply decided to hell with planning and gone straight for the plundering.

All in, and 100 percent certain of not only his welcome but his right to stay, to explore, to linger.

Passionate.

Devastating.

Relentless.

It wasn't until Natalia pushed forward, pulled his lower lip between her teeth, held her open palm to the column of his throat, let her nails bite the soft skin of his neck, that he pulled away.

Smiling up at her, his Adam's apple working beneath her palm, he said, "I'm at your mercy, Miss Vega. What do you intend to do with me?"

Such a small thing. Two syllables. Innocuous to most. A welcome respite to some. But to her? To Natalia, mercy was just a reminder of everything she was—and everything she could never be. On a heavy sigh, she pulled away.

His eyes creased at the corners, and recognition dawned that he'd said or done something to kill the moment. He pressed his mouth, still red and wet and inviting, closed. A little line appeared between his brows—a tiny expression, a ripple of sadness soon lost to the still planes of his face. Something most would miss. But this close to him, his heat still soaking her shirt, his breath still caressing her face, she saw it for what it was.

Regret.

She smoothed her thumb along the line, brushing it away with a gentle touch.

"You pulled your punches," he said, his voice raw and strained.

"You let me win," she accused, tracing her fingers across his brow, then down along the darkened stubble of his cheeks. It suited him, the barely there beard, the dark hair—as close to black as she'd ever seen—coupled with the electric blue of his eyes. It set him apart as striking. Clean shaven, he was beautiful. A high-end cologne ad come to life. But with day-old growth covering his cheeks, with his clothes rumpled from where she'd fisted the fabric, his chest still heaving as if he'd just stepped off the treadmill, Ethan held an allure no advertiser could hope to capture. Like a tiger stalking his prey—powerful, intent, wild. Utterly captivating in the way unique to only the most skilled hunters.

Beneath his gaze, Natalia shivered.

"Sweetheart, if this is what losing feels like, I'm prepared to let you win every single time." As if it took effort, he pulled his hand from her hair, brushed the line of her jaw with his thumb, then let her slide away and stand up.

"We need to talk." She turned her back to him and walked toward the kitchen. She picked up her gun off the floor, but only to set it on the counter next to the rounds. Whatever else he was, whatever else he might prove to be, for now, Ethan was no threat to her.

"Yes," he agreed, coming to stand beside her, "we do."

She could smell him—something clean and sharp, buried under the scent of a long day and little sleep. Not cologne or aftershave or even soap. Just life and the imprint living had left on him. Because it made her throb, made her fingertips twitch and her nipples harden, she walked away.

Much as Ethan invited Natalia to do something selfish, she had to put Ana Maria first. Funny, how after all these years, all the orders and the sacrifices, after all her uncle's rages and her sister's sweet requests, Natalia had never, not once, resented Ana Maria for any of it.

Until now.

For the first time, Natalia wanted to know what it would feel like to take something of her own. To indulge, just once, without thought or care for how her actions would spiral out to touch the only person in this world she cared about, which was why she forced herself to forge ahead. "Who are you, Mr. Somerton?"

"It seems you already know the answer to that, Miss Vega." He chuckled, though his voice remained low and rough. Good. She didn't want to be the only one struggling to put distance between them and passion out of reach. Didn't want to be the only one affected. The only one left wanting.

"A neat trick, by the way. Care to tell me how you pulled it off?"

She closed her eyes and drew a deep, steadying breath through her nose. She had a decision to make. From this moment forward, everything would be a balance. A careful dance of revelation, deception, and distraction. But which would serve her best? Both now and also in the long run?

She sighed and crossed the room to let the cold of the window soak her back. "I learned a long time ago—the best way to lie? Tell the truth. Except for the parts that really matter."

"Devil's in the details," he agreed with a nod. "The less you lie, the less you have to keep straight." He pinned her with a look. "And usually, the less likely you'll be caught."

"I knew the moment I met you that you weren't who you claimed to be."

"Really?" Ethan asked, smug condescension dripping from his tongue. Easy enough to recognize, as she'd tasted it on his mouth only moments ago—because, oh yes, he *had* been smug, had been sure of himself and his kiss. Rightfully so, it turned out, though she did her best to put it from her mind. "From the first moment?" he teased.

"Close enough. You were too practiced. You were looking for something. Reaction. Information." She shrugged. "I wasn't sure then, and I'm not sure now. But I knew you were more than some arrogant douche flirting for sport."

"Ouch." He grinned. "Some first impression I made."

"On my sister, yes." Natalia unsheathed her smile and delivered it like a cut against exposed skin. Just a taste, just a little sting. She had a thousand more to kill him with. "She thought your cocktail game quite charming."

"But not you."

"Not me." She tucked a strand of hair behind her ear. "Oh, it was clever, I'll give you that. But it wasn't thoughtless. You weren't flirting—you were profiling. Her and then me. What I want to know is why."

"A man who doesn't take the time to understand a beautiful woman doesn't deserve her."

"You didn't pursue a job within the cartel to get laid, Mr. Somerton. And from what I've read, it wasn't for money—your family has plenty." He drew back, just slightly, and she noted the vulnerability, tucking it away for the day it was useful. "It's not for power, not the sort that comes from big decisions or dangerous games." She tilted her chin and caught his gaze. "You want something—desperately, I imagine, or you wouldn't be here. I want to know what it is."

He poured another measure of whiskey, then brought the bottle to where she'd left her empty glass. Topping it off, he said, "Curiosity killed the cat."

"And satisfaction brought her back." She accepted the glass he held out to her, then followed him into the living room where he switched on a gas-burning fireplace and settled into a worn leather chesterfield. She perched on the arm of a matching chair but didn't allow herself the luxury of sinking into the deep cushions.

"I know damn well that every possible Internet reference you found online—at Penn or otherwise—would have told you my name was Ethan Sullivan—"

"A very neat trick, by the way." She repeated his earlier declaration, mocking him. She still hadn't figured out how he'd managed it, but it had confirmed what she'd long suspected. He wasn't working alone. Someone had backed his play, and judging by the lengths they'd gone to build him a cover, they had both money and resources. The move was too refined for a rival—cartels were more blunt-force trauma than laser-cut precision. And this had been precise. Calculated. Much like the man before her. Nothing had been left to chance, not if he could help it.

Government? Or something darker, something without rules or restraint. Private sector?

"But you went the extra mile, showed up in person. Why?" he asked.

She glanced at the flames, took another sip of whiskey, and, for the first time, allowed herself to truly consider just why she'd dipped into her emergency fund and purchased a last-minute ticket to Philadelphia. "I had to be sure." It was the thought that had driven her from bed in the early hours of the morning, followed her to Pennsylvania, all the way back to DC, and, eventually, into Ethan's condo to wait.

"Your gut called me a liar, but your heart couldn't condemn me for it?" he asked, watching her from his seat on the couch as if *she* were the mystery in the room.

"My conscience, maybe." She stood, strode into the kitchen, and retrieved the yearbook she'd stolen earlier that day. "I went looking for answers. For motivations. I wanted to understand who you were and what you wanted before I decided what to do with you."

"I have a handful of suggestions on that front," he said, dropping his head back against the sofa so he could grin at her. "But give me time and I'll come up with dozens more."

She scowled at him. "You're charming when you want to be. But there's something practiced about it, something almost impatient in the delivery. Like you can't quite believe you've got to bother in the first place." She strode back to the side chair but remained standing, crossing her arms over her chest and cupping her whiskey at her elbow. "I know when men are lying to me."

"Handy skill in a cartel, I'd imagine."

"There's no middle ground in this life. No compromise. No friends or allies or trust. Just enemies and the things they're willing to kill for." She stared down at him, unflinching, and tipped back the rest of her whiskey, letting the heat bite its way down her throat and remind her that where she came from, only two things defined a man: what he was after and what he was willing to do to get it.

"I want to know what made the man in this book"—she threw the yearbook at him like a Frisbee, biting back her grin as he startled to snatch it—"the man who graduated summa cum laude—"

"Fucking statistics courses," he grumbled, which only made her fight back a grin.

"You graduated from one of the best schools in the nation only to then join the navy as an officer. Why?"

"Would you believe as a 'fuck you' to the parents?" he quipped.

"Yeah. I would. If that were the only thing I'd read about you, I might even believe the experience turned you into something harsh and unforgiving. That you'd left that time in your life a mercenary looking to make a little money and burn a little adrenaline." She shook her head on a rough sigh. "You wouldn't be the first soldier of fortune to throw his lot in with a cartel."

"But you don't buy it?"

"No." She shook her head, trying to lay out everything he kept trying to sell her next to everything she'd read about him. None of it matched. None of it made sense. And one thing in particular stood out to her. "You pledged a fraternity your freshman year. But by your sophomore year, you'd walked away, joined a service-based organization on campus instead. Why?"

He shrugged and flicked his thumb along the rim of his glass. "Sold me a brotherhood but delivered bland parties, beer-pong tournaments, and nameless, faceless women. Wasn't for me."

"Uh-huh." She strode forward, jerked the yearbook from his hands, turned to the page she'd stumbled across detailing the 10K run he'd organized for charity. "Tell me about this," she said, slapping the book down into his open palms. "Because this, more than anything, I can't reconcile."

He glanced down. Ran a finger along a black-and-white photo of a younger, sweaty version of himself handing over a huge cardboard check to a cancer-research charity.

"Make me understand how a man like that, a brilliant, civic-minded veteran, goes from raising money for sick children to laundering money for one of the worst organizations on the planet."

He studied the picture she'd thrown at him, traced the edge of the check he'd stood behind all those years ago. He remained quiet so long that for an agonizing moment, Natalia wondered what she'd do if he refused to answer.

"*Ethan*, please . . ."

He glanced up, his gaze focusing on her face and pulling away from the memory she only now realized had captured him.

"I was eight when my brother died of a rare form of cancer," he admitted quietly, his voice a rough, broken thing. He watched her as she sank to the coffee table in front of him, tucking her legs between his open knees.

Natalia squeezed her eyes shut, her heart aching for the boy he'd been. "You were close."

"Yes." He nodded. "We were brothers; we found trouble or trouble found us, but we were together. We had each other's backs, best friends as our parents dragged us from one diplomatic posting to another." He shook his head, pain and sadness twisting his expression into something Natalia recognized but prayed she would never intimately know.

"Younger?" she asked.

Ethan barked out a laugh. "God no. Older by four years and never, ever let me forget it. Protective, annoyingly so. But my best friend, too." He glanced up, touched her with a look more intimate and knowing than his hands on her skin or in her hair. More familiar than his mouth on hers. "A role I think you're acquainted with."

The longing in his voice explained the fraternity and the military—special ops, she'd lay odds on it; Ethan wouldn't do anything by halves or settle for anything but the most difficult, challenging role—and raised so many more questions.

"The cancer ate at him. It was . . ." He glanced down between his knees, as if the area rug had suddenly become fascinating. "It was slow," he admitted. "A quick diagnosis but a long fight. And while my parents used it as a talking point, as a fund-raising effort, as a way to fill ten-thousand-dollar tables with wealthy donors, my brother slowly gave up. Slowly died," he said, his voice raw with decades-old guilt he should never have had to carry.

Natalia could imagine few things worse than losing Ana Maria. But being forced to watch as her vibrant, beautiful, headstrong baby sister died a slow, agonizing death, all the while knowing there would be no relief, no last-minute miracle? The horror kept her up at night.

Natalia laid her hand along Ethan's wrist; she needed to touch him as much as she needed him to believe her when she said, "You couldn't save him."

"No," he agreed, pinning her with that electric-blue stare. "My brother fought for a long time—held out longer than he should have, for me—but in the end, no, I couldn't save him." The admission left him in an angry rush, as if she'd wrenched it from him with cruelty rather than camaraderie. "But I *can* save another. A man no less deserving, a brother in name if not in blood. Will Bennett is suffering, Natalia. Every day is another step closer to the end, to the moment where dying feels like defiance. Like victory."

He turned his wrist free of her grasp, then grabbed her fingers, lacing them with his. "But this time I *can* save him," he said, the truth shining from his expression as pure and fierce and real as his kiss had been. "But I need your help to do it."

CHAPTER EIGHT

For a man who prided himself on careful planning and precise execution, Ethan sure had flung himself toward the edge of this cliff without thinking. He'd considered reading Natalia in—well, considered reading Ana Maria in, back when the program had named her as the mole within the cartel—but ultimately dismissed the idea as too dangerous, too reckless.

And yet, he'd still considered throwing his chips in with Natalia. Even gone so far as to present it as a potential path forward to the rest of the team.

But everyone had agreed—too risky.

But that was before. Before the reality of just how hard it was going to be to gain access to one of Hernan's computers had occurred to him. Before Ethan had come home to find Natalia in his living room, drinking his whiskey. Before he'd put his hands on her. Before he'd tasted her. Before he'd felt the beat of her heart, strong and fierce—a wild, untamed thing dancing beneath his fingers. Before she'd reached for him, in kindness, in solidarity, in commiseration. Her touch had elicited the story about his brother—a rarity in itself—but more, it had made the confession easier, the remembered pain less vicious.

Ethan had spent so much of his life amid the worst of humanity that he knew evil when he felt it. Recognized depravity when he saw it. There was nothing cruel or mean or cold about Natalia. Just a cautious reservation Ethan could respect, and a fierce love for a sibling he could both remember and admire.

As he let Natalia's fingers slip through his, as he gave her the room to sit back, to breathe, to absorb what he'd just told her, he cursed himself for a fool. Already, he missed the feel of her hand in his, the taste of her mouth, the scrape of her nails.

Will would accuse him of thinking with his dick. Hell, were their situations reversed, he'd accuse Will of the same.

But while Ethan couldn't deny his interest, his desire to take Natalia to bed, to leave his mark on her body and her mind, that wasn't why he'd asked for her help.

At the end of the day, if Ethan was sure of absolutely nothing else, he was sure that the love Natalia held for her sister rivaled the love Ethan held for his brother.

But as he stared at her, at thick chestnut hair she'd pulled up loosely in a rubber band, at the light of the fire dancing over her makeup-free face, at the way her lower lip still held the evidence of their kiss, Ethan realized that whether she knew it or not, little by little and piece by piece, Natalia was revealing herself to him.

He could do no less.

It could be a mistake, maybe the biggest he'd ever make, but he was willing to gamble his life and, more important, the life of someone he cared about, on the hunch that Natalia would do the right thing. It was, Ethan realized with the sudden strength of lightning-struck conviction, simply who she was.

He wondered if she even realized it.

"Tell me about tipping off the FBI, Natalia," he said, watching as her face shuttered with surprise. She stood, walked to the mantel, and let the orange glow of the fire paint interesting shadows along her legs.

"I don't know what you're talking about," she said after a heavy, pregnant pause.

Ethan leaned forward but managed to wrestle back the desire to go to her, to pull her close and twist the truth from her in far more intimate ways. "I don't believe you."

She rounded on him, fire in her eyes and at her back. "So?" she snarled. "I'm the one asking questions here—you're supposed to be explaining yourself, not the other way around!"

"All right," he agreed, leaning back and watching her pace. "I'll go first. My name is Ethan Somerton, which you already know," he added when she shot him a withering look. "What you don't know is that my company, Somerton Security, is a top government contractor."

She scrubbed her hands over her face but nodded as if she'd suspected as much already. Given the fact that she'd tracked him all the way to Penn off little more than a hunch, it hardly surprised him. Natalia's intelligence added a layer of intrigue to Ethan's attraction he could not have predicted. He usually preferred his women a little more simpleminded. Not stupid, just . . . straightforward and uncomplicated. They were easy to please and, when they became clingy, vapid, or demanding, easy to dismiss.

Natalia, Ethan knew, would be none of those things.

"Publicly, Somerton Security is primarily engaged in high-end private security—everything from full-time protection to special events to risk assessment," he explained, watching as she shifted from foot to foot, as if she wanted to pace but didn't want to show it.

"And privately?" she asked, shoving her balled fists into the pockets of her fleece.

"Privately, we work closely with the Department of Defense, Homeland Security, and the Justice Department. My team specializes in intel and, when the situation calls for it, can operate as an off-book Special Forces unit."

"Is the cartel under investigation?" she asked quietly, her shoulders tense and her expression carefully neutral.

"Yes," he confirmed with a nod. She sounded both cautious and hopeful, and for a second, Ethan wondered if she were playing him. "Though likely not in the way you imagine."

"And what way is that?" she asked, lifting her chin, her calm, patient regard evaporating beneath the heat of a challenge.

"I'm not here on behalf of the FBI or DEA or any other government agency you're familiar with." True, but only in the most technical sense. Ethan wasn't working with or for the DEA, but he didn't want to add that complication to their conversation unnecessarily or alienate Natalia before he could coax her to his side.

"A little less than a year ago, the US government sanctioned a raid against a cartel compound in the jungles of Colombia. During the course of that raid, one of our operatives was believed killed in action," he explained.

"Believed to be?" she asked. "Or was?"

"You know the answer to that, Natalia."

"Pretend I don't."

She hadn't outright denied it, but she hadn't confirmed it, either. Ethan didn't expect her to.

If she needed him to lay it out for her, to prove what he knew, he would.

"For almost a decade, someone within the Vega cartel has been sending in tips to the authorities, both local and federal." He set his drink on the table and stood, brushing the wrinkles out of his slacks. "Irregular—rare, even—but they keep coming. Those tips saved countless women and children from becoming one of the growing number of human trafficking victims in the United States. Dealing in people, it's a dark business," he said, watching her closely. "Drugs? Guns? The cartel may supply them, but they aren't directly involved with what people do with them. There's one degree of separation, at least." He paused, considered the weight of his next words carefully, debated if they'd be help or hindrance, then rolled the dice. "Your father didn't hold with that sort of business."

"No," she whispered, "he didn't."

"Seems someone within the cartel still agrees with him." Ethan watched for a reaction, a coy smile or a cutting glance, some subtle acknowledgment of what they both knew to be true. But again, she surprised him with both her subtlety and innocence. There was no smirk, no arched brow, just a pale-pink flush of pleasure—a young woman content in the knowledge her father would be proud.

"And you think those tips came from someone on the inside?" She tracked him as he stepped away from the sofa and around the large granite-topped coffee table, following his progress as if preparing to bolt. "I do."

When she pulled her hands from her pockets, settled into a stance that could mean fight-or-flight, he stopped moving. Let her relax. He was no threat to her, and they both knew it. But still, she remained wary, on guard. Though he was beginning to suspect that was her default setting—careful, watchful, assessing—he just hated that it was directed at him.

"Then you don't know half as much as you think. Do you have any idea what would happen if someone were caught feeding information like that to the authorities?" she asked on an angry hiss. "What my uncle would do to them if he knew?"

"I can guess," he said, thinking of what would happen if Hernan caught up with Milner, or even Natalia herself. "Which makes your actions all the more impressive."

"My actions?" she scoffed. "Please. I have nothing to gain from contacting the authorities about any of the cartel's dealings."

"Which is why I'm trusting you with the truth."

"You think anyone within a cartel does anything without their own best interests in mind?" She raised a single sculpted eyebrow and laughed, the sound bitter and desperate, like the warning mewl of a cornered cat that didn't want to fight but had claws and teeth at the ready. "Please. People choose this life because of what it can give them—or what they can take from it. There are no saints here, Ethan. If you believe otherwise, if you think anyone in this organization does anything out of the goodness of their heart, then you're a bigger fool than I thought."

"And yet, here we are." It took all the self-control he'd carefully cultivated over the years to maintain the distance she put between them—scant feet he could cross in the time it took to yearn for another taste of her. But whether he'd intended to or not, he'd trapped her—with words or kisses or unspoken threats, it didn't matter. Right now, he was the predator and she the prey.

He refused to press his advantage any more than he had to. More than anything, he wanted her to come to him.

"What's that supposed to mean?" she asked.

"Only that for someone entrenched in the cartel's way of life, you're awfully reluctant to condemn a man to death." He met her gaze, tried to convey his gratitude with a single look. She could have been the end of him; that she hadn't gone straight to Hernan, that she'd hesitated, spoke volumes about her character. "You have enough information to ensure I don't live to see the next sunrise, Natalia. One word to your uncle is all it would take; you know it as well as I do."

Her shoulders slumped as she heaved out a breath he only just realized she'd been holding. She looked tired but lost, too. Like every decision she made rested on her shoulders and her shoulders alone. It shouldn't have surprised him. As protective as she was of Ana Maria, he hadn't really expected Natalia to share her burdens, her fears, her worries. But then who did that leave? If she couldn't confide in her sister, who was left?

How the fuck had she survived this long?

The thought of her absolute isolation wrecked him and made it all the harder not to pull her close, notch her head beneath his chin, and whisper ill-advised promises and dirty possibilities in her ear. And then, when she was sated and sprawled, her olive skin aglow with sex and passion and the pleasure he'd racked upon her body, *then* he'd hear her whispered confessions.

Dreams. Fears. Regrets. He didn't give a damn; he wanted them all. Ethan had spent his entire adult life avoiding commitment and intimacy, only to finally desire it from the woman least likely to give it to him.

Pushing the thoughts away, he forced himself to stay the path, to keep his distance, and say, "You could have gone to Hernan with that yearbook, those campus newspaper articles. Those alone would have secured my death. But you didn't. You came here to me first. Why?"

Her eyes fell shut, and she swallowed hard. "I don't know," she whispered.

"I think you do." His resolve broken, he crossed the distance between them. She startled but didn't move away when he brought his hand up to cup her cheek.

"I think you knew I was lying but weren't sure why. I think you had to know the truth, that you couldn't have a man murdered without being absolutely certain he deserved it. I think," he said, meeting her whiskey-colored gaze when she opened her eyes, "that you have a steady hand when you need to, a curious mind when you want to." He kissed her forehead, just a brief press of lips, a small apology for what he was about to accuse her of. "And regardless of whether or not you like it or can afford it, I think you have a rigid sense of justice . . . and a soft heart."

"You're certain of that, are you?" she murmured against his throat. "Willing to risk your life on a hunch you can't possibly prove?"

He stroked his thumb across the corner of her mouth, willing it to lift again, to embrace an expression that wasn't built from fear and loneliness.

"Then let's look at what I *can* prove," he said, sliding his thumb along her bottom lip, tracing the mouth he so badly wanted to taste again. "Ten years ago, you were little more than an accomplished high school student. But something happened that changed all that."

He pulled his hand away, unreasonably pleased with the way her mouth dropped open and the ghost of a sigh left her. "Ten years ago, Hernan Vega arrived in the United States," he said, stepping back to give her breathing room and his control a chance to rebuild. "He killed your mother, your father. And in that moment he changed an extraordinary National Honor Society student into something else. Something darker. I don't need the details to know how desperate you must have been." He shook his head, wondering what he'd have thought of Natalia Vega had he met her in college—what she'd have thought of him.

"You'd have me believe you'd hand my life over to your uncle in a heartbeat if it served your purposes," he continued, focusing on the here and now instead of futures that simply were not meant to be. "Have me believe that you're what? Heartless. Vicious. Unrepentant."

Every muscle in her neck and shoulders seized, but she refused to move away from the fireplace—or meet his gaze.

"Wouldn't you?"

"Yes."

"But that would be little more than a convenient lie. An identity you slip on like armor. But it's not the truth." He knew she was so much more—even if she didn't.

"No?" she asked. "Then what is?"

"That while whatever happened all those years ago changed you, it didn't turn you into someone cruel. Someone heartless. It didn't twist you into a woman who'd kill a man on a hunch or ignore the plight of innocent people. Your uncle's betrayal left you as the last line of defense for Ana Maria—she was, what, twelve when your parents died?"

"My father died," Natalia admitted, her voice raw and wretched with memories. "My mother . . ." She shook her head, and he let it go.

"A child. A defenseless little girl who only had her big sister." Their pasts weren't the same, not even close, but too easily Ethan could imagine all the things he'd have done to save his brother. It was harder to imagine what costs he *wouldn't* have paid, what price he'd have deemed too high if it meant even one more day with Connor. "I believe that everything you've done since, every choice you've made, has been for *her*." He reached for her again, resting his hand atop her shoulder and brushing the curve of her collarbone with his thumb.

She wrenched away from him, and for the first time since he'd met her, Ethan saw what fear looked like on Natalia's face. It was only a glimpse, there and gone again in the space of a heartbeat, but it was enough to convince him he never, ever wanted to see it again.

"You don't know the first thing about my sister or me."

"I know the only thing that really matters, Natalia. I know that you'd do *anything* for Ana Maria. Protect her. Die for her."

"How typical." She sneered, backing away from him as if he'd demanded she fall to her knees before him. "Men like you are all the same."

"Men like me?" he asked, his own fists curling at his sides. She could accuse him of what she liked, but sooner or later, Ethan was going to prove just how wrong she was. Just how worthy, how worshipful, he could be.

"Powerful. Egotistical. So certain that just because you put your hands on me, just because you took my mouth or my body, that just because I *let* you do all those things, you know me. You. Don't."

Let him? The very idea rankled. As if she hadn't wanted it. Yearned for it. Demanded it with every countermeasure, every breathy moan, every slide of tongue. Fine. If she wanted to rewrite what lay between them, he'd allow it—but he'd be damn sure before he touched her again, before he took what they both knew she wanted to offer, that he'd make her ask for it. Plead for it.

A man's ego could only take so much. Until then, they had a conversation to finish.

"I know a lot more than you think," he said. "*You've* told me more than you realize." He stepped away, the heat from the fireplace soaking through his clothes to the point he was no longer comfortable. "I know that your first instinct is to protect your little sister—a habit so second nature I'm not even sure you realize the myriad ways you do it throughout the day." He shrugged. "Though your threat the other night wasn't exactly subtle."

"You'll have to forgive me," she snapped. "I took you for a man who thought charm and money were adequate substitutes for intellect."

"You made your point well enough," he said on an easy shrug. "But it was hardly necessary. Your love for Ana Maria was clear in the way you looked at her, the way your hand went briefly to the small of her back—protective, possessive, a warning in and of itself—the way you made sure she'd had something to eat. You love her."

"She's my sister."

Yeah, and were they talking about giving up the last slice of pizza, rearranging weekend plans, or some other minor, if not annoying, inconvenience, then he'd have let that comment slide.

"It's more than that, Natalia, and no lie will convince me otherwise." Ethan knew more than anyone that not all familial bonds were created equal. That not all siblings shared the same sense of closeness that he and Connor had or that Natalia and Ana Maria still did.

Hell, aside from the mandatory holidays or the rare benefit honoring his brother, Ethan rarely ever saw his parents.

He loved them, but would he die for them?

"I don't believe there's anything in this world you wouldn't do for your sister. To keep her safe. To see her happy." He watched her face, cataloging the expressions that played out upon smooth caramel-colored skin and wide toffee-colored eyes. Honesty. Regret. Love. But most of all, conviction, which he recognized in the subtle way her chin came up and her jaw clenched. "That's no small thing, Natalia. And regardless of what people claim, what they tell themselves and their loved ones, very few could live up to such a commitment, certainly not over the course of a decade."

"My father . . ." She swallowed hard, as if she never dared think of him, as if the simplest memory brought the untold pain of loss, but without the buoying measure of good memories to comfort her. "Family was *everything* to my father. Every dream I ever had, he supported. He never asked me for anything, not until his dying breath." Her voice caught, and she turned away from him. "I *promised* him, Ethan," she whispered, folding her arms across her middle and walking toward the floor-to-ceiling windows.

"And now that promise is your identity. I understand that." More than she knew. Ethan lived with the immense pressure that came with people who relied on him for their safety, for their lives. Knew the burden of disappointing them, of failing them. But he'd always tried. "I made promises, too, Natalia."

"To Will Bennett?" she asked.

"To him. To the men and women who work for me." To lead them. To guide them. To listen if they needed to talk. He'd never gone so far as to guarantee their safety—he knew he couldn't, not in the realm of special ops. Too much could go wrong. But he *had* made promises he'd believed he could keep. To stand by them. To have their back.

To always, always, bring them home—one way or another.

A promise he thought he'd fulfilled when he'd carried Will's flag-draped coffin off the plane.

He'd been wrong then, but he wasn't wrong now. Alive or dead, one way or another, he'd see Will home.

"You should know better than to make promises you can't keep," Natalia murmured, though it felt less like an accusation and more like a warning she willed herself to remember.

"I never have." Ethan didn't put much stock in platitudes or empty words designed only to make someone feel better. He preferred the truth, even when it had to be ripped off like a stubborn Band-Aid. But for the first time in his life, Ethan could see the appeal of reckless assurances. More than anything, right in that moment, he wanted to promise Natalia that he could free her of the cartel and the hold her uncle had over her. That he could guarantee a life beyond the violence and blood and constant threat of betrayal for her sister and her.

Such a vow was not only stupid but dangerous, too. But no more than the bone-deep desire he had to do it anyway. The feelings this woman stoked in him . . . primal, powerful, possessive urges he'd never thought to experience.

The smart thing to do would be to secure her secrecy and walk away. But just this once, Ethan found he didn't give a shit about the smart play. Not where Natalia was concerned.

"What do you want from me, Ethan?" she asked on an exhausted, resigned sigh.

"Your help," he said, joining her at the window. "I'd thought to simply dig through the cartel's financials—I'd hoped that would lead me to whoever is holding Will. I know something like that takes a coordinated effort . . . and a lot of money."

"It does." She turned, cocking her hip against the cool glass. "If your friend is still alive, he's likely being moved regularly or is being held in the jungle." She chewed at the curve of her bottom lip. "Either way, it makes him hard to trace."

"You said *if* Will is still alive. I had hoped . . . We only ever got the one tip, just a single video file that is months old at this point. Have there been others?" he asked. Part of him was relieved; if Will had died and Natalia knew about it, had seen it or heard something about it, then surely she'd have told him.

At this point, no news wasn't exactly good news, but he'd take it.

"Is there anything more you can confirm? Even if . . ." God, it was hard to say. He didn't even like contemplating it. But Ethan still had to ask.

Natalia studied Ethan's face, a little line bisecting her brow. Finally, she glanced toward the skyline. "Just the one file," she said quietly, "as far as I know, at least."

Ethan scrubbed his hands over his face, wiping back exhaustion and frustration and the nagging suspicion that Natalia was holding something back. He forced himself to ask the obvious, most painful question.

"If there've been no further video files, does that mean Hernan wouldn't need any more updates? That Will is most likely dead and buried?" It wouldn't change anything, not for Ethan, but he would regroup, come at the problem with less desperation.

What he wouldn't do was draw Natalia any further into a mess he'd created.

She didn't move, didn't turn her head or shift her stance, but she met his gaze in the reflection of the glass before her. "Your friend, he was Special Forces, like you?"

"Yes."

"So highly trained," she surmised. "With the mental as well as physical stamina to qualify for such a job."

"He is," Ethan agreed. "He knew what the risks were for every single operation he took part in. They train us for every eventuality, Natalia. Will would have known what to expect of capture. Would have some idea how to endure long-term captivity."

"Nothing prepares you for that kind of thing," she whispered, a shiver slipping away from her. "You think you know, but you don't. You can't. Not really."

"No," Ethan said, resisting the urge to slide his palm across her shoulders, to pull her back from memories he could see swimming just beneath the surface. "You never know what you can take until you have to endure it. But Will is highly trained—and possibly the most stubborn man I've ever met." Ethan smiled when she glanced at him. "A family trait. His sister's just as bad."

A ghost of a smile touched Natalia's mouth. "I bet I'd like her."

"She also thinks I'm an idiot, so you probably would."

"You try that lame cocktail come-on with her, too?"

"On my best friend's little sister?" he asked, barely suppressing a surprised bark of laughter. "Not on a bet." He tilted his head, studied the curious way Natalia watched him. "Unless you're jealous? Then I might have to change my answer."

She huffed and rolled her eyes, the mannerism so succinct, so clearly put out, that for a brief second she reminded him of Parker's cat. Ethan had rescued that ungrateful creature, but the beast still behaved as if Ethan were something he'd found in the litter box.

"My uncle is only ever patient when it comes to one thing." She glanced toward the door, ran a hand along her upper arm, then looked back up at Ethan. "Cross Hernan Vega and you're a dead man. He doesn't care how long you worked for him, how loyal you've been. If you fail, you die . . . but not before you beg him for the privilege."

"Will would never give him the satisfaction." Some men would, Ethan knew. But not Will. He'd turn it around, create strength where most would find only weakness. Hernan might believe that in withholding death, in forcing Will to beg for the end, that he was tormenting his captive. Will would see it differently. As his last, best "fuck you" to the man who'd captured him. His body might quit and Will might let go, but he wouldn't beg, not for his own life, at least.

"Then your friend is still alive."

"You're sure?" Ethan asked. Hernan Vega had the temper, the cruel streak, to keep a man alive if only to torment him with the promise of death. But did he have the patience?

"Yes," she said slowly. "But, Ethan, it's no life. You said it's been almost a year . . . that's a long time. Don't wish your friend alive at such a cost." She reached for him, placing her hand against his chest, and shook her head. "I'm sorry, but . . ."

He gripped her hand in his, pulled her knuckles up, and brushed a kiss against the skin there. "I know," he said when her mouth snapped shut. "But I have to assume he's alive, which means—"

"You have to find him." She pulled away but didn't turn to leave. "And you want my help."

"Hernan has a private network set up in the house; I need to access it."

She shoved her hands through her hair, pulling it free from the ponytail that had held it back. "Are you out of your mind?"

"It's not as bad as it sounds," he assured her. "I just need to load this"—he fished from his jacket pocket the thumb drive Parker had given him just before he left for the day—"onto any computer or device connected to the network. Five minutes on your computer or even your phone, that's all I nee—"

"You seriously think I have access to my uncle's private network? You can't be that stupid!" She spun, smacking his chest with the back of her hand. "Ever since the raid on his compound—you know, the one that was supposed to *kill* him?—Hernan has been twice as paranoid as ever before." The look she shot him could have peeled paint. "Thanks for that, by the way. Your team's incompetence has made him *so* much easier to live with."

"I'm trying to fix all that!" he yelled when she shoved at his chest. When she went in for seconds, Ethan caught her wrists and jerked her close. "I get it, okay? I fucked up." She tried to jerk her arms away, but he held firm. "I know. I know this isn't fair to you. I know what I'm asking you—"

"Do you?" she railed. "Because I'm not sure you have the first clue what you're asking me to do."

"I'm asking," he said, pressing her back against the cold glass when she tried to jerk away again, "for you to gain access to a computer—"

"My *uncle's* computer!"

"Fine, your uncle's computer for five fucking minutes, Natalia." He brought her wrists up over her head, then stepped in close so he could pin her body against the window with his. "Five minutes. Get me five minutes and I will get all the information I need to find my friend."

She turned her head to the side, so he laid his forehead against her temple.

"Please."

"Weren't you listening?" she cried, her entire body trembling against his. "Do you know what he'll do to me if I'm caught?"

"I swear to you, I will do everything in my power to protect you—"

"Protect me?" She wrenched to the side and stumbled several steps away before rounding on him, her hair a mass of heavy waves around her shoulders. "I thought you were smarter than this, Ethan. I thought you understood."

"Then explain it me."

"I have done every single thing my uncle has ever demanded of me, until now." The weight of her stare landed on him, rooting him in place.

Until I came to you first. Until I let you live.

She didn't have to say it; he could translate the set of her shoulders and the curl of her lips well enough. And even if he couldn't, her eyes, pleading and moist, would have given her away.

"I obey. But not because I'm afraid of him. Not because he'll kill me."

"I know . . . ," he said, taking a step forward even as she put more space between them. "I heard you. I know what he'll do. How he'll do it. I know and I'm asking you anyway, please. Help me do this."

"You don't know anything." She shook her head. "My uncle won't kill me, Ethan. That's not a punishment—it's just an end we've both expected for a very long time."

"Natalia . . ." How could she say such a thing? Contemplate the end of her life as if it didn't matter, as if it were inevitable.

"It's okay," she said on a trembling smile. "I made my peace with that a long time ago."

She sounded so resolved, so at ease with how and when she expected her life to end. It ate at him like slow-burning acid. Twenty-seven years old and she was as resigned to death as a woman who'd lived a full and wonderful life. But she hadn't, not yet, and if things stayed the course, maybe not ever.

And that wasn't something Ethan was prepared to live with. No matter what happened with Will, Ethan had to find a way to eliminate Hernan Vega from Natalia's life. If he could do it without her, if he could send her away somewhere safe, he would. But he knew, and so did she, that their best shot was if they worked together.

"I'm not afraid to die, Ethan, and Hernan knows that. There's only one thing I fear . . ."

I made a promise.

"Ana Maria," Ethan realized aloud.

"I told my father I'd keep her alive. That I would *protect* her. If my uncle suspects I've betrayed him, he won't kill me. He'll kill *her*. He will make me watch as he and his men take apart every good and beautiful thing I have left in this world. He will make me *beg* him. Do you understand?" she asked, tears welling in her eyes. "I am trapped in this life because I know what the cost of leaving would be. I won't pay it, Ethan. I can't."

He crossed the distance between them in three long strides, then pulled her close, her body tense but willing, and held her as she pressed her face to the lapels of his suit. When her shaking subsided, he pulled back just enough to brush away the few tears she'd allowed herself.

"I can't betray my sister, Ethan. Please don't ask me to."

He shook his head and cupped her cheeks, ensuring she met his gaze. "I'm not asking you to break your promise." He breathed her in, the fresh scent of magnolia and rain, and let it go. "I'm asking you to keep it."

"What?"

"It's like you said—you know the day is coming when your uncle considers you more a threat than an asset. But when he kills you—"

"Maybe I can—"

Ethan cut her off with a kiss to the crown of her head. "You can't. You know you can't. Maybe, if the fight were fair. But it's not. You know he'll send his best, and more than one. It's not a fight you can win, sweetheart." He pulled back. "What happens to Ana Maria then? How long until she, too, is a threat?"

"So, what, then?" Natalia asked, gripping his wrists but stopping short of pulling his hands away. "To hell with it all?"

"So wage the fight you *can* win."

"Your fight, you mean." She stepped back, slipping from his grasp like water through his fingers. "I'm sorry about your friend, truly I am, but don't ask me to weigh his life against my sister's. You'll come up short, and I won't apologize for it."

Ethan shoved his fists in his pockets. "I'm asking you to look beyond both of them and see the bigger picture." He sighed and went for broke. "Help me get the access I need, Natalia, and I promise you, I will do everything in my power to bring your uncle's empire crashing down around his head."

She smiled wistfully. "You think I've never considered it? That I haven't tried to do just that? It's a foolish dream. My uncle's too powerful."

"The *cartel* is powerful," Ethan corrected. "Your uncle's just a man. Men die, Natalia. At the point of a blade or at the end of a gun, they *die*."

She considered him, her eyes glassy but her expression open.

"You can't imagine the resources I have at my disposal. Whatever you've tried before, whatever you've considered, you've never had the benefit of the US government backing your play."

She glanced away from him, pulling her lower lip between her teeth. He wanted so much more for her than what the cartel could offer.

But she had to want it for herself, too.

"It's why you came here tonight," he realized aloud, slotting in that one last piece of the puzzle. "You didn't know who I was or what I wanted—but you hoped."

The corner of her mouth curled, and she glanced away. "You can't possibly promise to protect me, or even to protect my sister."

"I could send her away," he offered. "Remove her from the equation." He had the resources, the contacts. He could hide her—temporarily, at least.

"You know we can't. My uncle would never allow her to travel, and the moment he noticed her missing, he'd know." She shook her head. "But as a last resort, if things went bad . . . your team, your men, they could make her disappear?"

"Yes. Somewhere the cartel and your uncle would never find her."

"I'm not sure such a place exists."

"Tell me what you need from me, Natalia. I won't make you a promise I can't keep. It's not who I am, but I *can* help you. If you'll let me."

She stood there, still and quiet, on the edge of a tall cliff as he told her to jump. That he'd catch her.

"You've been alone for ten long years, but it doesn't have to be that way. Not anymore. Let's end this."

"I want that more than you could possibly know," she confessed.

"For Ana Maria," Ethan said. "But I want that freedom for you, too. You should have a shot at a future for yourself, a life of your own." He could imagine no one more deserving of a full and wonderful life.

"That's not important to me," she said, piercing Ethan's heart with the simple dismissal. As if she'd long ago stopped living, stopped dreaming, stopped wanting. Except tonight, for a moment in time, she had wanted something.

Him.

It was a thought that would keep him up at night.

"Then tell me what is."

She closed her eyes, took a breath, then opened them and pinned him with a clear, calm look. "I'll have only one promise from you, Ethan Somerton."

"Name it."

"If it comes down to a choice. If only one of us can live, Ana Maria comes first. Ahead of you or me or even Will. She's innocent. My sister didn't ask for this, doesn't even know the world is burning down around her."

"All right," he agreed.

"Say the words, Ethan. I need to hear them." She stared at him, the fierce flash of those whiskey-toned eyes softening as they traced every line and contour of his face. For something she could believe. For an oath. For hope.

"I promise," he said, the weight of the words settling heavily upon his shoulders. "If we have to choose, Ana Maria lives."

CHAPTER NINE

Dread should have slicked her palms with sweat, made her practiced movements rough and uncoordinated. But as always, as Natalia's fear escalated, as sweat broke out at the nape of her neck, as her thoughts tried to race out of control, her training took over. Her hands steadied, and she slipped her tension wrench into the lock, then followed it with her go-to rake. Lock picking was a skill—one Natalia practiced religiously on everything from combination locks to standard tumblers to handcuffs—but it was an art, too. Something that took instinct and a delicate touch—

The tumbler moved, little more than a sigh in the casing, but she had it. Two rakes of her pick, and she had it. A record, for her, at least.

It figured that the only lock in the entire world she'd be out of her mind to pick gave in with little more than a whisper of protest.

What was it her father used to say? *The doors to hell are wide open, but the entrance to heaven is sealed shut.*

Natalia turned the tension wrench and slid the bolt to the unlocked position. She took a breath, cast one wary glance toward the stairs at the end of the hall, and turned the tension wrench to the end shaped like a small flathead screwdriver. Slim but steady, the wrench outperformed most of the other tools in her kit built specifically for this sort of work. Which, she mused as she slipped the edge against the pin, was just as she liked it. Simple. Straightforward. A reliable multitasker.

If only everything in her life was so predictable and accommodating.

Leverage and a steady hand was all it took to edge the pin to the right. She twisted the knob, stood, and let herself inside.

Step one, down. Her path only got harder from here.

The door snicked shut behind her, throwing Natalia into an eerie midmorning twilight created by dark-paneled walls, drawn curtains, and burgundy leather. Odd, how so very little in this room had changed. The furniture, down to the huge Chippendale desk, the large wingback chair, and the sprawling hand-knotted rug, were all as they had been when her mother had decorated this room nearly twenty years ago.

Which was probably why Hernan hadn't changed anything.

But for Natalia, despite the decor that bore her mother's signature, this room would always remind her of her father.

It had been uniquely his domain, as evidenced by the heavy glass ashtray that still sat on one corner of the leather-topped desk. It had been the one place in the entire house her mother hadn't admonished him for what she'd playfully referred to as his "filthy mistress." Cigars, fat and sweet and pungent . . . and her father's favorite vice. They were, to Natalia's recollection, the only thing her father had ever denied her mother. So he'd smoked them here, in this room where so much of her father's time and attention had been sacrificed to the business.

Natalia had such fond memories of this room. Spread out on the rug, coloring as a child while her father learned to type on an old computer. Report cards, delivered with pride and expectation, and always filed away in the locked cabinet by the window with other "important things." Natalia traced her fingers over an arm of one of the chairs that faced the desk as she headed toward her uncle's desktop. So many memories rose to mind, but one always eclipsed the rest. The afternoon she'd entered, too excited to knock, and stood before him, nervous and proud, with a huge, flat envelope from Brown University. Her first choice, her future. At the time, it had felt so far away.

She couldn't have known how much would change.

But still, even as she sank into the chair behind what was now her uncle's desk, she remembered her father's hushed *I'm so proud of you,* mija, and his wry *But let's not tell your mother just yet. Boston is not as close to home as she'd like, eh?* For forty-eight amazing hours, it had been their secret. A mere day later, her father was gone.

It had taken Natalia ages to wash the gore from her hair, for her skin to rinse clean, for her tears to dry.

Her mother's favorite tablecloth—heirloom lace from Spain—and the one she only ever used for celebrations, had been ruined with the single bullet to the back of the head. One shot had stolen a beloved father, devastated a devoted mother, traumatized a little sister . . . and irrevocably changed Natalia's life.

Even now, so many years later, when Natalia thought back on that night, on her uncle's surprise visit, on her father's final words, it always seemed to blend with the innocent happiness of the days that had preceded it. Today, instead of pushing away the bittersweet memories, she embraced them.

Let the hurt, the anger, the rage bubble up within her. The time for cold detachment had passed. This risk? Breaking into her uncle's office, tampering with his computer, betraying him to Ethan and who knew who else? It changed things. Permanently.

Natalia had always known, from the first time she'd considered what it would take to slide her knife between Hernan's ribs, that there would only ever be one opportunity. That the first step toward aggression was the first step toward the end—one way or another.

She couldn't claim to be ready, and she was as terrified as she was committed, but Ethan was right. Every day her uncle grew more and more paranoid, more and more unreasonable, more and more violent. The time for caution and quiet submission had passed. If Ethan had done nothing else, he'd reminded Natalia her uncle wouldn't fight fair.

Neither would she.

Natalia plugged her headphones into the port, ensuring they would muffle any noise upon start-up, and turned on her uncle's computer. With the agonizing urgency of a computer several years out-of-date, the motor whirred, and the screen came to life.

The default icon appeared on-screen, her uncle's name inscribed inside, a password field waiting for authentication just beneath it.

Natalia plugged in the drive Ethan had given her, but for a long moment, nothing happened. The cursor blinked. The light on the edge of the thumb drive flashed. And Natalia held her breath as footsteps fell against bare wood floors, then continued from the top of the stairs and down the hall. They were light, not the heavy clod of her uncle, who'd left for a meeting Ethan had arranged to go over Milner's ledgers.

Footsteps passed the door again, this time pausing in the hallway.

Ana Maria, maybe? Natalia had seen her working on a term paper at the kitchen island downstairs.

Her heart hammered in her throat, and her hand hovered above the drive. It hardly mattered; no excuse she could possibly give would appease her uncle's suspicion or spare her his fury, were she caught.

So with bated breath and nerves she'd long grown accustomed to, she waited.

To be missed. To be caught. To finally, finally be free.

But the footsteps continued, echoing along the hall. The creak of a door—third one down, if she had to guess—confirmed it was only Ana Maria.

Natalia breathed again, relieved but jittery with adrenaline. So much could go wrong . . .

The light on the drive glowed solid, and the desktop appeared.

Now to wait. Each time she'd had Ethan walk her through it—what to expect, how to tell if it worked, how long it would take—Ethan had promised that five minutes was all the program would need to download itself. That the drive left no trace, didn't even open a window with a progress bar that had an agonizing countdown like in the movies.

Five minutes for the program to load. Five minutes to provide an all-access pass to everything the cartel did.

Five minutes to change her life forever.

After that, the first time her uncle sent an e-mail, accessed a cloud drive, or did something as benign as order another batch of cigarillos, the program would run, swiftly and silently, creating a door within his private network for Ethan's colleagues to access.

You'll know it's finished when the light stops blinking.

Yeah, she'd been staring at that blinking blue light for all of thirty seconds, and already she wanted to rip the drive from the port, pry open a window, and shimmy down the drainpipe. Every creak of the house, every sigh of the air conditioner, set her teeth on edge. But that blue light kept blinking, as agonizing as any progress bar could have been, and the door stayed firmly shut.

And really, *this* was the easy part; leaving would be a nightmare. But sitting here, watching that damn blue light flash like the steady thrum of a safety light on the back of a bicycle? That was just mind-numbingly boring.

God, she hated waiting. How did spies and undercover operatives handle the stress? Give her a good, straight fight with an armed and angry opponent any day. At least then she knew what to expect.

Dragging her gaze from the thumb drive, Natalia sat back in her uncle's chair, then forward again as it squeaked beneath her weight. She glanced at the light.

Still flashing.

She skimmed her gaze over to the time and date on the bottom right corner of the screen. Not even two minutes since she'd plugged in the device. *Great.*

Out of sheer boredom and a little curiosity, Natalia let herself scan the contents of her uncle's desktop screen. Jesus, didn't the man understand what folders and hard drives were for?

Obviously not. Hernan had everything from three versions of solitaire to old travel itineraries saved atop a stock background of a faraway beach. But one icon stood out among the rest. The same size as every other image, it was little more than a bland folder that she'd noticed only because of its placement on the screen in the upper right-hand corner, well away from the other files and folders.

She might have dismissed it but for the label.

Culo Americano.

American asshole.

Natalia glanced at the drive—still flashing—then at the door, still sealed firmly shut.

She didn't have to investigate that file to know what, or who, she'd find inside.

William Bennett.

Slowly, she slid the mouse across the screen, her finger hovering over the button.

She didn't *need* to open the file. Not really. She'd offered to open a private browser, to send an e-mail to herself or someone else, but Ethan had cautioned against it. The smaller footprint she left, the better, he'd argued. Less for her uncle to notice or wonder about. Less risk of getting caught. She'd let it go, if only because her uncle spent nearly every night in here, and because Ethan had assured her that once the virtual door was open, there would be no going back.

Still, he'd told her that nothing would be instant. That his team would have to sort through every file, review every e-mail. Parse through terabytes of data. Judging by her uncle's desktop, that was going to take a lot longer than any of them had hoped.

Chewing on her bottom lip, her finger poised like a scorpion's tail above the mouse, she glanced at the drive again. Still blinking. Still working.

She should let the file finish loading, shut down the computer, and walk away. Nothing in that folder would do her a damn bit of good. At best, she'd confirm what Ethan already suspected—that Will Bennett was alive and a prisoner of the Vega cartel. Opening this file, confirming what everyone already seemed so sure of, would only lend speed to a discovery Ethan was bound to make anyway. And worst-case scenario . . .

Worst-case scenario, she opened this folder to find that Will Bennett had succumbed to his injuries, infection, or Hernan Vega's final demand. It was, Natalia knew, a greater possibility than Ethan wanted to admit. Hernan wasn't particularly patient or clever when it came to subjugation and torture—but he employed people who were. People who would view Will as a challenge. People who could break him mentally if they couldn't break him physically.

At the very least, they'd enjoy the attempt.

And at the end of the day, it wouldn't matter if Will had died two months, two weeks, or two days ago, the result would be the same . . . Ethan would no longer have a reason to stay, and Natalia would have taken this risk for *nothing*.

She pulled the mouse away, watching as the cursor dejectedly slid down the screen.

There was no good reason to open that file and a thousand reasons not to.

But as Natalia watched that damn light flash, all she could think of was the expression on Ethan's face: agony and grief and bitter acceptance that he didn't know where his friend was, only that if he were alive, he was likely in a hellish prison of pain and fear and loneliness.

Not so long ago, Natalia had been in that same prison. Surviving day by day, hour by hour, waiting for something, anything, to change. To get better.

Or to end.

The only way it could have been worse was if it had been Ana Maria in her place. If Natalia had gone to bed every evening, woken up every morning, with the same litany of thoughts driving her.

Is she alive?

Does she know I'm coming?

Has she given up on me?

Living with that uncertainty, that helplessness, it would be a prison of a different sort but a prison all the same.

She could give Ethan answers *now*.

She didn't have to ask herself what she'd want him to do if the situation was reversed.

She opened the folder.

A new window appeared, a cascade of files dropping down to fill half the left-hand column. No names, no clever titles. Just a string of numbers it took her a second to recognize.

Dates—year then month then day. And military-style time stamps.

Twenty-four files in all, the most recent time and date from the week before.

Bile rose up the back of Natalia's throat. The file type—.avi—gave away exactly what she was looking at. Video files. A recorded history of torture and torment her uncle kept at his fingertips. A folder he visited often, given the digital history.

Disgust gave way to the hollow realization that she wasn't surprised. It was all too easy to imagine. Hernan, reclining in his chair, a lit cigarillo between his lips, the latest file open and playing. He'd relish it: the screaming, the pleading, the suffering.

Six months of files. Six months of agony. Of desperation.

Of defiance.

In Will, Hernan Vega had found something precious, something valuable. An opponent who wouldn't forfeit the game, wouldn't bend to his demands. A challenge.

Natalia shuddered. She didn't consider her uncle particularly smart or patient. He didn't have a head for numbers or logistics or the ever-changing demands of an illicit business. Neither was he attractive. More bull than stallion, he was a large man, taller than most in her family, but brash and graceless in his skin. In his youth, his size and his power, fueled by anger and the blood-deep conviction he'd been wronged at every single turn, he'd leveled his opponents. Now, the stairs winded him.

Were it to come down to a brawl, Hernan Vega would keep his feet, and his life, only as long as a man like Ethan Somerton allowed.

Ethan was an operator, perhaps not born and bred, but forged and hardened and utterly devoted to maintaining his lethal edge.

The same could not be said for Hernan Vega.

No. Natalia's uncle had been blessed with only one gift in this lifetime—fear.

He knew it better than anyone she'd ever met. Had taken the feral and malicious thing and made it his own. With a look, Hernan Vega could discern what held power over his opponents. Greed. Ambition. Love.

It didn't matter what weakness a man harbored in his heart or how carefully he hid it. Hernan Vega would find it and use it to pull him apart, piece by piece, until nothing remained but the desire for it all to end, no matter the cost.

That there were twenty-four files here—twenty-four tiny rebellions that made Natalia smile with mean satisfaction—meant that someone, somewhere, had driven her uncle to an unwelcome stalemate.

She'd never met him, but Natalia already liked William Bennett.

Assuming, of course, he was still alive.

She drew her mouse down the column, double-checking the dates and times. The time stamps varied, but the date the file was saved did not. Every Tuesday, without fail.

Would there be another one next week? Or would Ethan find he'd missed his window by mere days?

Only one way to be sure.

She glanced at the flash drive: still blinking.

Picking up a single earbud and placing it in her left ear, her right one still trained on the hallway, she opened the most recent file.

A man appeared in the center of the screen, far enough from the static camera that she could see the bottom of his bare feet where they rested against a dirt floor all the way to the top of his shaggy head. Cold, dark eyes stared out of a gaunt face smeared with dirt and blood and sweat wrung from the oppressive Colombian humidity. She found herself wondering what Will had looked like before he'd become a guest of the Vega cartel. Before he'd learned to embrace pain as a familiar friend. Before his hair had grown harsh and unkempt. Before a beard had grown in, thick and tangled, obscuring his expressions, his ears, his jawline, as effectively as the jungle undergrowth obscured the dead and decaying layers that had come and gone in the endless cycle of life, death, and rebirth the rain forest was famous for.

Caught in his own endless, unforgiving cycle, Will looked wild—cornered and trapped and waiting for the first opportunity to turn his fury upon those who held him.

Because he *was* furious, that much Natalia knew. Maybe some would look at this and see a man who'd shut down, who'd retreated, who'd given up.

But not her.

She knew too well what it looked like when someone harnessed the hate, the anger, the rage, to trap it and hold it and feed off it. It was a bitter meal—but it was also sustaining. Those weren't the eyes of a man who'd given up. He wasn't far away, tucked safely behind the comforting layers of his own mind.

No. Will Bennett swam just beneath the surface, watching, waiting—a shark in murky waters.

A man appeared on-screen, stepping in close to the metal folding chair Will had been secured to by wrists and ankles.

"*Listo para gritar, gringo?*" he asked, squatting down to eye level but ensuring he remained outside the camera shot. "All scream for *la hormigas*, eh?" He laughed, shaking a jar in front of Will's face.

Oh God.

Bullet ants.

Acid burned on the way up the back of her throat, dread and fear and memories as potent as if she'd made them that morning swamping her.

You failed. But you'll learn.

Her own scream echoed in her head as a high-strangled wail escaped through Will's clenched teeth and stubborn resolve. He'd scream—of course he would. If not now, then with each new bite, each new location, every one more sensitive than the last.

Intense and unrelenting as it was, the pain would fade. But the dread would not. It would only grow. Natalia shook out her hands, brushing away the ghostly footsteps marching across her skin, then set the video back to the start and closed the file. She couldn't watch. Not this. Already, her skin crawled, her eyes burned, and remembered pain flared on her thigh, on the inside of her elbow, on the thin, sensitive skin just behind her ear.

Every failure—and there'd been many in the early days—had merited a bite.

Fear for her sister's safety had made Natalia a devoted student. Fear of failure, of being told to put her hand in the jar—

Yours or your sister's. Choose.

That had made her a student possessed. Taken her knife work from passable to lethal.

Will would live, but she didn't need to watch. She had more than she'd hoped for—confirmation of life and a new file to anticipate. Now that she knew when to expect it, perhaps that would make it easier for Ethan's men to intercept and trace.

Maybe a single e-mail would end all this.

So many maybes.

The drive stopped flashing.

On a sigh, Natalia slid it free and tucked it back into the zippered pocket that usually held a spare set of keys when she ran or cycled on murky Virginia mornings. She went through the motions of shutting down the computer, unplugging and storing her headphones, and then, on quiet feet, she made her way to the door.

For a long moment, she lingered there. One hand on the brass knob, the other pressed flat to the smooth, solid wood. She breathed in on a count of four, exhaled on a count of eight. Did it again. And again. And again until her pulse slowed to a steady, even thrum, until the blood stopped rushing in her ears, until she was no longer deafened to the world beyond the door.

There was no way to be certain what lay on the other side of this door. If the hallway were empty or occupied. If someone would hit the landing as she closed the door—a door she still had to lock again from the outside. On a final, steady exhale, she turned the knob beneath her hand all the way to the left. Then, before she pulled open the door, she turned the lock on the knob back to the locked position so she could simply pull the door shut behind her. She'd have to reengage the dead bolt with her pick set, but this, at least, she could secure.

A wry smile curled her lips. If she stepped out into the hall to find she wasn't alone, to find her uncle had returned home early, to find death and defeat waiting, at least she'd know that she'd sent one final "Fuck you" to her uncle. Whatever else happened, Ethan had his access.

Victory in defeat.

On a breath, she stepped into the hallway and pulled the door shut behind her.

Fuck. Her breath left her in a rush, her palms going suddenly slick with sweat and nerves she'd held back until now.

The hall was empty. Thank God.

Turning, she withdrew her picks from the zippered pocket of her fleece and went to work on the lock. Why was it, she wondered as she struggled to get the tumbler to slide back in place, that securing a room she'd just broken into was so much more difficult than breaking in?

"What the *hell* are you doing?" Ana Maria hissed, her voice an unwelcome surprise that had Natalia fumbling tools she hadn't dropped in years. "Are you out of your damn mind?" her sister asked, her voice rising even as she fought to maintain a whisper.

Natalia stood, glanced at the stairs, then back at her sister. "Go downstairs, Ana Maria."

"You can't be serious."

Natalia turned back to the lock, her wrench and rake twisted in a way she hadn't intended. She shimmied them back and forth with a scowl. Stuck. *Great.* On a frustrated tug, the rake came loose, the three even waves irrevocably warped. *Dammit.*

The tension wrench, however, wouldn't budge.

"Go downstairs," she repeated, squatting so she was eye level with the tumbler, as if by some miracle she could see what the L-shaped tip of the wrench had caught on. "Now."

"What are you doing up here?" Ana Maria asked, striding toward her like an angry, flustered hen.

"Nothing." Natalia twisted the wrench, heaving an irritated sigh when the handle moved but the short end didn't. *Shit.* She couldn't leave it like this—but if she forced it, she risked breaking it off in the lock itself—something her uncle was sure to notice.

"Natalia." Ana Maria dropped a hand on her shoulder, her fingertips digging into Natalia's skin.

"I'm a little busy at the moment, Ana."

"*Natalia,*" Ana Maria repeated, her voice low and thick with tension.

Carefully, fingers slipping on the end of the wrench, she turned it a quarter to the right, straightening out the bend she'd created when Ana Maria surprised her. No way was she going to be able to relock the dead bolt—not with ruined tools. But there was a chance Hernan wouldn't notice that the dead bolt wasn't set. He could insert his key, turn the lock, and never realize there wasn't any resistance or, if he did, assume he'd forgotten to set the lock in the first place. She'd been careful, touched as little in the office as possible. Nothing would *look* amiss . . . she hoped.

Hope, the four-letter bitch of a word, hadn't done her a lot of favors over the years, but maybe, just maybe, she'd catch a break.

But that meant Natalia had to remove the wrench—and do it cleanly—because she was damn certain her uncle would notice if he tried to insert his key, only to find something that looked like a hairpin wedged in the tumbler.

On a prayer, she grasped the wrench between thumb and forefinger and *yanked*. "Oh thank fuck," she said, the curse falling from her lips as the wrench came loose in one mangled piece.

"Let's go." She stood, glancing up in surprise when Ana Maria didn't say anything. The second Natalia saw her face, sheet white, eyes wide, hand at the necklace around her throat, Natalia paused and forcibly swallowed down her fear. The hair along the nape of her neck stood on end, and as she turned toward the stairs, she knew what she'd find.

Carlos.

He stood at the top of the steps, his face inscrutable but his gaze alight with curiosity.

"Gatita." His voice was flat and toneless beyond the normal grating rasp, but his lips thinned and stretched into something that should have looked menacing and instead broadcast dark amusement.

"I—" Natalia swallowed, a hundred lies dying on her lips. Carlos wouldn't believe a single one of them. He stared at her; she stared back. She'd been caught, and she knew it. But she'd learned the hard way that there was little Carlos enjoyed more than sparring with her—and provoking her to reckless action. So though fear thrummed through her, a living, breathing torment, she held her ground and waited for him to make a choice.

"You play a dangerous game, little cat."

"I needed her help," Ana Maria rushed out. "My term paper," she said, grabbing for her messenger bag and flipping over the top flap.

"Ana, hush."

"No. No, it's fine." She brushed past Natalia, dodging the grab she made for Ana Maria's elbow. "I had to print it, see?" She brandished the paper as if that somehow proved something. "*Tio* lets me use his printer, but he wasn't here . . ." She trailed off beneath Carlos's dark stare. The scar near his mouth twitched as he glanced at her. He didn't say anything, just stared her down as she fidgeted as if he physically held her in place.

Finally, he looked up, directly at Natalia, and stepped aside to give Ana Maria access to the stairs. She took two wobbly steps forward, then glanced over her shoulder. "You're giving me a ride, right?"

Natalia dipped her head once and forced her feet to move, to carry her down the hall and within striking distance. When she drew even with Carlos, he stepped in to her, his lips near her ear. "Mind your footing; the ground moves as we speak."

She kept her eyes forward and put one foot in front of the other, until she was down the stairs and shrugging into her coat. Another warning. Another game.

And a reminder that he had her at his mercy.

CHAPTER TEN

They made it exactly three blocks—not even enough time for the heater to thaw out the car or soothe Natalia's nerves—before Ana Maria's patience dissolved and her curiosity seized her.

"What the hell, Natalia? His *office*? Do you have any idea what would have happened if anyone other than me had seen you picking that lock?"

Natalia cast her a furious glare. "Which is why you should have walked away when I told you to," she snapped. "We've talked about this before. When I tell you to do something, you do it!"

"He saw you, and you just stood there," she said, petulance pitching her voice high and sharp, like an angry, out-of-tune bell.

"No, I didn't. I can handle Carlos." She clenched the steering wheel in a white-knuckled grip and edged them onto the highway. Her heart pounded like a manic metronome. She'd been caught, and worse, she'd pulled Ana Maria into it, the one thing she'd wanted to avoid.

"But you didn't! One of us had to do *something*," Ana Maria hissed.

"But not you, Ana Maria." She took a turn a little too fast, then forced herself to relax. "Nothing can ever happen to you," she whispered, her voice an angry buzz of disturbed bees.

Judging by the way Ana Maria sat slumped in the passenger seat—her arms crossed over her chest, her brow furled, and her lips drawn in a pout—she was bracing for a lecture. *Good.* Natalia wasn't about to disappoint her. Today had been bad enough, dangerous but without immediate consequences. And if it had been an isolated incident,

Natalia might have been able to dismiss it. But Natalia couldn't ignore the suspicion that had been building within her since she'd confronted Ethan at his apartment.

Since he'd accused her of decency and kindness, of having a gentle heart.

Since he'd accused her of discovering the evidence of Will's captivity.

Because she hadn't. Until today, she'd never so much as glanced at her uncle's computer. She took every effort to avoid his presence and his office, where he was most likely to set down a directive she didn't want to hear or follow or live with.

So no, she hadn't discovered William Bennett, hadn't done anything to save him.

But she knew who had.

"I'm not an idiot, you know," Ana Maria said sullenly from the passenger seat.

"No, as a matter of fact, I *don't* know," she said, turning to glare at her sister. "Tell me about the American, Ana Maria. Tell me about the video."

The air in the car went heavy with the weight of the silence simmering between them, the efforts of the heater the only noise. Ana Maria tilted her head, staring out the window, her gaze fixed on the side-view mirror. Natalia pulled her focus back to the road. Forced herself to keep driving, to keep her hands on the wheel, to stay in control. Calm. Reasonable. When all she really wanted to do was throttle the sister she'd given up so much for to protect. How dare she take such a risk? How dare she gamble her future on a man she'd never met, on an outcome she couldn't possibly control?

How. *Dare.* She.

"I thought we'd settled this," Natalia ground out, fighting against anger and fear and a whole tidal wave of vicious, unfair thoughts. After everything she'd done, everything she'd sacrificed so that Ana Maria could have a life to be proud of. A life to protect. She shook her head. "You promised me, Ana Maria."

"So you're the only one allowed to have a conscience in this family?" she asked with a huff that ruffled her hair. "The only one allowed to take any risks, the only person who can do the right thing—"

"Yes!" Natalia exclaimed as she pulled onto campus. "Yes. That's the deal, Ana Maria. You don't involve yourself in the cartel. Not ever. Not for any reason—"

"But I *am* involved in the cartel," she whispered, the words a knife to Natalia's heart. "You can pretend that I'm not, that it doesn't affect me, doesn't touch me, but that's not true. You're just too stubborn to admit it."

Pulling into the garage, Natalia searched for a parking spot and the right words. Words that wouldn't drive a wedge between them. Words that wouldn't hurt, wouldn't bite, wouldn't reveal just how betrayed Natalia felt. She parked the car and killed the engine, her hands still white-knuckling the steering wheel as she fought a whole host of emotions she didn't know what to do with.

The realization that Ana Maria wasn't entirely wrong, that she *was* involved in the cartel. She didn't get her hands dirty, oh no, that was Natalia's burden to bear, but Natalia couldn't claim Ana Maria was free of it, either.

But mostly, she wrestled with the resentment. With the bone-deep exhaustion, with the things she didn't think about, the sins she didn't acknowledge but were lined up, miles deep, ready to tear her down the moment she stopped moving forward.

"It's not the same," Natalia whispered, staring through the windshield and into the shade of the parking garage. "Everything I do, I do it to keep you safe. To give you a chance at a life—"

"What life?" Ana Maria shouted.

Temper fraying like a wire holding too much weight for far too long, Natalia turned on her sister. "What life?" she repeated incredulously.

"How can you even *ask* me that? You have a car, college. Friends and volunteer work. You have freedoms I'll—"

"It isn't real, Natalia." Ana Maria sat there, calm and placid, her face smooth and open and so damn grown-up. As if she'd always felt this way but was only now voicing it, as if she were the adult, dropping a few harsh truths on a child. "I have *privileges*," she stressed. "And I'm grateful, I really am. You don't talk about it, but that doesn't mean I have my head in the clouds. That I don't know." She heaved a breath. "I see you when you come home late at night. I hear you sob in the shower. I know that every concession is bought and paid for with unspeakable things. But I'm no more free than you are."

Natalia shook her head against the tears stinging the backs of her eyes.

"Don't shake your head," Ana Maria snarled. "You know it as well as I do. You're just good at pretending. And you know what?" she asked, arching a brow. "So am I. I pretend I don't see what this life has done to you. I pretend I don't know what our uncle does. I pretend it doesn't disgust me—the way he killed our father, the way he raped and ruined our mother."

Natalia flinched, from the truth and from the way it dropped like lead from Ana Maria's mouth.

"I pretend that it's as you say, that she died in her sleep, that a heart attack instead of a handful of pills and our uncle's vicious obsession didn't drive her over the edge. That she didn't *leave* us with him."

Natalia released a ragged breath and, with it, just one of the tower of secrets she'd hid, unsuccessfully, apparently, from her sister.

"She was weak," Ana Maria continued, her voice icing over with long-held resentment. "She abandoned us, both of us, and I'll never forgive her for it."

"She tried—"

"No. You tried. You're still trying." The tension abruptly left Ana Maria's face, returning her to the girl Natalia recognized instead of the cold, unforgiving woman who'd just moments ago revealed the depths to which Natalia had failed to protect her. "I love you for it, I do. But it's not enough." She turned away, brought a hand up to smooth back an errant strand of hair. "I'm two semesters away from my degree, Nat. But what then? Do you think I'll have a job? An apartment? That I'll get to live paycheck to paycheck figuring out this whole being-a-grown-up thing? That I'll have a closet full of shoes and a pantry full of ramen? That I'll be allowed to make mistakes, fall in love, or have a family?"

"Purses," Natalia whispered. The thought was silly but the only one she could pluck from the turmoil in her head.

"Huh?"

"Shoes have never been your thing," Natalia explained, casting a long look at the ratty old pair of UGGs she'd bought Ana Maria more than five years ago. "You'd never go hungry for shoes. But I've seen you flip through the Louis Vuitton Christmas catalog. Watched you dog-ear the pages of *Vogue*. For the right bag, you'd eat peanut butter on crackers for a month."

That startled a shallow laugh out of Ana Maria, and though she shook her head in denial, her smile called her a liar.

"I want all that for you, you know?" Natalia said, speaking the only truth she really knew.

"A shitty apartment, a designer purse, and jars of peanut butter? I'm rethinking your birthday present."

Natalia released a shaky sigh, relieved to be back on familiar ground. And yet . . . and yet it felt as if everything had changed. As if the truth of their life had been named and shamed and put on display so that Natalia could no longer ignore it. It seemed that everyone was dead set on pointing out her shortcomings. First Ethan and now Ana Maria.

She was trying to find them a way out, goddamn it.

"I know," Natalia said for lack of anything more appropriate. "I'm working on it, okay? I need you to trust me."

"Like Garrison Coates did?"

As if she'd been punched in the gut, all of Natalia's breath left her in a rush. "That's not fair."

"He wanted to help us, Natalia," Ana Maria whispered, accusation sharpening her words to a lethal point. "He wanted to help us, and you killed him for it."

Natalia scrubbed her hands over her face. How had they gotten here? "We talked about that."

"No, *you* talked about it. I was just expected to accept it. To let it go. To pretend it never happened. As if I could ever forget." Ana Maria snapped off her seat belt, struggling with the strap in her anger. "Well, you know what? I am sick to death of pretending!"

She reached for the door, ready to storm out in a huff, but Natalia caught her arm and pulled her back, then engaged the locks. Then did it again when Ana Maria went for the unlock button. Then again and again and again in a petty war over the door.

"Enough!" Natalia roared.

Ana Maria stopped, settled into her seat, her breathing labored and her expression stormy.

"Enough," Natalia repeated in a whisper. "You think it wasn't hard for me? That I wanted him dead?"

"You didn't give a shit about him. If you had—"

"What? What could I have done differently?" Natalia asked incredulously. "Hernan caught a DEA agent in his home, in his business. Do you have any idea how much worse it could have been? What he'd have done if he'd caught him in your *bed*?"

Ana Maria's eyes went wide with shock, and a hand came up to toy with the tiny diamond necklace their mother used to wear.

"Yeah," Natalia sneered. "I knew about that. But I looked the other way because I want you to have every normal, wonderful thing in this life—sex included." God, what wouldn't she give to allow her sister to fall in love, to suffer a broken heart, to bounce back and do it all again. What wouldn't she do to share those moments, to giggle over a bottle of wine or cry over a pint of ice cream, all the while discussing men. She wanted those things with a desperation she couldn't express. And she did her best to give them to Ana Maria, to take comfort in the fact that even if her sister couldn't have the world, couldn't have everything, she could have so much more than Natalia did.

"I didn't know who he was," Natalia admitted. "Not until it was far too late."

"Like it would have mattered," Ana Maria grunted.

Natalia sighed, tucked her chin to her chest, and took a deep, steadying breath. "It might have," she admitted quietly. "I've thought about it, you know. What it would take to bring all this to an end, to set us free. I want that more than you can possibly understand."

"Just not enough to do anything about it."

Natalia shook her head on a rough sigh, pushing away the anger and the hurt and the betrayal. This, too, was her fault. She'd kept Ana Maria separate, sheltered. She couldn't understand the risks, the danger, the consequences, and that was as it should be.

Still, it hurt Natalia's heart. The urge to blurt out everything, to reveal what she was doing with Ethan, consumed her. Let Ana Maria carry some of the worry, some of the stress, just for a little while.

"I'm doing everything I can—"

"It isn't enough," Ana Maria snapped.

"And, so what? You thought you'd take the reins, send in that video? What was the point, Ana Maria? Where did it get you?"

Her sister stared at her with sullen eyes and a mulish expression. "It wasn't my idea. Garrison found it. He's the one who sent it in."

Natalia nodded. It made sense, she supposed, that Garrison Coates would have had a hard time ignoring William Bennett's plight. They were cut from the same cloth. Good, decent men who had paid dearly for trying to do the right thing.

"He got caught, Ana Maria. The second Hernan knew who he was, what he was trying to do, he was dead."

"Yeah. And you made sure of it, didn't you?" Ana Maria bit out, then popped open the lock and got out of the car.

Natalia followed, passing the keys over to her sister, numb to everything but the cold reality that Ana Maria knew so much more than Natalia had ever credited her with—knew, and hated her for it.

Ana Maria took a half dozen steps away, then stopped and turned, hiking her bag up on her shoulder. "I know you didn't have a choice," she acknowledged quietly.

"Do you?" Natalia asked, the frigid air of the parking garage slicing through her jacket but still far warmer than her sister's condemnation.

"Aren't you tired of it?" Ana Maria asked. "I want more than this, Natalia. More than a handful of shitty choices and shackles wrapped up and presented like freedoms. I want to see the world—or just spend a weekend in New York. I want to fall in love. I want to graduate and get my master's or find a job or backpack through Europe."

Natalia wrapped her arms around her middle. "I want those things for you, too."

"And I want him to pay for everything he's done to us."

Natalia went rigid with fear. It wasn't that she didn't feel the same, but to say it out loud? It felt too much like inviting death.

Ana Maria smiled at her, but it was sad and brittle and full of pity.

"You can't even hear it, let alone say it. And that's how I know you've given up."

What? She shook her head. "I'd never—"

"Not on me. No matter what else happens, I know you'd never do that. But you won't acknowledge what we both know—Hernan has to die, Natalia. He *deserves* it." She shook her head. "And worse? You don't talk about what *you* want. College. Medical school. Doctors Without Borders and foreign exchange programs. *You* used to dog-ear the pages of *Vogue*, drool over shoes too expensive to be comfortable or practical . . ." Ana Maria trailed off, her hands clutching the strap of her bag, her eyes blinking at Natalia as if she were some sad caged thing in a zoo.

"When was the last time you thought of the future? Of next week or next month or next year?" She took a slow step back. "When was the last time you wanted something for yourself?"

Two days ago. It felt like this morning and yet like another lifetime altogether. But when Ethan had put his mouth to hers, when he'd gripped her ass and pulled her close, Natalia had wanted to get lost in the moment. To get lost in him.

But before that? Before Ethan had stormed into her well-ordered life and tipped it like a snow globe? She couldn't remember; it had been so long.

"I want things, too, Ana Maria." Freedom. Heady kisses and lingering looks. Indulgent interludes and wild passion.

"Then, for fuck's sake, go do something about it," Ana Maria said, then went still and quiet. "Or I will."

Ana Maria walked away, ensconced in the comfort of her conviction. In the belief that there was still the possibility for something bigger, something better.

It was, perhaps, the greatest gift Natalia could have ever given her: hope.

Maybe it was time Natalia indulged in a little for herself, too.

CHAPTER ELEVEN

For the fifth time in the last hour, Ethan checked his phone, scowled at the blank screen, muttered a curse, and tried not to consider all the reasons why he couldn't focus.

Restless and far past the ability to focus on any more spreadsheets, transactions, or bank accounts, Ethan rose from his desk and strode into the kitchen—it didn't count as pacing if there was a destination. Pulling a bottle of water from the fridge, he screwed off the top and glanced out the window to a gloomy late-winter day in Washington, DC. Still early afternoon, it felt more like dawn or dusk, the city awash in a thin layer of gray. Gray clouds obscuring the sun. Gray concrete and buildings as far as the eye could see. Gray and barren trees that still hadn't seen the first leaves of spring.

Bland. All of it.

And so deceptive. There was so much to see—the cars, the people, the monuments that dotted the skyline—but none of it told him anything. Everything blended and blurred together, cast in the same gloomy hue.

It matched his mood.

Chugging down half the bottle of water, he forced himself to linger in the kitchen. To leave his phone on the desk that faced the windows. To run through every possible scenario that would explain why Natalia hadn't checked in.

They'd agreed, damn it. And he'd trusted Natalia to keep him in the loop. To not let him twist in the wind, caught between currents of worry and anticipation.

To not let him wonder if she'd been caught or hurt or killed.

Fuck.

He pushed out a ragged breath and gave in to the urge to pace.

And just what was his problem, anyway? This was his job. The life he'd chosen, the mission he'd trained for. He'd been here before. Stuck waiting as other people carried out plans and missions and operations that he'd devised but for one reason or another couldn't lead himself.

And yeah, those situations were always stressful, always carried a kernel of worry. But this?

This was agony—he just didn't understand why.

Was it the fear? The way her eyes had pleaded with him to find another path? The way she'd sighed and nodded, resigned to the reality that he was right? That she couldn't stay the course, couldn't keep living beneath her uncle's thumb—a reality she'd understood but not yet embraced? Because it had been there—the terror, the panic, a living, breathing thing she'd kept caged in her chest.

It was the same beast that beat against his rib cage now, a frantic, buried pulse of adrenaline and dread and fear that something had gone wrong. That Natalia wasn't coming back.

The idea bothered him—but not for the reasons it should.

Not because it would put him one step further away from Will. Not because it would mean that Natalia, who hadn't asked for any of this, had been caught because of him.

No, it was far, far simpler than that.

And far more dangerous.

Ethan wanted to see her again. To taste her mouth and touch her skin. To breathe in the scent of her hair and lick the salt from her neck.

He wanted to make her tremble and shake, to moan and plead. He wanted to know what those strong legs would feel like wrapped around his waist. Wanted to feel the sting of her nails against his back.

And then, when he'd worn her out, wrung every last drop of pleasure from her body, he wanted to watch her sleep. To stroke her skin and touch her hair and see what she looked like when fear and responsibility and all the other trappings of her life fell away.

Would the little line between her eyes disappear? Would her mouth go slack, her lips part? Would she turn to him, press her nose to his skin, and breathe in comfort and safety and strength until whatever tension he hadn't plied from her body slipped away?

Would a sleepy, love-worn Natalia be the calming presence Ethan thought she would? As steady and welcoming and ever changing as the waters of the Potomac in the predawn light?

He suspected she'd be all that and more. That when he took Natalia to his bed, pressed her against his sheets, drew his name from her lips, and fell asleep in her arms, he'd finally find something worth sleeping in for.

Something worth indulging in.

But she had to come back for him to find out.

And he should have heard from her by now. They'd agreed to wait—that the best time for her to access Hernan's computer would be during Ethan's meeting with the man. A meeting that had gone well. Hernan had been pleased with Ethan's progress. Interested in all the ways Milner had fleeced him, of which there'd been many. The man really was the most predictable sort of scum.

Hernan had officially brought Ethan into the fold. Promised him a list of cartel accounts and full access to their financials. He hadn't gone so far as to give Ethan total access, but if Natalia had done her job, that wouldn't be an issue.

If . . .

Hernan had left their meeting abruptly. He'd received a text, then made a call, and in the next breath he'd been climbing into the back of a black SUV. Cartel business, Ethan had assumed. As they'd nearly concluded their almost two-hour meeting, he hadn't thought much of it.

But that had been hours ago. And with each passing minute, more and more possibilities rose like specters from the mist.

Natalia should have checked in by now. Sent him a text, at least. How long did it take to send an "I'm fine" or one of those stupid little emotis or whatever they were called that Parker found so damn amusing?

Trapped with a sense of helplessness he didn't like and wasn't familiar with, Ethan gave up the urge and strode back to his phone. Halfway to his desk, someone knocked on the front door.

He paused just long enough to glance through the peephole and bite off a curse before he flung the door open and jerked Natalia inside by the lapels of her leather jacket.

"Hey!" she protested when he didn't release her, instead pushing her back up against the wall and holding her there with a hand to her shoulder. "Ethan—"

"Are you okay?" he demanded.

"Let go," she said, her hand coming up to pry at his wrist.

"Natalia," he warned, his gaze running over every inch of skin he could see.

She rolled her eyes at him. "I'm *fine*."

He released a ragged breath and stepped back. Anger replaced a half day's worth of worry, frustration, and fear.

"You were supposed to text me," he said, turning to stride back into the apartment and away from her. How he managed to step back instead of lean in and press her to the door, he'd never know.

Will would accuse him of mind-numbing restraint.

Parker would accuse him of weak willpower.

Ethan shook his head. Agreeing with the kid about anything outside the realm of tech called for day drinking.

"So sorry to have blown your carefully structured schedule," Natalia snapped, watching him as he crossed to the kitchen counter where he'd left the Jack Daniel's she'd helped herself to just days before. "I had other things to deal with."

"You were too busy to send a damn text?" Ethan asked, then immediately regretted it. Jesus, he sounded like an angry housewife who'd slaved over dinner only to let it go cold on the table. He poured a measure of whiskey into a glass, then tossed it back and let the burn soothe him. "I've been waiting to hear from you all day."

"Right," she said, striding forward, her gait clipped and angry. "For a minute there I forgot it was all about you." She dug something out of her pocket, then lobbed it across the counter. The flash drive skipped across the granite like a stone across a clear, calm lake, then bounced off the edge of the bottle of Jack. "You got your access, Ethan. You're welcome."

She turned and strode to the door, the full sway of her hips mocking him as she went.

"Stop," he muttered, pushing the words through a throat that felt like a cheese grater. When she didn't stop, didn't even falter, he thought about just letting her walk. It would be better. Safer. Easier, for her, at least.

But not for him. She'd invaded his space, his mind, his senses. Her scent—oranges and cardamom and something foreign, something interesting and potent and intoxicating—would linger to torment him. He'd see her spread out on the couch, pressed up to the glass, bent over his desk.

"Stop," he whispered, his voice little more than a broken plea. "For fuck's sake, Natalia, just stop."

To his astonishment, she did, turning to regard him with dark, liquid eyes and a neutral expression.

Ethan sighed, set his glass on the bar, and left the kitchen.

As he approached, she studied him cautiously, as if he were something new and unusual and concerning. She wasn't afraid of him. Just wary. As if she wasn't certain of her welcome or his desires.

That much, at least, he could clear up for her.

"I'm sorry, okay?"

Natalia shoved her fists into the pockets of her moto jacket and dipped her chin once as he slid closer. Clad in jeans, a deep-V T-shirt the color of wine, and that damn leather coat, her hair windblown and a touch of something red smeared across her lips, she looked like she'd stepped off some high-fashion magazine shoot.

"I was worried," he admitted.

She jerked her shoulders in something he interpreted as a shrug. "It's fine," she said. "You got your access." She swallowed hard. "I should go."

She turned and went for the door, but Ethan reached out to snag her wrist, halting her momentum. She froze, her gaze traveling first to his hand on her skin, then up his arm and to his face.

The tableau was a familiar one—the first time he'd reached for her, touched her, felt her skin beneath his had been across a bar. Had it been only two days ago? It felt as if a lifetime had passed since then. And yet so much of this woman remained a mystery to him. He didn't know her, not really. But he wanted to, which was a new experience in and of itself. With Natalia, he wanted more than a night of convenient release or simple satisfaction. He wanted to chart a course, take the scenic route, stop at every peak, valley, and canyon until, in this one intimate way, Ethan could claim a knowledge no one else could.

"Don't go," he said.

She studied him, but little by little, he could feel her pulling away. It was there in the way she smiled, something brittle and forced and so fucking polite it set his teeth on edge. "No. It's fine. I shouldn't have come by in the first place."

She didn't try to pull away, didn't fight his hold—*that* he could have dealt with. Instead, she just went limp, as if all the fight, all the fire, all the passion, had left her. She just . . . ceased. Like someone had smothered her flame and left her little more than a wisp of smoke that the slightest breeze could carry away.

"But you did," he countered, renewing his grip on her wrist. "Why?"

She jerked one shoulder in a half-hearted shrug. "To return the drive, I guess."

"I didn't need it," he replied, testing his hold and pulling her forward. She extended her arm but planted her feet, unwilling to move closer, to let him touch or hold her. Fine. He could work with that, too. "But then, you knew that already."

They'd talked it through a dozen times. Everything from the timing—they'd agree to wait for Ethan's meeting with Hernan to go over the accounts, an appointment Hernan would be sure to keep—to the method, to disposal of the drive. He'd been clear, more than once, that she should destroy it at the earliest opportunity. He didn't need it back, and she knew it.

"The program loaded, just like your guy said it would. But while it was running, I opened a few files. Will . . . he's still alive," she confessed. "There are more videos, and I just . . . I thought you'd want to know."

"I do," he said, stepping close, following her as she retreated but keeping hold of her wrist. "But you could have told me that in a text or over the phone. That's not why you're here." When her back hit the wall, when she had nowhere left to run, he leaned in, pressed his face to the hollow of her neck, breathed against the sensitive skin he found there, then whispered against her ear, "Why are you here, Natalia?"

"To see you," she breathed, strength returning to her limbs. "I wanted . . ."

Ethan pressed his hand against the wall above her head, let his body sway until he had her pressed to the flat surface, his hips pinning hers, her breasts pressed tight to his chest, her chin notched at his shoulder. "Tell me what you wanted, sweetheart."

"I shouldn't be here." She sighed, her stomach jumping beneath the fingers he trailed across her T-shirt.

"But you are."

"That's why, I mean. Because I shouldn't. Because I know better. Because it's selfish"—she stared up at him, her eyes molten, her expression unsure—"and because I want to, Ethan. Just because I want to."

Fuck me.

As declarations went, it wasn't the most passionate, wasn't the most complimentary. From any other mouth it might have sounded demanding or petulant or spoiled.

But from Natalia?

"The things you do to me," Ethan mumbled, wrestling with the urge to strip her, take her, claim her. Then do it all again. In his bed. In the kitchen. Over the desk. "And you don't even know."

She turned her head to the side, granting him full access to the long column of her neck. Submission. Surrender. He wanted to taste it, drink it down, commit it to memory. He scraped his teeth along the corded tendons and muscles he found there, licked up a stripe of goose bumps, bit gently after the shiver that elicited. And damn near came in his pants when she said, "Please. *Please*, Ethan, just . . . just *touch* me."

"Here?" he asked against her ear, stroking his tongue along one of the many curves he wanted to taste.

Her breath caught, the only response he needed.

"How about here?" he asked, putting a hand to her throat, his thumb brushing back and forth across her collarbone.

She jerked her chin up and down, her breathing harsh and ragged already.

"Yes," she breathed.

He brought his other hand to her shoulder, let his fingers touch behind the nape of her neck, his thumbs swipe back and forth against the dip at the bottom of her throat, reveling in the way she tipped her head back and stared at him through thick lashes and heavy lids. He had her pressed against the wall, his hands around her throat, his touch gentle and his grip loose. But that could change. At any moment, that could change.

Yet she seemed untroubled. Relaxed and willing—utterly content to let him hold her in the palm of his hand. Intoxicating, the control she allowed him. Not because he wanted it or because he demanded it of her, and not because this was a typical dynamic for him.

Ethan liked to think he varied his approach, customized sex for the women he took to his bed. That he wasn't the perfunctory asshole Natalia had accused him of being. Always, he took his cues from the woman he was with. If she liked a firm touch, he held her wrists or gripped her hair or jerked her hips. If she liked a gentle touch, he could stroke an orgasm from her with little more than the featherlight brush of fingertips. And if she liked the fantasy, the allure of the dirty deed done in darkness and privacy, well, he'd never run short of whispered promises or filthy demands.

Without exception, the women Ethan took to bed came first; their pleasure became his.

But this . . . this was a first.

Never had he so badly wanted to plunder. To possess. To control. Never had a woman elicited such a thrilling primal response from him. And now he knew why.

Natalia was different. Capable. Strong and fierce and a little bit feral. As Ethan held her still, cupped the back of her skull, felt the flutter of her pulse against his thumb, he knew it was only because she allowed it. With her, there would be no easy victories. No straightforward conquests.

Not unless she gave them to him.

It was a heady illusion, like taming a jaguar, seducing it to lick cream from the palm of his hand. An interlude. A fragile trust. And something that could only be granted, never taken.

Natalia had come to him. Wanted him. Put herself in his hands.

He spread his fingers, dipping them beneath the heavy leather of her jacket, and slid it from her shoulders, brushing his palms down the firm muscle of her arms.

"I like this," he rumbled, letting her jacket fall heavily to the floor. "Suits you. The cut. The weight. The scent. The feel."

She shuddered when his fingers disappeared beneath the hem of her shirt, then skated them across her stomach, teasing at the waistband of her jeans. "So very soft," he said, watching her eyes flutter and her bottom lip disappear behind straight white teeth. "It looks hardened, battle-scarred. But get close enough to touch . . ."

She obliged him, lifting her arms when he pulled up the hem of her shirt, revealing miles and miles of caramel-colored skin stretched over Colombian curves and well-honed muscles.

"Silk," he whispered.

He tossed aside the T-shirt, took in the simplicity of a plain bra made interesting only by what it held—and the fact that it clasped in front. He hooked his index finger beneath the clasp and pulled, watching as her chest heaved and her breasts spilled free. He brought his hands up, trailed fingertips along the underside, following the curve of lush, soft skin.

"So fucking beautiful," he said, watching her chew that bottom lip until it was swollen and wet and he couldn't help but take it between his and suck.

She gasped, her mouth opening, her body shifting. He put his hands on her hips to hold her steady, to press her back as he plundered that mouth that had teased him, tormented him, condemned him.

When she was gasping and clutching his shoulders, one of her long legs locked behind his knee, he pulled away just enough to study her.

"What do you want?" he asked, though he already had a thousand ideas of what he wanted to give her.

"Everything." She gasped when he tweaked a nipple, just to see it harden in welcome.

He didn't have to ask to know that Natalia had never done this before. Oh, he didn't believe she was a virgin, not by a long shot. She was too practical, too driven, too practiced when it came to baiting a man. She'd shown him as much when she skewered him over cocktails like olives on a plastic bayonet. It had been easy, efficient, and, worse, it had *worked*.

No, Natalia knew what to do with men, how to make them serve her purpose. How to manipulate them when the situation called for it.

But she'd never taken someone to bed as an indulgence, just because she wanted to, just because she could. Given what Ethan knew of her history, it had likely never even occurred to her.

Until now.

He'd never felt more powerful, more primal, more potent. It was as if she'd wrapped her hand around him and stroked his ego to a lethal point. Was it possible to return such a favor?

He didn't know.

But he intended to make it his mission to ensure two things where this woman was concerned. First, that Natalia would never again forget or bury or ignore her own desires. And second, that when that need built, when her thoughts turned to indulgence, to need, to desire, her mind turned to him, and *only* him.

"Everything?" he repeated, slipping a smile free as he popped the top button on her jeans. "Is that all?"

"To start," she replied, a rush of color climbing up her chest and throat. Not a blush, oh no, not from this one. Just heat and want and heady expectation. He followed it with a hand up the middle of her belly, through the valley of her breasts, and along the column of her throat until every breath, every swallow, bobbed and dipped against his palm. He let his thumb linger, then settle in the little dip beneath the corner of her jaw that welcomed him as if he'd always been meant to discover it.

He pulled down the zipper of her jeans, a slow, steady scrape of teeth when what he really wanted to do was yank and tear. But when her mouth dropped open and her eyes fell shut, he knew slow and deliberate would serve him far, far better.

"Both feet on the floor," he told her, nudging her with his hip when she didn't immediately loosen the leg she'd wrapped around the back of his. "Time to get these off." With one hand, he worked her jeans down, over her hips and across her thighs. They were too tight to fall the rest of the way on their own, but that was all right, he had what he wanted. For now.

He kept his hand on her throat, a gentle brace that was more reminder than restraint. When he pulled his index finger across her lips, she parted them, sucking one finger, then two. So wanton. So instinctive. And a terrible tease of just what that mouth could do. "Good girl."

He slid his free hand down across her chest, stopping to tweak a desperate nipple, smiling when teeth scraped the back of his knuckles, but the suction of her mouth increased. Finally, he let himself look down, watch as he pulled skimpy black underwear along smooth, strong thighs.

Her hips jerked when he exposed her to him, once, then twice, and for the first time she wiggled in his grip. "Too much?" he asked, pulling his fingers from her mouth and over lips she'd stained with something far stronger than lipstick. He'd have fun wearing it off. Later.

"Not enough," she moaned, undulating against him. "Don't tease me—"

She went to her toes on a gasp as he took the fingers she'd so greedily suckled and slipped them between folds slick with need. He didn't wait. Didn't explore or linger or taunt. Just plunged two fingers deep, immediately setting up a slow, pumping rhythm, using the edge of his thumbnail to brush back and forth against her clit.

"Oh God." She dropped her head back against the wall with a *thud*, shifted restlessly from foot to foot, and then, when she couldn't open her legs or hike a thigh over his hip, she grasped his shoulders and mewled as she came, riding his fingers and cursing his name.

Natalia stared up at the ceiling, taking in the exposed beams and unfinished air ducts, and tried to remember how it had come to this. How she'd wound up pressed to the wall, her pants around her knees, her inhibitions gone and her mind a pleasant buzz of, *When can we do that again?*

Because, dear God, did she want to.

Ethan dropped his head against her shoulder, bit at the skin he found there, and breathed her in as if it were the last taste of air life would grant him before a tidal wave sucked him under.

Natalia went for his belt, fumbling with his shirt, then simply yanking it from the slacks he wore so she could undo his buckle and then his pants. She shimmied as her fingers scrabbled. Stepping out of one shoe, then the other, she worked her jeans down, desperate to be free of them, to have the ability to lock her legs around his waist and pull him into her body.

"Wait, wait," he said, grabbing her wrists as she jerked down his pants and boxers. "Natalia, wait—"

She released his pants, let gravity take them to the floor, then tore at his shirt, absurdly pleased when buttons went flying, pinging across the floor and rolling to God knew where. She'd hoped it'd be weeks before he found them all, each one a torrid little reminder of what they'd done together.

"Natalia, honey, stop or I swear to Christ I'm going to fuck you against the wall."

"Do it," she urged him as his shirt spilled to the floor.

He cursed, then toed off his shoes and stepped out of his pants. She grasped the front of his undershirt and tore it open at the neck, letting it hang loose and open, her fists still gripping the cotton. He shrugged out of it and was on her again, grasping her wrists and pressing her back, attacking her mouth like a man possessed. His cock, hard and long, brushed across her stomach, where she was powerless to do anything about it.

"Let me touch you," she pleaded between bruising kisses. Touch. Stroke. Taste. She wanted all of it, and she wanted it now.

"No," he grunted, his hips flexing, his chest hair scraping over her sensitive breasts. "The second you touch me, I'm done. Do you understand? You'll ruin me, and I can't have that. Not before I'm inside you."

"Then do it, Ethan." She went to her toes to bring their bodies into alignment, then hiked one leg up over his hip, opening herself to him. His hips jerked, and his cock slipped across her core, each pass growing easier, faster, slicker. "Do it *now*."

He stilled, his entire body going rigid and still, curses spilling from his lips. He moved to step back, but she tightened the leg she'd locked behind his and jerked her fists free of his hands and grasped his shoulders. "No."

"Honey, I have to. We need a condom."

"I don't fucking *care*," she snarled, digging her fingernails into the muscle crossing his shoulders like a yoke. "I don't care about tomorrow. Or the day after that. I don't care about next week or next month or next year. Right now, the only thing I care about is right here." She reached between them and grasped his cock in her fist and brought the tip to her opening. "I want today. I want this moment." She hovered there, one thrust away from bliss. "Everything, all of it, the whole selfish indulgence. I want to feel all of it, Ethan."

He didn't make her wait, just thrust into her in one fatal plunge, a curse on his lips and his arms wrapping around her thighs.

He lifted her, and she locked her legs around the small of his back, crossing her ankles and holding on as he drove into her in a blinding rhythm that had her mouth falling open and her fingers scoring his back.

Her head fell forward, her hair spilling down around them in a curtain as the pressure grew inside her, building and building and building until it pushed everything else away to where it didn't matter anymore and all that was left was pleasure, rough and fierce and so fucking good she bit her lip until it bled and Ethan came inside her, marking her, intimately and irrevocably changing who she was.

For a moment, as they slid to the floor in a tangle, a sated heap of heavy limps, Natalia let herself imagine a life where this wasn't special or indulgent or selfish. A world where Ethan looked at her with heat and want and desire, a world where she could have him morning, noon, or night.

She hadn't thought of her own future in years. Leave it to this man—this wild, wonderful man—to fill it with sex and laughter and a desire so fierce she wondered if it were possible to survive it.

She hoped to God she got the chance to find out.

CHAPTER TWELVE

Somehow, after several hours and one very hot shower, they made it to the bed. Strangely, it had been slipping into Ethan's soft sheets and curling up against the man's broad chest that had set Natalia on edge. The sex? That she'd wanted and taken and enjoyed. Ethan had denied her nothing and given her so much more than she could have known to ask for.

She'd wanted the fantasy, the indulgence, the passion. Ana Maria had accused her of forgetting how to want, how to yearn for something new or better or different.

She'd been so wrong. There were a thousand things Natalia wanted. Dreams she'd cultivated as a child, plans she'd made to see the world and go to school and fall in love. Knowing she couldn't have them, that the best she could hope for was to pass them on to her sister, didn't mean she didn't still wish she could. Didn't still wonder what Italian pizza tasted like or if she'd excel in medical school or if New Zealand was the beautiful emerald amid a sapphire sea it appeared to be in travel magazines.

Knowing she'd never have those things, accepting that her life was different, that her goals had changed, didn't make her weak or sad or pitiful.

It just made her realistic.

Still, the accusation had sent her to Ethan, a path she might have resisted and a destination she'd never forget. But as wonderful as it had been, she couldn't afford to think that this was the start of something, that there was a future here, that she could get attached.

"You're thinking again," Ethan rumbled against her neck as he drew his fingers down along her arm.

"Only a little," Natalia replied, letting her body go loose and languid lest Ethan take it as a personal challenge—again—to set her at ease or, at the very least, to wipe away all thoughts of regret or unease or departure.

When they'd first tumbled into his bed, still damp from the shower, Natalia had expected another round. Yearned for it, even as muscles and nerves unused to such exercise or attention had simultaneously protested and cheered at the thought. But Ethan had surprised her and instead brought her an ice-cold bottle of water, then climbed in beside her and pulled her close.

She'd been naked with the man for hours. Let him touch her, stroke her, please her in ways she'd never even imagined, but the cuddling, that had done her in. Made her stiff and self-conscious. Ethan hadn't said anything, though it had been clear that he'd taken it as a personal affront and set himself to soothing one set of nerves while inflaming another. Turned out that Ethan's head between her legs, Natalia's fingers in his hair, drove every single thought from her head but one.

Wonder. Because there'd been nothing in it for him, not after an entire afternoon of sex. He was incredible but not a god. No, he'd put his mouth to work just because he'd wanted her to feel good, to linger a little longer in the moment they'd created. Then, when words failed her and muscles could no longer respond to basic commands, he'd tucked her in against him again, her head on his shoulder, one of her legs between his, and taken to stroking idle fingers up and down her back.

They stayed that way for a long time, until the sun set in a blaze of glory through his floor-to-ceiling windows and the city lights winked on, one by one until there was a sea of urban stars laid out before them.

But now reality was returning and, with it, unexpected consequences. Natalia had come here hoping for a singular experience. But she hadn't thought it through. If she had, she would have known there was no scenario in which she could have Ethan only once. There wasn't a whole lot that Natalia feared—losing her sister was really the only thing that came to mind—but that was because she'd so carefully denied herself any sort of attachment.

Now, whether he'd intended to or not, Ethan had given her things to think about. Like the next time they could do this. And the time after that. And the time after that. Surely it wouldn't, couldn't, always be this way? This potent. This good.

She'd miss him, she realized with a leaden drop of dread. Miss him in ways that weren't physical or primal, though her thoughts were sure to linger on those, too. Life, she decided, would be so much easier if she didn't like Ethan Somerton. Didn't respect him. Didn't wonder how a man who'd made a violent, lethal living could still be so wholesome and kind and loyal.

Acknowledging that dichotomy within him, the killer and the gentleman, the sinner and the saint, made her resurrect long-buried feelings about her own character. Reflect on the decisions she'd made—the ones she'd continue to make—and wonder if maybe she, too, could be more than the sum of her deeds.

She doubted it.

"I love the feel of your skin," Ethan said, drawing the sheet away from her back and stroking his fingers across her shoulders. "So warm and soft and strong."

She shivered, turning in to him and away from the fingers that slid over a scar that curved around her ribs. It was hardly the only one he'd found. She'd laid herself bare before him, in the middle of the afternoon, with the curtains open and the lights on. She didn't kid herself; Ethan had seen every single mark on her body, be it freckle or mole or scar.

She didn't mind, not really. Like so much else, she couldn't change them, couldn't take them back. They were a part of her, and Ethan could see them, could know they were there, but she didn't want him to touch them. To put his strong, capable hands on that part of her.

"Is this one sensitive?" he asked, brushing his thumb against the end of the raised skin along her ribs. "You shiver when I touch it."

"No, it's not sensitive," she said, sliding her palm up the expanse of his stomach and over his right pectoral. "Is this?" She brushed her fingers across the puckered flesh she'd mapped earlier. Raised and pink, it was healing and free of stitches but still new, still a recent memory instead of a distant reminder.

"It doesn't hurt, if that's what you're asking," he said slowly. "But it feels strange. It's not more or less sensitive, just . . . different."

She turned her head, pressed her lips to the corner of the scar, and wondered what circumstances had placed it there. "Gunshot?" she asked, though she suspected as much already. She'd seen these sorts of scars before.

"Yeah." He caught her hand, brought the tips of her fingers to his mouth for a kiss. "My vest caught the other two, but this one slipped in just above it." He pulled his fingers through her hair and down her back, then dropped a calloused palm over the scar at her ribs. "And this?" he asked, his fingers spreading as she tried to move away. "A knife, right?"

"Yes," she acknowledged. "A long time ago." She stilled beneath his hand, let herself relax against the length of his body, and prayed he'd drop it. She didn't want to talk about this. It would ruin the moment, shatter the fragile peace of their afternoon and evening.

It would remind her of things she did her very best to forget—and remind Ethan of all the reasons he shouldn't be with someone like her, even temporarily.

"Who hurt you?" he asked, pushing forward in a tone that was both curious and determined.

"It doesn't matter," she said, rolling away from him. She pulled the sheet to her breasts and sat up. "He's long dead."

"And this one?" he asked, tracing fingers along another raised line of healed flesh. "It isn't as smooth, as if the stroke wasn't clean."

"That's because it wasn't," she said on a sigh.

"And this one?" he asked, sliding his fingers up under the mass of wavy hair that fell down the length of her back, to press against the circle of raised skin.

"A cigar, but then you already knew that, didn't you?"

"We don't have to talk about it," he said, brushing against the raised skin, then sliding his hand down along the back of her arm.

"I'm not the one who brought it up," she snapped, staring out the window and wishing for the world to stay on the other side of that glass for just a little bit longer.

"You're a mystery to me, Natalia Vega," Ethan murmured, and sat up to press a kiss against her shoulder. "I know every inch of this gorgeous body. I know what you look like when you come, know the sexy Spanish curses and pleas that spill from your lips when you're seconds away but denied all the same." He pulled the sheet away from her grip, exposing her breasts. "I know the weight of these," he said, stroking the sensitive skin along an outer curve. "I know what you taste like, what your nails feel like. I've licked water from your skin and sweat from your throat. Is it any surprise I'd want to know more? That I'd want to know everything?"

No, no it wasn't. She returned his interest, after all. But it wasn't the same, not by a long shot. Getting to know Ethan would be a revelation, a wonder. This was a man who'd grown up privileged, who'd lost a brother, who'd committed himself to the military. He was a leader, natural born and gifted. There were layers to him, Natalia was certain, and there'd be darkness, too. Shadows left by grief and violence and life-and-death struggles. But the good would far outweigh the bad.

A white knight.

She couldn't claim the same.

She turned, pressing the flat of her palm to Ethan's chest and pushing him back against the stack of pillows, then shoved down her frustration and resentment. He wouldn't drop it, wouldn't just let them linger in the safety of knowing each other physically and leaving the rest to lie quiet and dormant. Which meant that once again she'd have to make the choice, the sacrifice. She'd have to push him away so that he didn't get attached. Didn't think she was something she wasn't.

Even now, staring down at him, she could see it written across his face. He didn't just want to know her; he wanted to save her. It was sweet and a little naive. And while the desire touched her, made her warm and happy in a way she couldn't remember feeling, it was also dangerous. She had to make him understand.

"This scar," she said, tracing her fingertip over the bullet wound that couldn't be more than several months old. "I'll bet you got it protecting someone."

He grimaced but otherwise didn't move. "It was a situation of my own making. If I'd been paying attention, if I'd listened, Parker would never have needed protection in the first place."

"He's your tech analyst, right?" she asked, the name familiar. "The one who gave you the drive?"

"Yeah." Ethan nodded.

"Was he hurt?" she asked, her finger moving back and forth over the scar on his chest.

"No, not that day, at least."

"Because you put yourself between him and the bullet," she stated, certain of how it had played out. For a man like Ethan, he'd think nothing of stepping into the path of a bullet to protect a friend. Hell, he probably wouldn't give a second thought to taking a bullet for a perfect stranger. "It's who you are," she said, sitting up to study his handsome face. "You're a good man, Ethan. Loyal. Protective. Honest." She brushed a lock of hair off his forehead, then reluctantly pulled away. "It's ingrained . . . and how I knew you'd uphold any promise you made."

Trusting him, even though it had been in her own best interest to do so, had still been startlingly easy. Though he was right that she couldn't stay the current course, couldn't continue to let things play out where her uncle was concerned, it should have been harder to accept his word. And yet, she knew that he'd keep his promise to protect Ana Maria—even if it meant putting his own man in jeopardy.

"And you aren't all those things?" he asked, grasping her wrist and linking their fingers. "Is that what you're telling me?"

"And if I am?"

"Then you're either lying or completely oblivious to the strength of your own heart."

She shook her head and tried to pull away.

Ethan tightened his hold and slipped his other hand to the nape of her neck to bring her close. "You're the most stubbornly loyal person I've ever met, Natalia. I know damn well there isn't a thing under the sun you wouldn't give to keep your sister safe. That there's nothing you wouldn't sacrifice to put a smile on her face. You're a good person, sweetheart, even if you don't realize it."

She pulled her fingers free, then circled them around his wrist and drew his hand to the oldest scar she carried, the cigar burn on the back of her shoulder. "This burn?" she said, letting Ethan trace the old wound. "I got it because I defied my uncle." She swallowed hard but forced herself to continue. "In the months following my father's death, I was confrontational. Angry—"

"Scared," Ethan supplied.

"Yes." She nodded. "And too sheltered to really understand what was happening. That I had to be careful. My father had always encouraged us to speak our minds, to be direct. It took longer than it should have for me to learn how to tread lightly." She bit her lip and drew a breath, her mind traveling back to those first early months. To a time she did her best not to think about. "Three weeks after he murdered my father at the dining room table, he moved us back to Colombia. Kept us under lock and key. Took my mother to his bed," she choked out, old tears clogging her throat before she could shove them down.

Ethan's eyes softened, and he brought his hand to her cheek. She turned away from the touch. She couldn't do this if he was nice. If he was gentle.

"Ana Maria didn't speak for *months*. Not a single word. Sometimes I worried she'd just waste away to nothing."

"But she didn't. She survived. Because of you," he said.

"Because of my mother," Natalia corrected him. "She pleaded with my uncle to send her to school or to at least hire her a tutor. It was the only time I ever saw them fight, the only time my mother railed at him for everything he'd done. He hit her—"

"And you went after him," Ethan realized aloud.

"With a cast-iron skillet." She could still feel the weight of it, the awkward balance, the cold metal digging into her fingers. "If I'd been older or stronger or had any idea of what I was doing, I might have killed him. I got in one good hit—across his shoulders, just clipping his skull." She ran a finger along the soft cotton of Ethan's sheets, stared at the way his chest rose and fell, watched as his face comprehended what would have come next.

"He let my mother go . . ."

"And came after you."

"Yes." She sighed and settled into telling the rest of the story. "He was furious, of course. I reminded him of my father, of betrayals more imagined than real. My mother pleaded with him, but . . ."

"He wouldn't hear it."

"He gave me to an associate he owed a gambling debt to," she whispered. "I don't think he ever expected to see me again."

Ethan sat up in a rush, reaching for her with agony in his eyes and comfort on his mind.

"Don't," she barked, pulling away. "I can't tell you the rest if you touch me."

"Then, for God's sake, Natalia, don't. I don't need to hear it—"

"Yes, you do." She pushed back, willing herself to make him understand. "You see my devotion to my sister as something altruistic. It's not. It's selfish, pure and simple. I made a promise, and I intend to see it through, no matter what it costs me"—she pinned him with a hard look—"or anyone else."

Ethan started to say something, then bit down on the protests she could see he wanted to make and said, "Okay. Tell me."

She smiled sadly at him. He figured he'd let her finish, let her say her piece, and then take apart the confession bit by bit and prove her wrong. She'd let him believe that a little bit longer.

"The night my uncle traded me for a gambling debt, it changed me," she admitted. "Forced me to make a decision. To choose a path." She tucked a strand of hair behind her ear. "I was so close to giving up. It would have been easy; he had his hands around my neck. All I had to do was close my eyes."

Ethan shifted, his face stricken, his fingers ghosting along her collarbone in apology, then disappearing before she could admonish him for it.

"Don't do that. Don't feel bad. I never once conflated the way you touched me with the way he did." She did her best to smile.

"I'm really glad you didn't give up, Natalia," he whispered.

"I couldn't break the promise I'd made my father." She pulled away, sat back, and let herself remember what it had felt like to die. "I couldn't breathe. Didn't know how to fight. I panicked," she admitted. "Dug at his face and, when that didn't work, grabbed for anything I could reach." Her fingertips had flown over the bed, scrambled against the table beside it, and found salvation. "I got ahold of a heavy crystal ashtray."

"You defended yourself," Ethan assured her.

She sighed and slid out of bed, wandering toward the huge windows. Idly, she wondered if anyone could see inside. "When I returned to my uncle, beaten and blood-smeared, I thought he'd kill me."

"What stopped him?" Ethan asked. "Your mother?"

"Greed." She glanced over her shoulder, watching as he slid to the edge of the bed and placed his feet on the floor. "I beat a man to death for the things he'd done to me. For the things my uncle had done to my family. I didn't have to. Could have stopped."

"That would have been an impressive feat for a traumatized teenage girl, Natalia."

Still, he wanted to believe the best of her. She shook her head. He was wrong; she'd had a choice. There was always a choice. And she'd made hers.

"Hernan spared my life, not because we're family, not for my mother who he professed to love. He did it because suddenly I was useful." She repressed a chuckle and rubbed her hands along her arms. "Suddenly, I had a skill set he could exploit. He gave me to his best *sicario*."

She didn't have to turn to catch Ethan's shock; she could see it all in the reflection of the glass. The way his head snapped up. The way he went unnaturally still. He didn't say anything, didn't come toward her, as he'd so clearly intended. *Good.* Maybe she was getting through to him.

She turned to face him, the cold of the window seeping into her back. "You were right," she said, drawing a finger across the scar he'd first touched, first asked about. "A knife did this," she explained, meeting his gaze and holding it. "I didn't know he was armed at the time. I was still young. Still inexperienced. But I learned . . . and I'm still here."

But only because they're not.

She didn't say it, but then, she didn't think she had to. Ethan wasn't naive. He knew what the cartel was, understood the sort of people who lived within its pull.

"Whatever you did, you did it because you had to," he said, rising from the bed and moving slowly toward her. "I believe that, Natalia, even if you don't. Tell me, what did your uncle threaten you with if you didn't comply?" He stopped directly in front of her, stared down onto her upturned face, and refused to understand the truth of her.

"You already know the answer to that."

"Ana Maria. Your weakness. One he's exploited for years." He drew his hands up as if to cup her face. He stopped, his palms hovering a breath away, the warmth of his touch on offer but so out of reach. "You didn't have a choice—"

"It's always a choice, Ethan. The same one, over and over and over again. Her life against someone else's." She placed a palm on his chest, absorbed the beat of his heart, strong and steady, into her skin. "You took a bullet to save a man's life," she said, stroking her finger over the scar one final time. "I buried a knife to save my sister's. Those are very different things."

"No, they aren't." He dropped his hands to grip her shoulders and pulled her close. "I've killed my share of men, Natalia. Sometimes I didn't even know the reason why. Only that my country had deemed them dangerous. I didn't ask, I didn't have to."

The text alert on her phone chimed, and she pulled away.

"Hernan ordered Ana Maria to sleep with you. To determine if you are who you claim to be."

"And you'd have me believe that's why you're here?" he asked. "To take her place?" He looked stricken, though the emotion passed as the events lined up in his head, the timeline no doubt reminding him that she'd come to him only after she'd had all the proof she'd ever need that he was a liar.

"He ordered me to kill you if I discovered you'd lied."

"You wouldn't hurt me, Natalia." He caught up with her as she stepped through the doorway and jerked her back to face him. "You could have. I don't doubt that. I imagine there's not much you can't do when determination sets in," he said with a wry grin. "But you didn't." He leaned down, pressed his mouth to hers, speared his fingers through her hair, then cupped her cheeks and stared into her eyes. "You'd never hurt me."

She brought her hands to his wrists and kept his gaze as she said, "You're sure about that? Sure that there's nothing in this world that could ever turn me against you?"

She gently pulled his hands from her face and stepped away.

"I trust you," he said, though the words were stilted and unsure, a declaration he wanted to believe but one he couldn't possibly be certain of.

"Don't," she said simply, then turned to find her phone.

Ethan followed her into the living room, though he didn't say anything as she slipped on her underwear, then pulled her phone from the pocket of her jacket.

"This conversation isn't over," Ethan said, something fierce and determined settling over his face. "*We're* not over. Not after today." He studied her but held himself back, as if he knew his touch was no longer welcome. "You don't see a future for us—"

"And you do?" she mocked him. "Based on what? A thumb drive and an afternoon of hot sex? There's nowhere to go from here, Ethan. Even if by some miracle I survive to see my sister free and my uncle dead, that doesn't change the facts. It doesn't change who and what I am."

"And who are you, Natalia Vega?"

"A—"

"Sister?" he interrupted. "Friend? Lover? A woman who'd risk it all on long odds based on the word of a man she barely knows? How about someone who'd help a man she's never met? Someone who'd provide a string of tips to the authorities just to spare a few women and children a fate she's all too familiar with?"

"It's a drop in the bucket, Ethan."

"But you did it anyway. Because it was the *right thing to do*. So tell me again who you are."

She read her messages, then fired off a response and sighed.

"You don't want to hear it," she said, pulling on her T-shirt. "Don't want to believe it." She picked up her jeans and cast him a resigned look. "You think of me as a victim. As a woman who fought back when cornered. It's simpler to imagine a knife to my throat or a desperate struggle. It's not always like that, but I guess I can understand why you'd have trouble imagining it." Understand, and even appreciate his effort to paint her as something more, something worth saving. "It's just not true, but I suppose there's only one way you'll understand. Get dressed, Ethan," she said when he didn't move, just crossed his arms and stared at her as if he could out-stubborn her. "My uncle has summoned us." Which meant he knew she was here. It didn't surprise her, not really. She hadn't tried to hide it, and he'd all but told her to find a way into Ethan's bed, but it still left a sour taste in her mouth. As if Hernan's shadow had darkened an otherwise wonderful afternoon.

And it *had* been wonderful, every last second of it.

But now reality hovered, just beyond the door, ready to snatch Natalia away again.

In some ways, she was grateful. It would be like ripping off the Band-Aid—quick, clean, and less painful to do it now and do it fast. Ethan had to understand.

"Natalia—"

"You can't save everyone, Ethan."

"Not everyone. Just the people who deserve it."

But she simply wasn't one of them. She just had to make him see it.

Buttoning her jeans and then shrugging into her jacket, Natalia said the only thing she knew would shut down Ethan's desire to argue. "Stephen Milner's been found."

CHAPTER THIRTEEN

Nothing good ever happened with tarps taped to the floor—it was the one stalwart consistency in her life, though she couldn't call it comforting. Just depressingly familiar. She took a breath and forced herself to walk to the far side of the room, away from the single bare bulb swaying overhead, away from her uncle, and away from Ethan Somerton.

And as far as she could possibly get from the man, already broken and bleeding, tied to the room's only chair. Natalia had no love for Stephen Milner, though part of her had hoped to avoid this. Still, he'd known who he was doing business with. And whose money he'd stolen. Milner's choices—and no one else's—had led them here.

But now, because he'd failed to do his job, Natalia was faced with doing hers.

"*Venga.*" Carlos placed a hand between Ethan's shoulder blades and shoved, propelling him farther into the dimly lit room. Ethan didn't complain, just straightened, pulled his shoulders back, and followed Hernan inside. He'd been quiet on the ride over, but then, what was there to say? He wasn't a stupid man; he knew what awaited him, understood what would happen to Stephen Milner, even if he didn't yet grasp the finer points of how it would all play out. Natalia took up a spot against the far wall and forced herself to look away from Ethan.

"What's going on?" Ethan asked Hernan. Remarkably composed given the barely recognizable man taped to a chair, he stepped lightly, the covered floor whispering rather than announcing his approach. He swept the space with a discerning, curious gaze, but there wasn't much to see beyond bare, windowless walls and two steel-framed doors—the one Carlos had shoved Ethan through led to an alley where the three SUVs they'd arrived in idled. The other, Natalia assumed, led to an empty factory or warehouse. A Vega holding, no doubt, which she did her best to avoid.

"We're dealing with a few loose ends," Hernan said as the heavy steel door behind him closed with a *thud*. He straightened the lapels of his jacket and made his way to the center of the room, the heavy plastic shifting and cracking beneath every step. "Your predecessor," he said, nodding to Stephen Milner. "Though I imagine he's difficult to recognize."

Natalia stared straight ahead but let her gaze go loose and unfocused. She didn't need or want to see, though she couldn't hope to avoid it forever. Just more kindling for the nightmares.

"Mr. Milner," Hernan said, clapping a hand to Stephen's shoulder in a gesture that was as patronizing as it was paternal, "was my accountant for more than ten years. He cleaned our money, and in exchange, I made him rich. And despite my generosity, he stole from me." Hernan sighed and shook his head. "He's here to answer for his crimes."

"N-no, I . . . ," Milner croaked through chapped, bleeding lips.

Natalia couldn't even claim surprise at the state of the man before her. When Hernan had texted her, demanding she escort Ethan to this location, she'd *known* what was coming. Hernan had only one use for her, and one way or another, his demands tended to end the same way. A life gone. A piece of Natalia sold and consumed and destroyed. But also because when she'd arrived, her uncle had opened the car door and smiled at her. Offered his hand as she'd stepped outside. It was a courtesy he always offered Ana Maria but rarely something he bestowed on Natalia. That gesture alone would have told her he was in a good mood. That he was happy to see her, which happened only when he was excited, poised to exact justice for a slight against him. It was, Natalia knew, when he felt most potent, most powerful.

And when he was the most predictable.

It was a goddamn cliché, really. The warehouse. The torture. The cheap theatrics Hernan believed bought obedience and cultivated fear.

"Please, I c-c-can tell you—"

"I thought we were past this, Stephen," Hernan said, his inflection flat and smooth, as if he'd stated a fact or statistic he'd heard on the evening news. "Past the denials and the excuses. I was told you were ready. Was I misinformed?"

"Please . . . ," Milner mumbled, his tongue thick with dehydration. He'd been here awhile, Natalia realized—hours, certainly; days, maybe. "I know th-th-hinges."

Beneath the bruising and the blood, the heavy, slurred speech, and the way his head drooped and rolled as if it had grown too heavy for his shoulders, it was hard to tell just how long Milner had been at her uncle's mercy.

It hardly mattered. He was down to minutes. Natalia knew it. Hernan knew it. And judging by the constant stream of pleas and lies that fell, half-voiced and pitiful, from Milner's broken mouth, he knew it, too.

"M-m-mercy," Milner pushed out between cracked and bleeding lips. "Please."

A shiver stole down Natalia's spine. She locked her muscles, kept her arms crossed, did her best to check out of the next several minutes.

"All in good time," Hernan agreed, squeezing Milner's shoulder. "But not yet. Not for you."

Milner settled even as Ethan shifted from foot to foot, the near-silent whisper of plastic beneath his feet reminding Natalia that he was here. That Hernan had brought him to bear witness to what happened to those who cheated him. If Hernan intended to shock him, he'd get his wish. Just not in the way he imagined.

She pulled her gaze away from Ethan's and back to her uncle and Stephen Milner's final moments.

"You want his job?" Hernan asked, turning his attention to Ethan and stepping away from Milner.

"I do," Ethan replied. Calm and collected, he let Hernan approach him in an arc, circling in close like a shark. Ethan didn't move. Didn't flinch. Barely seemed to track Hernan as he passed behind him.

Natalia knew better. When it came to her uncle, Ethan didn't need to watch him. Hernan's heavy breath, his footsteps—loud and a touch uneven under the weight of a man who drank too much and exercised too little—gave away his progress.

"I made that sack of shit rich, but he took what didn't belong to him. Now you'd have me believe you're different."

"N-no, p-p-please! I—"

Hernan nodded, his gesture clipped and efficient. In unison, two men Natalia knew on sight, but not by name, moved, one grasping Milner's right hand and prying his index finger from his fist, the other stepping forward with a pair of industrial kitchen scissors used to cut through chicken bones.

Milner's scream bounced off the cinder-block walls, echoing in the dying wail of a tortured animal as his index finger dropped to the plastic-covered floor, joining three others. The steady *tap tap tap* of blood against the ground matched the angry beat of her heart.

"I'd thought the money enough to buy his loyalty," Hernan continued. "It certainly bought him luxury. A life he'd never have achieved on his own. But then, there's a fine line between self-interest and greed. Wouldn't you agree?"

"People are predictable." Ethan shrugged. "Men like him," he added, inclining his head toward Milner, "especially so."

"And what do you know of 'men like him'?" Hernan's forehead creased until heavy brows cast shadows over dark eyes.

"I know that they're soft and that they've never had to fight for anything. A man like that takes risks without the education of consequences. It makes him lazy. And stupid." Ethan shifted his stony stare from Milner to Hernan and said, "And, if you're paying attention, predictable."

"You think I should have known?" Hernan asked, the challenge slipping from his tongue like the rattle of a snake's tail.

Tread carefully, Natalia thought. Her uncle had an explosive temper and a constant need to prove his control, his power. He didn't respect those he considered weak—one of the reasons Milner had stolen so much for so long. Her uncle had assumed he needn't watch Stephen, didn't need to worry that the soft corporate lackey with eyes for fast cars, fine things, and fresh-faced company would have the balls to rip him off.

If there was anything Natalia could grant her uncle, it was that he didn't make the same mistakes twice.

Still, if Ethan's goal was to work his way into Hernan's good graces, he would gain nothing by playing a simpering, greedy coward—something Natalia suspected Ethan knew already and was exploiting. Instead, Ethan would have to convince Hernan he was formidable—but uninterested in more than he was being offered. A delicate balancing act, and not one a man could pull off without careful planning.

Ethan, she knew, had come prepared.

"The signs were there," Ethan said with a shrug, as if he didn't hear the near-constant whine from Milner's throat.

Shivers racked Milner's immobilized body—though whether it was from the trauma or withdrawal from the cocaine addiction he'd nursed for more than a decade, Natalia couldn't be sure. At this point, it hardly mattered.

"Were they?" Hernan asked.

"If you chose to look." Ethan stepped forward, moving closer to Milner, walking on blood and vomit as if he didn't notice or care.

"At a glance, everything about Stephen Milner looks average and boring, from his imported silver sedan to his twenty-third-floor condo off DuPont Circle. He's habitual, settled into his routine." Ethan glanced from Milner to Hernan. "I didn't have to look very hard to find his weaknesses. Or figure out how he spent his money."

"Explain," Hernan demanded.

"He hid the coke habit well enough—a recreational if consistent user. It didn't impair his ability to do his job, but it wasn't something he could kick, either. Not with the sort of access he had to high-end product."

"My product, you mean."

"It shouldn't surprise you. Nothing more predictable than an addict with access."

"But it wasn't just the drugs," Hernan said. "It wasn't just my merchandise disappearing up his nose."

"Of course not. His addiction's not that simple. Truth is, there's nothing remarkable about a man like Stephen Milner. He's just like every other overindulged, middle-aged American out there. Mommy and Daddy told him he was special. That he could be anything, do anything, have anything. And he was dumb enough to believe it." Ethan sighed and settled into a relaxed position, his arms crossed beneath his chest. "A man like Milner always expected to be successful. Thought it his due. From the moment you started lining his pockets with money, he started wondering what else he could buy. Who else he could outpace. For a man like that, the addiction isn't about drugs or money or sex—it's about what makes him feel powerful. Big. Important. And that's never about what he can afford, it's about what's just beyond his reach."

"N-no, I—" Another scream, another finger, and Milner fell quiet but for a few mewling cries.

"New car every eighteen months—always an upgrade, always half the lease term. He's moved how many times in the last ten years? Six? Seven? Always to a bigger place with a better view. But it was never enough. He was never satisfied. Not with the call girls. Not with coke or the expensive cases of imported wine."

Ethan pinned Hernan with a steady stare.

"You thought you bought his loyalty," Ethan continued, "but he'd already sold his soul to greed. It would never have been enough. He'd always want more. Eventually, he felt bold enough to take it. I don't know if he became complacent, overconfident, or both, but somewhere down the line, Milner began skimming from cartel transactions to feed his habits. When he got away with that, ego reigned where caution should have."

Ethan stepped away from Milner, turning more fully to address Hernan, who looked both furious and intrigued. Competence and arrogance: it wasn't a combination her uncle was used to. The men in his employ tended to fall into two categories: sycophant or sociopath in need of an outlet.

He kept both busy.

"How much of your coke went up his nose?" Ethan asked. "Do you even know?"

"I do now," Hernan said. "Once you provided a detailed overview of the money he'd taken and the places he'd spent it, he became very willing to answer questions."

Ethan rolled his neck, the *pop-click-crack* of vertebrae loud in the small room. "He was a long-standing client of a well-known madam. But when the call girls lost their shine, what then? Where did he turn to find the bigger rush, the better thrill? The thing about an illicit rush is that the more you indulge, the less forbidden it becomes. So when call girls became little more than expensive girlfriends, he turned to some of your other business ventures to quench his thirst, didn't he?"

That, more than anything, was why Natalia couldn't drum up any sympathy for Stephen Milner. He'd made his bed. On more than one occasion taken some terrified underage boy or girl to it. As often as possible, Natalia interceded, placed a call, tipped off the authorities. But it wasn't enough. It never would be. So, like with all other aspects of her life, she settled for what she could secure even as she longed for more.

"And who's to say I won't have the same problem with you?" Hernan asked, though anger had fled his expression.

Ethan shrugged. "You're not a man who repeats his mistakes."

"And yet, it would seem you missed something."

Hernan stroked his chin and considered Ethan with a quiet, shuttered expression Natalia didn't care for. It wasn't like her uncle to hold back, to play things close to the vest. She relied too much on his impatience and transparency. If that were to change . . .

Ethan's facade slipped, and surprise, however brief, stole across his face. Ethan had done his homework, that much was clear based on how well he'd played her uncle. He'd presented himself as a careful blend of ego and proficiency—confidence that bordered on arrogance but was held in check by a strict work ethic. Ethan Sullivan was the culmination of all of Ethan's strengths and none of his weaknesses. The man in the room with her right now didn't care about the greater good, didn't keep his promises because personal ethics demanded it of him. No, the man standing on the opposite side of a soon-to-be-dead man was unforgiving and lethal. He would understand Natalia, respect her choices.

But then, the man before her was a lie.

The man who'd taken her to bed, the one who'd promised to save her sister, the one who'd bled for a seventeen-year-old girl he'd never known—he was real.

And he was far too good for Natalia. And soon enough, he'd know it.

"Did I?" Ethan asked, a biting smile curving one side of his mouth. "Scant days, with limited access to accounts, I suppose it's possible."

"You have something to tell me?" Hernan stepped before Milner and stared down as the man worked to bring his chin up. Harsh yellow light spilled across his face, adding depth and color to a man so pummeled that identification, were his body dumped on the coroner's steps, would be unlikely. "I'm ready to hear it."

Milner heaved in a breath, then let it go on a wet, heavy exhale. "I c-c-can tell you." He nodded as if to himself and licked at his swollen lips. "Valuable information. I—" He wheezed and coughed, his head dipping as blood loss and shock worked against him. "More missing. Money."

"My money?" Hernan asked, the edge of his voice turning sharp. "Who?"

"D-d-don—" When his words failed, Milner just shook his head. But it was enough. He didn't need to say anything more; even Natalia could piece it all together. Assuming he wasn't lying, Stephen Milner had not been the only person stealing from Hernan Vega. She marveled that so many could be so *stupid*.

"M-m-millions."

"But you don't know who? Are you sure?" Hernan asked, then nodded and stepped back so one of the men could remove Milner's pinkie. "Let's try to jog your memory."

The wail came out as little more than a raspy plea. Natalia forced herself to remain still and detached. It would be over soon. And quickly. It was the best Milner could hope for and the only thing she could offer him.

"How much money is missing, Stephen?" Hernan demanded.

"Not sure . . . millions," he replied, his teeth chattering, cold and shock and pain shutting down his systems.

Hernan turned back to Ethan, rage riding his jaw and shoulders, countering the evening's alcohol that had so far kept Hernan relaxed, buzzed, and as even-keeled as he was capable of.

"Seems you missed something after all, Mr. Sullivan."

Natalia watched as the muscles at Ethan's jaw flexed and popped. He stared at Milner as if weighing the truth of his words. For the first time since he'd entered the room, he looked unsure. Caution rode him, from the steady stare to the tense jaw to the set shoulders. But he wasn't surprised, Natalia realized. Not by the revelation, at least. What did he know?

And what hadn't he told her?

Had he known about the millions Hernan had not? And if so, how was that possible? Hernan had given him only Stephen's financials, and if Stephen hadn't stolen the money, then Ethan would have had no transaction to follow.

Had his team already discovered something with the program Natalia had installed? She doubted it. There hadn't been nearly enough time—Ethan had said that it would take days to copy and sort through all the information. And anyway, she'd been with Ethan all afternoon and well into the evening. She'd know if he'd talked to his team.

It was with a stunning sense of betrayal that Natalia realized Ethan had lied to her, by omission, at least. It hurt, given the level of trust he'd demanded from her. But worse, she was surprised. She swallowed down the inconvenient emotion. She'd trusted him, and while she didn't believe that trust was entirely misplaced, the depth to which she'd placed her faith in him was beyond naive.

"Anything to say?" Hernan asked Ethan, stepping back and away from Milner. "This morning, when you provided your review of Milner's accounts, you assured me that you'd caught everything. A lie? Or are you just stupid?"

Ethan bristled, his striking eyes going straight for Hernan. "You demanded an accounting of Milner's actions, and I supplied it. If someone else has stolen from you, I'll track down the transactions and identify them, too. But I can't find transactions on accounts you've locked me out of."

For a long moment, Hernan and Ethan stared at each other, neither blinking nor moving or speaking. A challenge thrown and a challenge accepted. How her uncle would respond, Natalia couldn't be sure.

"I-I can find it," Milner offered, picking up his head to stare at Hernan and Ethan, desperation lending him strength. "S-s-spare me. I'll—"

Hernan struck out, the back of his closed fist snapping Milner's head to the side. "You dare to barter for your life?" he thundered. "And with my own money!"

"No! I-I—"

"I've taken the fingers that touched what was mine. I should—"

"No! *Please.*" Milner's chest heaved under the weight of each terrified breath. "There's more."

"More money?"

Milner's head jerked from side to side, loose and heavy, but a clear no. "T-timing. Transaction . . . a week before the hit."

Shock and fear stole the air from Natalia's lungs. Surely not. A coincidence, it had to be. Except, age and experience and criminal enterprise had taught Natalia there was no such thing.

And judging by the way her uncle went still and silent, barely breathing, his face devoid of all expression, he had leaped to the most dangerous conclusion and embraced it.

Someone had tried to assassinate her uncle at his compound in Colombia, and now, if Milner's implication was to be believed, it had been bought and paid for with Hernan's own money.

It made sense, but *fuck.*

No one outside the cartel had known the coordinates of Hernan's compound, and the sad truth was, Hernan had no shortage of enemies. People he'd slighted or insulted. Men he owed money to.

"With my own money," Hernan mumbled. *"Cobardes."* Slowly, he turned back to Milner, his voice calm but his hands bunched into fists. He was growing desperate. Cornered. If it were an internal power grab, what were the odds it wouldn't be a clean sweep? That she and Ana Maria weren't considered dangerous due to association or proximity?

"Is that all?" Hernan asked, his tone turning silken. "Stephen?"

"Y-y-yes."

"Finish," Hernan snapped, and turned away.

Gaze trained on the far door, Natalia felt her chest rise and fall in steady measures. She didn't flinch when Stephen lost his thumb. Didn't react when his scream broke, his voice all but abandoning him. Just stood there, waiting, her gaze focused on the far door, on the world outside this tiny room, on better things—her sister's smile, Ethan's kiss, the way he looked at her like she was something special, something he wanted to understand and embrace and protect—as Stephen lost what remained of his fingers.

"You say you're better than *him*," Hernan said to Ethan as Milner's head lolled forward, as if barely attached to his shoulders. "What is that going to cost me?"

Natalia allowed herself to focus beyond the agony and the stench of blood. To consider the problem looming instead of the one coming to an end.

"What you paid him," Ethan said, his gaze passing briefly over Natalia, "plus twenty percent."

"And why shouldn't I simply kill you? Who's to say I can't find someone better?"

"It isn't easy to find a man who's comfortable with your line of work—and clearly, I'm not squeamish when it comes to your business dealings."

"And why is that, Mr. Sullivan? Why should I trust you, when I clearly should not have trusted him?"

"You shouldn't, and you don't," Ethan countered, as if he were simply bartering over a boardroom table. "But you need me, and right now, that's enough." Ethan took a step closer to Hernan, holding up against the scrutiny, rallying under the open threat.

It was the right play. At this point, he'd pushed too hard, dared too greatly. If he crumpled, Hernan would go in for the kill.

"You thought to buy loyalty; it didn't work," Ethan said.

"And now?"

"Now you'll know that every time I handle cartel funds, every time I move money or shift accounts, *he* will be the first thought through my mind. You hope fear will succeed where money failed."

"Strange that you don't seem more concerned about Mr. Milner's condition." Hernan studied him as if he didn't quite know what to make of Ethan's steady calm.

"I'm a practical man. I knew who I was dealing with long before I accepted your interview. I'm only surprised he's still alive."

"And if I put a gun in your hand, told you to rectify that?"

"I'd remind you what you pay me for—and what you don't." He didn't hesitate, didn't even consider it.

Natalia wondered what he'd do if Hernan ordered it anyway. If, when push came to shove, he'd kill to maintain his cover. Maybe. Milner was dead either way. And Ethan had killed people, he'd told her as much. But still, it was one thing to kill a man who had a gun to your head—or the head of someone you loved—it was instinctive, reactive. Live or die. But it was quite another to make a decision, to have time to consider it, to weigh one life against another. That was cold calculation . . . and far harder to justify.

"Everything at a price," Hernan said.

"Yes. Though we both know you don't need me to kill him." Ethan's gaze wandered to Milner, as the scent of blood and sweat and urine hung in the air. "You've got what you wanted."

"And what was that?"

"A man guaranteed to act in his own best interest," Ethan said simply. "I brawled my way through school," he continued. "Paid my way through college in drugs and fights and bets. A man like Milner could never appreciate the dangers of his position." Ethan met Hernan's stare head-on. "I can."

Yes, Natalia agreed, he could. But it wasn't because he came from the same broken, eat-what-you-kill background as Hernan did. He was too self-aware. Too collected. Hernan, at the end of the day, was a scavenger. A man who stole what he believed he could keep. Wild. Reckless. Ruthless. But he wasn't self-possessed enough for the long game.

He wasn't relentless enough to pursue a greater goal or bigger picture.

But Ethan was. She just hoped he hadn't lied to her about what that endgame was.

"Find my money and identify who took it, Mr. Sullivan, and the job is yours." Hernan stepped in close, the breadth of his chest and shoulders pressing Ethan to give, to step back. He didn't. "One week from today, you deliver the thief. They die . . . or you do. Do we understand each other?"

Ethan didn't say anything, just dipped his head in acknowledgment, as if Hernan Vega hadn't just promised to kill him should he fail. As if he hadn't just seen how such a death would be meted out.

Satisfied, Hernan turned back to Milner. "And you?" he asked. "Are you ready to give me what I want? Or should I have the men fetch some ketchup?"

"P-p-please," Milner begged, licking his cracked and bloodied lip with a swollen tongue. "N-n-no more. P-please," he whispered.

"Beg me. Beg me to end your pathetic life."

Milner wheezed, his lidless eye dilated and unfocused. "M-m—"

"You'll have to do better than that," Hernan said, "or perhaps I'll take your toes—"

Milner squealed and cried, rocking back in his bonds as Hernan crushed the tip of Milner's bare toe beneath his shoe.

"Try again."

"M-m-mercy," Milner pleaded through a broken voice. "P-p-please! Mercy."

"Granted," Vega said, turning and walking out the door. Natalia pushed away from the wall and slipped out the blade Carlos had handed her before she'd entered. Resolved, she crossed the room in three long strides. She didn't look at Ethan. Couldn't stand to see his expression, be it horror or sadness or just the vacant stare of a man who no longer considered her as anything more than an asset.

For just a little while longer, she wanted to hold on to the look Ethan had cast her at the party as she'd walked away. To the way his eyes had softened as he'd touched her. To the way he'd so clearly wanted to protect her from old wounds. The man who'd held her, coaxed her to pleasured heights she'd never known, cared about her. Wanted good, wonderful things for her.

It had been a long time since anyone had wanted something for her just because they thought she deserved it. She wasn't ready to lose Ethan's interest, his conviction that she deserved better, that she was worth saving.

As always, she pulled to mind the image of Ana Maria, crowing over her college acceptance, the dean's list, the keys to the almost ancient Prius that to Ana Maria meant freedom and to Natalia meant safety. It was the only reminder Natalia needed. The only source of strength she could afford.

She didn't hesitate. And she didn't miss.

Stephen Milner slumped against his bonds, dead before Natalia had removed the blade from between his ribs.

She glanced up, forced herself to meet Ethan's gaze—shuttered and sealed, the playfulness his handsome face had once held, gone. She doubted she'd ever see it again.

And hated that she'd miss it.

Resolved to everything her life was and everything it could never be, Natalia turned and walked away from a man she never should have allowed herself to have.

Mercy comes for us all.

CHAPTER FOURTEEN

"Well, good morning to you, too," Parker said when Ethan didn't so much as pause on his trek down to his office. "Brought you a fresh cup of coffee."

"You want to die before eight in the morning?" Ethan was far too tired to put up with Parker's antics this morning. He hadn't slept for shit, tossing and turning for a handful of hours before giving up and stumbling into the shower and determining to head into the office. And was it any wonder why? Somehow, in the hours he'd spent tangled with Natalia Vega, in all the myriad ways he'd considered her a threat—a distraction, a potent desire he was near helpless to resist—he'd never really considered her dangerous.

Or capable of cold-blooded murder.

Turned out, discovering that the woman he'd buried himself in was more well-trained killer than cartel hostage could keep a man up at night. Who knew?

Ethan sure as hell hadn't. He'd been blindsided—and he had no one to blame but himself.

"Not eight a.m. for me. More like—" Parker tilted his head back and stared at the ceiling tiles, his lips moving as he listed off a string of half-mumbled numbers that, knowing him, could have been anything from train schedules in Tokyo to strings of code to high scores from Jungle Gem. "Three in the afternoon, maybe?" He dropped his gaze to where Ethan sat behind his desk. "Wait, what day is it?" Parker asked.

As usual, Ethan couldn't be 100 percent sure Parker was joking. It was always so damn hard to tell, but given the way the corner of Parker's mouth twitched and the fact that he wasn't restlessly shifting from foot to foot, an addled mess of caffeine and sugar-fueled artificial energy that would put to shame a six-year-old high on birthday cake, ice cream, and laser tag, Ethan figured Parker was probably kidding.

Maybe.

Oh hell, he didn't know or care; Parker was Georgia's problem these days, and Ethan made a concerted effort to stay as far away from their nocturnal habits as physically possible.

Besides, Ethan had enough to deal with.

"Brought you the good stuff," Parker said, placing the tumbler on the desk in front of Ethan and pushing it forward with a single fingertip, the bottom of the mug making a high-pitched grinding sound as he did. "Black, just the way you like it."

"You've got fewer brain cells than a goldfish with Alzheimer's if you think I'm falling for that a second time."

"Nah." Parker dropped into the chair across from Ethan's desk, lounging against the backrest in a way that couldn't possibly be comfortable and had Ethan reconsidering the merits of sending Parker to basic training for his posture alone. "We both know I screwed with the mug again, but how, I wonder?" Parker let out a lengthy sigh, cracked his neck, and made to put his feet up on the edge of Ethan's desk.

"Do it, and I swear on—"

"Coffee?" Parker asked, dropping his feet with an unrepentant grin. "Your set of James Bond DVDs? Hmmmm, what else would Ethan Somerton swear on?" He snapped his fingers. "Got it. The rigid stick lodged—"

"Sorry I'm late," Georgia said, shuffling into the office and taking the open chair next to Parker and thereby saving the man's life.

She sat on a heavy sigh and pushed a hand through her disheveled mass of hair that had Ethan grinding down on an unwanted tactile flashback of what Natalia's hair had felt like spread across his chest, clutched in his fist . . .

"You started yet?" Georgia asked.

"Just got around to giving Ethan his coffee," Parker explained. "He's pretending he doesn't want it, even though I went all the way down to that shop he likes."

"I've had coffee," Ethan grunted.

"Well, I haven't," Georgia said, reaching for the tumbler. "You mind?"

"Nope," Ethan said at the same time Parker blurted out, "I'm not sure that's the best idea . . ." He trailed off as Georgia cut him a look that could have castrated better men.

"You want to talk to me right now about bad ideas? Really?" Georgia asked, her hand curling around the cup and her expression defiant.

Parker shook his head, his eyes wide.

"Didn't think so," Georgia said, then twisted off the bottom and slapped the batteries on Ethan's desk. Ignoring Parker's muttered "killjoy" she took a sip of coffee, sighed, then said, "Well, you called us in at this ungodly hour; I assume there's a reason?" even as Parker muttered something that sounded like "killjoy" beneath his breath.

Ethan shook his head, too exhausted to do much more than take note of how to neuter Parker's endless supply of annoying mugs in the future.

"Stephen Milner's dead, for one."

Parker sat up straight in his chair, but Georgia just met Ethan's gaze over the rim of her coffee cup and took a sip. If she was surprised, she didn't show it; her expression was just resigned, maybe a little curious.

"When?" she asked simply.

"Last night."

"You're sure?" Parker asked. "Isn't it possible Hernan's lying to save face?"

"No," Ethan explained reluctantly. It still surprised him, every now and then, how incredibly kind Parker could be. That even after all the years he'd spent in government, in special ops, in digging through the very worst of humanity's habits and appetites, he still took each and every death so personally. Though, to be fair, Ethan had seen this one coming. "I was there," he said, holding Parker's gaze. "He's dead."

"Right." Parker sighed and sat back in his chair, his gaze going vacant.

"We talked about this," Ethan said, even as Georgia laid a hand on Parker's arm.

Parker rallied, sat up straight, brushed off whatever thoughts were plaguing him. "No, I know. We made the right call—Milner wasn't exactly innocent, but we're the ones who tipped Vega off to the fact he'd been stealing from him. We needed access to the cartel, and this made sense, but we're still the reason Milner ran—and the reason he was caught."

"No," Georgia corrected him. "Milner ran because he was greedy enough to take a job with a cartel, then stupid enough to rip them off. You said it yourself when you told me everything you'd dug up on him—all his habits, all his weaknesses. He wasn't a good man, Parker. The embezzling was the least of his crimes."

"I know," Parker said, lacing his fingers with Georgia's. "But we outed him, and he died for it. I knew it was a possibility, knew what Vega would do if he caught up with him. I just don't like knowing that I had a part in that, however small it was."

Calm and steady, Parker turned back to Ethan, who nodded once. Parker had been in this role a long time, and for the most part, he weathered it well. His ability to compartmentalize, to be analytical and decisive when it mattered, was one of Parker's greatest strengths—and something Ethan respected him for beyond measure. He'd been in both roles, after all. The man who gave the orders and the man who carried them out. There was a certain degree of comfort in taking orders. In trusting the chain of command to do its job. It was simpler, for sure. Far easier to carry out the order when you trusted the man giving it.

Too bad Natalia couldn't say the same. She knew damn well any order her uncle gave was born of spite or cruelty or maliciousness. There was no greater good, no faith that at the end of the day her sins were in the service of something better, something justifiable, something righteous.

It was an unfair comparison, Ethan knew. He just didn't *care*. Natalia hadn't hesitated or objected. Just stepped forward and slipped her knife between Stephen's ribs like she'd done it a thousand times before.

For all Ethan knew, she had.

Had she gone home to second-guess her actions? To wonder if there had been a better way? Did she feel even a tinge of the remorse that Parker did?

Ethan doubted it.

Parker still struggled with the negative aspects of the decisions he made because he was a good person. It would never be easy for him. Never become second nature. He would never take for granted the power he held—especially not after Charles Brandt had traded on Parker's program, getting rich on death like it was some common commodity to be traded on the open market. For better or worse, regardless of what it cost him, Parker would never find it easy to weigh one life against another.

But that was something that *had* become second nature to Natalia. She'd told Ethan as much, too. Stood in his bedroom, naked and vulnerable, and *told* him, plainly, succinctly, what she was.

He just hadn't believed her. Hadn't wanted to, if he were honest with himself.

Not that any of it did a damn thing to change the fact that Ethan still felt betrayed. Not so much by Natalia, but by his own instincts. Because he'd looked at her, wanted her, let himself have her—and then lied to himself about who and what she was. Convinced himself she was just a stronger version of Ana Maria.

A victim.

Someone to save. Someone he *could* save. Someone who wanted an out.

He'd never felt so foolish.

Or so inadequate.

"Anyway, I didn't call this meeting," Ethan said, pushing thoughts of Natalia as far away from his mind as possible. "You did," he said, nodding at Parker. "Care to tell me why?"

"I have good news," Parker said, excitement driving him forward to the edge of his chair and propelling his foot up and down. The bottom of his ancient, lucky Chuck Taylor flapped and squeaked, but as much as the noise annoyed Ethan, he also knew it almost always heralded intel he needed to hear.

"You've found something on Vega's computer network?" Georgia asked, leaving the question she really wanted to voice to linger unsaid in the room. Ethan heard it anyway, and he had no doubt Parker did, too.

Parker glanced at her and shook his head. "Too soon for that. We're monitoring everything that comes and goes via the network, but on our end, mirroring everything he has stored takes time. Then we have to search it." He shrugged. "It's like looking for a needle in a thousand haystacks that have been blown to straw and have to be reassembled."

"The good news, Parker," Ethan reminded him.

"Right. Got it." He sat back, but the pleased grin never left his face. "Your girl came through for us. Big-time."

Ethan bristled. "She's not my girl."

Parker stilled, the repetitive *squeak, squish, squeak* of his shoe coming to a sudden halt. "Oooookay," he said. "Just going to point out you didn't ask who I—"

"The vein in his head is starting to throb, Parker," Georgia warned. "Just get to the point."

"Fine. Those files Natalia told you about?" Parker said, glancing back to Ethan. "The file names you then sent to me? They're basically a golden ticket."

Georgia straightened, turning to Parker with a cautious, guarded expression. Ethan couldn't blame her. They'd come so far, and that "break" had always eluded them.

"I thought they were just video files," she whispered.

And fuck, Ethan hoped Parker hadn't let her watch them. Ethan had seen the original, of course, and Natalia, once he'd allowed her to use her mouth for something so mundane as talking, had explained what she'd found. He'd notified Parker immediately, but still. Ethan had assumed that the videos would provide little more than fuel for future nightmares and proof of life.

"Nothing's *ever* just a file, babe," Parker said with a smile. "Because Natalia noted the folder name and a few of the file names, searching for them was easy. Thank her for that—it might have taken days to retrieve the data otherwise."

Thank her? Not likely. Even if Ethan hadn't just watched her kill a man, he had to acknowledge that going anywhere near Natalia's orbit was a colossally bad idea.

He didn't have to know if Natalia was good or bad or something caught in between. The bottom line, Ethan couldn't predict her. Couldn't be sure which way she'd turn, what path she'd take.

And worse, he couldn't be 100 percent certain of what he'd do if she betrayed him.

Best just not to find out.

"Anyway, she was right, the files come extremely regularly, like clockwork, even."

"Can you trace the source?" Georgia asked hopefully.

Parker shook his head. "Not of the files themselves. At least not yet. And anyway, that's not what's interesting about them."

Parker heaved in a breath, and Ethan braced himself for whatever came next. Because if history was any indicator, it was bound to be a double-edged sword. Otherwise, Parker would have blurted it out in an excited rush by now.

"When I was digging through the code underlying each file, I realized that a few of them were different. The files come every week, yes, and judging by the time and date embedded in each file, these guys operate on a strict timetable. Made me wonder why," he admitted.

"And?" Georgia asked.

"He's live streaming it," Parker said, promptly resuming the repetitive leg bouncing. "Not every week, but every other, almost without fail, he watches the interrogation live." He glanced at Georgia, a satisfied, determined grin pulling up a corner of his mouth. "And that I *can* trace," he said.

"You're sure?" Ethan breathed.

Parker nodded. "Positive. The minute they stream the next file, I've got them."

Ethan sat back in his chair, stunned. This was so much more than he could ever have asked for. He'd hoped that accessing the cartel's financial transactions would lead Ethan to who Hernan was paying to hold Will. That the paper trail would take him all the way to Colombia and, ultimately, bring his friend home. But this? This was so much better. This wasn't an area to explore or a person of interest. This was *Will*.

This was victory.

And Natalia had made it happen.

Fuck, he didn't have the first clue how to process that.

"How—" Georgia stopped, swallowed hard, then started again. "How close?"

"Inches? Feet?" Parker shrugged. "I'll have coordinates—I could tell you what room they're broadcasting from."

"And you're sure you can trace it? It's not encrypted?" Ethan asked, still afraid to believe this whole nightmare could finally, finally, be over. For Will, at least.

"Oh, it's encrypted. They're using a platform on the dark net. Normally, it would be a tall order, even for me," Parker admitted. "I know I make it look easy, but the truth is, hacking is mostly a matter of patience, diligence, and persistence. It takes *time*, and a lot of it. Which is why I'm so damn grateful that Natalia got bored or restless or just curious as a cat with all nine lives left. Because now we *have* that time."

"To get a team in place, ready to deploy the minute we have coordinates," Ethan said, thinking out loud. "It's a good bet Will is still in Colombia—when is the next live stream scheduled?"

"Five days from now," Parker answered.

"I'll get Ortiz to put a team together—"

"I called him this morning. He's already on it."

Ethan nodded, unsurprised in the least that Parker had anticipated him. "In the meantime, I'll continue to pursue the financials." No choice, really. Now that Hernan had demanded Ethan find who'd stolen millions more that Milner had either hidden or ignored, he'd want consistent updates. And on the off chance Parker couldn't trace the live stream or something went wrong, then Ethan needed to cultivate a backup plan.

Either way, it forced Ethan to ask some difficult questions and pursue answers he didn't really care about. He knew, of course, where the money had ended up—lining Brandt's pockets—but who had bought the hit on the compound?

Given what Ethan knew of Hernan, there was no shortage of people who wanted him dead.

And one who stood out among the rest.

In more ways than one, everything seemed to come back to Natalia Vega.

"You'll thank her, won't you, Ethan?" Georgia asked, studying him carefully from across the desk. He'd seen that look before, not so long ago, as she'd sat before him in the lobby of Parker's loft, asking questions he either couldn't or didn't want to answer.

"Yes," he said, clipping off the word the way he hoped to snip off the conversation.

"I feel like you guys are having a discussion without me," Parker said, turning his head from Ethan to Georgia and back again. "I'm missing something," he said, his forehead scrunching and his glasses slipping down his nose. He pushed them back up with his index finger.

"It's nothing," Ethan said, ignoring the knowing glance Georgia sent him. "Do you have the bandwidth to run another outcome through the program?"

"Bandwidth?" Parker choked out. "Do you even know what that means?" he asked on a laugh. "Ethan, if you're trying to relate to me as a peer, it's a little late and frankly scary as fuck."

"Yes, I know what it means," Ethan grumbled. More or less, anyway. "And you didn't answer the question."

"Yeah, sure. System's already primed for the cartel, so adjusting the query should be simple enough. Why? What's up?"

"It would seem," Ethan said slowly, turning things over in his head for the hundredth time since he'd found out the night before, "that someone within the cartel not named Stephen Milner stole millions. Hernan has tasked me with finding the money and naming the thief."

"Great," Parker groaned. "Like we don't have enough to do."

"What aren't you saying?" Georgia asked.

"Given the timing, it looks like the money was used to take out a hit on Hernan. A *failed* hit," he explained, shooting Georgia a significant look. He wouldn't need to spell it out; she'd make the connections on her own.

He'd assumed—they all had—that an outside party interested in Hernan's demise had bought that South American raid from Brandt.

And why not? Vega had plenty of enemies, both here and abroad. Given Brandt's connections, his worldwide contacts, and his willingness to do just about anything to make a buck, the possibilities were so endless that Ethan hadn't focused on *who* had purchased the outcome. It had seemed like an invitation to tumble down an endless rabbit hole that, even if he got lucky and found the end of, was unlikely to lead him back to Will.

Of all the things that should have surprised Ethan the night before—the torture, the missing money, the murder—only one thing truly had.

Apparently, there was a fox in the henhouse—Ethan just hadn't bothered to look.

Ethan pushed away his frustration. Every time he turned around, there was another indictment against his own shortsightedness.

"You need Parker's program to tell you someone within Vega's organization would want him dead?" Georgia scoffed.

"Hardly. What I need is to narrow down the suspects, make sure I don't get caught out." Again.

"Narrow down?" Georgia asked, arching a brow at him. "Or rule out?"

"What's the difference?" Ethan asked.

"You narrow down suspects," Georgia said. "You rule out allies . . ."

"Yes, well, in the cartel, everyone's an ally until they slip a blade between your ribs." Ethan winced. He should not have said that out loud. For one thing, he knew Georgia was fishing, but for another, it also wasn't entirely true. Ethan had no doubt that, whatever else she might be, if Natalia came for him, if the ground shifted beneath their feet and they found themselves enemies instead of allies, she'd have the decency to let him see her coming. There might be a knife to the heart, but he didn't think she'd bury it in his back.

Another stupidity on his part, to believe that Natalia wasn't duplicitous, that if she tried to take his life, she'd be *honest* about it. Hadn't he already learned this lesson? With Brandt? With his parents? With every poor choice that had led him to this moment?

Betrayal never came from enemies—only those he trusted enough to let close.

"I see," Georgia said, then turned to Parker, passing over the tumbler of coffee she'd stolen. "You mind?"

"Seriously, you want another?" he asked, staring at her with a bemused expression.

"Yes, Glow Stick, I want another."

"How long you going to hold that against me?" he asked, planting his feet on the floor with a *plop*.

"Months," she said simply. "Possibly decades."

He sighed and rose from his chair. "Fine, but I'm getting you tea. Too much caffeine makes you grouchy."

"Bring me watered-down mulch and find out what happens."

"See what I put up with?" he asked Ethan on his way out.

"Full caf, full fat, extra chocolate, or whatever. And a scone!" Georgia shouted after him.

When Parker had left with a little wave and a muttered "You could have just said you wanted to talk to him alone, you know," Georgia turned back to Ethan.

"Glow Stick?" Ethan asked.

"Trust me. You don't want to know," she muttered with a shake of her head. "*I* didn't want to know," she grumbled.

Georgia cracked her knuckles—one of the many tiny habits and mannerisms she'd picked up from Parker—sat back, and said, "You slept with her."

"I don't know what you mean," Ethan said, turning back to his computer and pulling up his e-mail.

"Sure you do," Georgia said.

"No," he corrected her slowly, enunciating very clearly, "I don't."

"Uh-huh," she said, lacing her fingers together over the top of one knee. "You know how many times I've seen you petty, Ethan?"

"About as many times as I've seen you drunk, Georgia."

She snorted. "I'm a better drunk than you are a butt-hurt princess."

"Butt-hurt princess?" Ethan asked, shocked at both the phrase and the casual way Georgia had lobbed it at his head.

"Oh, let's not pretend that's exactly what's happening here. You only act like this when you get your pride in a knot," she explained. "You slept with Natalia Vega, and now you're taking petty to heights that would impress Taylor Swift."

"Now I know you're spending too much time around Parker," he said with a shake of his head.

"Probably. But that's not the point."

"Apparently, my sex life is," Ethan said, snapping his fingers across the keys of his keyboard in a frustrated flurry. "Remind me, when did my sleeping habits fall under your purview?"

"Oh, I don't know," Georgia said, leaning back in her chair. "About the time you accused me of thinking with my vagina."

Ethan choked, and Georgia smiled. "That's not exactly the way I remember it."

"No? We were at FedExField, it was cold as balls, and you accused me of . . . do you know? I'm not actually sure what you accused me of. Breaking Parker's delicate constitution with the power of my Kegels, I think."

"Oh God, stop. Just . . ." Ethan waved her off. "Just stop. I'm sorry, okay? I never should have questioned your . . . professionalism. Is that what you want to hear?"

"Not really," Georgia said with an unrepentant grin. "I'm much more interested in what led you to Natalia Vega's bed—and why you're acting like a love-scorned schoolgirl over it."

Ethan shook his head. "What's it going to take to end this conversation?"

"The truth," Georgia said on a shrug. "You owe me that much, at least. Will's my brother, Ethan, and if you're compromised, someone on the team should know about it."

"And what makes you think you're the best candidate for that?" he asked.

"Because I'm the only person in the office who knows that sometimes falling into bed with someone isn't an accident or a mistake or a miscalculation—it's necessary. Inevitable. The best, worst decision you'll ever make . . . ," she said, her voice trailing off into something a little fond and a little exasperated. She caught herself, pulled away from whatever thought or memory teased her, and looked at him. "I also know how much it screwed with me."

For a long time, Ethan stared at the woman sitting across from him without saying a damn thing. He didn't need a polygraph to read the truth on Georgia's face. He'd had a first-row seat to just how much falling for Parker had screwed with her—and how much it had changed her.

Oh, it hadn't softened her. Georgia remained the same snarky, short-tempered, suffer-no-sexist-bullshit woman she'd always been. But she smiled more. Interacted with the team in a way that felt seamless and organic rather than stilted and practiced. Parker stared at her as if she'd hung the moon, climbed up there, then peppered the sky with a twelve-gauge full of buckshot until the light bled through the darkness just for him. And in turn, Georgia brought out a confidence in Parker that Ethan had only ever hoped to catch glimmers of.

There'd been every conceivable reason the two of them wouldn't, couldn't work. Too similar in all the ways that could break a relationship, and miles apart on the rest, to say nothing of the fact that they'd come together under some of the worst circumstances imaginable.

And yet . . .

They'd survived it all, and not for the first time, Ethan wondered if they would have had they not been together. United, Georgia and Parker were one of the strongest teams Ethan had ever seen. From what should have been a disaster had sprung something rare and inexplicable. Something that, in the privacy of his own mind, Ethan could admit he *envied*.

The trust. The closeness. The constant awareness that pulsed between them.

Teammates. Partners. Friends. Lovers.

Why was it only now that he realized he wanted that, too?

"I slept with her," Ethan admitted, surprising himself with the confession, though Georgia just let the corner of her mouth pull up in the barest hint of a grin. "It complicates things."

She nodded. "Sex usually does. But that's not the problem, is it?"

"No," Ethan said on a rough sigh. "It isn't."

Georgia rolled her eyes. "Are you really going to make me drag this out of you? Because I can send Parker on an endless number of errands until I do."

"She murdered Stephen Milner."

"Okay," Georgia said simply.

"And probably Garrison Coates, too." And there it was, the piece that had lodged in his throat, choking him with the truth.

"I see."

"You see?" Ethan asked, swiveling his chair to stare at Georgia head-on. "I tell you that I think she killed a DEA agent and that's all you have to say?"

"You're surprised?" Georgia said slowly, as if she were just puzzling out the crux of the conversation.

"Hell yes, I'm surprised!"

"For fuck's sake, why?"

Ethan steepled his fingers, then braced his elbows on the desk and took a deep breath. "Seriously? I tell you I take the woman to bed only to watch her kill a man in cold blood, realize she's probably done far worse, and you act like I'm the weird one for being caught off guard?"

Georgia snorted. "You didn't take a woman to bed—you took *Natalia Vega* to bed. Are you really going to sit there and tell me you didn't at least suspect what she was? That it wasn't part of what attracted you to her in the first place?"

He suppressed a wince, the honesty inherent in the statement scraping against his skin like sandpaper. Everything about Natalia had screamed competence, precision, danger—and all of it had baited him, stirring up something primal and dark and potent.

Georgia shook her head on a snort. "Christ, Ethan, you are not this dense. We ran full reports on the entire Vega organization—"

"And revealed next to nothing about Natalia."

"And you never stopped to wonder why that was?" Georgia asked incredulously. "Come on. I might have bought that she was an innocent caught up in her uncle's schemes if we hadn't turned up so much information on her younger sister. Ana Maria, we were able to profile. So much so that the program eventually named her the informant."

"Incorrectly named her the informant, you mean."

"Do I look like Parker?" Georgia asked with a raised eyebrow. "The program was wrong, it happens. But as Parker is so fond of reminding me, it can only paint a picture with the colors at its disposal. Natalia Vega was never a part of that palette. Are you really going to tell me you never wondered why that was?"

Oh, he'd wondered. But for the most part, he'd dismissed Natalia as nothing more than an idle question mark. Going into the mixer that Whitney, Smith and Brindle had thrown, Ethan had anticipated two people: Ana Maria and Hernan. It wasn't until he'd actually met Natalia that she'd truly occurred to him as a person of interest. And from the moment she'd turned that acid-laced tongue against him, he'd formed his own impressions of a woman too smart for her own good and too decent to have any real role in the cartel.

"I did," he admitted with a shake of his head. And he *had* wondered who she was. What role she had to play. But why had he missed the obvious? He shook his head, sorting through the memories of the first night they'd met. What had he failed to see? Twenty minutes in her company and Ethan had known Natalia was not a woman to be dismissed. That her intellect was matched only by her devotion to Ana Maria. And later, when she'd broken into his house, taken him to the ground, lobbed a yearbook at his head, he'd seen her drive. Her determination to go to any and all lengths to satisfy her questions.

And finally, as she'd let him hold her against the door, as she'd sucked his fingers and begged for his touch, he'd seen her honesty, the raw, unguarded edge she hid from everyone—including herself. She'd pleaded with him. For release. For pleasure. For a heady afternoon that common sense should have forbidden but desire had demanded.

He'd seen so many shades of Natalia Vega. Fierce, determined, sexy, resigned. But even now, even as Milner's face swam to the forefront of Ethan's mind, he still struggled to acknowledge Natalia as the assassin she was. Because even as she'd delivered the killing stroke, even as she'd looked at him, steady and sure and so utterly certain he'd turn his back on her, she'd still worn an air of vulnerability that defied logic.

"I thought she was trapped," he said quietly.

"You thought she needed a rescue," Georgia corrected. "Where do you keep that huge white horse of yours, Ethan? The boat shed? A parking spot downtown?"

"What's that supposed to mean?"

"Oh, please," Georgia said, reclining in her seat and flicking her fingers at him dismissively. "The contradictions in your personality start and stop at Ivy League accountant and Navy SEAL. The rest of you, I'm afraid, is all too predictable."

"Is that so?" he asked, revisiting the merits of just firing the infuriating woman. How had she even goaded him into this conversation in the first place?

"The big, bad Navy SEAL has a rescuing-people fetish. Who's shocked?" She cut him a quick grin. "Admit it. You took one look at Natalia Vega and decided she needed a savior."

And if he had? She *did* need help. Even if she was reluctant to admit it.

"She's trapped in that cartel, Georgia. As long as her uncle controls Ana Maria, Natalia's at his mercy, and he knows it. But I'm supposed to just look the other way? Just use her for our own ends and screw the costs she'll pay?"

"Wow. Defensive much?" Georgia asked. She crossed an ankle over a knee and laced her fingers atop it. With a grin, she said, "You know what your problem is, Ethan?"

"I've got mouthy employees who forget who signs their checks?"

"Don't take that tone with me—you've had this coming for months."

He shooed her on with a hand. She was right, and they both knew it. Just a few short months ago he'd sat in the lobby of Parker's loft and so condescendingly told Georgia he knew what her problem was. Ethan could only imagine how much she was enjoying this.

"Your problem, Ethan Somerton, is that you are one hundred percent white knight. Hell, even that ginormous tank you refer to as an SUV is white." She sighed like he was the dumbest person on the planet. "My point is, everything is good or bad with you. Right or wrong. Villain or victim. People are either worth saving or deserve destroying. There's never any middle ground, Ethan."

God, she made him sound like an uncompromising hard-ass, which was probably true when it came to running operations or training new employees. But it was hardly a fair observation when applied to the entirety of his life. Hell, the very nature of his job ensured he was constantly operating in shades of gray, but before he could say anything, Georgia continued.

"Don't bother. You'll make some half-hearted attempt at denial, but why? It's not always a bad thing, being so self-assured. It makes you decisive. Gives you the ability to act where others would debate. Your conviction does you credit, Ethan. I mean that," Georgia said, her tone warm and kind even as her expression told him she was about to deliver a vicious combination. "But it also leaves you with a rigid way of viewing things. It's why you had such a hard time reconciling what happened between Parker and me. It's why Brandt's betrayal caught you so off guard. It's why you wouldn't tell me that you suspected Will was still alive . . . and it's why Natalia Vega has turned you inside out and upside down."

"She's killed people . . . *innocent* people—"

"I'm not excusing it. God knows, if it had been Will, I could never forgive it."

"But?" he asked, praying it was something that would help him make sense of the mess of emotions running in tangled lines through his head.

"But *why* did she kill him, Ethan? And more importantly, what would you have done in her shoes?"

He sucked in a breath. If it had been him? If it had come down to a choice between Garrison and Connor? The answer, pushed up on a churning wave of anger and helpless rage, came far easier than he was comfortable with.

"Now imagine being forced to make that choice at seventeen. At eighteen. At twenty. Then again and again and again until it's just the frigid reality of your life." Georgia stood and brushed imaginary lint off her slacks, then stretched as if she'd just ended the conversation rather than started one. "Truth is, Natalia doesn't fit into your black-and-white world, Ethan. I don't know her, and I really can't imagine what just the simple act of surviving the last ten years has cost her, but I simply don't have it in me to condemn her."

What hadn't it cost her? Ethan wondered. What price hadn't she paid? What price would be too much? He knew the answer already, felt it like a blow to the chest. Natalia was prepared to give up anything—everything—to save Ana Maria.

But not to save herself.

Only now did Ethan understand why. That Natalia wasn't a saint or a martyr. She didn't worry about her future because she didn't believe she deserved one.

If Ethan knew nothing else about her, if the sum total of his interactions with her had been watching her kill Milner, he might have believed it, too.

But he'd seen too much. She'd *shown* him too much, whether she realized it or not.

The gentle way she touched her sister. The string of anonymous tips that she'd have him believe were trivial but had spared others the scars and hurts Natalia wore daily.

The way she'd come to Ethan, demanded answers, and, in the end, spared his life. It had been a stupid, foolish, risky thing to do.

But she'd done it anyway.

There was so much there to like, to respect, to find worthy.

But she couldn't or wouldn't see it.

"She tried to tell me," Ethan said as Georgia stood on the other side of his desk, "that I couldn't save her. That I shouldn't even try."

"Natalia Vega doesn't strike me as the sort of woman who needs to be saved in the first place."

"She's not." Short of the woman standing in front of him, Ethan struggled to come up with someone stronger, more resilient, more capable of taking care of herself than Natalia.

"Then what the fuck are you doing?" Georgia asked with a grin.

"I wish I knew." Because as enlightening as this conversation had been, it still left him with an unsolvable riddle. "She doesn't need me to save her, I get that. But she won't save herself, either. She doesn't believe she deserves it, not after everything she's done."

"Does she?" Georgia asked quietly.

Ethan let himself view the night before from Natalia's perspective. Watched as her face shuttered. As she pulled her knife. Stared at the gentle slope of her heart-shaped face as she'd done the one thing she'd believed could convince Ethan she wasn't worth it.

And for the first time, he saw her for everything she was—determined, lonely, strong, and so goddamned scared to let him help her. So fucking afraid to believe there might be more. That she might deserve better.

"Without question."

"Natalia doesn't need a white horse or a knight in combat boots and tactical gear. She doesn't need to be rescued or saved, Ethan. Any woman who does—she's not for you." Georgia smiled and pulled open the door as easily as she'd just pulled apart the tangled mess of his thoughts. "Natalia just needs to know that someone wants all those things for her."

"I don't know how to convince her she deserves them," he admitted.

Georgia cut him a condescending glare. "You're going to let something so trivial stop you?" She shook her head. "I took you for a man who likes a challenge."

"You know I do."

"It's not going to be easy, and it's bound to get messy. You can't afford to be half in on this, Ethan. It's not fair to her."

"It's like you said—with me, it's black or white. Right or wrong. All in or all out."

"She worth it, then?" Georgia asked.

He didn't hesitate. Didn't think it over. Just said the first thing that came to mind. "Fuck yes."

He didn't need data or history or a lengthy backstory—he just needed his gut. And it had told him, loud and clear, over and over, that Natalia was special.

Now he just had to make her believe it.

And he knew just where to start.

CHAPTER FIFTEEN

Cold air seared her lungs. Her heart hammered. Her arms ached. Sweat had long ago soaked through her undershirt and clung to her skin, creating a moist layer of damp heat between the still-frigid grip of late winter and her. Everything ached with fatigue and exertion, but Natalia went for another combination.

Jab, cross, left hook.

Right cross, left hook, right cross.

Jab. Jab. Jab.

The bag, old as it was and suspended from the ancient carport in the back, took the abuse without complaint. But it wasn't enough. Not to banish the memory of Stephen's last breath—or the way Ethan's face had gone cold and dark and distant. Not anger. Not shock. Not even judgment had crossed those handsome features. Just . . . a quiet regard as he'd followed her out of the building. A casual glance—one that hadn't lingered or cut or even really made an effort to look right through her. A single nod, a blank expression, and Ethan had dismissed her from his life as if he hadn't systematically dismantled hers.

As if she hadn't believed him.

Trusted him.

Slept with him.

He'd stripped her bare and inspected the pieces with nimble fingers and heated stares. Tasted her moans and devoured her pleas. And he'd believed, for an afternoon, at least, that she was something beautiful. Something wondrous. It had been in his possessive touch—the hand wrapped first around her neck and then around her heart—in the way he'd stroked idle fingers over her skin, tracing imaginary lines and wondering about all-too-real scars.

She'd known it couldn't last. That sooner or later he'd see her for who she was instead of who he wanted her to be.

She just hadn't expected the loss to haunt her. To hurt her when she woke, alone and cold and aching for something she'd only had once but would miss for the rest of her life.

So she attacked the bag, hoping that exertion and bone-deep fatigue would chase away the sense of loneliness that had been her constant companion but only now felt like an enemy.

And she ignored the handful of texts saying, "We need to talk" and "Call me" and "This isn't over." Because it *was* over, and she had no intention of dragging it out. If Ethan needed something—more access, different files, a password—then she'd do her best to give it to him. They'd made a deal, after all, and she'd hold up her end because even after everything, she still believed he'd hold up his.

But no more. If he needed something, he could just come out and ask.

Natalia took a break, grabbed a drink of water, and glanced up, counting lights. Second floor, two windows from the right, her uncle's office.

The dim glow of his desktop lamp lit the window. *Great.* He'd been spending more and more time in his office. Drinking. Cursing. Yelling. Ever since Stephen's bombshell revelation of stolen money, Hernan had been spinning out. She didn't need to have her ear pressed to the door to know why. He'd lost millions, but not of his own money. Oh no, that would have been inconvenient, dangerous only in that it made it known he was vulnerable. Weak. But he'd lost millions of the cartel's dollars—and now Colombia knew, too.

She tossed her water bottle to the corner and went back to the bag.

So many outlets to choose from. Her uncle's stupidity. Ethan's predictability. Her *own* stupidity.

She settled on the last one and put together a combination that would leave her aching tomorrow.

"So angry," Carlos said, stepping in close to hold the bag for her. "But with yourself?" he asked, peering at her around the bag. "Or the accountant?"

"Milner was a complication. I killed him. End of story," she huffed, wiping away the hair plastered against her forehead, and launching another volley of hits.

"You did not spread your legs for Milner."

She stopped midswing to stare at him.

He laughed. "You confirm it."

"Think so?" she asked, shifting her weight back and forth, wondering if she would ever have any secrets from this man.

"Always, your eyes go to him. Watching. Waiting. Wanting." He grinned. "Passion and anger—always the same for you."

Jab, uppercut, cross.

"I wanted to know who he was." She shrugged. "I parted my legs, and he opened his mouth." Nausea clawed at the back of her throat, the lie toxic, even if necessary, and close enough to the truth that he might believe it, because she *had* wanted to know Ethan. "Can't say I didn't enjoy it."

"You surprise me, *gatita*."

She grunted.

"Bad time to become reckless."

"Tell it to my uncle." She exploded against the bag in a final combination, then stopped, the scent of the night and sweat and frustrated effort filling her nose as she pulled at the Velcro of her gloves with her teeth.

"Colombia sent the message."

She paused in unwrapping her hands to stare at him. She wasn't surprised. How could she be? The cartel had sent Carlos when it had been a missing accountant and stolen funds. But now there was another thief and *millions* gone.

"When will it happen?" she asked, forcing herself to start with the easiest, most straightforward question and not go racing headlong into all the others buzzing through her head like a swarm of angry wasps.

"He's been given three days." Carlos shook with silent laughter. He'd never been impressed with Hernan's barked orders or general lack of respect. "Generous, no?" His white teeth flashed and bit through the dark like the warning of a predator circling in close.

"And Ana Maria?" she asked lightly.

He shrugged.

"No one cares for a pretty, harmless little girl," he finally said. "Your sister poses no threat and holds no appeal. Colombia wants their money, *gatita*." He measured out a look, one that carried the weight of a warning. "And no future threats."

Message delivered, he turned and walked away.

Pretty, harmless little girl.

So the family might spare Ana Maria, at least.

But not her.

Any hope for Natalia rested with a man who could barely look at her. She snorted out a laugh. Karma had come to collect in the worst way.

She could roll the dice. Take Ana Maria and run. Spend the rest of her life in one anonymous hellhole after another, waiting for the day Carlos or someone like him finally tracked her down. She might last months. A few years, if she had money. But in the end, death would come—and charge her for the trouble.

It was an old reality, one that hovered constantly, right at the edge, waiting for the day she grew audacious enough to yearn for something more, something better.

Even if Hernan died, no one left the cartel without permission. No one ran—not if they expected to live. Colombia would chase her to the ends of the earth, if only to prove a point. Fear. Control. Penance. They were all absolutes in the cartel. Nothing had changed.

Except that wasn't *entirely* true, she thought as she headed back to the house and slipped inside, climbing the back stairs—an old, twisting turn of creaky wood meant for unseen servants and careful feet. Ethan. He'd brought so much change to her life in the span of days that stretched to weeks if she was generous. But he had the resources, the money, the contacts—everything she lacked for a clean getaway.

But could she still trust him to keep his promise?

Where Ana Maria was concerned, yes. Ethan had given his word, and he wore how much that meant to him on his skin like a tattoo for the world to see. In his hands, Ana Maria would be safe.

But would he extend the same courtesy, the same protection, to Natalia—a murderer, a disappointment, a dream he'd taken—only to wake to the ugly reality? Maybe. At least if she had something to barter with. Problem was, she'd already given him everything he'd asked for. Help. Access. Sex. What could she possibly offer him that he didn't have already?

Nothing.

She turned the knob to her bedroom, dropping her house key in the little porcelain dish on her dresser, and froze. For the second time that night, the hair on the nape of her neck stood on end. But this time, the fear didn't follow.

Just a vague sense of surprise and a punch of lust that raised a flush on her skin. As if she were one pulse point, one nerve ending, one single desperate thought, her body throbbed at the sight of Ethan sitting in the little wooden chair by the window.

"Shimmy up the drainpipe?" she asked, keeping her voice low. He had no business in this house—let alone in her room—and while he probably thought he could justify it, Natalia wasn't willing to risk their exposure.

"Lattice by the window," he explained, still and composed and utterly convinced of his welcome. "Sturdier than it looks."

"My mother wanted climbing roses," she said with a shrug. "Surprised it held your weight."

Ethan shook his head, the glow of the porch light through the window catching his grin. "I used the stairs—you're not the only one who can pick a lock."

She toed off her running shoes and set her aching feet against the bare wood floors. "Why are you here, Ethan?"

"You didn't answer my texts." He watched, his electric-blue gaze a lightning flash of silver in the near darkness, as she pulled the zipper down on her fleece, revealing the skintight tank top and sports bra she wore beneath it.

"There's nothing to say." She tugged her hair from the rubber band, letting her ponytail spill down her back.

"I disagree."

Of course he did. The man had been contrary from the first— completely implacable and utterly convinced he had all the answers. "Fine. Say it and leave."

He rose and came toward her on silent feet, his head cocked to the side as he studied her retreat around the bed.

"You're defensive," he noted. "What is it you expect to hear, Natalia?"

Nothing good, that was for sure. That Ethan had come to her after the way they'd parted the other night could mean only one thing: he wanted something. But whether he needed her help or he just wanted to make sure she knew the score, she couldn't be sure. Either way, she'd rather just get it over with. One way or another, her time with Ethan was coming to an end. And if it was selfish of her to want this one thing to go smoothly, painlessly, if she wanted to let go of him gracefully so that maybe, just maybe, she could preserve the memory of what it had felt like in his arms?

Then, fine. She'd be selfish.

Natalia turned her back on him, as frigid a dismissal as she could manage, and headed for the Jack and Jill bathroom that led to an empty guest room.

"I'm cold, tired, and hungry. Just tell me whatever was so important that you thought breaking into my uncle's house was a good idea, and then get the hell out so I can take a shower." She flicked on the lights and avoided the mirror, instead going straight for the shower, sliding open the old frosted door and turning the water to scorching—the steam would soothe her tired muscles, and the noise would hopefully drown out their voices.

"You've been avoiding me," Ethan said slowly, as if he was parsing out the words, discarding the majority, and stringing what was left into a sentence that made sense only to him. "And now you're going for cold and nonresponsive. It doesn't suit you."

"And what does?" she asked, turning on him but keeping her voice low and level.

"Passion. Fire. Desire." He toed the door shut behind him, then stalked forward, forcing her to step back, right up against the closed and locked door that led to the guest room. He crowded her in, his hands braced on either side of her head. "Me."

She opened her mouth to . . . to what? To argue? To fight? To tell him to please, please, go away? Or to beg him to put his mouth on her skin, his fingers in her hair, his mark on her heart. Already she felt as if she wore him against her skin, as if he'd imprinted himself there, a clinging warmth that lingered even as life around her grew colder. It was torture.

She wanted more.

"Ethan—"

"You deserve so much more than this life, Natalia," Ethan growled, his voice tumbling out of him like the roll of distant thunder, a gathering storm snapping at the horizon as if ready to devour everything in its way. "Why don't you see that?" Agony pierced his expression, his face tightening and jaw flexing as he rubbed his cheek along hers, a lion greeting his mate.

He ran his palms along her shoulders, down her arms, his hands firm and sure where she'd expected a gentle slide of skin. But then, Ethan didn't strike her as the careful, gradual sort. No matter what he'd thought of her, if he'd believed her weak or cornered or trapped, he'd never treated her that way. Not really. Never coaxed her with sweet words or gentle touches. Hadn't seduced her with gradual, considerate regard.

When he put his hands on her, like now, his palms on her hips, his fingers digging into her flesh, he made himself known. A firm touch, a steady grip, a hard mouth. He handled her, kissed her, came undone inside her without pretense or caution or restraint.

She wondered if he'd ever had that before. A woman he could be himself with. A partner he could pin down, stretch out, spread wide— a lover he couldn't break, a woman who'd not only let him be rough and wild, demanding and controlling, but match him in intensity, ferocity, lust.

An equal.

"What will it take? How do I convince you? Make you believe that you're more than your uncle's demands or your sister's keeper or your father's daughter? How do I make you see yourself as I do?" he asked, his words as close to a desperate plea as she'd ever heard from him. He dug his thumbs into the soft flesh beneath the arc of her hip, nipped his teeth at the pebbled skin along her neck. Whispered, "Tell me." He rubbed his hips against hers, breathed in the scent of her sweat-damp hair, and sighed as if it were the smell of home. "I'll do anything."

"*Show* me."

CHAPTER SIXTEEN

Show me.

Ethan took a breath. Then another. Then used nerveless fingers to pull up the hem of Natalia's tank top.

Show me.

God, the things those words did to him. Did she understand the task she'd laid at his feet? The burning need within him to complete it? The inescapable fear that this would be the single greatest failure of his life?

Show me.

He didn't know if he could, he thought as she lifted her arms and allowed him to remove her shirt, leaving her in compression pants and a zip-front sports bra that made his mouth water. How did he capture all this? How could a conversation ever convey what stood before him?

The strength.

The resilience.

The conviction.

Because the more he thought about it, the more he realized that was simply who Natalia was. A woman of conviction. She'd found her true north a long time ago—in the love she had for her sister—and let it guide her through the darkness. How could he fault her for that? How could he, a man who'd spent a significant portion of his adulthood mastering the art of killing, judge her for it? Joining the navy had been his choice. Becoming a SEAL, his goal. He'd worked and risen and advanced all the way to the top of an off-book unit that *specialized* in profiling the enemy . . . and then eradicating them.

Natalia had faced her own choices—and she was right, she'd made them. Over and over and over again, until she'd lost all sight of the girl she'd been or the woman she might someday become. But she'd done so for reasons Ethan could not only understand but respect.

So no, he didn't see a murderer. Someone who'd grown cold and hard and jaded.

He saw his future.

Now, he just had to share it with her.

It might take a lifetime to convince her, but he could think of no worthier pursuit.

"I like this," he said, flicking the end of the zipper with his index finger. "Sexy."

She huffed with a roll of her eyes. "Functional."

He nodded. "Fun."

He pulled the zipper down and clear of the catch, then watched as her breasts—too generous for his hands unless he spread his fingers wide—tumbled free. "So damn beautiful."

Beneath the weight of his words and the heat of his gaze, her nipples hardened. He slid his palms across the top of both of them, keeping his touch little more than the light scrape of calloused skin over blooming arousal. A tease. A promise. He pulled away the bra and let it drop to her feet along with his heart.

God, this woman.

It wasn't that she stood before him half-naked, her nipples hard, her mouth parted in need.

It was that she wanted to be there. That she let him strip her down, even as he was fully clothed, even as she was still unsure of his motivations, his intentions.

Bravery. She was just too close to see it.

"I love your skin," he said, tracing fingers along her ribs, alternating the pad of his finger and the press of his nail on each mound and groove as he went. "So soft. And it just goes on and on and on." Like sloping, shifting sands, restless and undulating, forever moving and changing and never relinquishing the ability to surprise.

He could get lost in the graceful slope of her curves. Spend a lifetime mapping each and every dip and bend and valley, only to discover there was still more to learn. He dropped to a knee and hooked his fingers in the waistband of her pants, then slowly drew them, and the underwear she wore beneath, down her legs.

He leaned close, bestowed a kiss, stole a taste, drew a gasp.

"Into the shower," he ordered hoarsely, the taste of her spreading across his tongue and urging him to dive, devour, and demand.

But this wasn't about him or even about sex—at least not in the simple terms he usually used to define such an act. This was about her, about pleasure and the promise he'd made to show her everything he saw when he looked at her.

Ethan reached out, slid open the opaque glass door, then stood and turned Natalia toward it. He braced his hands on her hips, sucked up a mark on her shoulder, then said, "Go, I'll follow you."

A promise made, and after a long, molten look, she stepped inside and under the spray.

He stripped, kicking his shoes and clothes beneath the counter where a chair should have been, then joined her.

Oh fuck.

She stood there, her back to the jet of water, her head tilted back, the long column of her throat exposed as she rinsed her hair. Ethan reached out, drew a finger down a curling, wet tendril, tracing it over her collarbone, across her chest, around the outside arc of her breast, then followed a steady stream of water lower, across her navel and over her mound. When he dipped his fingers low, slid them across her clit, she opened her eyes.

"I love touching you. Watching you come alive. Feeling the beat of your heart here," he said, sliding his fingers across her entrance. "You gasp and your eyes go wide and that's when I see it."

She blinked at him, her gaze back to half-mast with lazy lust and curious interest.

"Surprise. Like you'd forgotten or, worse, never knew what this felt like." He curled a finger, slid it all the way inside her on one smooth stroke. She went to her toes, gasping, her teeth biting at her lower lip and her hands coming to his shoulders. "There it is. Want. Shock. Raw, honest need."

He added a second finger, then set a slow, steady rhythm. Unhurried. As if he had all the time in the world with her. Untrue, of course—life and danger, promises made and broken and still to be kept hovered just outside, waiting to pull them apart. Even Ethan, with all his careful planning, couldn't change that. He couldn't suspend Natalia in an endless moment, couldn't stop time to convince her how deserving she was. But he could come close.

He could draw out the pleasure, bring her right to the edge. It would take all the devoted, unselfish skill he possessed, but if he held her there, trapped in pleasure—and the unfulfilled promise of something more, something greater—he could make time stop, and in the quiet, as the world spun on without them, he'd begin the assault not on her body but on her soul.

And he knew just where to start.

He went to a knee, kissed the flat of her belly, let his thumb brush against her clit.

She canted her hips, sank her fingers into his hair, begged for his mouth with a restless sway and a breathy cry. He'd give it to her, but not in the way she expected.

He leaned forward, kissed the arc of her hip, then moved up along smooth caramel skin until he found his goal. The moment he tasted it, licked water from the edge of the slashing scar along her lower ribs, she jerked, her body going tight and tense and distant.

He curled his fingers, firmly stroking her back to arousal, to desperation, and when she couldn't fight him anymore, couldn't pull away or hide or run, he opened his mouth and used teeth and tongue and every ounce of desperate resolve he possessed to lay waste to that fucking scar.

To prove, once and for all, without question or doubt, that there wasn't a single part of her that he didn't see, that he wouldn't own and cherish and pay homage to.

She shuddered, and he brushed his thumb over her clit once, twice, then realized this wasn't the wild, reckless tumble of orgasm. It was something so much more potent, something stronger and, if he had to guess, far scarier.

Tears. Release of another kind. But he could still give her more, give her everything.

"Natalia," he said, sinking down to sit and press his back against the end of the tub. It'd be a tight fit, but he could make it work, see them through to the end. "Oh, honey." He withdrew his fingers, gripped her hips, eased her down until she straddled his legs. Her body shook, and she bit her lip, tears escaping unbidden down her cheeks in a cascade of emotion he used his thumbs to wipe away.

When she rose to her knees, tried to impale herself on his cock, he grabbed her hips and plumbed the depths of a control he'd never known. He'd meant to settle her, to dial things back, to slow things down. To hold her. Comfort her. To stroke her back for as long as time—or the hot water—held out.

She wasn't having any of it. She rose again, defying his hold, and stared down at him with a look he'd never seen before: something fierce and wild and tinged with desperation. Agony. Ecstasy. And right there, slipping just beyond the edge of her control, the admission that she wanted so much *more*.

"You started this," she told him, canting her hips so the head of his cock slid through wet folds. "You did this to me, touched me, kissed me, *broke* me," she whispered on a raw, wet sob. "Now finish it—finish it, Ethan," she demanded. "Or I will."

He splayed one hand over her scar, the other across a shoulder, and eased her down, pushing her to take his length in one long, hot slide that had him wondering what sort of karma he'd banked that kept him from coming on the spot.

He tried to thrust his hips and promptly lost traction, sliding down the tub a few inches. "I—There's not enough room. I can't move."

"I can," she whispered, dropping her mouth to his as she flexed her hips, then rose and fell like an undulating wave that intended to sweep him out to sea. She set a pace for both of them, something that started calm and a little uneven as her tears stopped and his thumb stroked the marred flesh that now belonged to him.

"You're a beautiful woman, Natalia Vega," he said, drawing a hand from the base of her throat and down her chest before sliding his fingers lower and stroking her clit in time with her thrust. "In every single way that counts."

Her hands clenched, her nails digging into the skin along his shoulders. She shook her head and doubled her pace.

"Yes," he corrected her, taking his fingers away until she bit out a cry and twisted her hips, grinding herself against him in the desperate pursuit of the edge.

When she didn't find it, when he denied them both what they really wanted, her resolve snapped. "What do you want from me?"

Right now? He wanted her to come undone, to fall into an orgasm so fierce that she milked his cock of every last ounce of come he'd ever produced. But he needed something from her, something important, something special, first.

"One thing," he said, then clenched his teeth when she lifted almost completely free, then sank down again, rubbing the sensitive head of his cock in the process. "Give me one thing and I'll let you come."

"Anything."

"I want to know one selfish thing that isn't about the promise you gave your father or the love you have for your sister. Tell me one thing you want but believe you'll never have."

Tell me so I can find a way to give it to you.

It would be like a drug. An addiction. It had started already, he realized. When she'd come to his loft under the pretense of returning the drive, that had been the beginning. She'd taken something for herself—and it had scared her so badly she'd tried to run him off.

But now he knew her playbook, knew how fiercely she fought against a selfish hope.

So one thing at a time, big or small, silly or profound, he'd draw from her the things she wanted, secretly dreamed about, then collect the pieces and lay them like a breadcrumb trail to a future of her own choosing until she could no longer see the way back.

"Tell me," he demanded.

She stilled, her eyes closed and brow furrowed, and left him there to wait, trapped in her heat and her grip and her moment of indecision.

Finally, when he worried she'd balk or he'd come or the water would grow cold and uninviting, she said, "An apartment." Her eyes were closed, her thoughts far away, even as her body was right here, still rocking, still seeking. "Something tiny that I could afford on my own. A big bed and a better view." Her fingertips curled into his shoulders, as if she were physically trying to keep her feet on the ground and her thoughts from something dangerous. "To wake up one morning, warm beneath the weight of a heavy down comforter, a puppy at my feet, with a long, lazy day ahead of me with nothing to do and no one to worry about. A perfect day," she sighed.

He smiled, pushed a heavy mass of hair over her shoulder. "And am I there?"

She grinned, her mouth unfurling into the promise of something warm and wicked and fully realized. "I kicked you out to walk the dog, fetch coffee, and hot, fresh croissants."

She shifted her hips, resuming her pace, a heated flush the color of spilled wine spreading across her chest.

He put a hand to her throat, brushed a thumb above the dip of her collarbone. "Consider it done, Natalia. No matter what it takes, no matter what it costs, that day is yours."

She stared down at him, swallowed hard, and finally, finally, hope dawned bright and clear on her face.

Victory.

And now, the reward.

He urged her to move, to ride him, to throw her head back and take what they both wanted.

It took three strokes and one whispered promise of just what she'd have to do for that croissant, and they came undone as he intended to ensure they'd do everything else.

Together.

As if they had the time—and the safety of true privacy—Ethan and Natalia lingered until, finally, the hot water went tepid, then cold. As they climbed from the tub, Ethan wondered how they'd made it work in the tiny old garden tub with sliding glass doors . . . and decided he was immediately renovating his own bathroom to include a huge, sunken jetted tub.

He intended to do this again. As often as possible.

Natalia, silent since she'd shuddered and come in his arms, handed him a large towel from the linen cabinet next to the sink. When she withdrew another, Ethan set his aside, took hers, unfurled it, and began drying her off.

She jerked beneath his hands, looked at him like he'd lost his mind, then rolled her eyes on a huff.

"I don't need you to take care of me, you know," she said quietly.

Now that the shower was off, they'd have to be more careful, and really, Ethan did need to be going. Regardless of what he'd already said, coming here had been a risk, albeit a calculated one.

"Doesn't mean I don't want to do it," he whispered, draping the towel around her shoulders and reaching for the one he'd set aside. "I'm not going anywhere, Natalia."

"For now," she corrected him, tucking the towel around her breasts and securing it with a fold. She reached for the large-toothed comb on the counter, and he caught her wrist.

"No. Don't do that. Don't assume you know how I feel. Ask me, and I'll tell you. But don't put your guilt or doubt or insecurity in my mouth." He ran a hand along her arm, then pulled away. "You thought what happened with Milner would drive me away—it didn't. I'm here."

But why?

She didn't need to ask the question for him to discern it on her face. Little by little, piece by piece, she was coming back to herself, time was moving forward, and doubts were setting in.

Ethan repressed a kernel of disappointment that he wasn't so blindingly good in bed he could completely shift the axis on which Natalia's world spun on that alone. But he was committed, and he suspected that he was going to have a lot of fun bringing Natalia to his way of thinking.

And he wanted that, he realized. The long road. The courtship. The ups and downs and fights and frustrations. The future stretched out before him, and for the first time, Ethan could see something that wasn't all work, all the time. More, he could see himself sharing it with someone else. Trips and dinners and casual Sunday mornings where he bribed Natalia out of bed and down to the water with the promise of fresh pastry.

Hell, he could even see the dog—so long as it wasn't something she planned to cart around in her purse, anyway.

So yeah, he was all in. Which meant dismantling her defenses as quickly and efficiently as possible.

"Say what's on your mind, Natalia." He retrieved his clothes and pulled on his underwear and then his jeans.

"Nothing, it's fine."

"It's not," he said, reaching for his shirt. "You're looking for something to explain my presence, to justify why I'd come to you now that I know what you are."

"A murderer, Ethan. Say it, it doesn't offend me."

"No," he said slowly, "but it does hurt you, and that I won't do."

She jerked the comb through her hair on angry, frustrated strokes. "What do you need from me?"

Ah. There it was. Not "What do you want from me?" but "What do you *need*?" She thought he'd come back for Will, for access or information. It was a sensible conclusion but one easy to dispel.

"Not a damn thing," he said softly as he turned her to face him, cupped her face, and dropped a simple kiss on the end of her nose. When surprise lined the skin beside her eyes with a hint of laughter, he knew he'd chosen the right gesture. As passionate as this woman was, casual affection doled out often would be the way to her heart. She simply wasn't familiar with it. "You've done everything I could have asked for, and because of you, we're only days away from bringing Will home."

"You know where he is?"

"Not yet, but we will," he explained. "The files you found? Turns out that every other week, your uncle watches the interrogation live. We can trace that, Natalia. Locate Will with an accuracy you can't imagine. We're setting up now so we're ready for the next broadcast." He dropped his forehead to hers. "You did that. Gave us the answers we needed."

"I just plugged in a drive," she said, lacing her fingers around his wrists but turning her cheek into his palm. "Your team took it from there."

"No, you don't understand. The access is great, and we're scouring your uncle's systems now. But it was the file names you brought me, the interrogation videos you watched, that did this." He frowned. "Why did you watch them?"

She shrugged, but he didn't let her go. She hadn't needed to view the files, to subject herself to their content. To have proof of one more life she couldn't save. So why?

"I saw the files, knew what they were by the title. And I just . . . If it were me, if Ana Maria were missing, if I didn't know . . . I'd want to have answers as soon as possible, even if"—she swallowed hard—"even if she were gone, I'd want to know."

Ethan released a breath, his curiosity satisfied and replaced with a warmth and appreciation for the woman before him. She'd done it for *him*. So he'd know, one way or the other, if Will was still alive.

He placed a kiss on her mouth, then drew back to look at her. "And you'd have me believe only the worst of you, Natalia Vega." He kissed the side of her mouth. "Five days from now, your uncle is going to get another video, and we're going to bring Will home. After that, no matter what it takes, I'll see everyone who ever hurt you wiped from your life."

"Five days?" she asked, her brow furrowing in confusion rather than the relief he'd expected.

"Five days," he confirmed. "And then I'll turn the full power of my company on your uncle."

She shook her head. "No—"

"Yes," he hissed, stepping toward her when she backed away. "I won't leave you in this life. I can't."

"No, Ethan, you don't understand," she said, her face clear and her voice firm. "My uncle, he's mismanaged the business for months. Years, even. And now there's money—a *lot* of money—missing that he owes Colombia."

"I know," Ethan said. "Milner said as much."

"You don't understand. Hernan's out of time—they've given Hernan three days to pay—one way or another."

Three days . . .

Time, you vicious, vicious bitch.

"He doesn't have the money . . ."

Fuck. It would seem Hernan Vega's luck had finally run out—which meant so had Will's . . . Goddamn it.

"The cartel doesn't take this sort of thing lightly," Natalia explained. "His death will not be handled quietly. People will know—"

"And there will be no need to send another video," he finished for her.

"The cartel will tie off loose ends—"

He snapped his gaze up to hers. "And you . . . Are you a loose end?"

"I don't know."

Shit. How had everything gone to hell so damn fast? Just minutes ago he'd been buried in this woman, thinking of a future that was one Labrador shy of perfect.

"I'm getting you out of here. Now."

She pulled away. "You can't. I can't. If Ana Maria or I disappear, it'll look like Hernan's running. They'll kill him now, and you'll lose your best shot at finding your friend."

His body drew tight with frustration, ready to fight a battle he didn't know how to win.

"It's *okay*," she assured him. "They'd never stop looking for us. You leave with permission—or not at all."

"Permission?" Ethan snarled. "They're not going to give you *permission*."

"Things have changed, Ethan. Hernan's lost position, and the people who've lost patience, they liked my father. They won't hurt Ana Maria. There's no reason to. She's innocent, and she's a Vega. To some people, that still matters."

"And you?" he asked roughly. "You're a Vega."

"It's different." She tried for a smile, something to soothe him, which only pissed him off. "Ana Maria's not . . ."

Dangerous. A murderer. Lethal.

Fuck.

"But if he pays?"

Natalia shrugged. "He lives and nothing changes."

That wasn't happening, not even if Ethan had to pull the trigger to make it so. But that was a problem for another day. Right now, he had to figure out how to buy time or find money. Thank God he specialized in the latter. And he was already looking, just not hard enough. Parker's confidence that he could trace the live stream had made it seem unnecessary. A waste of time and resources. He'd done just enough to keep Hernan off his back, but Ethan had focused on Will, on transactions that would lead to him.

He hadn't given a shit about Hernan's missing money. Maybe he should have.

Now he had three days to find—and retrieve—millions. To say nothing of the fact that he'd need to out the thief to spare Hernan. To prove, beyond a doubt, that someone else had moved against the cartel.

It would mean another death, another Stephen Milner on his conscience. He just didn't give a shit. Whoever had taken the money had known the risks and done it anyway, and at the end of the day, if it freed Natalia, there was no price Ethan wouldn't pay.

He pulled on his shoes, laced them up, then stood to memorize every last piece before him.

"What are you going to do?" she asked.

"I'm going to find the damn money, bring Will home, and keep every last promise I've made to you." He crushed his mouth against hers, drank her in, committed the taste to memory. They were so, so close to everything either of them could have hoped for.

He'd be damned if karma came for Hernan Vega early and screwed them all.

CHAPTER SEVENTEEN

"I brought coffee," Parker said, his voice flat and tired as he walked into Ethan's office.

He pulled a cup from the cardboard carrier he held and slid it across Ethan's desk, label side first.

Well, fuck. Either Parker had figured out how to hack 50 percent post-consumer cardboard or he was too damn exhausted to screw with Ethan's caffeine. Arriving with untampered coffee could only mean Ethan would need it to wash down the bad news.

"Kolaches, if you're hungry." He tossed a white paper bag, grease spots lining the bottom, on the desk.

"What time is it?" Ethan asked, suddenly starving and tearing into the to-go bag for the first food he'd had that wasn't trail mix in . . . hell, he had no idea and didn't care.

"Isn't that my line?" Parker dropped into a chair and took a deep pull of his own to-go cup.

"You don't have the market cornered on pulling all-nighters, no matter how much you like to pretend otherwise."

Parker withdrew his phone. "I'm going to need you to speak slowly into the microphone and say that again."

"I'm sure you'll manage to remind me." Ethan leaned back in his chair, polished off the kolache, and rolled his neck from side to side. Everything hurt, which annoyed the crap out of him. He could double-time it through tropical heat under the weight of full gear, row the entire length of the Potomac, tackle an ultra-marathon and sleep like a baby after. But thirty-six hours at a desk and he felt like a sixty-year-old man longing for a recliner, a cold beer, and a flat-screen.

"What's on your mind, Ethan?"

"Questions I can't seem to answer."

"Answers you don't like are still answers."

Ethan suppressed a wince. *Great.* In addition to aging three decades in the span of two days, he'd also become transparent.

"Relax. No one's cracked your poker face."

"Stop reading my mind, it's creepy."

"Makes you feel close to me, doesn't it?" Parker smirked. "Like brothers from another mother."

"Please, please, never say that again."

"Surest way to shut me up is to start talking."

True. And maybe laying all the pieces out on the table would simplify things, help him find a way forward that didn't feel bleak or impossible or somehow worse than if he'd never gone looking for answers in the first place.

Because he had—after countless hours, endless searching, and employing every single trick he knew—found *plenty* of answers.

He just hadn't thought solving one problem would lead to so many more.

"Bro from another ho . . . ?"

"I know who stole from Hernan Vega," Ethan blurted out. Parker wouldn't stop, he'd just get more creative, and Ethan really would kill him.

Apparently satisfied, Parker sat back and laced his fingers across his stomach. "Show your work," he said with a wry grin that had Ethan wondering just how often someone had said the same to him.

"For starters, Stephen Milner *vastly* undersold how much money had gone missing. To be honest, I'm not sure he had any idea just how pervasive this was."

"Before he died, he implied that a lump sum of money had gone missing—and had been used to purchase the failed hit on Hernan, right?" Parker asked, picking at the hem of his jeans.

"Right. The timing is too suspicious to dismiss, but the money used to buy the outcome from Brandt was just the tip of the iceberg and, if I had to guess, unplanned and rushed, which is why Milner caught it in the first place." Ethan sipped on his coffee and tried not to let his mind wander. "The reality is, someone has been systematically stealing from Hernan Vega for years."

"How much money we talking about?" Parker asked. "Millions?"

"Rough estimate?" Ethan asked, rubbing away the headache pounding along his temples. "A hundred and thirty-five million."

Parker choked, and Ethan allowed himself a second to bask in the glow of shocking Parker into silence.

"A hundred and . . . How the hell do you not notice you're missing a hundred million dollars?"

"The sheer amount of money that moves through the major cartels on an annual basis, coupled with Hernan's poor business management, created the perfect storm for embezzlement. All someone would need is the right kind of access and the balls to attempt it."

"But a hundred million?" Parker asked, shock still lacing his voice.

"It's not nearly as much as it sounds." Ethan shook his head and leaned forward, bracing his elbows on his desk. "Let me put it into perspective. The cartels, for all that they have a well-deserved reputation for violence, aren't stupid. After the rise and fall of El Chapo, they evolved. Most of the major organizations operate, more or less, like legitimate international businesses with an always in-demand product. Rough estimates indicate the Mexican cartels alone pull in anywhere from forty to fifty billion dollars annually." Ethan sat back on a sigh, realizing just how impossible it really was to dismantle a cartel. Cut one head off and two more popped up in its place. "Just for reference, that's more than the annual gross revenue reported by companies like Coca-Cola."

"Holy shit," Parker breathed.

"Yeah. And while the Vega cartel isn't operating in Mexico or pulling in anywhere near forty million dollars—they simply can't match the scale—they are one of the big three enterprises operating out of South America, with a market share of nearly a billion dollars annually."

"And I thought I was rich." Parker blew out a breath.

"Now consider that moving drugs is an export game, and you won't be so surprised to hear that of that billion dollars annually, the United States operation is drawing in roughly two-thirds of that gross profit. That's just over six hundred and fifty million dollars a year flowing through Hernan Vega's piece of the enterprise."

"Let me guess—he's keeping it all in his mattress."

Ethan snorted. "No. Most of the major cartels evolved to the point that they have extremely lucrative relationships with some of the foremost international banking institutions in the world. It's why they need staff accountants like Stephen Milner to manage those associations and transactions."

"Aren't there laws preventing that kind of thing? Penalties for institutions caught doing business with the cartels?"

"Sure, but proving it is a nightmare because these cartels have become experts at laundering money through a multitude of private holdings and shell corporations. By the time the money lands in the last account, it's almost impossible to back-trace it through all the channels and prove it's dirty." Ethan sighed, his head spinning with the sheer number of companies associated with the Vega name. "And as you can imagine, the banks involved aren't exactly getting in line to roll on some of their most profitable, not to mention dangerous, clients. It usually takes months, if not years, of investigating to secure the appropriate orders to demand information. Even then it's a long shot." Which the DEA had learned the hard way. They'd sacrificed untold resources, both monetary and physical, lost an agent, and for what? At the end of the day, they'd turned up nothing that could do more than bust a few low-level thugs who wouldn't turn for love or money. Not when the cartels had taken such pains to establish exactly what happened to a snitch's family.

"Okay, so that puts the sheer numbers into perspective, I guess, but doesn't explain how it went unnoticed."

"A few things made that possible. First, Hernan wasn't paying attention to the accounts the way he should have—he over-relied on his accountant for that. In turn, that provided Stephen Milner the opportunity to line his pockets and cover his tracks. And finally, this was a well-planned, well-executed, systematic assault targeted specifically at how the cartel does business," Ethan said, awe filtering into his voice without his permission.

"Sounds like someone's got a real chubby for the numbers," Parker chuckled. "They won't keep you warm at night, Ethan."

Crass, but not entirely untrue. The thief had shown a remarkable amount of skill, creativity, and, most impressive, restraint when setting up the embezzlement scheme. If Ethan hadn't gone looking for it, if Milner hadn't been searching for a way to save his own skin, if the thief hadn't grown desperate and screwed up, it might have gone on for years.

"You'd probably stand and salute, too. There's a neat bit of coding involved you'd appreciate."

"Seriously?" Parker asked, sitting forward, the promise of someone else's technical exploits drawing his interest.

"The embezzlement was almost entirely automated—it's why it was so hard to find, even when I was looking for it. It's also what made it possible to steal so much for so long without anyone noticing."

"How so?" Parker asked, cocking his head to the side.

"Most of the time, people are caught embezzling for one of two reasons: something stands out as abnormal, or there's a pattern in the transactions that doesn't make sense or shouldn't be there."

"But not in this case?"

"No. It's what made figuring out what the hell was going on so damn difficult. There was a surprising amount of restraint here."

"I'm not sure I'd call stealing a hundred million dollars 'restrained.'"

"You're letting the number blind you, but that didn't happen overnight. That was the result of years of systematic siphoning."

"The code you mentioned," Parker said.

"Yes." It still surprised him, just how sophisticated a job this had been. Maybe it was Hernan's heavy-handed presence or Stephen Milner's general ineptitude, but Ethan had expected something sloppy—and as a result spent the better part of forty-eight hours looking in all the wrong places for all the wrong things. "In the end I had to import five years' worth of cartel transactions into a custom report and sort by everything from date to size to transaction type." He was exhausted just thinking about it. "It was the last one that yielded the results I needed. Transaction fee on transaction fee on transaction fee."

"I don't get it," Parker admitted. "Aren't transaction fees a normal part of banking? God knows I pay out the nose anytime I so much as want to transfer money."

"And therein lies the elegance of this. Transaction fees *are* common, and more than that, they're generic—"

"Which means easily overlooked."

"Right. Especially if you keep the increments small."

"So . . . what, you're saying that someone stole a hundred million dollars by charging five bucks a transaction?"

"No. I'm saying someone stole a hundred million dollars by charging anywhere from a half a percent to twelve percent of any given transaction amount."

Parker let out a long, low whistle. "Automation at its finest—a laughably simple solution with devastating results."

"So that kind of program would be easy to write?"

"Easy?" Parker asked. "Depends on who wrote it, but yeah. It's not particularly complex—the tricky part is the automation, and employing multiple percentages to differing fees. But if someone had the skill—and understood international business transactions and what sort of fees might be attached—it would be easy enough to pair transaction types to percentages, deploy the program, and send the 'fees' to a destination account." Parker leaned forward and snatched the bag of kolaches off the edge of Ethan's desk. "I'm assuming you found that."

"Yeah. A private brokerage account nestled neatly within a few dozen other Vega holdings."

"Wait, so you're saying Vega's missing money is in a Vega account?"

"That's what I'm saying. It's hiding right there in the portfolio. Between what's been siphoned into it and the conservative rate of return, it's actually worth more than the original amount stolen, which further insulates it from discovery."

"So, wait, are you saying Vega stole from *himself*?"

Ethan shook his head. "Technically he'd be stealing from the business, but by 'hiding' the account among other Vega holdings, it certainly looks like Hernan is self-dealing—intentional, I'd imagine, on the part of the person who did this. A scapegoat and plausible deniability in one stroke of genius." Every single step had been thought out, meticulously planned and executed. Ethan couldn't help but be a little impressed.

"Okay, so assuming Vega doesn't know about the account that's literally right under his nose, why don't you just, I don't know, do your job as his accountant and enlighten him to its whereabouts?" Parker asked. "Then he returns the money with a nice interest payment on top, the cartel's satisfied, and we get the few days we need."

"That was my first thought, too," Ethan conceded. "But I wasn't going to go to Vega unless I was absolutely sure of what I was dealing with."

"Why do I get the feeling this is about to get annoyingly complicated?" Parker asked.

"Consider it payback for all the times you went on and on and on about tech shit no one but you understands or cares about. But in the interest of your attention span, I'll keep this short." Ethan drummed his fingers against the glass desktop, considering the easiest way to explain. "After Isaac told us what he'd learned from the DEA, I requested all the financial disclosures the banks had provided over the course of their investigation, and because the DEA can be reasonable when they think it might lead to a high-profile arrest and have nothing to lose, they complied."

"And now you've proven that regardless of how many Ivy League–educated forensic accountants the DEA has on staff, they don't have you."

"Keep stroking my ego. I'm still not authorizing whatever overpriced, unnecessary gadget you want Somerton Security to pay for."

Parker fell back in his seat on a huff.

"But yes. As always, context proved key. If I hadn't been looking at that account specifically, I'd have missed something, too." Ethan scrubbed a hand through his hair and drained the last of his coffee. "When the siphoning started, the account holding it was an already established but inactive shell corporation. It saved the thief the trouble of forging all the necessary paperwork to create a company and establish a new international bank account. Smart. It was far easier to forge the paperwork to convert that account into a trust."

"So Vega 'opened' the account," Parker said, using air quotes, "but doesn't actually have any authority to access it."

"Exactly. The trust was constructed too neatly. It becomes eligible to access on one of two eventualities: Hernan Vega's death, or upon both beneficiaries reaching the age of twenty-five."

"But why?" Parker asked. "Why would you steal all that money but be unable to access it?"

"It all depends on what your goals are. I think this account was intended to be a golden parachute." It was the only thing that made sense, that someone had begun thinking about the future, about freedom, and acted accordingly. "Besides, by setting it up this way and making access so restrictive, it reinforces the idea that Hernan himself set this up. That he, and not the intended beneficiaries of the account, had redistributed the money. Like I said—remarkable restraint."

"But that restraint is what caused the problem, right?" Parker asked, his foot bouncing against the carpet as he spoke. "Because if the account was inaccessible, the money for the hit had to come from somewhere else."

"Far as I can tell, it looks like an opportunity presented itself—I still haven't quite figured out how Brandt ties in to all this—and rather than play it safe, our thief rolled the dice and made a much bolder, and harder-to-conceal, money grab."

"Which is how Milner stumbled across it," Parker finished for him.

"Pretty much. It was sloppy, no time to funnel it through enough accounts to make it disappear, and since Milner was already moving things around to conceal his own theft, it was easy enough to spot."

Parker grimaced. "Am I the only one with a massive headache?"

"Hardly. You can't imagine the Gordian knot this was to untangle."

"But you did, and because you didn't like the answers you found, you asked me to cue the program for you." Parker stared across the desk at Ethan, all trace of humor gone from his face. "And I'm betting that even though the DEA's paperwork would have confirmed who the beneficiaries on that account are, you already knew."

"Suspected." Ethan nodded, his stomach turning over with the inescapable conclusion he'd come to long before he saw it written down in black and white. "Natalia and Ana Maria Vega."

"Any chance Hernan had some sort of crisis of conscience for all the shit he's done and opened this account for them as insurance?"

"No way." Of all the ludicrous scenarios he'd considered, that one had been the easiest to dismiss.

"Which means," Parker said, wincing as Ethan saw the full impact of the realization hit him, "that one of them has stolen a hundred million dollars from the cartel—and isn't likely to give it up."

"I came to the same conclusion." Eight hours ago, then had proceeded to jump through every scenario he could possibly come up with, ranging from the idealistic to the downright insane, to draw another conclusion. But sometimes the simple answers were the best.

"Well, fuck," Parker said on a rough sigh. "That explains the outcome you had me run and the results I didn't really understand."

"I needed to be sure, Parker." Though even as he said it, Ethan realized he was, and that nothing Parker's program did or didn't say was going to change that. If he'd learned nothing else in the last two weeks, it was that sometimes a man had to trust his instincts—even if it twisted his guts with the force of a poisoned assault.

"It's not her, Parker. Natalia wouldn't keep this from me. It's not who she is."

Parker smiled patiently, for the first time ever unaffected by the idea that maybe, just maybe, his program didn't have *all* the answers. "Show your work."

Ethan took a breath, unexpectedly grateful that Parker was willing to let him say his piece, to work it out for himself.

"I trust her," Ethan said simply. "She didn't have to tell me about the files—she did it because she wanted me to know, as soon as possible, if Will was alive. Then, when I told her that we were close, days away, she corrected *me*. She knew damn well it'd send me straight down the rabbit hole after the money."

"It's like you said, though, the theft was incredibly well done. She could have simply been confident that either you wouldn't find it or that by the time you did, it would be too late."

Maybe, but none of that felt like the woman he knew. There was no pretense where Natalia was concerned. It may be battered and more than a little bruised, but she still wore her heart on her sleeve. And while Ethan had believed her when she'd said she would do anything to save her sister, he didn't think *this* would have ever occurred to her.

"What are you thinking?" Parker asked.

"That if Natalia set up a rainy-day fund, she'd have been more conservative in the percentages—I doubt that stealing tens of millions, let alone hundreds, would even have occurred to her. Too risky. She's conservative by nature, always looking for the safest way forward."

"And?" Parker prodded.

"And if Natalia set up a trust, she'd never have put her own name on it." Ethan swallowed, hated thinking, let alone saying, what he knew to be true. "Natalia has never believed there was a future for her beyond the cartel. She'd have set up Ana Maria, given her a way out, but expected to pay for it with her life."

"You're putting a lot of faith in a woman you've known for two weeks, Ethan. How can you be sure? Especially when Natalia has both the skills and the access to pull off something like this, to say nothing of the motivation. Can you say the same about Ana Maria?"

"Natalia and Ana Maria are both trapped, Parker."

"But only one of them is cornered, Ethan. Only one of them is dangerous. Only one of them has a history of hurting people, killing people, to get what she wants."

Ethan shook his head on a rough sigh. It made sense, he just couldn't bring himself to believe it. He *knew* Natalia, goddamn it. Had watched her sleep, felt her come, heard her cry. She was the best of them, of all of them, and he would believe that until his dying day.

"I'm in love with her," he admitted aloud, caught off guard by the stunning realization that it was true.

"Most people would tell you that's a dangerous thing to be. That it clouds your judgment and opens you up to betrayal."

Ethan cast a steady look at Parker. "But not you."

"Not me," he agreed. "I fell in love under similar circumstances. And while I never had reason to doubt Georgia's loyalties, it wouldn't have mattered. I knew how she made me feel—about her, about myself, about my abilities—in her, I saw the truth of who I am . . . and there's no greater honesty than that." He stood and stretched, his waffle-weave Henley bunching as he did. "People say love makes you weak, but I disagree. What I have with Georgia? It made me stronger. More resilient. More comfortable in my own skin."

All true—Ethan had seen it. More, Parker had done the same for Georgia.

"That kind of love? It's the most honest thing I've ever experienced. If that's what you have, it doesn't matter where it came from or how fast it happened—trust it, Ethan."

"I promised her," Ethan said, thinking back on that night Natalia had broken into his apartment. "I promised that if it comes down to a choice, Ana Maria lives. No matter what. If I betray that, if I tell Hernan what she's done, he'll torture her to get to the money." No matter what choices Ana Maria had made or why she had made them, Ethan wouldn't wish that upon her . . . and he'd never forgive himself for putting Natalia through that. "I won't break the promise I made. I can't. Not even for Will," he whispered, the betrayal slicing him open with a blade forged from friendship. "If I save him, Ana Maria dies and I lose Natalia forever. But if I keep my mouth shut, Hernan dies and I lose Will forever." He blinked away the sting of frustration and stared up at Parker for answers Ethan knew he didn't have. "My hands are tied."

"Yours are. But Natalia's aren't," Parker said simply. "We need time, which means we need money—the only person who stands a chance at convincing Ana Maria to do the right thing is her sister."

"This will kill her, Parker. Everything she's done, every choice she's made, it's been to protect Ana Maria. To find out she's been stealing funds for *years*? Natalia will question everything."

"Maybe it's time she did," Parker offered softly. "Because while you're afraid this will kill her, I think it just might set her free. Finally give her permission to treat her sister like the adult she is—and pursue a life of her own."

A life with me.

He didn't have to say it; Ethan heard it all the same.

Now, he just had to have faith that at the end of it all, when he stole the only truth Natalia knew, that she'd love him enough to forgive him for it.

CHAPTER EIGHTEEN

"I don't believe you." Natalia shook her head, then wiped sweaty palms against her pants and stood. She shuffled around the coffee table and circled as far away from Ethan as she could manage. She didn't know how to look at him. Didn't know what she'd do if he reached for her.

How could he do this to her?

"Yes, you do," he said slowly, rising from the club chair he'd dropped into shortly after she'd arrived at his apartment.

When he'd texted her, asked her to slip away, to come to him, she'd prayed for a miracle, that he'd found the missing money, that he'd forged a path to that future he'd promised her.

She should have been more specific in her prayers. Because this? This wasn't a path forward; this wasn't one step away from a tomorrow so bright and potent it practically buzzed beneath her skin. This was destruction—couldn't he see that?

"No." She shook her head and pulled the sleeves down on her pullover, hooking her thumbs into the loops on the cuffs. "Everything you just described . . . It's no easy thing, Ethan. It would take so much skill, so much ambition, to pull it off. Ana Maria's just a kid. She wouldn't—couldn't—do what you're suggesting." For God's sake, they were talking about a kid who'd never broken curfew, who held a near-perfect GPA, who'd hadn't so much as had an overdue library book.

"You still see her as a child, as the little sister you promised to protect, but she's twenty-one, Natalia," Ethan said, following her over to the window but stopping feet away, as if he knew that each word he uttered placed another foot between them. "She's smart—smarter than even you or I gave her credit for—and she has as much reason to hate the cartel as you do."

She shook her head and turned her back on him to stare out at the bright midafternoon sky.

"But a hundred million dollars? An automated program? Large-scale embezzlement?" Natalia barked out a laugh that cut her throat with the edge of hysteria. Ana Maria wouldn't so much as slip a twenty from Natalia's purse without asking, but now Natalia was supposed to believe she'd been the mastermind behind a nine-figure theft? It was ludicrous.

Impossible.

And the only answer that made sense.

She knew it. Had understood where all this was going when Ethan had been only halfway through his careful explanation.

"The program is simple enough for someone who knows what they're doing," Ethan explained. "Any bored college kid with a laptop and too much time on their hands could write it up. How many of those do you think your sister met at George Washington? How many would have been all too willing to do her a favor, no questions asked?"

Ethan moved closer, circling in with logic, tightening the noose with facts.

"She's a double major in international business and accounting. She's made the dean's list. Twice."

All true. All things Natalia had taken such pride in, almost as if they'd been her own accomplishments. In a way, they had been. It was because of her, because of the sacrifices she'd made, that Ana Maria had been given the opportunity to go to college in the first place.

And now Ethan was saying what? That the very education Natalia had wanted so badly for herself, had worked so hard to give her sister, had been key in corrupting her?

"I never even saw her coming," Ethan said with a rueful shrug. "From the beginning, I dismissed her out of hand. Couldn't imagine a world where that sweet, unassuming kid could be anything other than what she appeared. God, she had me snowed." Ethan heaved out a rough sigh and settled into a restless pace in Natalia's peripheral vision.

"There's not a deceitful bone in my sister's body," Natalia argued, her voice firm even as doubts flooded in. There'd been a time when Natalia and Ana Maria had told each other everything. After their mother died, there'd been no one left to talk to, no one else to rely on. There'd been no secrets between them.

Except that wasn't entirely true. Ana Maria had invited a man into her bed, a *federal agent*—and said nothing. Not until it was far too late for Natalia to caution her against it. Not until there was nothing she could do to save his life or spare her sister's heart.

But that had been young love. A relationship too dangerous to acknowledge to anyone.

Natalia had her own experience with that now.

But to systematically steal from the cartel? To set up their uncle as the fall guy? To do that over the course of *years* and say nothing?

Natalia couldn't fathom it.

When she shook her head, searching for an argument that rang true, Ethan cut her off.

"She had the access, Natalia. The right education. And most of all, she had the perfect cover. I knew the moment I met you that you were so much more than who you appeared to be. That I'd be stupid to take you at face value. That there were depths to you most would never see. Why did I ever assume it would be any different with your sister?" he asked, shifting toward the window and coming more fully into her line of sight. "You raised her. Protected her. And she watched you become what you needed to in order to survive. Is it any wonder she did the same?"

"So . . . what? You're saying everything was a lie? That I don't know my sister at all?" The words tasted bitter against her tongue, but did that make them a lie? She didn't know anymore, and that made her queasy.

"Of course not. But everyone—you included—looked at Ana Maria and saw a beautiful, fragile little girl. Someone harmless. Someone who wasn't a threat. There's power in that. Ana Maria understood that, then turned it to her advantage."

No one cares for a pretty, harmless little girl.

How many times had Natalia thought the same? That her sister's innocence, her kindness, her nonthreatening nature, protected her? How many times had she encouraged Ana Maria to remain docile and accommodating and quiet?

To be invisible.

But when had she, too, stopped seeing her? Stopped paying attention?

"She would have told me, Ethan. I would have known."

"But she didn't."

Which was the hardest part of all this to understand. Ana Maria knew the things Natalia had done for her, the price she'd paid for basic freedoms like a car and college and a reasonable curfew. And yeah, she spared her sister the worst of it, the gruesome details that could serve only to make Ana Maria feel guilty for a choice that was purely Natalia's. But still.

Natalia had kept nothing from Ana Maria.

Now Natalia was forced to wonder what else Ana Maria had lied about. What else she'd hidden.

Because if Ana Maria had successfully stolen more than a hundred million dollars from the cartel, Natalia had to wonder—had it all been worth it?

At the end of the day, Natalia had made a promise to protect her sister. A promise she'd taken seriously. Natalia had done everything in her power not just to keep Ana Maria physically safe but to shelter her from the violence. To put her through school, let her get a job, get her a car.

All because, to Natalia, keeping Ana Maria safe meant taking every hope and dream and wish for a future that she'd ever had and passing them along to her sister. She'd wanted so much more than the cartel life for Ana Maria.

But now it looked like what she wanted hadn't mattered at all.

If Ana Maria had done what Ethan said, then she was as trapped in the cartel as Natalia had ever been.

And they would *kill* her for it.

"There're only two beneficiaries on that account, Natalia. And we both know you never touched a dime of your uncle's money."

Defeated, Natalia closed her eyes against the emotions making her sick. "What do you want from me, Ethan?" Natalia asked, her shoulders heavy beneath the weight of a no-win situation. No matter what she did next, it would be the wrong thing. To help Ethan was to betray her sister—and the promise Natalia had made to her father. To shield Ana Maria was to let Hernan—and, by extension, Ethan's friend—die. Once again, someone else would pay for the choices Natalia made.

Because of her, someone else would die.

"What do I want?" Ethan asked, fire and frustration and the snap of his patience striking through his voice. "I want you to realize that not everything is about your sister. I want you to finally understand that not all promises can be kept," he railed. "I want you to acknowledge that you've already done so much more than your father could ever have asked of you!"

She swallowed hard against the panic climbing her throat and seizing her shoulders, rooting her in place even as she wanted to hit the pavement at a dead sprint and never, ever stop.

"Even yours?" she asked quietly, wondering for the first time why Ethan had drawn her here in the first place. To warn her, yes. But of her sister's betrayal—or the one he was about to make?

"Mine?" he asked, bewildered.

"You made promises, too, Ethan. To your friend. To me." She looked at him over her shoulder, wishing her eyes weren't heavy with the sting of tears. Wishing she knew what she'd do, who she'd choose, if it came down to it.

If we have to choose, Ana Maria lives.

The oath had slipped from his lips without the tang of a lie to taint it. She'd known then, as Ethan had stood there, promising her the only thing she'd ever have asked him for, that he was someone special. That he'd keep his word.

It had been the first crack in her resolve. The first chink in her faith that the only person she could truly trust was Ana Maria. But if she'd been wrong about that, wrong about a sister she'd practically raised, how could she possibly put any faith in Ethan?

How could she believe, for even a moment, that he'd choose her—not her sister but *her*—over the life of his friend? Because that was the only reason he could possibly have for holding his tongue. For not immediately informing Hernan, and by extension, the rest of the cartel, of Ana Maria's duplicity.

A man would have to love a woman beyond all reason to do such a thing.

How was she supposed to believe she'd earned that sort of devotion?

"You think so little of me?" he asked, his voice low and hurt and begging her to turn and face him. "You still have so little faith in me?"

When she couldn't bring herself to move, he came to her, pulling her around and bracing her back against the windows, his grip firm and undeniable. For a long moment, he studied her face, searching for what, she didn't know.

"It's not me you don't believe in," he concluded without victory. "I made you a promise, Natalia. But even then, even before I knew the taste of you, the lines of your body, the depths of your heart, even before you let me see all of you, I made that promise for *you*. Not because I thought Ana Maria was innocent and not because it was the right thing."

He shook his head and let go of her. "I wanted to give you something no one else could, even if I didn't really understand why. I asked for your faith, and I know what a gift it was. I won't squander it."

Her heart, which had been lodged in her throat from the moment she'd realized just how much danger Ana Maria was in, dropped to her toes. For so long she'd believed her heart closed, consumed with the sort of love and devotion that could never be rivaled. And she'd been okay with that. Content to live a life dedicated to someone better, more worthy, than herself.

But then Ethan had stormed into her life with cheesy cocktail come-ons and bright, mysterious eyes. He'd been a challenge, an anomaly that didn't make sense . . . and dangerous from the start.

She just hadn't understood the ways he'd destroy her, or how fast she'd come to care for him, or how much she'd long for his regard.

The fall had been so fast, so sharp, so effortless, that sometimes it didn't feel like falling at all. It felt like the embrace of fresh, warm linens and the comfort of a familiar smile and a casual hello.

Ethan felt like home, and she didn't know how to give that up.

She reached for him, grabbed his forearm, pulled him back to her.

"I've never asked her for anything," she said, stepping into his chest, breathing in his scent, committing the feel of his embrace to memory. "But I'll ask her for this. For the money. For *you*."

"I always knew you would, Natalia." He brought his arms up, held her close, kissed the top of her head. "But I don't want you to do it for me or because it's the right thing. I want you to do it for *us*. Let's end this for Will, for Ana Maria, but most of all, let's end this so that we can start something new. Together."

She stifled a sob, kissed him on the mouth—one last, long, lingering taste to tide her over—then slipped from his arms. She couldn't tell him how much she wanted that—the day he'd promised her and every one that came after it. Ethan *believed* in her, *trusted* her, and in placing his faith in her, he'd offered her redemption.

She'd prove herself worthy of him if it was the last thing she ever did.

◆ ◆ ◆

"Hey," Ana Maria said when she spotted Natalia lingering on the steps leading up to the economics building. "Were we meeting for lunch today? It's after three. You must be starving if you've been waiting for me."

She bounced down the remaining steps, a tote on one shoulder, her hair tumbling out of a half-hearted topknot. She looked exactly the same as she had that morning on the way out the door, but she felt like a stranger.

Ana Maria pulled to a stop with a wide grin. Just this morning, that same smile had been something Natalia basked in. A warm, simple thing that was a physical reminder that Ana Maria, at least, was still whole. Now she looked at it and wondered what lay dormant beneath. Wondered what she didn't see.

"Natalia?" Ana Maria asked, her smile crumpling and her brow furrowing. "Is something wrong?"

Yes. Yes, something was very, very wrong. "Take a walk with me?"

"I've got another class in a couple of hours, and I was going to swing through the library beforehand. Can this wait?" she asked, shifting her bag from one shoulder to the other.

It took every ounce of restraint Natalia had not to thumb away the red friction burns on her sister's shoulder. To scold her one more time about the merits of a backpack over a purse. Instead, she simply said, "It can't wait."

"Okay." Ana Maria fell in step beside Natalia, a curious but otherwise-patient expression on her face.

Did she have any idea what was coming? Did some part of her know that her secret had been exposed? Natalia pushed away the questions. God willing, there'd be time enough to worry about learning Ana Maria's tells. Hopefully, someday in the not-too-distant future, Natalia would be able to look at her sister again without wondering if she knew her. Without wondering if she was being played or lied to.

When they turned south on Twenty-First Street and the noise of heavy traffic ensured a private conversation, Natalia said, "I know about the money."

Ana Maria didn't falter a step, didn't blink, didn't gasp. She acted for all the world as if Natalia had simply said, *I remember where I left the keys* or *Let's have Thai food for dinner* or *Don't be late*.

"How did you find it?" Ana Maria asked, her happy expression slipping into something more practical, morphing her into someone older, the adult Natalia knew she was but rarely saw.

"Does it really matter?"

"The accountant, then," Ana Maria concluded. "Can't say I'm surprised. I thought he might be a problem—especially after you started sleeping with him."

Natalia's skin tingled with embarrassment, and the thrum of stop-and-go traffic matched the erratic beat of her heart.

"Yeah. I know about that," Ana Maria admitted in a bitter imitation of something Natalia had said to her not so long ago. She hiked her bag up her shoulder and huffed, the little puff of air ruffling her bangs. "I suspected he wasn't who he said he was, figured he was FBI or DEA or maybe even Interpol. You sleeping with him only confirmed it." Ana Maria cocked her head to the side, pinned Natalia with a smug, brittle look. "Guess I'm not the only one keeping secrets."

"How did you know?"

"That you were sleeping with him?" Ana Maria laughed. "Please. The chemistry between you was palpable from the start—the two of you were destined to fuck or fight or both."

Natalia winced at the casual way *fuck* slipped from her sister's mouth. Another confirmation that when it came to Ana Maria, Natalia had only half the picture.

"But I also knew there was no way you'd go for casual sex, even if it was what you wanted." Ana Maria shook her head as if the very idea was alien to her. "Which means this isn't casual, which also means whoever Ethan is, he's not some cartel lackey. No way Natalia Vega spreads her legs for a man she can't respect," she said, her voice dipped in scorn that had been bottled and aged, as if she'd been storing it up for years. "How am I doing so far?"

Sick of the lies, surprises, and second-guessing, Natalia shrugged. "That pretty much sums it up." Her sister had made it sound crass and a little virginal—as if Natalia had been saving herself for true love—but that didn't make her wrong. Natalia would never have taken Ethan to bed, let him touch her, see her, know her, if she didn't respect the man he was.

"So what do you want to know?" Ana Maria asked, sidestepping around a woman with a stroller, giving the chubby-armed toddler a little finger wave. "How I did it?"

"I know the how—Ethan was able to explain that part—I want to understand the why."

"You're kidding, right?" Ana Maria stopped Natalia with a hand to her arm, jerking them both to a halt. "Why? Why *not?*"

"But if anyone besides Ethan had caught you, the consequences, Ana Maria—"

"Are no different from the ones we face every single day, and you know it!" She lowered her voice to a whisper, a grinding, angry rumble that sounded like a machine turning over after being left to rust. "Every day *Tío* gets more violent, more paranoid. It's only a matter of time before he lashes out at one or both of us. And even if he doesn't, the cartel is done with him. You don't hear the rumors, you don't see the warnings. But I do. People are careless around me, they don't think I'm a threat, they don't think I'm dangerous." She stared Natalia down, fire in her eyes and heat in her voice. "They're. Wrong."

You're wrong. Ana Maria didn't have to say it; Natalia heard the condemnation anyway, felt it like a blow to her solar plexus she should have expected but still hadn't seen coming.

Ana Maria started walking again, her pace hurried but her steps choppy with anger. "Colombia has lost patience with *Tio*; it's only a matter of time now."

Hours. They were down to *hours*. And though Natalia wouldn't weep for her uncle, wouldn't give a second thought to his death if it weren't for Will, it still rattled her to hear her sister speak so cavalierly about what was to come. Did she not understand that she'd been the one to set this whole thing in motion? That she'd set up their uncle for this fatal fall by embezzling money from his accounts?

"Because of you, Ana Maria. Because you *stole a hundred million dollars*," she whispered through an angry snarl.

Ana Maria shook her head once. "No, this has been a long time coming. Hernan thought Papa was weak, that the choices he made in running the business proved he'd gone soft. But even though Papa had lost revenue by cutting off streams of income he didn't like, he made the others safer, more reliable. In the end, profits would have increased. But *Tio* convinced the right people he was better suited. That Papa was too busy playing at being legitimate to seize the right opportunities. *Tio* set Papa up, and then they killed him." Ana Maria shoved her hands beneath her armpits, her arms crisscrossing her chest. "But what goes around comes around. And now Colombia regrets their greedy decision. Where Papa managed the business, *Tio* ran it into the ground. If it weren't the money, it would be something else. Six months, a year? It doesn't matter. All I did was accelerate the timeline."

"Then, why take it at all?" It was just one of the questions Natalia couldn't answer on her own. Nothing about Ana Maria had ever seemed superficial or pretentious. She'd never asked for designer clothes or fancy cars. What could she want all that money for?

"Because I *could*," she snapped. "Because he's taken *everything* from me, every good decent thing in my life he destroyed. My parents. My childhood. My—" She cut herself off, her denial strangling her voice to the point that for a moment she sounded like the startled twelve-year-old girl who'd just witnessed her father's murder. "Even my *sister*. He took it all, so I wanted to take something from *him*." She stepped to the side, letting a woman on a cell phone pass between them, then closed the distance again. "Then one day, I asked if I could use his computer to print a term paper, and I realized he trusted me. That I could do *anything* and he'd never even *think* to blame me." She shrugged, stopping to glance in a storefront window and wipe the smeared mascara from beneath her eyes. "In the end, it was all so easy. And now, finally, someone's noticed. It'll be over soon. I can't say I'm sorry."

Natalia rubbed a hand over her face, parsing through everything Ana Maria had just told her, looking for anything that rang untrue. Relief, cold comfort that it was, trickled through her. Bitterness. Anger. Revenge. Those were things Natalia could understand, and they were so much better than the alternative. Than realizing that Ana Maria had acted out of greed, out of a sense of entitlement. As it was, she was right at the edge of crossing a line she couldn't come back from.

"I need you to release the money, Ana Maria."

Ana Maria turned to stare at her over her shoulder. "I named you as a beneficiary, too, you know," she said gently, as if that mattered. As if that softened the blow somehow. "It's enough for us to start over somewhere far away, somewhere the cartel can never find us—if they can even be bothered to look."

For the first time that afternoon, Ana Maria's expression relaxed, her eyes lighting with excitement and transforming her into the barely grown woman Natalia knew so well.

"They don't care about us—they never have. They'll always believe *Tio* stole all that money. The trust dissolves the minute we empty it—I arranged *everything*," she explained, pride infusing her cheeks with a pretty flush. "And now that you know, we can plan. Decide where to go, what to do."

Natalia shook her head against the shocking realization that Ana Maria thought the cartel would let her walk. That somehow, despite everything, she still managed to believe that they would ever allow Natalia to live.

But even now, as her sister turned to face her, excited with the promise of everything they could do and have together, Natalia couldn't bring herself to tell her that.

"I need the money now, Ana. A man's life depends on it."

Ana Maria's excitement fled, and she studied Natalia as if searching for answers written across her body.

"Don't tell me you're doing this for *him*."

"It's complicated—"

Ana Maria waved her off. "I don't care—"

"I just need to buy a little time—"

"I don't care—"

"An innocent man will die if they kill Hernan. Don't you understand?" Natalia said, then grabbed Ana Maria's hand and pulled her down a narrow dead end caught between two redbrick buildings.

Ana Maria wrenched her arm away. *"I don't care!"* she thundered. "I don't *care* about some man I've never met. I don't *care* about our uncle. I don't *care* what Ethan Sullivan wants!"

"But I do," Natalia admitted on a hushed whisper.

Astonishment stole across Ana Maria's face. "You fell in *love* with him."

Since it was an afternoon of confessions and no part of her could deny Ethan, Natalia just nodded.

Ana Maria laughed, her voice rich with contempt. "I knew you were naive, but I had no idea you could be so stupid."

Only hours ago, Natalia would have found the idea of Ana Maria calling her naive insane. Now, it just felt like a half-hearted jab but hardly untrue.

"You think he loves you—"

"He does, I know he does—"

"He *needs* you, Natalia. There's a difference. And when all this is over and he's got no more use for you, you'll realize that. Realize it and thank me," Ana Maria declared, as if she were decades older, as if her heart had been battered one too many times. "One man's life is not worth a hundred million dollars or the freedom it will buy."

"Then, do it for me. Do it because I'm asking, begging you to. Please, Ana Maria, please release the money."

"Why? Why should I give up the fortune of a lifetime to help the man you love, when you wouldn't so much as lift a finger to save the one I did?"

"What?" Shock rippled through her, rooting her feet to the pavement, sending her heart pounding. But she didn't ask who, didn't need to. In her gut, she already knew.

They were sisters, after all; it should come as no surprise they had similar taste in men.

"You thought it was just sex, didn't you?" Ana Maria sneered. "That Garrison was just using me to help the DEA gain entry into the cartel. But he *loved* me. He wanted to *save* me." Tears welled in Ana Maria's soft blue eyes, then spilled down her cheeks. "He told me everything. Things about the case, about his life, even things he'd overheard at work. Rumors about a program that could topple entire organizations—criminal or legitimate—in an afternoon. He told me that for the right price, we could *buy* our way out. He even gave me a name." She wrapped her arms around her waist, ignoring the way the tears kept coming. "But I didn't believe him. How could I? It all sounded so insane."

Ana Maria shivered, but Natalia knew it wasn't the chill that lingered in the early-spring air. It was regret, a desperate wish that she could go back, do things differently. Her body's way of railing against the helplessness that threatened to break her. Natalia was all too familiar with the feeling.

"But then he got caught photographing those shipments, and you *killed* him—"

"I had to, Ana Maria," Natalia rushed out, desperate for her sister to believe it. To understand that if there'd been any other choice, she'd have taken it. She'd had no idea that Ana Maria had fallen in love with him. No clue it was anything more than young infatuation. But it wouldn't have mattered. If there'd been another option, Natalia would have taken it. "There wasn't any time—I didn't even know until I was dropped off at the warehouse. I would never intentionally hurt you—"

"It doesn't matter," Ana Maria said, sniffling, then wiping away her tears. "After that, I swore I'd do whatever it took to ruin our uncle, to destroy him the way he'd destroyed me." She flicked her fingertips free of the moisture, as if the tears were somehow beneath her. "The hit was expensive—and risky. I'd set up the trust too neatly to access it at the last minute—but it would have all been worth it if he'd died like he should have." Ana Maria sighed, as if the inconvenience of it all weighed her down. "But it doesn't matter now. What's done is done, and this will all be over soon."

"Ethan loves me, too, Ana Maria."

"He *needs* you. There's a difference. That money is *ours*, Natalia, recompense for every cruel thing that man did to our family. It's a new life; I won't let that go. Not even for you."

"Ana—"

"I have class," she said dismissively as she pulled her hair down from the messy bun, raked her fingers through it, then resecured it with an elastic. As if that gesture alone could put everything right.

"Ana, *please*," she begged, even as her sister turned and walked back toward the street.

"Neither one of us should deviate from our normal routines right now," she said with a casual glance back. "I'll be home for dinner. I'll bring a pizza."

And just like that, Ana Maria turned right and headed back up Twenty-First Street, as if nothing was wrong, as if she hadn't just broken Natalia's heart.

Natalia pressed herself against the worn brick at her back and struggled through the surge of emotion attacking on all fronts. Disappointment. Failure. Sadness.

But mostly, she wrestled with the realization that she'd known how this would end. Known that if Ana Maria had gone to such lengths to pull this off—and to keep it from even Natalia—then she wouldn't let the money go so easily.

She just hadn't expected the bitterness. The anger. The callous disregard for the fact that Natalia had never asked for any of this. That she'd given up her whole life on the hope Ana Maria might someday have one of her own.

Natalia swallowed.

Her sister was angry, and on some level, she probably thought she was doing the right thing. In a matter of hours, Hernan would be dead; Ana Maria could practically taste the freedom on her tongue. Maybe, if there was time, Natalia could convince Ana Maria that there were other ways. That Ethan would help them.

They were out of time, and Natalia knew of only one way to buy more of it.

She withdrew her phone, punched in Ethan's number, waited for him to answer.

"Natalia?"

"You told me once you could protect Ana Maria. That you could give the order, have her picked up, and hide her so well no one would ever find her. Did you mean it?" she asked.

Ethan was quiet for a beat, then said, "Yes. Why—"

"George Washington University. She'll either be at the library or the economics building." Natalia clenched her phone in nerveless fingers. "I need you to pick her up. Now."

"Send me her phone number. I'll have it traced and send someone to pick her up," he said, snapping off instructions in a way that reminded her that this was who he was. This was what he did. "What's happening, Natalia?"

She didn't answer right away, couldn't. She knew what he'd say. Instead, she put him on speaker, pulled up Ana Maria's contact card, and sent it to him.

Seconds that felt like unfulfilled lifetimes passed before he said, "Got it. I'll send someone on the way to her location. Now tell me what's happening," he demanded.

"She won't release the funds," Natalia admitted, "and I don't have time to change her mind."

He cursed, and she smiled, picturing his face, mentally tracing the lines of his frown, the curve of his lips, the break in his nose.

"You've kept your promise, Ethan. Now I'm going to keep mine."

"Natalia—"

"Goodbye, Ethan."

She hung up before he could say anything, before he could curse or scream or beg, before he could tell her it wasn't worth it, that she didn't have to.

Before he could tell her that he loved her.

She turned off her phone and dropped it as she exited the alley.

Less than twenty-four hours until that live stream came through. Without the money, Hernan would be dead in twelve.

Unless, of course, Carlos believed someone *else* had stolen it in the first place.

CHAPTER NINETEEN

"You can't keep me here," Ana Maria snarled the moment Ethan walked into the tiny, windowless conference room that Ortiz had banished her to with a curse and a demand for hazard pay. Apparently, Ana Maria carried pepper spray and was well versed in how to use it.

Her sister's doing, no doubt.

Just the thought of Natalia, of the surge of fear that had swamped him the moment she'd hung up on him, had him clenching his fists and biting back angry words and brutal demands that wouldn't get him what he wanted. Panic, potent and powerful, an emotion Ethan had far too little experience with, flooded his bloodstream. It had been there for hours, thrumming through him with each beat of his heart, whispering dark warnings about all the things he couldn't stop, all the hurt he was helpless to prevent.

He knew what Natalia had done. Had known the second she'd said goodbye. Like it was some sort of gift. Like she'd miss him. Like this wouldn't destroy him as surely as it would her.

And he was *furious* with her. Had she heard nothing he'd said? Understood none of what he wanted so badly to impress upon her? Never, not under any circumstances he could fathom, would he have asked this of her.

She'd gone to her uncle to confess. To buy him time. To save Will.

God*damn* her.

Didn't she understand what this would do to him?

What she *meant* to him?

If she survived this, he was going to kill her.

Or marry her.

But first, he had to save her, which meant he needed to turn the snarly, angry, bitter woman across from him into an ally. He could only hope Ana Maria possessed a fraction of the loyalty for Natalia that her sister held for her.

"We don't have a lot of time, so I'm going to make this simple for you—"

"I'm not giving *you* the money, either." Ana Maria sat back in the conference chair, shifting her weight from side to side so it spun 180 petulant degrees in either direction. "You can keep me in here all night, if you like. I only have to hold out until morning, then it won't matter."

"Your sister will be dead by morning," Ethan snapped out, the urge to say *Screw diplomacy* and *Fuck explanations* fighting against his resolve. Above all else, he needed Ana Maria's help, which meant he needed to hold on to his patience and smother his fear.

Ana Maria stilled, the defiant petulance draining away until only insecurity and surprise remained. "What are you talking about?"

"Why do you think we picked you up?" Ethan asked on an angry snarl. "She came to you for help, and you turned her away—"

"She came to me for a hundred million dollars." Ana Maria slammed a delicate fist against the table, then jumped at the sound of the *thwack* that reverberated around the room. "For a man she's never even met. And all because she was dumb enough to buy into whatever bullshit you sold her."

He wouldn't stand there and justify the things he'd told Natalia, wouldn't prove the depth of his feelings to her angry little sister. There wasn't time, and the only person who deserved to hear it was—

He swallowed hard and pushed beyond the surge of panic that if he didn't play this right, if he didn't fix it, then he'd never get a chance to prove anything to Natalia at all.

He'd thought they had time.

He swore he'd never take that for granted again.

"She came to you for help. For loyalty. She trusted you—and why wouldn't she?" he snarled, his voice a biting condemnation. "Has she ever denied you *anything*? Her only mistake was believing that you loved her as much as she loved you." At the end of the day, Ethan didn't blame Ana Maria for stealing the money or setting up her uncle or wanting so desperately to have a life of her own that she'd pay any price. But that she could turn away her sister for any reason at all enraged him.

Natalia deserved so much better than the both of them.

"You don't know the first thing about us!" Ana Maria stood from her chair and leaned over the desk, staring Ethan down. "You think I don't know what she's done for me? I know *everything*. I know that she'd kill herself to keep the people she loves safe, to make them happy. It had to *stop*."

On that, at least, Ethan and Ana Maria agreed.

"I built us a future, a way out of the cartel; all we had to do was wait for Hernan to die and we could *walk away*." She sat back down hard enough to send the chair skidding across the floor. "But then you come along and suddenly she's ready to throw it all away. And for what? Love?" She scoffed. "Please. You're just using her to get what you want."

"You don't have the first clue about what I want from Natalia," he bit out, forcing his voice into something cold and flat. "And you're a damn fool if you really thought that the cartel was ever going to let Natalia walk away."

"No one's ever given a damn about us."

"No one's ever given a damn about *you*. Except Natalia, who made sure that no one would ever so much as glance in your direction," he ground out. "But your sister is deadly—that makes her either threat or asset and nothing in between." Ethan sighed, forced himself to take a breath, to take a step back, to remember that whatever or whoever else she was, Ana Maria was still the most important person in Natalia's life. And right now, she held the key to saving it. "They never would have let her walk away, Ana Maria. Your sister understood that." He pulled out one of the unoccupied chairs and forced himself to sit. "She's been prepared for that for years. So when you told her no—"

"I—"

Ethan held up a hand. "It doesn't matter why. Not anymore. When you told her no, Natalia did the only thing she thought she could. She turned herself in and took the blame for everything."

All the color drained from Ana Maria's face. "She wouldn't—"

"Of course she would. Putting herself last, saving other people, it's the thing that comes most naturally to her."

"They'll kill her for this . . . ," Ana Maria whispered, her fingers coming up to toy with the necklace at her throat.

"Yes," Ethan agreed. "But not until she gives them what they want."

"Then, why?" But even as she uttered the words, Ethan saw the truth dawn across her face. "She thinks she can buy you enough time to find your friend," she realized aloud. "She did this for *you*."

"It doesn't matter why she did it. It doesn't matter if I deserve it. She didn't see a way out for herself, but she saw one, no matter how slim a chance it is, for someone else. *That's* who your sister is." Selfless. Relentlessly devoted to the people she cared about.

How had she ever thought herself irredeemable?

"She's tenacious, I'll give her that," Ethan acknowledged, even though it pained him to do so. Never could he have imagined that Natalia's strength of will, her absolute conviction, could be turned so brutally against her. "She'll last long enough for my team to find our man."

"And then?" Ana Maria asked.

"And then she'll tell them what they want to know, and if she's lucky, they'll kill her quickly."

Ana Maria dropped her head into her hands, scraped her fingers through her hair, shuddered once, twice, and then when Ethan was sure she'd fall apart, when he thought he'd have to comfort her enough to bring her back from the brink, to gain her cooperation, she surprised him.

"I never wanted this." She looked up, pinned him with a soft cornflower-blue gaze, and said, "I'll release the accounts."

He heaved out a relieved sigh. The money wouldn't help them—it was far too late for a solution that simple. But that she'd offered . . . Whatever else Ethan might feel about the woman sitting in front of him, he had to at least acknowledge that at the end of the day, she valued her sister's life at more than a hundred million dollars, and that was no small thing.

"It's not that easy. Even if we could get all the money wired in time, they'd never let her walk out of there alive."

"So, go. Get. Her."

"We've tried, goddamn it!" he roared. "You don't think I've looked everywhere? I sent a team to the house. Every holding we know about has been checked out. Wherever she is, I can't find her."

"You have to," Ana Maria whispered, horror pushing her voice through a cheese grater. "Ethan, you have to."

"I can't," he said, the weight of the truth threatening to drown him. "But you can."

"Me?" Ana Maria shook her head. "I know a lot more than people realize, but I've never been directly involved in any facet of the business. I don't know where shipments come in or deals are made."

"I don't . . . That's not what I need." He needed a miracle—another, better option. But in lieu of that, he'd have to make do with what he had. He only prayed Natalia would forgive him for it.

"Your sister's a fighter—"

"A nice way of saying stubborn as a mule," Ana Maria muttered, then flushed, as if she hadn't intended to say as much aloud. She probably hadn't. The words had slipped out fond and exasperated, as if she'd said them a hundred times before.

"That, too. But she's strong, and, more important, she's driven. Maybe the most driven individual I've ever known." Which was saying something, considering the people he worked with every day, each and every one of them at the top of their respective fields. "She's not going to give in, not until she's sure enough time has passed."

"They're going to hurt her," Ana Maria whispered through the fingers she held to her mouth.

"They're going to try to break her—your uncle's good at that. Looking into someone, finding their fears, using it against them. But Natalia only fears one thing."

"Losing me," she realized aloud. "I'm her weakness—"

"And her strength," Ethan countered. "But yes. You're the key, and as long as they don't have you, they don't have a way to make Natalia talk."

Ana Maria stared at him, her eyes wide, her throat working around a swallow. "But if they had me," she said, working it out without his help, "then *you'd* have a location. They'd take me to her, use me to hurt her, to make her talk."

"I'd never let that happen, Ana Maria. We'd be with you the whole time," Ethan said, doing his very best to allay her fears even as his own built with every passing second. "The minute you confirm Natalia's there—you only have to say her name—we'll break down the doors to get to you."

"So I'd, what, wear a wire?" she asked, her voice small, her posture every bit the frightened kid.

"We can do a lot better than a wire, but yes, we'd set you up with a GPS tracker and an audio stream. We'd be right behind you the whole time."

"And once I'm inside, what then?" she asked, chewing the edge of her fingernail ragged.

"Then we end this. For good," he assured her. "You and your sister are the only ones walking out of there alive."

"What about your friend?" she asked quietly.

"We're down to hours now. Less by the time we set this whole thing in motion. If we're careful, if luck is on our side, no one will know your uncle's dead until far too late."

"And if luck *isn't* on your side? If doing this costs your friend his life?"

Ethan closed his eyes against the guilt, against the unfairness of a choice he never should have had to make. Will or Natalia. Loyalty or love. If he lost Will, a part of Ethan would no doubt die right along with him. But if he lost Natalia . . . if he lost Natalia, then that was it, he was done. Knowing that she'd walked in there certain of what she'd face, carrying around the understanding that she'd done it for him, was too much. He wasn't strong enough.

So in the end, the choice was easy, may Will forgive him for it.

"I choose her," he said. And he'd keep choosing her, over and over and over again, until she realized where she belonged. That she could count on him. That when he made a promise, he kept it.

"So do I," Ana Maria said, rising from her chair and tugging down the sleeves of her shirt. "Let's go get my sister."

"Do you remember why I like this position, *gatita*?" Carlos asked, his question less a raspy whisper of sound and more a grating physical touch, uninvited and unwelcome.

"No?" He clucked his tongue, his breath a moist puff of air on the back of Natalia's neck. "You never did take to this, did you?"

He completed his circle, sidestepping until he appeared before her, blurred through sweat and traitorous tears and something heavier that tried to seal her eyes shut. It didn't matter. She didn't need to see. Didn't want to know. It would all be over soon. Until then, if she closed her eyes, let her mind drift and her body sway, she could picture Ethan.

Mentally unpack the depths of his smile, the layers of colors that made up his eyes, remember the texture of his hair beneath her fingers.

"Always so eager to finish the job, always too merciful to draw it out." Fingers, blunt and unwelcome, stroked down her abdomen, jerking her back to the present. The movement, small as it was, was enough to lay ruin to the precarious balance she'd found.

"Ah," Carlos sighed as Natalia stiffened, her entire body one long line of fire as every muscle stiffened and cried out as one. "And now you remember."

Oh, she hadn't forgotten. How could she? She'd been here hours, her arms stretched high, her toes barely brushing the floor. Her uncle might have bound her to a chair, left her immobile and utterly at his mercy, helpless to move or flinch or evade. In his unimaginative mind, he equated complete control with absolute power.

Carlos was not so limited.

He preferred his captives to have a hand in their torture. To work against their own instincts, their own interests.

So when they'd dragged Natalia in here, already bruised and bleeding and half-unconscious, he'd shoved the sturdy metal chair to the corner, stripped her of her shoes and jacket, and strung her up until only the balls of her feet made contact with the floor.

If he'd simply left her there, agony would have set in within a matter of hours, the position wrenching her shoulders and stretching her chest until the simple act of breathing became a torment.

He hadn't left her there, but neither had he needed to get creative. There'd been no pliers or needles or shocks. Just fists and the punishing sway of her own failing body. Still and calm, she felt the pain ebb and flow through her until it became a pulsing but predictable wave. But if she moved? If she let herself shy away from his touch or flinch from a blow, her entire body cried out in agony. As the hours passed, he'd hit her less, hurt her less—but found more and more ways to ensure she inflicted suffering upon herself.

She wanted to hate him for it but had expected no less . . . and far worse.

"You must be hurting, *gatita*." As if she were a prized thoroughbred, he ran a palm across her stomach, over her hip, along her flank. He stroked across muscles that quivered and bruises that throbbed, but his touch was impersonal and efficient, as if he were looking for a lameness that had come on overnight and without warning.

This time, she kept her feet, let herself lean into his hand and use him for the energy it took simply to maintain her balance.

He *tsk*ed and withdrew. She swayed, then relaxed, letting her arms take her weight so her feet wouldn't move. Small corrections, little adjustments—it was the best she could do.

"*Me duele hacer esto.*" He sighed, his grating, roughened voice somehow more fluid in Spanish than in English. "Hurting you brings me no joy, *gatita*."

Strangely, Natalia believed that.

The moment she'd told her uncle what she'd done, he'd turned on her, his rage a living, breathing thing. For a moment, she'd thought he'd kill her quickly, if brutally, and finally, finally, everything would be done.

But no. He'd stopped. Handed her over to Carlos with a cold, "Break her. Then kill her. But not until after she releases the money."

No one could claim Carlos hadn't done his job, no matter what her uncle screamed during his brief rage-fueled appearances. But where Hernan had been blinded by his pride, lost to his rage, Carlos knew her. In some ways, Carlos knew her better than almost anyone else on the planet. He'd made her, after all. Taught and punished and pushed until lessons became ingrained and fears distant.

All but one, anyway. And he understood that. Knew that without Ana Maria, Natalia could not be made to talk. Not with the knife at his hip or the gun at his back. And because for him this would always simply be a job and nothing more, he took his time, inflicted the pain, but took no pleasure in it.

He'd kill her, they both knew he would, but Natalia was grateful he wouldn't make it any worse than it had to be. That he'd left her clothed, kept her whole. It was a strange thing—perhaps not gratitude but a grudging respect for a man who had ruined and saved her in turn.

"Are you thirsty, little cat?" Carlos asked, pushing a sweaty tangle of hair away from her face. "Would you like water?" He snapped his fingers, held out a hand, and, a moment later, the cold rim of a water bottle touched her lips.

She opened her mouth, let the water run over her tongue and coat her lips, but precious little made it down her throat.

When he took away the bottle, she heaved out an agonized breath, then fought, her chest rattling like an ancient, failing water heater, to draw another.

"Hush," Carlos said, running a soothing hand across ribs she was certain were broken, though if they'd cracked beneath her uncle's foot or Carlos's fists, she couldn't be sure.

She suspected the former. For all that Carlos was brutal, there was a reluctance there. A degree of restrained disinterest. Still, when he bunched his fists, torqued his body, he went for maximum pain and minimal damage. She couldn't die before she gave up the money, not if her uncle wanted to save his own skin.

It hardly mattered. The choice would soon be taken from all of them. Each wet, raspy pull of air was smaller and harder fought than the last.

Natalia was ready.

"You're drowning, you know," Carlos said, stepping back to study her face, to trace the edge of a bruise, the split in her lip. "Slowly, your chest fills with blood and your lungs collapse. It need not be so painful, *gatita*." He leaned forward, skimmed a finger along the outside of her arm and down to dip between the grooves of two ribs. "The knife would be fast, I promise. The pain"—he snapped his fingers—"gone." He shook his head. "Will you not tell me what I ask?"

"No."

He sighed and turned away. "Always so stubborn," he said, his voice fond but exasperated. Strange, to think that the man who'd taught her to kill, to survive, would be the one who killed her. He wouldn't regret it, that was an emotion he'd shut off a long time ago, but she didn't think he'd have chosen it, either.

"A different question, then," he said, stepping closer until he could bend his knees and look up into her eyes for the answers he sought. "Why?"

When she blinked, long and slow and tired, he continued.

"I ask myself this. Why?" His expression didn't change, didn't become curious or frustrated or annoyed. But she knew that she'd surprised him, that he'd believed from the start Hernan was guilty. "Money does not drive you, little cat. Only loyalty."

It bothered him, she realized, that he couldn't figure out what had driven her to this. He'd grown too used to life in the cartel. Too comfortable in the expectation that everyone was always out for themselves. He'd grown up poor, fought for everything he had, and even after a decades-long career—a rarity unmatched within the Vega cartel—he had only his reputation to show for it. He could understand loyalty, but only in the basest terms. He'd never bite the hand that fed him, but it was born of necessity and not desire.

Carlos was, and always would be, a product of his roots.

Just as Natalia was a product of hers.

There was no answer she could give that he'd understand.

Because though she'd forgotten what it felt like, she'd been raised in a loving home, with parents who had supported her, believed in her. People who wanted more for her. And though so much had changed, and even if she'd forgotten what it was to bask in the warmth of someone else's faith, someone else's pride, Ethan had reminded her.

When she'd believed the worst of herself, Ethan had forced her to acknowledge the best. To remember that she hadn't chosen this life. That she hadn't always been hardened and cold and lonely.

And now, each passing minute, every agonizing breath, was a step back to the woman she wanted to be. The price she had to pay to wipe the slate clean. To do the right thing for the people she loved.

Beneath the weight of her desire to be the woman Ethan believed her to be, her resolve hardened. It would be enough to see her to the finish line, a threshold she could finally see, one she expected to cross in minutes rather than hours.

A door behind her creaked open, then slammed shut, the heavy, labored footsteps heralding her uncle's return.

"Anything?" he barked.

"No."

Curses fell like hailstones against a metal roof, drowning out everything but the agony in her shoulders, in her chest, at her side.

"I want my goddamn money, you whore!" he shouted, kicking her legs out from beneath her and startling a cry from her mouth. "And finally, you'll give it to me." He stepped in front of her, waited the long moments it took for her to stop flailing, to stop gasping for air like a fish on a hook, and for her to find the strength to lift her head and meet his stare. "Bring in the sister."

No!

Natalia jerked back, watching in horrified silence as two men escorted Ana Maria into the room.

A sob—shattered, wet, and broken—tried to expel the jagged pieces of her heart. Ethan had *promised* her. Sworn he'd have Ana picked up and detained. Why hadn't he?

She closed her eyes, tugged at the shackles digging into her wrists, whined at the way her feet slipped and slid against the floor. Ethan wouldn't have let them take her; he would have kept his word. Which meant . . . which meant . . .

"Natalia," Ana Maria whispered, her voice a ruin of shock and horror and fear.

She couldn't do this. Couldn't watch as they took Ana Maria apart. Ana was the reason for *everything* Natalia had ever done. Good or bad, right or wrong, Natalia could shoulder it because no matter what, she could never regret ensuring Ana Maria had the life she deserved. But now that was about to be torn to shreds. If Ana Maria died, it would all have been for *nothing*.

"Look at me," Ana Maria said, her voice pushing past fear and turning sure and steady and clear as a church bell. "*Natalia*, look at me."

Natalia opened her eyes, met her sister's gaze.

Ana Maria smiled. "You were right. He—"

The single door into the room burst open on a *bang*, slamming against the rough cinder-block walls hard enough to swing wildly back in the other direction, but not before something sailed through the door, bringing noise and fire and chaos with it.

Silence descended, smothered beneath the hazy, high-pitched ringing in her ears. Somewhere beneath that, as if she heard it from the bottom of a pool or through a dozen walls, voices shouted and shots rang out.

Natalia blinked, her vision foggy, as if she'd opened her eyes into the sun and temporarily blinded herself. Slowly, her senses came back to her, sound following sight. Four men—two who'd watched as Carlos had beaten her, two who'd dragged Ana Maria through the door only moments before—lay dead on the floor.

And Ethan stood before her, a man she didn't know at his back. She swallowed back an apology or a plea or a sigh of relief—it was hard to tell beneath the mess of pain and confusion and exhaustion. His mouth moved, terse words she didn't understand falling from his lips.

She forgot herself, tried to take a swaying step forward, only to be jerked back by a strong arm and a brutal grip. Too late, she felt the knife at her throat, the edge biting into her skin.

"Stay, *gatita*," Carlos said against the shell of her ear. "Stay and live a little longer."

"Natalia," Ethan said, his words for her but his focus on Carlos, "don't move, honey."

Relief twisted her lips, trying to muster the energy for a grin, but the humiliating bite of exposure—she was utterly helpless, completely reliant on someone else—stole her focus. She'd been prepared to die alone, to have that dignity at least, but now Ethan stood before her, barely able to look at her.

"Mentiroso!"

Hernan's roar pulled Natalia's gaze to the corner of the room where he stood, clutching Ana Maria to him like a shield, his arm around her neck, a gun in his hand. The man who'd followed Ethan into the room had his own gun up and at the ready, but even if he was an expert marksman, the risk was too great, Ana Maria too much of a target.

She pulled uselessly at the rope binding her wrists. She needed to . . . She couldn't . . . Oh God, she couldn't reach anyone. Couldn't help anyone.

"Hush," Carlos said again. "Your role in this is done, and now I will hear the truth."

"Let her go," Ethan repeated. "We can settle this without the women."

"I don't think so." Carlos leaned close, his chin nearly settling atop her shoulder, his knife still pressed to the column of her throat.

"I have what you came for. Let her go and I'll wire the money."

"How did you come by the money?" Carlos asked. "She gave it to you?"

"Does it matter?" Ethan didn't so much as take a step, though his body shifted, as if he had to fight every instinct he had to hold his position.

"To the cartel? No. Colombia sees only guilt and retribution. They do not care for why."

"But you do," Ethan said.

"I do." Carlos loosened his hold, the knife nicking Natalia's throat pulling away enough for her to heave in a shuddering breath. She coughed, wet and thick, then wheezed as she tried to pull in another breath. "Explain. And for her sake, do it quickly."

"Natalia never touched the money."

Natalia whimpered through an agonizing breath. "No, Ethan . . ."

"Shh. He says what I already know," Carlos whispered. Then to Ethan, he demanded, "Who?"

"Hernan, of course."

"You lie!" Hernan shouted from the corner of the room, an angry bull facing the sword. Ana Maria jerked and cried, her hands pulling fruitlessly at her uncle's forearm.

"To steal but not spend, to take but not run—it requires discipline. Control. Hernan does not have these things. Colombia knows this. I know this. If you have the money, as you say, then Hernan did not take it." Carlos shifted, used the weight of his arm around Natalia's throat to push her down, forcing her chest to expand and the pressure to drive the air from her lungs on a strangled wail of agony.

"Stop it."

"Then, tell me."

"I took it!" Ana Maria blurted out, her voice panicked and scared. "I took it."

"Bitch!" Hernan shoved his gun into Ana Maria's ribs. "I'll kill you both!"

She jerked sideways but brought her gaze to Natalia's, her face scared but her eyes determined.

"You're dead the second you pull that trigger," the man behind Ethan said, sliding forward another step.

"He is dead anyway," Carlos pronounced. "Too careless for too long. It is time for change."

"I don't have the money!"

"But you lost it," Carlos said, his voice a rolling tumbler of gravel. "To a bad accountant. To *agentes federales*. To a woman. For that, you will die." Carlos shifted, tilting his head to the side as if considering Ethan. "You object?"

"I need him," Ethan acknowledged. "He has something of mine."

"Ethan . . . please," Natalia begged, though for what—her sister's life, her own freedom, Will's safety—she couldn't be sure. But this had to end, and Carlos didn't need to know these things. She didn't know what he'd do with the information, if he'd care or cut his losses. There was nothing in it for him, no reason to do anything other than what he'd come to do.

"You knew this, *gatita*?" he asked against her neck. He *tsk*ed, a familiar cluck of tongue that said she'd both disappointed and amused him. "I warned you."

He had. About love. About loyalty. About the weakness it bred within her. He'd meant Ana Maria, but it applied to Ethan, too. And now he knew it.

"And what would you give me?" Carlos asked. "What is his life worth to you?"

"Nothing. I needed only time—" Ethan pinned her with a look. "Time I was given. I have no need for Hernan Vega."

Relief, nearly as sweet as fresh, crisp air, filled her chest. She'd done it. Bought him the time he needed to find his friend. She hoped Ethan brought Will home. That he found comfort in his friend.

Natalia only wished she'd be able to meet him.

"And hers?" Carlos asked, flicking the point of his knife to Natalia's throat. "What would you give me for this life?"

"Anything," Ethan declared. "Everything."

"My little cat." He stepped away and withdrew his knife. "One more fight," he said, his voice a fond goodbye, "and then no more." He put his blade to the rope at her wrists. "If she fights and lives, so be it," he declared, the rope loosening, then fraying, her heels touching the ground. "But Natalia Vega is no more. Yes?"

"Yes," Ethan agreed.

"He dies now," Carlos said, nodding to Hernan as he continued to cut at the rope binding her.

Hernan shouted, pulled his gun up, and aimed straight for Carlos and her. Natalia watched, stunned and proud and horrified, as Ana Maria jerked her hand from his arm; withdrew the switchblade Natalia had given her so long ago; turned to the side, giving her room to bury the knife in Hernan's thigh, twisting her wrist and severing the femoral artery, as Natalia had taught her.

Hernan released Ana Maria as the rope holding up Natalia snapped, dropping her to the ground like a stone into a pool of fire and agony. She turned to her side, drew a breath, fought for another, and gasped like a landed fish.

Hernan glanced down, the gray of his pants already wet and heavy with blood. It would take only minutes. And from the look on his face, her uncle knew it, too.

"Bitch," he spat, pulled his arm to the right, and fired two rounds before the man behind Ethan put a bullet through his head.

All the fight Natalia had left hit the floor with Ana Maria's body, the echo of the bullets impacting her back like fists against a heavy bag. "Ana . . ." Natalia twisted, gasped, and tried to pull herself across the floor.

"Check on her, Ortiz," Ethan said, his gaze still fixed on Natalia. "It's okay," he said. "It's all right, she's going to be fine."

"She's alive," Ortiz said, "but we need to get Liam in here *now*."

"You will wire the money?" Carlos asked. "I do not wish to return."

"On my word, it's done," Ethan said, falling to his knees beside Natalia, his hands trembling as he reached for her. "It's all done."

Carlos stepped over her and toward the door, then glanced back. "Goodbye, *gatita*." And then he was gone, through the door and out of her life like a ghost.

"Ana—" She turned her head, looked for her sister, but couldn't find her through the chaos of men pouring into the room.

"Shh, shh," Ethan said, rolling her to her side. "Just breathe. Ortiz is with her. We're going to take care of you both. Just stay with me, Natalia."

He brushed hair from her face, cupped a palm against her cheek.

"Why? Why did you do this?" he asked, his face contorted in pain and confusion. "I never—You should never have . . . ," he said, picking up her hand and kissing her knuckles.

She blinked at Ethan, black spots dancing in front of her eyes. "Your friend . . . the right thing."

"I've got a team on the way—"

"Hey, let me take a look." A man with red hair appeared at her side, gentle hands checking her over, a soft voice asking her to breathe—he might as well have asked her to fly.

"Liam?" Ethan asked.

"First ambulance is here!" a voice shouted from the door.

"Liam!" Ethan repeated.

"They're both critical," he replied. "Both out of time—you need to prioritize one and triage the other."

"Ana . . ."

"Second ambulance is minutes out, but I need to know who to take, Ethan."

"Can't both go?"

"Ambulance can only carry one critical patient, Ethan, the crews need room to work."

Oh God. No. *No.*

"You *promised* . . ." Natalia forced her chest to expand, to fight for the air to breathe one last burst of life into her sister.

"I know," Ethan said, dropping his forehead to hers, torment deepening the grooves on his face until she barely recognized him. "I'm sorry. I'm sorry, Natalia."

She squeezed his hand. Tried to tell him it was okay but didn't have the words or air or energy to do more than grasp his fingers.

"Forgive me," he whispered as more men and women and equipment poured into the room.

Then, as she'd known he would, Ethan looked her in the eye as he buried the knife in her heart.

"Over here!"

CHAPTER TWENTY

Two Weeks Later

"Ahoy, Admiral Coxless," Parker declared, interrupting the classic rock blaring through Ethan's headphones and intruding on what was supposed to be a quiet morning on the water.

Too tired to protest the fact that Parker had hacked his phone—again—Ethan just pulled his oars through the water on a sigh. "Promoted me, have you?"

"Well, you're the navy man, so I'm sure you'll correct me if I'm wrong, but isn't that how it works?" Parker asked, the noise of a coffee grinder churning through the background. "If you're the captain of two coxless vessels, then that makes you an admiral, right?"

"I only own the one single scull, Parker." Ethan dipped his oars in the water, keeping his stroke smooth and even. Being out here, the sun still a pink slip of light on the horizon, was the closest thing to rest he'd managed in the last several weeks. Nothing settled him. Everything hurt. And the reminder of failure was everywhere.

"Yeah, I wasn't referring to a second boat."

"Didn't think so." Too tired to humor Parker, Ethan cut to the chase. "What do you want?"

Parker paused, all noise from the other end of the line going quiet. There was no clanking of mugs, no whir of beans, no clatter of spoons. Just Parker, still and calm, as if he were seriously considering the next thing to come out of his mouth. It could mean only one thing—Ethan was going to hate whatever Parker had to say.

"What do I want?" Parker asked, the rattle of a drawer full of clinking silverware accompanying the sarcasm. "I want to know where Georgia hid my Keurig, because this damn French press takes forever. I want my artificial sweetener, frozen pizzas, and Mountain Dew to magically replace the organic sugar, chicken breasts, and kale. And I definitely want to stop losing rock-paper-scissors to the entire office," he grumbled. "Statistically that shouldn't even be a thing." He sighed and ran water in the sink. "But since Georgia likes her coffee fresh and does all the grocery shopping, I'm just going to have to learn to live with the first two. I'll revisit the rock-paper-scissors issue at a later date—I'm sure Ortiz, at least, is cheating—but until then, a bet's a bet. I lost, so I get to call the boss on his—how did Georgia put it?—butt-hurt-princess routine."

Ethan didn't bother to object. What was the point? He wasn't stupid. He'd been nothing short of an asshole at the office. Even Georgia, who typically gave as good as she got, had been avoiding him.

"Nothing to say?" Parker asked. "No protestations from the BHP?"

"What's the point?" Ethan asked, his scull slipping silently through the water. "You're going to tell me what you think, regardless."

"True," Parker agreed, the whistle of a teapot sounding in the background. "And hey, if you're not going to fight me on what an asshole you've been lately, then I can jump straight to the good part."

"Which is what, exactly?"

"Fixing it, of course." The refrigerator door creaked, then closed, and Parker mumbled, "She thinks she's so smart, pouring out the flavored creamer and replacing it with fat-free half-and-half laced with cinnamon. Like I won't notice when my coffee doesn't taste like a snickerdoodle."

There was a long pause, then a heavy sigh. "Don't tell her I said this, but damn, fresh-ground is the way to go."

"Enjoy your coffee, Parker."

And leave me in peace.

"Do *not* hang up on me. If I have to track you down to your river of solitude, I'm gonna be pissed."

Ethan adjusted his stroke, straightening out his scull when it slid through an unseen current that pulled it to the right. He didn't want to talk to Parker. Didn't want to hear about what an asshole he'd been. And he definitely didn't want to hear about how none of it was his fault. But most of all, Ethan didn't want to think of Parker pouring a second cup of coffee, of meandering down the hall, still fuzzy and sated from a good night's sleep, and slipping in bed beside the woman he loved.

Ethan was unaccustomed to jealousy, despair, or defeat. And until he learned how to deal with each of them, it was better for everyone if he kept his distance.

Ethan hung up, then powered off his phone for good measure. He made it a quarter mile upstream before Parker's voice interrupted the quiet.

"Seriously? You thought turning off your phone would work? On me?"

"Worth a shot," Ethan grunted.

"Please. I updated the hardware on all our team's equipment months ago. Short of taking the battery out and dumping it in the river, you're a captive audience."

"Don't tempt me—"

"Do it and I swear to God I'll start hacking into your home security system. I'll critique *everything*. The way you brush your teeth, the way you fold your underwear—and I *know* you've got one of those little board things just for that perfect center crease—I'll be like an über-opinionated AI you can't get rid of."

"You're already an über-opinionated AI I can't get rid of."

"So then we agree—resistance is futile."

Ethan was 90 percent certain that based on the delivery, Parker was making some inane pop culture reference; he just didn't care enough to ask. In any case, it would only prolong the inevitable.

"How long are you going to let this continue, Ethan?" Parker asked, the question a soft, toneless statement in Ethan's ear, so at odds with the quippy banter Parker relied on for socialization. "How long are you going to punish yourself?"

"I'm not punishing myself."

"Wow. So we're just straight-up lying to each other now. Okay, then. Gloves off." Parker pulled out one of the bar stools flanking the kitchen island, its legs scraping against the floor. "Regardless of what your ego may have led you to believe, you are not God. You are not all-seeing, and you are not responsible for every single person who enters your orbit." Parker sighed as if Ethan had told him to slow down and use small words. "None of what happened is your fault, Ethan."

"She *died*, Parker. Because of me. Because of choices I made—"

"That's bullshit, and you know it."

No, no, he didn't know it. Ethan had made the decision to go undercover. To read Natalia in. To ask for her help. And then he'd been dumb enough to get close. To let something that should have been strictly business turn personal. He'd made promises, goddamn it. And he'd broken every single one of them.

And what had it all been for? Yes, Hernan Vega was dead, the cartel done with the DC area, but that wasn't why Ethan had taken the job in the first place.

"What was it all for, Parker?" Ethan asked, finally giving voice to the thought that had been plaguing him. "Tell me how the last month and a half hasn't made everything worse instead of better."

Tell me how I haven't made everything worse.

"You act like Will's dead, Ethan—"

"We don't know that he isn't." The thought kept him up at night, poring over topographical maps, searching the Internet for chatter.

"I promote you from captain to admiral, and you advance from princess to drama queen—no one could ever accuse you of being anything short of ambitious."

"I'm serious—"

"Yeah?" Parker snarled. "Well, so the fuck am I. Will isn't dead, Ethan. You've read the reports, you know that as well as I do. We got there too late! We missed him by hours, a day at the most, but to focus on that is to ignore what's important—he walked out under his own steam, Ethan. A whole host of forensics at the scene tell us as much."

Ethan had read the reports. Reviewed what little footage had been recovered, studied each and every photograph. All indications said Will had walked out of that hellhole alive. But where was he? Who was he with?

And why hadn't he come home?

"His captors were all dead, Ethan. A sniper saw to that."

"Then, where is he, Parker?" Ethan asked, his muscles burning, sweat dripping into his eyes as he pulled himself upstream against a current that kept trying to push him back down again.

"I don't know," Parker acknowledged, dropping his voice a degree or two. "I wish I did. I wish Georgia didn't jump every time her phone rings. I wish I never caught her staring out the window or scanning the faces of the people we pass on the street. I wish I had all the answers, I really do." Parker took a long sip of coffee. "I don't know where Will is or what he's doing—but he's a Bennett, which means he'll come home when he's goddamn good and ready and not one second before." He cursed beneath his breath, then with a smile lacing his voice, said, "It's a family trait."

Yeah, yeah, it was. Ethan wasn't sure he'd ever met two more headstrong people in his life—Will and Georgia could try the patience of a saint—but they were loyal, steadfast, and eventually they made the road to where they needed to be.

"He'll find his way back."

"Georgia did," Ethan acknowledged. "After everything, she came home." And now Ethan felt as if he'd never really known her at all. As if for years he'd seen shades of who she might be, who she could be, if the circumstances were right. He'd thought to give her that with a job—he could never have imagined it would take something else entirely.

But he couldn't argue with the results. Georgia and Parker just *worked*. They compensated for each other's weaknesses, bolstered each other's strengths. And for a sliver of time, Ethan had tasted that kind of relationship. Recognized it for the addictive drug it was. But learning to live without it, forcing himself to move on, was proving far more difficult than he could ever have imagined.

"And Natalia didn't, is that what you're saying?" Parker asked.

"I don't think it needs to be said at all."

"God, you're an idiot sometimes." Parker sighed.

Ethan didn't have to be in the same room to know that Parker had shoved his glasses halfway up his forehead so he could pinch the bridge of his nose. It was his go-to reaction whenever Ethan asked for a technical explanation, or help resetting his password, or deploying an update on his phone.

"She died—"

"Yes," Parker snapped. "Ana Maria died. I was there, if you'll recall, sitting next to you in the hospital while we waited for news. But Natalia *lived*. You worry so much about where Will is and what he's doing, but you know *exactly* where Natalia is and have done *nothing*."

That wasn't true at all. Ethan had called in every single favor, asked Isaac to jump through flaming hoops of fire, and all so Ethan could assure Natalia's safety. It had taken some convincing, but in the end Natalia had been declared dead and granted a new, ironclad identity—courtesy of Parker—in exchange for consulting with the DEA on cartel operations.

Last Ethan had heard, she'd been set up with a stipend and a tiny studio apartment in Arlington.

"I know exactly where she is, Parker."

"Which begs the question—why the fuck aren't you with her?"

Parker didn't understand, but how could he? He'd met Natalia just once, and only to go through the process of wiping away her old life and replacing it with a new one. He'd gone the extra mile, arranging for Natalia to have more than just a new identity—providing her with a past, a history, adding layer upon layer upon layer of protection. Ethan hadn't even had to ask; Parker had just stepped in and done it.

Coupled with the fact that the cartel had their money and every assurance that Hernan and his nieces were dead, Natalia would be safe. Could have the life she'd wanted, complete with a tiny studio apartment and the freedom to pursue what made her happy.

He wanted that for her. Even if it didn't include him.

"I promised her, Parker. Promised that if it came down to a choice, that I would save Ana Maria." Ethan sighed, sweat slicking his skin as the sun crested the horizon, spilling light and warmth across the water until it sparkled.

"Right. Because that's how it works," Parker muttered.

"She only ever asked me for one promise, and at the end of the day, I broke it." He didn't regret it. Not really. How could he, when somewhere, right now, Natalia was safe, tucked up in bed, warm beneath the weight of a down comforter? Soon she'd wake, have some coffee, and face the day.

He wanted to be with her. To roll her over and stroke her back. To bring her coffee. To take her to breakfast. But if that was the price he had to pay for putting her first, for loving her enough to save her life, then he'd pay it. Gladly.

But still, he worried about her constantly. It would be hard now. He understood that for Natalia, this unexpected freedom would be a new kind of hell. But it would fade, and she'd find her way.

And likewise, Ethan would find a way to let go. To let someone else stroke her skin, kiss her good morning, bring her croissants. If that was the price he paid for knowing she was alive, he'd accept it. Learn to live with the ache her absence had left in him.

"Right. And I promised Georgia that glow-in-the-dark condoms were just as good as the regular ones."

Ethan choked on surprise and air and a laugh that felt like a rusted penny lodged in his throat.

"Glow Stick?" That little anecdote made so much more sense. How Georgia kept from strangling Parker in his sleep, Ethan would never know.

"Not the point," Parker continued, and Ethan could practically see the tips of his ears going pink. "The point is that you still haven't figured out that the only one who expects you to be perfect, the only one who expects you to live up to your word a hundred percent of the time, is you." Parker snorted. "Wherever he is, Will doesn't blame you, Ethan. He's not angry or hurt. And I don't believe that Natalia blames you, either. Not really."

"Her sister meant everything to her—"

"And she was dead the moment those bullets tore through her back. One of them nicked her aorta—you heard the doctor—no amount of time would have made a difference . . . But for Natalia? That time *mattered*. Probably even saved her life."

Yes, but Ethan knew she'd resent him for it all the same. That if anger didn't widen the canyon between them, grief would. No matter how much he hurt, no matter how many times a day he found himself reaching for his phone or driving through her neighborhood, Ethan would not make this any harder for her. His door was always open—even if she chose to keep hers closed.

"She knows how to find me," he said, pulling through three strong, deep strokes, extending his legs and tightening his core.

"I never pegged you for a quitter—how disappointing."

"You gave Georgia the space she needed," Ethan grunted, letting his scull slide the final few yards up to the dock. "As I recall, you were adamant that you give her the time and space to figure out what she wanted."

"Because Georgia, God love her, has to figure shit out for herself. I *have* to give her the space to get comfortable with change. I had to sit back and pray that at the end of the day, she'd be brave enough, strong enough, to come home. To love me. That's just who she is—confident and self-assured once she's made a decision, but a stubborn neurotic mess while she gets there." Parker's words might have been annoyed, but his voice was all warm affection. "Why do you think she still pays rent on that apartment she never visits? Why do you think I haven't put a ring on her finger when we both know I'm going to? I give her time and space because it's what she needs, Ethan, and I'm always, always going to put what she needs *first*." He grew quiet for a long beat, only the sound of the *tap* and the *clank* of his mug filtering over the line. "You seem a bit slow this morning, so let me spell it out for you—Natalia's never going to come to this realization on her own, and I think deep down you know that."

Did he? He'd certainly considered the possibility Natalia would never reach out, never find a way to forgive him for everything that had happened. But that wasn't really what Parker was saying.

"The *one* time you repress that pesky saving-people urge," Parker said, his eye roll almost audible.

"She doesn't need me to save her, Parker. She never did, and your better half was the one to point it out."

"And if I recall correctly the recap of that conversation," Parker said, drawing out his words like an irritated teacher repeating something for the fifth time, "she also pointed out that Natalia just needed someone to remind her that she was worth saving *in the first place*.

"She's grieving, Ethan, and not just the loss of her sister. She never got a chance to mourn her parents, either. And now, on top of all that, she's got to find a way to reconcile all the guilt that's been eating her up for years."

"She's got nothing to feel guilty for," Ethan snarled. She never had. He regretted that he'd ever had even a second of hesitation about that. "Nothing."

"Easy, killer, *I* know that. You know that. Hell, the entire team knows that. But does she?"

She couldn't possibly. Ethan had seen the regret she carried, the guilt she refused to acknowledge. And he knew, without a shadow of a doubt, that Natalia would have a hell of a time living with the fact that, in the end, every single terrible decision she'd been forced to make hadn't saved her sister.

"She'll blame herself," Ethan admitted.

"Yeah. Sounds familiar, doesn't it?"

Ethan snorted but climbed onto the dock without protest or denial.

"Now you tell me—if I hadn't thrown paper instead of rock, would you have gotten out of your own way long enough to see the situation clearly?"

Ethan let the silence answer for him.

"Yeah, that's what I thought." Parker groaned as if he were stretching. "Lucky for you, you've got friends who love you enough to hack your phone and explain all the ways you're a moron, and all before dawn."

"Sun's up, Parker."

"Fine. All before a second cup of coffee. Point is, Natalia doesn't have that. So if you want her to walk through your door at the end of the day, if you want to wake up next to her every morning, if you want the chance to make, break, and keep an infinite number of promises, then you better fight for her, Ethan. Because she's not in a place to fight for herself."

"You're right."

All movement abruptly ceased on the other end of the phone. "Come again, please?"

"I think once in this lifetime was more than enough," Ethan replied. But it was true. Parker, as usual, had managed to worm his way to the heart of the issue and make something that looked complicated sound simple.

Fight for her. It wouldn't be easy. And she might not be ready. But Ethan specialized in the impossible.

The dishwasher door creaked, and the top tray rattled as Parker pulled it out. "Ugh. I keep telling her to stop rinsing—I can never tell if these are clean or dirty!"

Ethan huffed, pulled his scull from the water, and made his way to the slip he used for storage with the beginnings of a grin. There'd been a time, not too long ago, when Parker had owned nothing but coffee mugs, paper plates, and plastic forks. Domesticity looked good on him, even if it did make him insufferably smart in new and irritating ways.

"Fine. If they're clean, they're just getting washed again," he grumbled. "We good? Do I need to physically come get you and drag your ass out to Arlington?"

"We're good," Ethan confirmed, though he wasn't headed to Arlington just yet. He had some stops to make first, another set of promises to keep. And one lingering question that surfaced above the rest.

"Hey, Parker?"

"Yeah?"

"You said you promised Georgia that glow-in-the-dark condoms were just as effective . . ."

"Heartbreak made you a bit slow, didn't it?" Parker laughed. "You never even noticed when Georgia took herself off the fieldwork rotation and took on consulting."

Holy. Shit.

"I . . . Congratulations? May Georgia have mercy on your soul? I hope the couch is comfortable?"

"Yes. To all of it," Parker laughed. "It's wild, man! I duplicated code! Now go get your girl. I'm about to be a positive male role model, which means I need *my* positive male role model to get his shit together."

And on that slightly terrifying bombshell, Parker hung up, leaving Ethan to wonder how so much had changed so fast.

And what changes were still to come.

CHAPTER TWENTY-ONE

As she trudged up the last flight of stairs leading to her sixth-floor studio, Natalia tugged the rubber band from her ponytail and let her hair have its way. One mile or ten—or in this case, simply a walk around the block, all her battered lungs could handle—it didn't matter; her hair never held. She'd cut it, but it was thick and curly, and Ana Maria had always said she'd look like a poodle with a bowl cut if she tried.

Natalia stopped at the top of the stairs, braced a hand against the wall, and took a deep breath, forcing back the sting of tears. She told herself that she was still recovering. That things would get easier. She was halfway there—she didn't roll over in the middle of the night only to wake herself with protesting ribs and livid bruises.

She missed the pain.

The ache of storm-cloud bruises.

The tug of healing muscles.

She'd known what to do for those things. Ice. Rest. Heat. Yoga.

For weeks, she'd focused on healing. At getting her strength back and walking up a flight of stairs without wheezing for air. It had given her something to do, a way to spend the endless stretch of days that felt both alien and oddly threatening.

Now, all but the worst of the bruises had healed, and she could take deep, long gulps of air without pain or coughing fits. She was, more or less, back to normal.

Except normalcy was as foreign to her as freedom. And as isolating as prison. Long nights passed with the glow of the television and the absence of the drugs that had brought sleep, and the days stretched on with hours upon hours of lonely nothingness.

Natalia didn't know what to do with herself. Had no clue who she was in this new, stranger world. And she just couldn't seem to muster the energy or curiosity to change that.

What was the point?

She'd lost everything, and though the future lay before her, unencumbered and wide open, all she could think of was that it wasn't supposed to be this way. That she'd stolen this from someone else, someone more deserving. None of this was hers.

She didn't want it.

And couldn't waste it.

So she ran. And read—she'd found a used bookstore around the corner—and wondered how she'd fill the next six decades.

A job, she supposed. Something menial, because what else was she really qualified for? Maybe college, if she were lucky enough to get her finances in order and her feet beneath her. But she expected that would only remind her, again, that she was different. An outsider. How was she supposed to go from the cartel to campus?

Tomorrow's problem, she decided.

Natalia pushed open the fire door at the end of the hall and headed toward her apartment. Halfway there, her attention on the key she'd attached to the lanyard sewn into her jacket, she froze, nerves and instincts and the bone-deep pull of something she'd never, ever forget tugging at her.

Her gaze down, she saw his legs first. Stretched out where he sat against her door, they were long and lean and encased in casual dark-wash jeans that looked as if they'd been tailored. Sitting next to him was a cardboard carrier with two coffee cups. A white paper bag sat on top, the opening closed in neat, precise folds.

Coffee and croissants.

Promises and pretty pictures.

Consider it done, Natalia. No matter what it takes, no matter what it costs, that day is yours.

She might have had the strength to turn Ethan away. To leave him standing on her doorstep with pastries and coffee. To ignore his set jaw and the guarded way he watched her approach. He'd come to fight for her, and she'd be lying if she said a part of her hadn't hoped he would. She'd turn him away; it would hurt, but she'd do it.

Why should she get to be happy?

But as always, Ethan was one step ahead of her and too damn smart for his own good. Because draped across his lap, chewing on the edge of his jacket, was a gray puppy with toes dipped in white and a tail that never stopped moving.

He'd bought her a dog, damn him.

He stood, tucking the puppy beneath his arm and lifting the coffee carrier by the base. The bag on top wobbled, then settled. "Hey," he said, the puppy in his arms wiggling and stretching, desperate to smother his chin in enthusiastic kisses.

"Cute dog." What else could she say? She knew what she *should* say, had rehearsed all the words that would drive him away. They'd tumbled through her head often enough, mean-spirited stones that could pummel and break and destroy until nothing remained but the scatter of guilt and blame and loss. He'd take it, too. She knew he would. He'd stand there and let her rail, let her blame him, let her hate him.

If it made her happy, if it made her whole, he'd do it. For her.

"Pit bull," he explained on a shrug and a smile. "Too often misunderstood. Mistreated. But so very, very loyal."

Her throat closed. She didn't deserve him, but she wanted him more than her next breath. Wanted to wake up tomorrow secure in his arms and in the knowledge that he'd be there for all of it. The grief, the sadness, the overwhelming realization that she didn't know who she was anymore . . .

But as always, when he looked at her, she knew who she wanted to be.

But that all felt so out of reach now.

"Can I come in?" he asked when she stepped around him to slide her key into the lock.

She tried to shake her head, to give voice to a shattered *no*, but a paw landed on her shoulder, and tiny teeth pulled at her hair. She shrugged instead. She pushed open the door and toed off her shoes. She glanced around and forced back a wave of embarrassment. The studio was clean, but that was all she could say for it. Everything was a shade of brown or beige, from the bare walls to the kitchen counters to the worn-down wood flooring.

A blank slate.

"I don't really have anywhere for you to sit," she said, wishing she'd made her bed or at least straightened out the duvet and tucked in the sheets on the air mattress in the middle of the floor. Aside from that, the only furniture she had was a television she'd scavenged off the Internet and a solid wood dresser she'd bought off a moving neighbor. A can of paint—yellow, like her mother's stove—sat next to it, but she hadn't yet found the energy to start stripping layers away and replacing them with something new.

"I have water." She pulled open the fridge, uncomfortable in the silence Ethan had brought with him. Why wasn't he talking? Surely he had a thousand things to say. *Thank you. I'm sorry. I miss you. Forgive me.* She didn't care; she just wanted him to start so it could all finally, finally be finished.

Then she could grieve everything, all at once, one final time.

She turned, a bottle of water in her hand, to find him leaning against the counter, teasing the puppy he held with a finger, but his focus was trained on her.

What was he waiting for?

She held out the bottle of water, but he just shook his head.

Fine. She twisted the top off on an angry jerk, drank half the bottle, then slammed it down on the counter. "What do you want?" she asked, anger pushing the words out like the crack of a whip.

"That, for starters," he said, scratching the dog behind the ears. "The anger. The resentment. The honesty. I told you once, Natalia, and I'll say it until you hear me: cold indifference doesn't suit you. You're so much more than that."

"I'm tired." She tucked a strand of hair behind her ear. So, so tired. The sort of bone-deep exhaustion even sleep didn't touch. "I don't want to fight with you, Ethan."

"What do you want?" he asked, stroking a broad hand along the puppy's back. "Do you even know?"

"I want my sister back." She tried for angry, aimed for bitter, but instead her voice came out sad, resigned, as if she were asking a question she already knew the answer to.

"I know you do," he said, leaning forward to push the puppy into her arms. "I'd do just about anything to bring her back to you, Natalia. I know you blame me—"

"I don't blame you, Ethan," she said, inhaling the scent unique to puppies. "The surgeons told me it wouldn't have mattered in the end. That they couldn't have saved her."

He pulled a coffee from the carrier, his jaw flexing as if his brain told him to bite back words his heart urged him to speak. "I didn't know that when I made the decision," he admitted, then took a long sip of coffee. "All I knew was that you were dying. I promised you, Natalia. I gave you my word that if it came down to a choice, Ana Maria would live." He pinned her with a stare, bold and blue and painfully honest. "I couldn't do it. And I want you to know, need you to understand, even if I could go back, if I could change my mind and save her life . . . I wouldn't do a damn thing differently. Because even if you hate me, even if you never let me in—you're here. You're alive. I'm not ever going to regret that, regardless of the circumstances that led to it."

"You chose me," she whispered, stroking soft ears and fighting against the guilt and fear and insecurity that said that couldn't possibly be true. That she was undeserving. That after everything she'd done, she didn't have the right to be happy. It was why she hadn't gone to him. Why she hadn't called or dropped by. Why she'd lain awake at night, missing his warmth, his touch, his conviction.

She'd needed him. To come to her. To fight for her. To believe in her.

"I *love* you, Natalia," he snarled. There was no soft admission, no gentle declaration. Everything Ethan did was designed to provoke, to challenge—his love was demanding and fierce and passionate.

Hers could be no less.

"I love you," he repeated. "And yes, that means I choose you. Ahead of anyone else, always. No matter the circumstances, I will choose you over and over and over again until my devotion settles into your skin like a well-healed, hard-earned scar. Until you know, down to the very marrow in your bones, that if you have nothing else, you have me."

He sighed and set his coffee aside.

"But that means you have to choose me, choose us, too. You have to find a way to believe that you deserve every good, beautiful thing in this life, Natalia. I can show you and remind you and teach you—but I can't believe it for you."

"I want to," she admitted, pressing a kiss to the puppy's head, then setting her on the floor to attack the laces on her running shoes. "I'm scared." An odd confession, even to her own ears. For the first time in her life, she had nothing to fear and no one to worry about. But worry consumed her. "What if I'm not . . . What if I'm never more than . . . ?"

"Than an adoring sister?" Ethan asked. "Than a devoted daughter?" He pushed away from the counter, closed the distance between them, tilted her chin up so he could look her in the eye. "If you are never more than the woman who walked to her death to save a man she'd never met, then you will still be the strongest, most beautifully selfless person I've ever known."

"Ethan . . ." She went up on her toes, seeking his mouth, his touch, his warmth.

He put his hands on her shoulders, pushed her feet back to the ground.

"But I want more than that," he said, staring into her eyes with that uncompromising electric-blue gaze. "I want you to be selfish, Natalia. I want you to remember what it is to dream and fight and live. And I want you to do it with me."

"I don't know who I am anymore or who I want to be." She swallowed, recognizing the crossroad beneath her feet. There was no going back, no starting over. No blank slate and clean history. The past was there—it would always be there—but she could move forward. Had to, really.

For Ana Maria, who'd want her to be happy.

For her father, who'd loved both his daughters.

And for Ethan, who'd seen her, loved her, chosen her . . . when no one else had.

But most of all, for herself. Because if she hadn't earned the right to be happy, if she didn't deserve the man before her, then she could easily spend the rest of her life in the pursuit and think of nothing more worthy of her time.

Ethan loved her, believed in her, and because Natalia believed in him, too, she found the strength to believe in herself. In them.

"I don't know who I am," she repeated, finding her feet, her voice, her heart, "but I want to find out. With you."

The breath left him in a rush, and in the span of a heartbeat, he was on her, pushing her up against the refrigerator and taking her mouth as if it had required every single drop of self-control he possessed to wait for her to come around, to catch up, to decide to be happy.

But no more. No more waiting. No more fear.

She kissed him back, bit the full curve of his lower lip, eased the sting with a gentle kiss.

When he pulled back, his forehead against hers, his hands gripping her hips, his breathing hard, he said, "I was prepared to fight for you. To come back tomorrow and the next day and the day after that. To ply you with croissants and coffee, to test your restraint and steal your smiles. I'd have done it, you know, no matter how long it took, no matter how hard you made it, I'd have fought dirty—"

"You brought me a puppy, Ethan. I think you entered the ring with weighted gloves."

"When it comes to you, I'm not ever going to fight fair." He kissed her temple. "I made you promises, Natalia, plural. And I know I broke one, but I'm here to keep the other. And if you'll let me, I'll spend the rest of my life making you promises—and doing my damnedest to live up to them."

She reached for him, lacing her fingers together behind his neck.

"I love you," she said against his mouth, tasting the truth of it on her tongue, then saying it again, stronger, clearer, louder. "I love you, and I'll only have one promise from you, Ethan Somerton."

"Name it."

"From now on, we choose each other."

He kissed her deep and long, his mouth eventually curling up in a smile. "Done."

ABOUT THE AUTHOR

Elizabeth Dyer likes her heroines smart and snarky, her heroes strong and sexy. An attorney and recent coffee devotee, Elizabeth spends the majority of her time tucked into a corner table at Starbucks or pinned beneath her (overly affectionate) bullmastiff. When she isn't working or wrestling the dog, Elizabeth can be found writing the kinds of sexy, suspenseful books she most loves to read. A born-and-bred Texan, Elizabeth resides in Dallas, where she indulges in Netflix marathons, Instagramming her dog, and brunch. *Definitely* brunch. Adorably awkward, Elizabeth hates the phone as much as she loves social media—especially hearing from her readers. Follow her on Twitter (@lizdyerwrites) or Instagram (@elizabethdyerwrites).